D1446894

THE VALANCOURT BOOK OF HORROR STORIES

THE VALANCOURT BOOK OF
HORROR
STORIES

edited by
JAMES D. JENKINS & RYAN CAGLE

VALANCOURT BOOKS
Richmond, Virginia
2016

CONTENTS

EDITORS' FOREWORD   7

AUNTY GREEN   John Blackburn   9
MISS MACK   Michael McDowell   16
SCHOOL CROSSING   Francis King   34
A PSYCHOLOGICAL EXPERIMENT   Richard Marsh   49
THE PROGRESS OF JOHN
    ARTHUR CRABBE   Stephen Gregory   63
THE FROZEN MAN   John Trevena   68
CALIFORNIA BURNING   Michael Blumlein   91
LET LOOSE   Mary Cholmondeley   130
OUT OF SORTS   Bernard Taylor   149
THE HEAD AND THE HAND   Christopher Priest   160
THE GHOST OF CHARLOTTE CRAY   Florence Marryat   176
THE GRIM WHITE WOMAN   M. G. Lewis   195
THE TERROR ON TOBIT   Charles Birkin   204
FURNISHED APARTMENTS   Forrest Reid   218
SOMETHING HAPPENED   Hugh Fleetwood   242
THE TARN   Hugh Walpole   258
THE GENTLEMAN ALL IN BLACK   Gerald Kersh   273

ACKNOWLEDGMENTS

The Editors acknowledge with thanks permission to include the following stories:

'Aunty Green' © 1977 by John Blackburn. Originally published in *Cold Fear*. Reprinted by permission of The Estate of John Blackburn.

'Miss Mack' © 1986 by Michael McDowell. Originally published in *Halloween Horrors*. Reprinted by permission of The Otte Company and The Estate of Michael McDowell.

'School Crossing' © 1979 by Francis King. Originally published in *The 20th Pan Book of Horror Stories*. Reprinted by permission of A. M. Heath, Ltd., and The Estate of Francis King.

'The Progress of John Arthur Crabbe' © 1982 by Stephen Gregory. Originally published in *Illustrated London News*. Reprinted by permission of the author.

'California Burning' © 2009 by Michael Blumlein. Originally published in *Asimov's Science Fiction*. Reprinted by permission of the author.

'Out of Sorts' © 1983 by Bernard Taylor. Originally published in *The Dodd, Mead Gallery of Horror*. Reprinted by permission of A. M. Heath, Ltd., and the author.

'The Head and the Hand' © 1972 by Christopher Priest. Originally published in *New Worlds Quarterly 3*. Reprinted by permission of the author.

'The Terror on Tobit' © 1933 by Charles Birkin. Originally published in *Terrors*. Reprinted by permission of The Estate of Charles Birkin.

'Furnished Apartments' © 2016 by The Estate of Forrest Reid. Published by permission of Queen's University Belfast and Johnson & Alcock, Ltd.

'Something Happened' © 2016 by Hugh Fleetwood. Published by permission of the author.

EDITORS' FOREWORD

Since 2005, Valancourt Books has made available almost 400 neglected classics by dozens of authors, most of them out of print for decades, sometimes even for a century or two. Our catalogue includes Gothic novels from the late 1700s and early 1800s, Victorian 'penny dreadfuls' and 'sensation' novels, vintage mystery and horror fiction from the 1920s, '30s and '40s, rediscovered gay interest fiction from the mid-20th century, and more recent horror and science fiction from the 1970s, '80s and '90s. The idea behind this anthology was, "What if we distilled the best of each part of our catalogue into a single volume? What would a horror anthology spanning two centuries, and featuring only Valancourt authors, look like?"

This book has something for fans of each section of our catalogue. Those who have enjoyed our Gothic Classics series will surely find Matthew Gregory Lewis's rare ghost story in verse, 'The Grim White Woman', to their liking. If, like us, you love a good, old-fashioned Victorian horror story, you'll relish the creepy tales we've included by authors hugely popular in their day but now little known, like Florence Marryat, Richard Marsh and Mary Cholmondeley. Readers who have appreciated our efforts to rediscover lost gay fiction will be pleased to find contributions from authors such as Forrest Reid, Hugh Walpole and Francis King in this volume. Of course, no horror anthology would be complete without stories from some of the great contemporary masters of horror like Michael McDowell, Bernard Taylor and Stephen Gregory. But perhaps the biggest surprise for some readers will be the excellent tales by writers not normally thought of as 'horror authors', like Christopher Priest, Michael Blumlein and Francis King.

In choosing the stories for this book, our foremost goal was, of course, to select ones that are well-written and fun to read. However, we have for the most part tried to avoid stories that are widely available in other anthologies, as well as ones included in other Valancourt volumes. Of the seventeen stories in this book, two have never been published before anywhere and five others are reprinted here for the first time outside the collections in which they originally appeared. The others, we think, are uncommon enough that they should prove new to most readers.

Drawing on our deep catalogue and showcasing the talents of a number of fine writers we've had the honor to publish over the last twelve years, this anthology is a Halloween treat dedicated to all of you who have supported our publishing projects over the years, and we hope you will enjoy reading it as much as we have enjoyed putting it together.

JAMES D. JENKINS & RYAN CAGLE
Publishers, Valancourt Books
August 2016

John Blackburn

AUNTY GREEN

Undeservedly neglected in recent years, JOHN BLACKBURN *(1923-1993) was a key figure in British horror in the 1960s and '70s, drawing upon his work as an antiquarian bookseller and his knowledge of medieval folk tales and myths, which he updated in innovative ways in his fiction. Though his novels were often horrific, it is difficult to label Blackburn as solely a 'horror' novelist: generally, his works featured an unclassifiable mix of horror, science fiction, thriller, and mystery. Much of his early fiction tends toward the genre of the Cold War thriller, but by the late 1960s Blackburn had more fully embraced horror in his novels, turning out a stream of successes, including* Children of the Night *(1966),* Bury Him Darkly *(1969),* Devil Daddy *(1972), and* Our Lady of Pain *(1974). Though his reputation waned after his death, during his lifetime he was recognized by the* Times Literary Supplement *as 'today's master of horror' and by the* Penguin Encyclopedia of Horror and the Supernatural *as 'certainly the best British novelist in his field'. Fifteen of Blackburn's novels are available from Valancourt. 'Aunty Green' first appeared in Hugh Lamb's anthology* Cold Fear *(1977) and is reprinted here for the first time.*

'SLOW DOWN, SMITH. I told you my appointment's not till eight and I don't want to arrive early.' It was a lovely evening. The hills gay under the setting sun, a waterfall foaming at the head of the valley and trees swaying in the breeze blowing from the sea. Very beautiful, but Sir James Crampton did not appreciate scenic beauty and he scowled through the rear window of a Rolls Corniche. He had once known the district much better than he knew the back of his own hand and he hated it. Every hill, every tree, every stream and field and farmhouse sickened him.

'Fork left at the church when we get to the village, Smith.'

Sir James spoke with authority because he was a knowledge-able, authoritative man, and he owned things. Since leaving the orphanage all he touched had turned to gold and his current assets included a prosperous civil engineering firm, a fleet of lorries, a large number of flats, houses and office blocks, and over three million U.S. dollars earning tax-free interest in a Swiss bank account. He also owned the Rolls Royce and its driver, William Smith, who was his slave; body, soul and mind.

Good, loyal Bill Smith, who'd better remain loyal, or the police would hear about his sexual habits. Crampton had paid off the last prostitute Smith roughed up, but he'd taped a recording of her complaints and the tape could set Bill up . . . up in a dock at the Central Criminal Court – the Old Bailey.

Yes, Sir James Crampton, K.C.M.G. (awarded for services to the export drive) had many enviable chattels: machines and money, men and women, bricks and mortar, but there were other possessions no one would envy. An army of malignant cells was consuming his lungs and liver and emotion had already consumed his soul. Anger directed against an old, frail woman he hadn't seen for thirty-five years.

'Turn right at the next crossing and then fork left again, Smith.' Crampton's voice rasped the orders, but the voice of memory was far louder and more domineering. *'Turn round and face me, Jimmy . . . Bend over and take your punishment, Jimmy . . . Fetch me the fork, you deceitful little swine.*

'Aye, that hurt didn't it, but evil children should suffer and there's a line of poetry to describe you, Jim Crampton. "He must be wicked to deserve such pain." '

The fork stabbing his arms and thighs, the whip slashing his buttocks, the woman's expression while she pressed his fingers against the portable oil stove. Worst of all, the creatures swim-ming under the cupboard. ' *"He must be wicked to deserve such pain." '*

Why had Aunty Green (she'd told him to call her that after the council appointed her and Uncle his foster parents) believed he was wicked? Had her dislike made him imagine he was a murderer, and had he talked in his sleep? If so, he'd talked nonsense. He had not wanted to kill his own parents, though he wasn't sorry when he regained consciousness in the hospital and a nurse told him they were dead.

'Bang, you're dead.' The Rolls was passing a public house and Sir James thought of another car and another pub. An old, rusty Ford parked outside the Jolly Gardeners and a lonely boy waiting; Mum and Dad had promised they were only stopping for a *quickie*, but they were staggering when they finally came out and he must have waited two hours for them; trying to read a comic under the interior light and playing with his toy pistol. There was only one cap left in the pistol and surely its tiny report couldn't have caused Dad to lose control of the car and swerve into the bus? The long wait had made him angry, but he didn't really mean to harm Mum and Dad. He was joking when he pointed the muzzle against Dad's ear and shouted, 'Bang, you're dead.'

Just a bitter, childish joke and nobody had criticised him. The police and the magistrates were sure that alcohol and a faulty steering system were responsible for the crash. The nurses and the doctor and the lady from the Children's Care Department were all sorry for him. Everyone was sympathetic and kind ... Everyone except Aunty ... Aunty Green, the witch of his nightmares.

'I know you are glad to be rid of your parents, Jimmy, and I don't dislike you for that. I don't even blame you if you did kill 'em, because drunken sots are no loss to the world. But bad people breed bad children and I can recognise a bad child. You're a bringer of evil, Jim. You fooled me at first, but I've rumbled you now. I sensed your badness the moment you stepped into this house.' Aunty had tilted his face towards her own and he saw her eyes penetrating the flesh and bone and probing the mind behind them. *'Aye, I know you, James Crampton. You're a Jonah and a born hater, but you'll bring no bad luck here. Not if I can help it.'*

Was he bad – was Aunty telepathic, Sir James wondered? She certainly seemed able to read his thoughts and the ability cowed him even more than the physical tortures which started after bad luck did come and Uncle died.

'*You hate us, don't you, Jimmy? You'd like to do me a mischief. To take everything away from us and leave me with nothing.*'

Partially true statements, though it was unfair to say that he'd planned Uncle's death. Uncle Green was a boorish lout, but he hadn't really resented him. Not his fault that Uncle had tripped over a ball he'd left lying on the landing, fallen down the stairs and broken his neck. Careless, short-sighted Uncle . . . Careless, tormented Jimmy.

'*You did it on purpose, Jim. You killed my husband deliberately, and now you'll pay for him. The oil stove's nice and hot, so let's go into the kitchen and have a feel of it.*'

He'd paid all right. Sir James flexed his fingers. He had paid in full, and been too frightened to tell the teachers or the Child Care Officer what Aunty Green did to him. She was a witch who could read his thoughts and sear his brain as well as his body. He'd suffered patiently until breaking point came and knowledge came too. The realisation that, though Aunty dominated him mentally, he was physically stronger. That wonderful day when she failed to force his fingers against the paraffin heater. He picked the heater up and threw it at her.

Aunty Green survived the fire which scarred her face and turned Wildmere Cottage into a blackened ruin, but she didn't dare to say how the fire had started. Silly, cruel Aunty went quietly to hospital. Wicked, lucky Jimmy remained quiet at the orphanage. Mrs Green was virtually a pauper. Sir James Crampton was a knight of the realm and a multi-millionaire.

'We're still early and you're driving too fast, man.' They had crossed a bridge. Sir James consulted his watch and growled at the chauffeur again. Smith was eager to complete the journey because he'd been promised a reward at journey's end. The harlot's tape-recording which could put him behind bars.

Prison bars – an unpleasant cage, but nothing compared to the cage he had experienced himself. The dark walls of the cupboard above the disused well. The creaking floorboards screening the shaft of the well, though not the smell of the water. Sour, stagnant water with sour things in it; soft slimy things though they had jaws and claws and tentacles. He knew they were there – Aunty Green had described them to him. She had also told him that the floor was weak and rotten. If he fell through the floor, those things would have him.

But he hadn't fallen and he never would. Somebody else would go screaming down the well shaft. Somebody else would plummet into the sour water, and there was another poem as appropriate as Aunty's: a poem concerning execution. '*He shall hear the stroke of eight and not the stroke of nine.*' That was why time was important. The grandfather clock which was Aunty's pride and joy, had been chiming eight when she first shut him in the cupboard and neither of them would hear nine strike this evening. The miles and minutes were creeping on and the place of execution was in sight.

Wildmere Cottage! He'd almost forgotten the place till current pain revived early anguish. He hadn't thought about Aunty for years till the specialist diagnosed cancer and he suddenly knew what must be done before he died. But as soon as he did know, his minions had received their orders and carried them out. An agent established that the ruined cottage had remained unoccupied and the land was for sale. He paid far more for that land than it was worth, but to hell with money. What did a few thousand pounds matter to a doomed millionaire with a single mission to accomplish? Michael Gallagher, his chief foreman and another loyal retainer, had restored and renovated the cottage to his exact specifications; new roof, new plaster, new doors and floorboards. But no floorboards covered the shaft of the well and Tom had fitted the cupboard door rather tightly. Far too tightly for a frail old woman to loosen. He would have to open the door for Aunty himself, and he'd laugh while he watched her go through it.

The trap had been baited and set. He'd even provided replicas of the original furnishings as far as he could remember them, and there was a grandfather clock in the hall and a portable oil stove in the kitchen. All the trap lacked was a victim. If Aunty had died he'd be deprived of revenge and his preparations and hopes would come to nothing. That anxiety had persisted for weeks and months, but he needn't have worried. The private detective agency traced her to an old people's home in South London. His solicitor called on her.

Old homes ... old people! The second hand of his watch seemed to be racing now and, despite his tension, James Crampton smiled. The old are supposed to have long memories, but Aunty Green was an exception. She had forgotten the fear and misery her sadism had caused him. She believed he'd forgiven her and wept tears of joy when the lawyer told her that he'd purchased the cottage and the dear old home was at her disposal. Foolish Aunty would weep less joyful tears when she toppled down to the things under the cupboard.

Mike Gallagher had reported that the well was empty apart from a few feet of water at the base of the shaft, but Mike was wrong. The things were there and they were hiding in the slime; waiting for Aunty ... waiting to clutch and claw and savage her!

A horrible way to die, but after she died he'd be able to die himself; die painlessly. A child's cap pistol had destroyed his parents, but there was nothing childish about the pistol in his overcoat pocket. One bullet from the revolver would end pain and give him peace. How much better than the lingering Golgotha of cancer.

'Stop by that gate on the left, Smith, and then you can go home and relax. I'll not be needing you, or *this* any longer.' Crampton continued to smile as the Rolls stopped and he handed his chauffeur the incriminating cassette recording, but his smiles vanished after the man opened the door for him and he stepped out.

'*Open the door and go into the cupboard, Jimmy,*' said the voice of torment. '*Naughty boys must be locked up alone in the dark, and I wonder how long I'll keep you locked up, an hour, a day ... maybe forever? But, however long, you'd better not try to escape, Jim Crampton. If you move a muscle the floor will collapse and down you'll go. Down to them that's waiting.*' Them – the dark – alone – forever. '*He must be wicked to deserve such pain.*' Dusk was gathering, the tail lights of his car were tiny specks on the horizon, and far off in the distance he heard a church clock strike the hour.

'*The stroke of eight and not the stroke of nine.*' He'd kept his appointment to the minute and he would not be alone for long. Though the path ahead of him was dark, the cottage windows were brightly lit. Aunty was at home and he was going home. A home he dreaded, but the place where he'd find peace, and the heavy revolver swung comfortingly against his thigh while he strode forward to obey destiny. Aunty – the well – then the bullet. No more anger, pain or bitterness ... No more nightmares. Only a void; dreamless sleep and tranquillity.

A welcome prospect, so why didn't he grasp it? He had rung the bell and his summons had been obeyed. Aunty Green was expecting him and she had led the way to the kitchen. A small, weak old woman with scar tissue still visible on her brow and cheeks while she halted beside a replica of the oil stove that had maimed her. A pathetic, defenceless little woman, who smiled pleasantly at him, but the woman he hated; the witch he had come to kill.

So why couldn't he kill her? Why had his hands become paralysed? He might be ill, but disease hadn't affected his muscles yet and his fingers were on a door-knob. Why wasn't he strong enough to release a jammed door and throw Aunty into the cupboard?

Was she too small, too weak and defenceless perhaps? Too old and pathetic? Was it possible that she was innocent and had never harmed him? Did he suffer from a persecution complex; paranoia?

Difficult problems, but soon solved. The woman crossed over to him, the years slipped away and she was no longer old or pathetic. She was a fiend whose eyes could penetrate his skull and brain and read the thoughts behind them. She had known his intentions from the moment the lawyer called on her. She knew that there was no floor over the well shaft. She knew he was a child again.

'Open the door and go into the cupboard, Jimmy,' said Mrs Green, and Sir James Crampton obeyed.

Though he didn't go alone. Strength returned as he stepped to meet the things at the bottom of the well. Wicked Jimmy clutched Aunty's arm and dragged her down with him.

Michael McDowell

MISS MACK

Of the many authors rediscovered by Valancourt, none has proven more popular with readers than MICHAEL MCDOWELL *(1950-1999). McDowell's writing career was relatively short – his first novel,* The Amulet, *appeared in 1979, and his last in 1987 – but quite prolific: under his own name and various pseudonyms he published some thirty volumes of fiction during this span before turning his hand to Hollywood screenwriting* (Beetlejuice, The Nightmare Before Christmas). *His Southern Gothic novels* Cold Moon over Babylon *(1980),* The Elementals *(1981) and* Blackwater *(1983) are among the finest horror novels of their era and are now rightly considered classics of the genre. 'Miss Mack', McDowell's first published short story and one of only a handful that he wrote, first appeared in Alan Ryan's anthology* Halloween Horrors *(1986) and is reprinted here for the first time. Those already familiar with McDowell's work will notice the story shares settings in common with* The Amulet *and* Cold Moon over Babylon; *on the other hand, those unfamiliar with McDowell's work won't remain so for long, we think, after they read this delightfully creepy tale. Eight of McDowell's novels are available from Valancourt.*

WHEN MISS MACK SHOWED UP IN BABYLON in the late summer of 1957, nobody knew what to think of her. She had come from a little town called Pine Cone, and had a brother back there who did ladies' hair in his kitchen. Miss Mack was a huge woman with a pig's face, and short crinkly black hair that always looked greasy. Her vast shapeless dresses of tiny-patterned fabric seemed always to have been left too long in the sun. She always wore tennis shoes, even to church, because, as she candidly admitted, any other sort broke apart under her weight.

She wasn't old by any means, but a woman of such size and such an aspect wasn't regarded in the usual light, and nobody in Babylon gave any thought to Miss Mack's age. For seven years she had traveled all over Alabama, Georgia, and Florida, doing advance and setup work for the photographer who came in and took pictures of the grammar school children. She had been to Babylon before, on this very errand, and the teachers at the grammar school remembered her. Now the photographer was dead, and Miss Mack returned to Babylon. She showed the principal of the grammar school her college diploma and her teacher's certificate from Auburn University, and said, 'Mr Hill, I want you to give me a job.'

Mr Hill did it, not because he was intimidated, but because he had a vacancy, and because he knew a good teacher when he saw one.

Everybody liked Miss Mack. Miss Mack's children in the third grade adored her. Having inherited the itinerant photographer's camera, Miss Mack took pictures of every child in her class and pinned them to the bulletin board with their names beneath. Miss Mack's strong point was fractions, and she drilled her children relentlessly. Her weak point was Alabama history, so she taught them the state song, and let it go at that. On the playground, Miss Mack played with the boys. Infielders cowered and outfielders pressed themselves right up against the back fence when Miss Mack came to bat. At dodgeball, Miss Mack rolled the ball up inside her arm so tightly and so deep that it seemed buried in the flesh there. She unwound the ball so quickly and flung it so hard that the manliest boys in the center of the ring squealed and ducked. Miss Mack's dodgeball could put you flat out on the ground.

Because all teachers in the grammar school were called by their students 'Miss,' it was a matter of some speculation among her pupils whether or not she was married. When one little girl brought back the interesting report that Miss Mack lived alone in one of the four apartments next to the library, the children were all nearly overwhelmed with the sense of having delved deep into the mystery that was Miss Mack's private life.

Miss Mack's private life was also a matter of speculation among her fellow teachers at the grammar school. The first thing that was noticed was that, in Mr Hill's words, she 'kept the Coke machine hot,' dropping in a nickel at every break, and guzzling down a Coca-Cola every chance she got. It appeared that Miss Mack couldn't walk down the hall past the teachers' lounge without sidling in with a nickel – she kept a supply in the faded pocket of her faded dress – and swilling down a bottle at a rate that could win prizes at a county fair. Miss Mack's apartment was not only next to the library, it was next to the Coca-Cola bottling plant as well. Wholesale, Miss Mack bought a case a day, summer and winter, and declared that, in point of fact, she preferred her Cokes warm rather than chilled.

Every weekend Miss Mack disappeared from Babylon. It was universally assumed that she drove her purple Pontiac up to Pine Cone to visit her brother, and maybe sit with him in the kitchen, swilling Coca-Cola while he fixed ladies' heads. But Miss Mack once surprised them all when she said that most weekends she went fishing. She drove all the way over to DeFuniak Springs because DeFuniak Springs had the best trout fishing in the world. She had a little trailer – the itinerant photographer's van with all the equipment jettisoned – parked on the side of some water there, and every weekend Miss Mack and three cases of Coca-Cola visited it.

Despite her alarming and formidable aspect Miss Mack quickly made friends in Babylon, and the friend she made earliest was the other third-grade teacher, Janice Faulk. Janice wasn't but twenty-two, just out of college, short and cute and always smiling. It was thought that Janice had a whole bureauful of white blouses with little puffed sleeves, because she was never seen in anything else. She wore little sweaters and jackets loosely over her shoulders, held in place by a golden chain attached to the lapels. Janice had loved every minute of her two years of teaching. Her children loved her in return, but tended to take advantage of her, because Miss Faulk could be wheedled into just about anything at all.

Mr Hill, the principal, was even thinking of wheedling Janice into marriage. He had taken her down to Milton for pizza a couple of times, and they had gone to the movies in Pensacola, and he had asked her advice on buying a birthday present for his mother. Mr Hill, a thin man with a broad smile, didn't think it necessary to say anything more just yet. When the time came he didn't doubt his ability to persuade Janice up to the altar. After all, he had hired her, hadn't he? And he had always made sure she got to teach the smartest and best-behaved kids, right? Janice was just the sort of impressionable young woman to imagine that such favors ought to be returned, with considerable interest. Mr Hill had even told his mother of his intention of marrying Janice Faulk, and Mrs Hill, a widow living in an old house in Sweet Gum Head, had heartily approved. Mrs Hill in fact told her son he ought to propose to Janice without delay. Mr Hill saw no need for haste, but a little later he was sorry not to have taken his mother's advice.

The next time Mrs Hill spoke to her son on the subject of Janice Faulk – the following Halloween – Mr Hill listened carefully. And he did exactly what his mother told him to do.

For what Mr Hill hadn't counted on in his sanguine projection of easy courtship and easy marriage was the friendship of Janice and Miss Mack.

One Friday morning recess, the bully of Janice's class had fallen on the playground and split open his head on a rock. Janice had been about to run for Mr Hill, but Miss Mack was right there, kneeling on the sandy ground, lifting the boy's head onto her lap, bandaging it as coolly as if she had been a trained nurse. Janice began to come to Miss Mack for other help and advice. Soon she was coming for the mere pleasure of Miss Mack's company. Janice's mother was dead, and her father worked five weeks out of six on an oil rig in Louisiana. She lived alone in a little clapboard house that was within sight of the grammar school. She visited Miss Mack in her apartment between the library and the bottling plant, and Miss Mack visited her in the lonely clapboard house. In Miss Mack's purple Pontiac they went to the Starlite drive-in. If they saw horror movies, Miss Mack held Janice's hand through the scary parts, and told Janice when it was all right to open her eyes. Miss Mack thought nothing of getting up from the supper table, and driving straight down to the Pensacola airport for the mere pleasure of watching the planes take off and land. On the four-lane late at night, Miss Mack came up right next to eighteen-wheel diesels, and made Janice roll down her window. Janice leaned her head cautiously out, and shouted up at the driver of the truck looking down, 'You want to race Miss Mack?'

Miss Mack, in short, knew how to show a girl a good time.

By the summer after her first year of teaching, Miss Mack and Janice were inseparable friends, and an odd-looking pair they made. Miss Mack's appearance was vast, dark, and foreboding, and people in the street tended to get out of her way. She gave somewhat the impression of a large piece of farm machinery that had forsaken both farmer and field. Janice Faulk was petite, retiring, faultlessly neat, like the doll of a rich little girl – very pretty and not often played with. Both women, in consideration of the extra money and the opportunity to spend nearly all their time together, took over the teaching of all the summer remedial classes in the grammar and junior high schools. As if five days a week, all day long, were time insufficient to indulge the happiness they felt in one another's company, Miss Mack began taking Janice off to DeFuniak Springs every weekend.

Gavin Pond, left to Miss Mack by the itinerant photographer, was no more than five acres in extent, surrounded on all sides by dense pine forest. One end of the pond was much shallower than the other, and here a large cypress grove extended a dozen yards or so out into the water. The little trailer, still bearing the name and the promises of the itinerant photographer, was set permanently in a small clearing on the western edge of the pond. Directly across was a little graveyard containing the photographer, his ancestors, and his kin by marriage. A dirt track – no more than two gravel-filled ruts really – had been etched through the forest all the way around the pond. At compass-north it branched off toward the unpaved road, a couple of miles distant through the forest, that eventually led into the colored section of DeFuniak Springs. Altogether, Gavin Pond was as remote as remote could be.

Miss Mack and Janice arrived at the pond every Friday evening, having stopped on the way only for a coffee can of worms and a rabbit cage of crickets. They unloaded the car, fixed supper, and played rummy until ten, when they went to sleep. Next morning they rose before dawn, ate breakfast, prepared a lunch, and went out in the little green boat that was tethered to one of the cypresses. All morning long they fished, and piled up trout and bream in the bottom of the boat. Janice thought this great fun, so long as Miss Mack baited her hook and later removed the gasping fish from it. The two women beneath their straw hats didn't speak, and all that could be heard were the kingfishers in the cypress, and the cage of crickets sitting in the sun on the hood of the Pontiac. Miss Mack liked the sound, and said they chirped louder when they were hot.

At noontime, Miss Mack rowed over to the little cemetery. There among the Gavin graves, the two women ate sandwiches and drank Coca-Cola, though Janice, deliberately to antagonize her friend, sometimes insisted on Dr Pepper instead. Over this lapse of taste, Miss Mack and Janice passed the time in pleasant and practiced argument. In the heat of the afternoon, they returned to the trailer. While Janice napped, Miss Mack sat in the Pontiac – hot though the vinyl seats were – and listened to the baseball game over the radio. This weekly indulgence necessitated always carrying an extra battery in the trunk against the possibility of failure. In the late afternoon, they sat out in folding chairs by the pondside, talking, talking, talking and slapping at mosquitoes. Miss Mack had a large stick across her lap. Every time Janice screamed and pointed out a snake, Miss Mack leaped from her chair and killed the creature with a single blow. She lifted its mangled body on the stick and waved it before Janice's face in retaliation for the Dr Pepper.

Once Miss Mack killed a rattlesnake in the same manner, hesitating not a single moment in running up to the creature and cudgeling it as ferociously as she would have attacked the most harmless king snake. She sliced off its head and rattles, skinned it, cut out its single line of entrails, and then coiled it up in a buttered skillet and cooked it. She made Janice swallow two bites, and she ate almost all the rest herself.

But most evenings they ate the fish they had caught that day, Miss Mack consuming far more than Janice. After supper they played more cards, or read each other riddles out of paperback books, or just talked, talked, talked.

They drove back to Babylon on Sunday afternoon, arriving sometime after dark, tanned and weary, but already looking forward to the next weekend.

Mr Hill knew of these trips, and Mr Hill didn't like them one little bit. Through her friendship with Miss Mack, Janice had changed, and – so far as Mr Hill was concerned – not for the better. Janice no longer wanted to go to Milton for pizza, because Miss Mack didn't like pizza and Janice had decided that she didn't like it either. Janice no longer considered it a wonderful privilege to be asked to go to Pensacola to a movie, because it was so much more fun to go to the airport and watch the planes take off and land, and try to guess which relatives waiting in the coffee shop would go with which passengers coming through the gate. Mr Hill didn't even get to see Janice in church on Sunday morning, and sit next to her, and hold her hymnbook, because on Sunday morning Janice was fishing out at Gavin Pond with Miss Mack, getting burned by the sun and eaten up by mosquitoes. Mr Hill, in short, was worried. He feared that, because of Miss Mack's influence, Janice would refuse his offer of marriage. Mr Hill's mother, to whom he confessed his anxiety, said, 'Miss Mack will never let Janice go. You got to take back what's rightfully yours. And if you cain't think of anything, then you come on back to me, and I'll *tell* you what to do.' Quite beyond any consideration of his fondness for Janice Faulk, Mr Hill had no intention of allowing his comfortable plans to be thwarted by a fat woman with greasy black hair and a face like a pig's.

One day in August, right after a meeting of the teachers preparatory to the beginning of the academic year, Mr Hill said to

Miss Mack, 'You gone keep going out to your fishing pond after school starts, Miss Mack?'

'I sure do hope so,' replied Miss Mack. 'Even though we probably cain't get away until Saturday morning from now on.'

Deftly ignoring Miss Mack's *we*, Mr Hill went on, 'Where is that place anyway?'

'It's about ten miles south of DeFuniak Springs.'

'Hey you know what? My mama lives in Sweet Gum Head – you know where that is? I have to go through DeFuniak Springs to get there. One of these days when I go visit my mama, I'm gone stop by your place and pay you a visit.'

'I wish you would, Mr Hill. We have got an extra pole, and an extra folding chair. This weekend I'm gone put your name on 'em, and Janice and I will start waiting for you.' Under normal circumstances Miss Mack's hospitality would have been extended to Mr Hill's mother, but in her travels through the Southern countryside, Miss Mack had heard stories about *that* old woman.

Though Janice and Miss Mack returned to Gavin Pond every weekend in September and October, Mr Hill didn't come to visit them there. Finally one day, toward the end of October, Janice said to Mr Hill, 'Mr Hill, I thought you were gone go see your mama sometime and stop by and see Miss Mack and me out at the pond. I wish you had, 'cause now it's starting to get cold, and it's not as nice. We're going out this Halloween weekend, but that's gone have to be the last time until spring.'

'Oh lord!' cried Mr Hill, evidently in some perturbation. 'Didn't I tell you, Janice?'

'Tell me what?'

'You're gone be needed here at the school for Halloween night.'

'Saturday?'

'That's right. I was gone get Miz Flurnoy to do it, but her husband's getting operated on in Pensacola on Friday, and she says she cain't. Gallstones.'

Janice was distraught, for she had intended to savor this last weekend at the pond. She came to Miss Mack with a downcast countenance, and told her friend the news.

'Oh, that's not so bad,' said Miss Mack. 'Tell you what, we just won't go out at all until Sunday. We'll make just the one day of it.'

'No sir!' cried Janice. 'I don't want you to miss your weekend on my account. You were going out there long before you knew me, and I certainly don't want you to miss your final Saturday out there. Sunday's never as good as Saturday out at the pond, Miss Mack – you know that! You go on, and I'll drive out on Sunday morning. I'll be there before you get up out of the bed!'

Early on Halloween morning, Janice appeared at Miss Mack's door with a paper bag filled with sandwiches. When she answered the bell, Miss Mack fell back from the doorway in apparent alarm. Janice was wearing a Frankenstein mask.

'Is that you under there, Janice? 'Cause if it isn't, I'm sorry, Whoever-you-are, but I don't have a piece of candy in the house. I ate it all up last night!'

Janice removed the mask. 'It's me, that's all!' She handed Miss Mack the bag of sandwiches. 'I sure do wish I were going too,' she sighed.

'You come tomorrow,' replied Miss Mack, 'and you bring me some Halloween candy. I sure do love Snickers, and they go great with Coca-Cola.'

Miss Mack drove off alone in her purple Pontiac, and Janice went to the school cafeteria to begin decorating for the children's Halloween party that night.

At Gavin Pond, Miss Mack altered her routine not one bit, though she admitted to herself, sitting alone in the little green boat in the middle of the pond, that she wished Mr Hill had chosen somebody else to help with the Halloween party that night. She sorely missed Janice's company. Without her friend, Gavin Pond seemed to Miss Mack a different place altogether.

Just when Miss Mack was thinking that thought for the two hundredth time, she was startled by the sound of an automobile driving along the track that went all the way around the pond. Miss Mack looked up, but could not see the car through the screen of trees. She rowed to shore, hoping very much that it was Janice come to join her after all.

It was not. It was Mr Hill.

'I had to pick up some things from my mama last evening,' said Mr Hill in explanation, 'and I thought I'd stop by on the way back home.'

'How'd you find us? This place is about two hundred miles from nowhere!'

'Us?'

'Just me,' said Miss Mack. 'I'm just so used to Janice being out here, that I said *us* by mistake.'

'Too bad she couldn't come,' remarked Mr Hill. 'Well, it was Mama who drew me a map.'

'Your mama! How'd she know about this place? Gavin Pond's so little and so out-of-the-way they don't even put it on the county maps.'

'Oh, Mama's lived around here all her life. My mama knows every square foot of this county,' replied Mr Hill with some pride. 'And my mama said to tell you hi, Miss Mack.'

'Your mama don't know me from Jezebel's baby sister, Mr Hill!' exclaimed Miss Mack in a surprise unpleasantly alloyed with a sense – somehow – of having been spied upon.

'My mama,' said Mr Hill, 'has heard about you, Miss Mack. My mama is old, but she is interested in many things.'

'I had heard that,' said Miss Mack uneasily. Miss Mack had also heard that the things that Mrs Hill interested herself in withered up and died. But Miss Mack did not say that aloud to Mr Hill, because Mr Hill evidently loved his mama. He visited her often enough, and was wont to say, in the teachers' lounge, that he always took her advice, and when he didn't take her advice, he should have. Miss Mack just hoped that Mrs Hill hadn't given her son any advice on the subject of herself and Janice Faulk. Miss Mack liked Mr Hill well enough, but she knew jealousy when she saw it – in man or woman.

Miss Mack cooked some bream for Mr Hill's lunch, and they

sat and talked for a while in the folding chairs. Miss Mack said how sorry she was that the ball season was over.

About four o'clock Mr Hill gathered himself up to go. 'It sure has been pleasant, Miss Mack. Now I know why you and Janice come out here every single weekend. I'm just real jealous.'

'We are pretty happy out here,' returned Miss Mack modestly.

'Hey, you know what? It's Halloween. Aren't you gone be scared, being out here all by yourself?'

Miss Mack laughed. 'Janice came over this morning wearing a Frankenstein mask, and that didn't scare me one little bit. I've stayed out here all by myself lots and lots of times. Before I knew Janice, I was out here all the time by myself. You don't have to worry about me.'

'I'm glad to hear it. Listen, I got to get on back and help out Janice at the school.'

'You go on, then. You give her my best, and tell her not to forget my Snickers.'

Miss Mack went inside the trailer as Mr Hill drove off. She was clattering with the pans, or she would have been able to hear that not very far from the trailer, Mr Hill stopped his car.

In the pine forest it was almost dark. Mr Hill had just turned onto the track that would lead him back to the dirt road to DeFuniak Springs. He killed the ignition, got out quietly, and opened the trunk. He took out a small corrugated box filled with heavy black ashes mixed with cinders. The rank odor and the lumpish consistency of the blackened remains suggested not the sweeping-out of a coal-burning fireplace, nor a shovelful of some ash heap, but rather something organic, recently dead or even still living, which had been burned, and burned with difficulty.

With a measuring cup that he took from a paper bag in the trunk, Mr Hill scooped out a portion of the cinders and the ashes, and sprinkled them in one of the ruts of the track that led away from the pond and toward the road. Then he poured a cupful into the other rut, and so alternated until he had distributed the ashes and cinders evenly. Then he tossed the measuring cup and the cardboard box back into the trunk of the car and shut it. Taking then a piece of yellow notepaper from his shirt pocket, he unfolded it, held it close to his eyes in the decreasing light, and in a low voice read the words that had been written upon it. From the same pocket he took a single calendar page – October of the current year – and set fire to it with his cigarette lighter. After this was burned, and the ashes scattered on the ground, Mr Hill pulled from his trousers a child's compass and a cheap wristwatch – such items as are won in ring-toss booths at traveling carnivals. He checked that the compass needle did indeed point north. He put the wristwatch to his ear to hear its ticking. He dropped both into the heaps of ashes, and crushed them beneath the heel of his shoe.

As Mr Hill got quietly into his car and drove slowly away, the twilight was deepening into night. The piles of ashes began to blow away. The heavier cinders alone remained, dull and black and moist. The broken springs and face and glass of the wristwatch and compass gleamed only faintly. At a little distance, Miss Mack's crickets in their rabbit cage produced one loud, unison chirp.

Miss Mack fixed more fish for supper. Afterward she cleaned up, and settled down to work a couple of crossword puzzles at the table, but soon gave this over. She had much rather be playing cards with Janice, or trying to guess the riddles that Janice put to her. She went outside, and looked up at the sky. She wore a sweater because the nights were chilly in October. There was a new moon, but the sky was so clear and so bright with stars that Miss Mack had no difficulty in discerning its circle of blackness against the black sky.

She went back inside and went to bed earlier than was usual with her. She was lonely and told herself that the sooner she got to bed, the sooner she might rise. She intended to get up very early, in expectation of Janice's arrival.

Miss Mack awoke at six, or at least at what her internal clock told her was six o'clock. But it obviously wasn't, for the night remained very black. Miss Mack could see nothing at all. She rose and went to the door of the trailer and peered blearily out. It was still deep night, and when she looked toward the east – directly above the little plot of Gavin graves on the far side of the pond – she could discern no lightening of the sky. Miss Mack thought that she had merely been so excited by the prospect of Janice's arrival that she had risen an hour or so before her time. She was about to turn back into the bed for another while, when she suddenly noticed, in the sky, the same black circle of moon as she had seen before.

It hadn't moved.

Miss Mack was confused by this. The moon rose. The moon set. It never stayed still. Perhaps, she attempted to tell herself, it had moved a little. In that case, she had been asleep not eight hours but perhaps only one. That would also explain why it was still so dark. Yet she felt as if she had slept for six or seven hours at the very least.

Miss Mack went back into the trailer and lay down again. If she had slept for only an hour, then she ought to go back to sleep until morning. Perhaps she would be waked by the horn of Janice's car.

But Miss Mack couldn't go back to sleep. She wasn't tired now. She was hungry. She wanted breakfast. So, thinking how foolish she was, she lighted a lamp, and set up the little stove, and cooked bacon and eggs and ate them all up. She stood once more in the doorway of the trailer, and looked out across the pond.

The sky was no lighter. The moon had not moved.

Miss Mack said aloud, 'I am dreaming. I am asleep in the bed, and I am having a dream.'

She looked at the bed behind her, as if she thought she might indeed see her sleeping self there. She looked back out at the night. She pinched her arm, and held it next to the lamp, watching the flesh turn color.

Nervously, she opened a Coca-Cola, and pulling a sweater over her nightdress, walked out to her car, got in, and turned on the radio. There were only two stations on the air, so she knew it *was* very late at night. More stations came on at four or five with the farm reports. So it had to be earlier than that. She went to WBAM in Montgomery, and got the announcer.

Halloween night – don't let the goblins get you! Lock your doors and close the curtains, boys and girls! It's 2 a.m. and don't walk past any graveyards. This next song goes out to Tommy and Julie, it's . . .

Miss Mack turned the radio off. She was relieved in the main, for at least she knew the time. But still she was puzzled by the moon. She looked up at it, and for a second, was joyed to see that at last it had altered its position. Waking up in the middle of the night always leaves you in a confused state of mind, and she had only made matters worse by eating breakfast at one-thirty in the morning. Sighing, and trusting that *now* she would surely be able to sleep, Miss Mack got out of the Pontiac and slammed the door shut with a grateful bang. She smiled up at the moon – and all her relief washed suddenly away. The *moon* hadn't moved, only *she* had. When she went back to the door of the trailer, and looked again, it still hung the same distance above the top of the same cypress as before she had prepared her untimely breakfast.

Miss Mack returned to the trailer and lay down a third time. Her nervousness she carefully ascribed to the strangeness of being up and about so late at night. She willed herself to sleep, slipped into unconsciousness, and woke at a time that seemed at least several hours later. Certainly she suffered the grogginess and physical lassitude attendant upon too much sleep. She went hastily to the door of the trailer.

The moon had not moved.

This time neglecting her sweater, she ran to the car and turned on the radio. WBAM was playing music, and she turned to the only other station. She heard the end of a song, and then the announcer came on.

And here's the 2 a.m. wrap-up of some of the day's top stories . . .

She turned the radio off.

She sat very still in the front seat of the car, with her chin immobile upon the steering wheel, staring up at the moon, attempting to trace even the slightest movement. She could see none at all.

Miss Mack, with nothing else to do, fixed more bacon and eggs. As she cooked, and as she sat at the table and ate, she refrained from looking out the door at the moon. She saved that for when she had carefully cleaned up. She went with conscious bravery to the door of the trailer and looked out, taking great care to stand exactly where she had stood before so that any slightest alteration of position would be detectable.

The moon had not moved.

It was still 2 A.M. on WBAM, and on the other station as well. This time she listened to the song that was dedicated to Tommy and Julie, and then turned to the wrap-up of some of the day's top stories.

Not much happened on Halloween.

With sudden resolution, Miss Mack ran back to the trailer, quickly dressed, and came back out to the car. She started it up, and backed onto the track. The crickets were in their cage on the backseat, and they brought the voice of the forest along with them. Miss Mack would return to Babylon, and tell Janice that it hadn't been any fun at all, alone on Gavin Pond.

The lights of the car were a little dim – that came from playing the radio so much, and running down the battery. She no longer kept a spare in the car, because ball season was over, and there hadn't been any need for the extra security.

Miss Mack's relief was so great, just to think that she was getting away from Gavin Pond, that she did not realize that she had missed the turnoff until she found herself passing the graveyard on the far side of the pond.

Don't walk past any graveyards.

Miss Mack sped up. In another minute or two she had gone all the way around the pond and was passing by the trailer again. The turnoff was only twenty yards or so beyond the clearing. She put the lights on bright, and slowed considerably.

Before she found the turnoff, the headlights were glancing off the Gavin tombstones. She had missed it again.

Miss Mack went around the pond seven times, looking for the turnoff, and she missed it every time.

That was not possible. She had never once overlooked it

before. It was a perfectly obvious break in the trees. The car lights at night would glance off the silicate pebbles in the ruts.

The car lights were growing dimmer with each succeeding turn around the pond. She could tell this by the amount of light that was reflected off the tombstones. The moon didn't move. The chirping of the crickets in the backseat grew clamorous. Miss Mack threw the car into park suddenly, reached over into the back, and flung the cage out the window.

It hit the trunk of a tree, and must have broken open, for the chirping dispersed. Miss Mack immediately regretted her action. Having given Mr Hill all the fish she had caught the previous day, having consumed all her bacon and eggs in the course of the two nervous breakfasts, she had now nothing to eat. And she had just disposed of the bait she might have used to catch more fish. It was little comfort to remember that fish didn't bite at night.

Miss Mack drove around more slowly now, and even began to look for the track leading to the DeFuniak Springs road on the opposite side of the pond from where she knew it to be. She pinched her fat arms until they were bruised and raw, hoping with each attack to wake up in any place but this.

Miss Mack realized suddenly that not only was she wearing down her battery, she was using up her gas. She had very little left. She hadn't looked at the odometer when she first attempted to drive away from Gavin Pond – why should she have? – but she suspected that she had already driven thirty-five or forty miles. On a straight road, that would have carried her all the way back to Babylon.

The moon hadn't moved.

Miss Mack stopped the car by the trailer, got out, and went inside. She sat down exhausted on the bed. She went to sleep again, and slept for she knew not how long. She hoped that when she waked it would be day, that Janice would wake her by knocking on the door of the trailer. She hoped all this had been a dream – it certainly had the qualities of a dream – and that she might precipitate its ending by rendering herself unconscious within its confines.

She waked, and it was night. Without daring to look at the moon, she went back out to the car. It started, but sluggishly. WBAM was still dedicating a song to Tommy and Julie, and she had very nearly memorized the 2 A.M. wrap-up. Miss Mack drove around and around the pond, and the Pontiac's wavering headlights fell in brutal alternation, now upon the metal trailer, now upon the white Gavin tombstones. She was no longer even looking for the turnoff. She drove as fast as she could around and around the pond, until the car, out of gas, rolled to a standstill just beyond the graveyard.

Miss Mack tried the radio one more time.

Faintly came the song for Tommy and Julie. She listened to it all the way through, thinking, If he plays another song, then I'll *know* that time is passing, and I'll be all right. If he starts over again, then I'll *know* that I'm dreaming.

The battery failed on the last notes of Tommy and Julie's song.

The car lights, which she had left on, faded to blackness.

Miss Mack got out, and turned back. She walked past the graveyard, and slowly along the track from which the turnoff had unaccountably and indisputably disappeared. All the way back to the trailer, she stared at the ruts in the earth, and kept her mind solely upon the turnoff – she did not wish to miss it in her distraction. But the turnoff was not there. She did not stop at the trailer, but continued around again, until she came to the Pontiac, still ticking away its heat.

Don't walk past any graveyards.

From this point, it seemed useless to keep on in the track. She struck out into the pine forest, heading directly north, to where the dirt road led up to DeFuniak Springs. Her way and her speed were impeded by tangled undergrowth and briers. The forest and the night were so dark that she sometimes walked directly into trees, not having been able to see them. Yet swiftness was not of such concern as was the maintenance of her direction. She forged straight ahead, knowing that if she only walked far enough, she would get *some*where.

She had lost sight of the darkened moon, for the canopy of

tree limbs was too thick to permit her to see it. But it was behind her, she knew, and she took some comfort with the reflection that she was walking away from it. At last, after she had walked about an hour, Miss Mack came to a little clearing in the forest. She caught a glimpse of dark water – but even before she had seen the trailer and the gleaming tombstones on the far side, she realized that she had returned to Gavin Pond.

She made another attempt, and struck out directly southward. There was a farm road probably no more than a mile distant, with some old tenant-farmer shacks on it. Miss Mack no longer cared whether they were inhabited or not. If only she could reach that road she would be safe.

She walked for a time she knew not how to measure. It might have been for thirty minutes, or it might have been for hours. And even more carefully than before, she maintained her direction – of that she was certain.

Yet once again, she came upon the clearing in the forest, the trailer, the glint of tombstones on the other side of the water.

For the first time in her life, Miss Mack felt real and uncontrollable fear. By no means could she get away from Gavin Pond. There was no turnoff from the circular track. All ways out through the forest led directly back to the clearing. She had no food in the cabin, and no bait with which to fish. Her lamp oil would not last forever, and tomorrow morning would never come. Miss Mack's one hope was that she was asleep and dreaming. With this single thought, Miss Mack went inside the trailer, lay down upon the bed, and went to sleep. When she waked, it was night – still Halloween night. The moon hadn't moved.

Francis King

SCHOOL CROSSING

FRANCIS KING (1923-2011) *was one of the most distinguished men of letters of his generation, publishing fifty volumes over a sixty-four year career, comprising novels, story collections, poetry, criticism and autobiography, and he was also well known as a book reviewer and theatre critic. His early novel* The Dividing Stream *(1951) won the Somerset Maugham Award for best novel by a young English writer, and two later books,* A Domestic Animal *(1970) and* The Nick of Time *(2002) were nominated for the Booker Prize. At first glance, King, who was known for his literary fiction, much of it gay-themed, might seem out of place in an anthology of horror stories, but as critic Paul Binding has written, King had a 'darkly penetrative vision of existence', and a tendency toward the dark and macabre runs though much of his fiction. Though he was not a prolific author of horror stories, King wrote a half-dozen or so fine ones, including 'School Crossing', a wonderfully understated tale that first appeared in* The 20th Pan Book of Horror Stories *(1979). Unlike some of the stories in this volume, King's is rendered more chilling by what is left unsaid: Why did Mark lose his post at the school? Why does he hate his children so much? Why does he wear eyeglasses for which he has no medical need? Even if its ending is not entirely unforeseen, this story still packs a punch and will linger with readers long after they have finished it. King's first six novels are available from Valancourt.*

THESE DAYS IT SEEMED as if his glasses were never clean. Yearning, importunate or mischievous, the small hands would reach out, soiling and smearing; and it was as if they soiled and smeared everything at which he looked. The garden at which he had laboured for many years, the house filled with the antiques inherited from his first and now dead wife, even the youthful face of his second wife: all seemed to have lost their pristine bloom. 'Don't!' he would ward off the hands. But the twins would think this some kind of game and, laughing hysterically, twisting and lunging, they would hurl themselves upon him. Sometimes he would be rough with them, repelling them with all his force, and then a bewilderment would suddenly freeze their half-formed features and he would see the same bewilderment on the face of their mother, as though he had all at once changed into someone else. He was always wiping the glasses. On a handkerchief. On the end of his tie. On a paper-tissue or a table-napkin or a sheet of lavatory paper. But the imprints of those two pairs of hands perpetually renewed themselves, just as the imprint of those twin lives now perpetually marked each hour of his existence.

It must have been the glasses: the obvious explanation. The glasses and some freak of light as the late sun filtered down through a jagged line of conifers on that late autumn afternoon. It was the old drive that he knew so well, up the hill from the town. He had passed the Smugglers' Rest, with its faked creosoted beams, its plastic chairs and tables set out in the hope that some hardy travellers might be tempted to eat or drink outside, its neat hedges, neat flower-beds, neat paths; then the low line of red-brick Council houses; then the notice, glinting briefly in the setting sun, SCHOOL CROSSING. School, his school. Or what he had thought of as being his school until they had taken it from him. Teaching English part-time to foreigners now, he tried not to think of that brutal dispossession. Never went near the school. Never wished to see any of his former colleagues, unless a little furtive, a little guilty, a little shame-faced, they themselves sought him out. Never spoke about it, not even to Clare, the young science teacher whom he had married.

SCHOOL CROSSING. The Aston Martin, which he could no longer afford to run, leaped effortlessly up the hill; and suddenly, for a moment, there they were, boys and girls straggling across the road. Faces turned at the sound of the engine. Some drew back, others scuttled over to the further side, jostling, ungainly, undignified. But why should they be out of school as early as this? School holiday? No. He had braked to a halt.

And then, to his amazement, he had seen that there was no one
there at all. The late sun glinted on the crown of the road; the
conifers soared up on either side, their green encrusted here
and there near their summits with rust; somewhere far off an
owl hooted. Odd. He could have sworn. But it was the glasses
of course. He took them off, fumbled in his pocket for a handkerchief, found he had none and then, as so often, used the end
of his tie. The tie seemed only to make them worse, leaving a
halo over the left lens where before there had only been a streak.
The sun sank with a strange abruptness, as though that patch of
fire on the crown of the road had been doused with an invisible
pail of water. Behind him a van was hooting. He looked in the
mirror and saw that the driver looked like that Mason boy, son
of a butcher, who had been one of the ring-leaders.... But he
wasn't going to think of the school, never, ever.

He engaged the gears and the car leapt forward, like some
beast suddenly unleashed to seize its prey. Odd.

He did not tell Clare. One of the twins, the boy, had grazed
his knee in a fall; and the other twin, the girl, had somehow
contrived to break a Crown Derby cup. He had to hear about
both accidents and he had to pretend that he cared more about
the knee than the cup. Would he have mentioned what had
happened on the hill if he had come home to peace instead of
turmoil? He did not know. Probably not. There was a lot that
he never mentioned to Clare: a whole secret life of hurt feelings, humiliation, disappointment and resentment. She herself
was so candid, telling him all her most intimate thoughts and
feelings, that she could not guess at the depth of his lack of
candour.

'A good day, Mark?'

'Oh, not too bad. Not too bad.'

He had picked up the *Times*; but as he was opening it, the
boy twin began to scramble up on to his knees. One hand went
out, crushing the paper. A shoe kicked his shin. Then the other
hand was at his glasses. The child crowed with pleasure. Mark
wanted to fling him from him. But instead he forced himself to

laugh as he held the child's arms, one in either hand, and asked him: 'Well, how is that knee of yours?'

Again the child tried to lunge; but his father held him firm. Then the girl came up from behind and her greasy fingers. . . . He looked across at Clare and he could hardly see her face. The smears seemed to be across it, not on his glasses.

'Oh, do take the children upstairs or into the kitchen or somewhere.'

She got up silently and again he fumbled for the handker-chief that he had not got and again he raised the end of his tie.

Several days passed before it happened again. Now it was dark and he was returning from a farewell party given by a group of jolly, noisy students from Norway. They had kept fill-ing his glass even though he told them, 'Look I've got to drive home. I don't want to be breathalysed, now do I?' He felt old and tired; a sour envy had invaded him, like the aftertaste of the acid Spanish wine, for the youth not merely of the students but also of his colleagues. He wondered how soon he could decently make his escape. A plump coquettish girl, with a downy moon-face and eyes of an arctic blankness and blueness – she had always sat just under his desk, arriving at class long before anyone else in order to secure that place – had swayed up to him and enquired tipsily: 'You do not dance, professor?'

'My dancing days are over.'

'But you will dance with me? A last dance?'

He shook his head. He forced himself to smile. 'Neither a last dance nor a first dance. Not after all these years. Not even with you, my dear.'

Surprisingly she had seemed not to be angered but delighted by the rebuff. It was what she must have expected. She laughed, throwing back her head and showing large, white, even teeth. Then she told the others: 'Professor Clark says that his dancing days are over! He will not dance with me!'

'Shame!' cried one of Mark's colleagues, a spotty boy whom he particularly disliked.

'Oh, come along, Mark!' another colleague, a girl, cajoled

him, taking him by an arm and attempting to drag him among the dancers. He had never asked her to call him Mark and he always tried to avoid calling her by any name, surname or Christian name. Some of the students began to clap her as she tugged and tugged at him, her face growing red under its swaying fringe of jet hair. But he would not yield. 'No, I'm not going to dance. But you can give me something more to drink.'

A Norwegian boy splashed some more of the vinegary white wine into his glass.

Well, it could have been that wine. Because he had been a little drunk as he had walked out, long before any other of the teachers, into the frosty December air. He had dropped the car-keys and he had felt uncomfortably top-heavy as he had searched over the asphalt of the yard for them, the tips of his fingers grazing themselves on its uneven surfaces. It must have been that wine and not his glasses, because as soon as he had got into the car, he took off the glasses and wiped them on a corner of a handkerchief that was still neatly folded in the trouser-pocket in which he had put it before setting out. Yes, it must have been that wine. What else could it have been?

It was misty as he drove up the hill and he passed only one car, crawling beetle-like ahead of him. He liked that surge of power as the Aston Martin devoured the little Fiat or whatever it was. It gave him a feeling of exhilaration; it never failed to do so. Which was why he had kept the car while at the same time urging on Clare a number of economies. The daily, holidays abroad, drinks before dinner, the laundry for his shirts: all must go before that car would go. Now that his joints so often ached and were stiff with rheumatism in the mornings, now that he found himself out of breath at the top of a hill or even of the stairs, now that one set of tennis, one swim, one orgasm, was enough for him, he found a compensation in the undiminished ferocity and pounce of that engine.

He could not see the crests of the conifers because of that pervading mist; at times he could hardly see the sides of the road as it curved up to the brow of the hill. The trees seemed to have merged into huddled, opaque masses as the fierce headlights picked them out. SCHOOL CROSSING. The cat's eyes winked at him and then died as he raced past. Slam on the brakes. Their terrified faces. Some began to run. Others frozen. The tyres screeched. The car all but went out of control. He peered into the mist, the car door half-open and one leg hanging through it into the icy air. He had been about to rush out and shout at them. You bloody clots! Couldn't you hear my engine? Didn't you see my lights? And what are you all doing at an hour like this? Don't tell me that you're coming home from school! You might have got yourselves killed! But there was no one there, no one there at all; no target at which to direct his near-hysterical shock and rage.

He heard a chug-chug-chug behind him and the little beetle crawled up past the sign, slowed, all but stopped and then passed on. The driver was probably saying to himself, Odd. Why should he have stopped there? Alone too. But he seems all right. Better not to get mixed up in whatever it is. Perhaps he just wants a piss. The silence closed round the coughing of the little engine as it disappeared from view.

He raised the end of his tie; took off his glasses. But of course it had been the wine, it must have been the wine.

After that he began to dread having to pass the notice. But there was no other way to drive up from the town to the house: not, that is, unless he made an enormous detour. Enormous and costly too – that car devoured petrol with the same greed that it devoured the distance between itself and any other car. It was some silly kind of optical illusion. The trees with the sun low behind them or with the headlights thrust against them. Some trick of shadow. And the fact that he was tired, the glasses, the wine. Nothing odd about it really. As a child, waking up and seeing what seemed to be a stranger seated in the chair, a dark, humped stranger, with a white luminous face, he had screamed and screamed and screamed; but all it was (his mother rushing in) was his own clothes with the moonlight on them. . . . Silly. She had said that to him. Silly, silly boy. Why it's *nothing*!

It was nothing. But still the dread remained. As the Aston

Martin climbed effortlessly up the hill, he would feel his mouth go dry, his heart would start to thump and he would peer ahead, wondering . . . would it happen again this time? But days passed and it did not happen and soon that tension of both the body and the brain no longer gripped him. He had still not spoken of what had happened to Clare or anyone else; and now he would not do so, since obviously it was not going to happen again.

Going into the town one Saturday to shop, they left the two children for a moment in the locked car while they changed their books at the library. It had been a day of nagging rain; and when they returned, they found that the seats of the car, its sides and even its roof were imprinted with the marks of small muddy feet. He could understand how, without meaning it, they might have soiled the seats by scrambling over them or even the sides by kicking out; but to reach the roof they must have made a deliberate, malicious effort. 'Christ! What the hell have you been doing? Look at this! Look! Look!' He pointed here and here and here and the twins cowered and giggled, while Clare, in an effort to placate him, her face suddenly pinched and grey with apprehension, pulled a tiny, pathetic wad of a handkerchief out of her handbag and began to make ineffectual efforts to wipe away the mess.

'You'll only smear it! Leave it! I'll see to it when I get home.'

'It'll all come out. You'll see. . . .' As so often, her fear of him made her turn on the twins. 'Oh, stop that silly sniggering!'

'Why can't you control these bloody brats?'

'They're your brats too.'

But somehow, deep inside himself, he never thought of them as his brats at all. They had come too late; and they had come unwanted.

Clare took the girl on her lap, leaving the boy in the back of the car. The boy was her favourite and so it was the girl to whom she gave this kind of preferential treatment. 'Look, pet. I've got this lovely book for you. Look. That's a dog like the one that Ann has got, isn't it? A big dog, with a big bushy tail. And big teeth. But a friendly dog. Like Anna's dog. A dog with long,

long ears.' From time to time she would glance sideways at him with wary apprehension, wondering whether he would forget about the stains all over the interior of the car or whether they would make him difficult for the whole weekend. He drove thinking, Christ, what inanities!

The car seemed even smoother and even more powerful than ever; and that began to soothe him, as he pushed it up the steeper and steeper gradient, passing one car after another. Everyone seemed to have been shopping; every car was laden with children and baskets and carrier-bags and dogs and toys. SCHOOL CROSSING. There was a ramshackle saloon ahead of him, just beyond the notice; and then, as he pressed the accelerator to catch it up too and leave it in his conquering wake, suddenly, without any warning, the children began to stream across the road. In twos and threes. Shouting to each other. Laughing. One boy pushing another boy into a tall, solitary girl.

The impact of the braking threw the boy twin forward so that he struck his forehead on the seat in front. Fortunately Mark and Clare had both fastened their safety-belts, and the girl was secure in Clare's hands. The boy began to whimper, rubbing his forehead with a look of bewilderment on a face that had begun to pucker. Cars passed, the cars that they themselves had passed. Faces looked round. What a bloody silly place to stop! That's the way to cause an accident. Idiot. Someone hooted.

'Are you all right, darling?' The child began to wail. Clare touched the spot with blunt, cool fingers. 'Does it hurt?' The child wailed louder.

'He's not hurt. You know how he always makes a fuss over the smallest things.'

'He could have been hurt. Badly. What on earth did you stop like that for?'

'Didn't you see. . . . ?' He broke off.

'See? See what?'

He thought quickly. 'The hedgehog.'

'Hedgehog?'

'In the middle of the road. I was afraid I'd run over it.'

'I saw nothing.'

'I saw it, Mummy! I saw it!' the girl began to shout. 'I saw it! Big, big hedgehog!'

The boy was sobbing now. Clare said to the girl: 'You'd better climb over to the back and change places.'

'Why?'

'Because he's hurt his forehead.'

'No!'

'Now, Sally, do what I tell you.'

'It's my turn to sit in front!'

'You sat in front last time.'

'Didn't.'

'Did.'

Oh Christ! It was with a cold, murderous rage that he engaged the gears and once more resumed the journey home. Would they never allow him any peace? Such was his fury against them that he hardly thought of those phantoms suddenly emerging out into the road. It was only later that he began to worry.

Bill Edmonds – 'Big' Bill as he was known all over the town to differentiate him from his partner, also Bill, who was small and fox-like – had once been Mark's closest friend as well as his doctor. Perhaps he still imagined that he was Mark's closest friend, since he was not particularly perceptive; but Mark had never felt the same towards Bill since that whole school business. Bill had not been loyal; or at least not loyal enough to say 'my friend, right or wrong.' His view that Mark had been partly wrong he had never concealed from him, even though he had conceded that Mark had also been partly right. 'You can't run a comprehensive as though it were a small and select grammar school. You know exactly what you're doing and a lot of that staff of yours have no idea what they're doing at all. But that doesn't mean that you can ride roughshod over them.' Later, when the affair had smashed Mark's career and smashed so much else, it had also smashed the peculiar intimacy that had joined the two men. They went on seeing each other; Bill went on prescribing drugs for Mark's blood-pressure, his insomnia and hay-fever; Mark went on tutoring Bill's bored, backward daughter in mathematics during the vacations; the two couples went on entertaining each other to dinner and going on holidays together and playing tennis with each other. But, as far as Mark at least was concerned, the friendship had ended.

Now Bill said: 'Well, I'm damned if I can find anything wrong with you. The blood-pressure's a little lower in fact. The heart is fine.'

'I must have imagined it.' A statement more than a question.

Bill shrugged. 'Some trick of the light,' he said.

'I've thought of that. But it's happened at different times of the day. I mean, if it was a trick of the light, then if the light then changed, if it was coming from a different direction or a different source. . . .'

'Your guess is as good as mine.'

'I suppose one might call it a hallucination.'

'Well. . . .' Bill laughed, one massive buttock perched on the edge of the desk while he scratched at the other. He was always scratching himself.

Mark stared down at his linked hands and then darted an upward look. 'You don't think. . . . Well, this isn't the beginning of a – a breakdown is it?'

'Christ no! I'd be much more worried if you were hallucinating all over the place at all times of the day. The fact that it's just that one particular spot and just that one particular hallucination. . . . But, in any case', he added hurriedly, 'hallucination is not really the word for something so trivial.'

'Then what is?'

Bill did not answer that. 'You've been through a difficult time. Months ago, I know. But the after-effects of that kind of traumatic experience are often delayed. I should guess that you're a bit run-down. Liable to get depressed. Tired.'

'Well, those children certainly never let me sleep after six or seven!'

'Let me give you a tranquilliser.'

When Mark's first wife had been dying, Bill had also given

her a tranquilliser, since there was nothing else to give her. 'A happiness pill' he had called it to Mark; and certainly, whether because of her faith or because of that pill, she had died reasonably happy, when not in pain.

'Oh, I don't think. . . .'

'Now come on! Half my patients are on tranquillisers. Nothing to it!'

Mark had the prescription made up; but he pushed the bottle into the back of a drawer and forgot about it.

The hallucination (if it was a hallucination) now came more and more frequently until it was happening almost every day. As he stepped into the car, sometimes even during his class, he would ask himself, I wonder if I'll see them today. They even appeared when he was giving another of the teachers, whose motorcycle had broken down, a lift up the hill. There they were ahead of him (he had purposely slowed the car, just in case), straggling out over the road with their brief-cases, trailing scarves, knee-high boots and loads of books. He could hear their loud immature voices and hear their loud immature laughter over the purr of the engine. He stopped and watched them, oblivious of his passenger, as they crossed over from the footpath to the lane on the other side. Some of the faces he had never seen before; they had come to the school since his day. Others he recognised and those he hated.

'Anything the matter?'

'What?' The last of them had gone. He attempted to pull himself together. 'I was – was looking at that owl in the tree over there. He's often there at this hour.'

'You must have the most fantastic sight. I can hardly see a thing.'

'It's as though he waited for me. Every evening.'

'Well, imagine that!'

Mark released the hand-brake. Suddenly he felt the sweat icy on his forehead, on his neck and in the small of his back.

He and the famous ophthalmologist had been at the same

Oxford college together; but there had always been a faint con-descension even then from the spectacularly gifted man to the one far less gifted, and now it had grown more marked. The ophthalmologist, thin and sharply handsome, with his modish clothes and his modish haircut, might have been at least ten years younger than the schoolmaster.

'Fancy deciding to start a family so late in life! I'd no idea. It's as though I'd suddenly decided to get married.'

'Well, we didn't really *decide* to start a family. It just hap-pened.'

'Still, it must be fun.'

'Up to a point.'

'I don't really care for children myself. Or animals.'

Mark nearly said, 'Neither do I.' But some impulse of loyalty to Clare, not to the twins, restrained him from doing so.

'Which must mean that I have a shocking character,' the ophthalmologist went on, obviously not believing anything of the kind.

When he had finished his examination he said: 'Well, *I* can't find anything amiss.'

(Mark did not care for the emphasis on the pronoun. Who did he think could find anything? A psychiatrist?) 'The eyes are perfectly normal for a man of your age. In fact, I don't think I'd have even prescribed those glasses for you. You could easily do without them.'

'Then what . . . ?'

The other man shrugged. 'You might have floaters. People with short sight often do. They're maddening things and, if you start to think about them – to become too conscious of them – they can cause you a lot of misery. I had a patient once, a woman, who even advertised in *The Times* for a cure for them. But there isn't one, of course. As I'd told her.'

'I've had floaters. I know what you mean. But they could hardly account for my seeing a number of school children and seeing them in detail. . . . Could it?'

The ophthalmologist, who wanted to get home before going on to Covent Garden, sighed and shrugged. 'You might be haemorrhaging slightly from the eyes from time to time. Though I see no evidence of it. I've often thought that that's all that Joan of Arc's visions amounted to. She never menstruated, you know. But she might have bled instead from the tissue of the eye. It's not unknown. Not at all. I had a woman patient who did precisely that.'

'You don't suggest that I'm menstruating from my eyes?'

The two men laughed; but Mark's laughter was nervous and strained.

'Good God no! And in any case, you'd have reached the menopause by now and the bleeding would be over.'

Again they both laughed.

The ophthalmologist put his arm around Mark's shoulder. It was as a patient that he thought of him now, not as a friend, and the gesture was a purely professional one. 'I should guess you need a holiday. You look rather strained. You've aged a bit since that last Gaudy. Why not go away for a holiday?'

'I might do that.'

'I should ignore the whole thing. Drive through your vision! Why not? Prove to yourself that there's nothing there at all.'

'Yes.'

The ophthalmologist realised that, so far from encouraging his patient, he had only discouraged him further.

Mark had left his car in the station car-park. When he went to reclaim it there, he found two schoolboys examining it carefully. These schoolboys were not from the comprehensive but from the posh preparatory school a few miles outside the town. Mark knew that from their caps.

'That's a lovely job you've got there.'

'Super.'

'Fantastic.'

Mark put his key in the door, smiling at them, saying nothing. He felt that somehow he must appease them.

'Must cost a fortune to run.'

'What's the fastest you've done?'

'Oh, I've no idea. But she's fast.'

'I bet she is!'

They hung around; probably they wanted him to offer them a ride. But he did not do so. He slammed the door and thought, you're like those others. Just like those others. Except that you wear those caps and you sleep in dormitories instead of at home and you have that disdainful upper-class drawl. I hate the lot of you. It was you who smashed me. Smashed me.

He drove off, not even bothering to look at them again.

It was a beautiful December afternoon and he ought to have been happy at the thought of going home after a day in a London that seemed to him, with each visit, to become more and more noisy, more and more crowded, more and more squalid. But he was not happy. He thought of that lucky ophthalmologist, who had been wise enough not to burden himself with a wife and children; who had visited the Caribbean for his last holiday and was going to visit East Africa for his next; who had been about to go to Covent Garden to see *Traviata*. Back home, Clare would complain that the dishwasher had broken down again or that a bulb needed replacing; the children would have broken something or lost something or soiled something; the stain would still be in the centre of the sitting-room carpet; the seat of the chair on the left of the fireplace would still be sagging; he would still be able to see where Clare had stuck that Crown Derby cup inexpertly together.

The Aston Martin began to leap up the hill. Would they be there, waiting for him among the trees? In a curious way, he felt that his fragile, failing body was now somehow fused with the strong, ever-powerful one of the car. I should ignore the whole thing. Drive through your vision, why not? Prove to yourself that there's nothing there at all. What's the fastest you've done in it? Well, I'm doing over seventy now and on a gradient like this. Lovely job. Super. Fantastic. His heart was now the throbbing heart of the engine; his nerves trilled with each of the explosions that sent it hurtling onwards.

SCHOOL CROSSING.

I should ignore the whole thing.

The impact was terrible. The car ploughed on and on. Then

at last it jolted to a stop. Staring out ahead of him, he thought, This must be what is meant by seeing red. The whole windscreen was smeared with blood.

Or were the smears only on his glasses?

Richard Marsh

A PSYCHOLOGICAL EXPERIMENT

One of the most prolific authors of the late-Victorian and Edwardian periods, RICHARD MARSH *(1857-1915) produced some 83 volumes of fiction and 300 short stories during his career, including as many as eight books a year at the height of his popularity. Born Richard Bernard Heldmann, he began his career as an author of fiction for boys, published under the name Bernard Heldmann. But following a conviction for passing bad checks and a term of eighteen months' imprisonment with hard labor, Heldmann began a new career as 'Marsh', his mother's maiden name. He is best known today for his horror classic* The Beetle *(1897), which was published the same year as Bram Stoker's* Dracula *and for a quarter-century outsold Stoker's book, until* Dracula *was adapted for a now-classic 1931 film. But Marsh was more than just a one-book wonder: his vast output comprises work in almost every genre, from horror to crime to comedy to romance, and much of it remains well worth reading. His horror novel* The Joss: A Reversion *(1901) bears comparison with* The Beetle, *and the eerie thriller* The Goddess: A Demon *(1900) is a compelling and unsettling tale. But Marsh may have been at his best in the field of short fiction: he excelled both in tales of horror and the supernatural and in blackly comic stories, with the two sometimes merging, as in the collection* Curios *(1898), in which rival antique dealers pursue strange artifacts. His best horror fiction can be found in the collections* Marvels and Mysteries *(1900),* The Seen and the Unseen *(1900), and* Both Sides of the Veil *(1901). Valancourt has republished thirteen volumes of Marsh's novels and stories, including* The Seen and the Unseen, *from which the present story is taken.*

THE CONVERSATION HAD BEEN OF MURDERS AND OF SUI-CIDES. It had almost seemed as if each speaker had felt constrained to cap the preceding speaker's tale of horror. As the talk went on, Mr Howitt had drawn farther and farther into a corner of the room, as if the subject were little to his liking. Now that all the speakers but one had quitted the smoking-room, he came forward from his corner, in the hope, possibly, that with this last remaining individual, who, like himself, had been a silent listener, he might find himself in more congenial society.

'Dreadful stuff those fellows have been talking!'

Mr Howitt was thin and he was tall. He seemed shorter than he really was, owing to what might be described as a persistent cringe rather than a stoop. He had a deferential, almost fright-ened air. His pallid face was lighted by a smile which one felt might, in a moment, change into a stare of terror. He rubbed his hands together softly, as if suffering from a chronic attack of nerves; he kept giving furtive glances round the room.

In reply to Mr Howitt's observation the stranger nodded his head. There was something in the gesture, and indeed in the man's whole appearance, which caused Mr Howitt to regard him more attentively. The stranger's size was monstrous. By him on the table was a curious-looking box, about eighteen inches square, painted in hideously alternating stripes of blue and green and yellow; and although it was spring, and the smoking-room was warm, he wore his overcoat and a soft felt hat. So far as one could judge from his appearance, seated, he was at least six feet in height. As to girth, his dimensions were bewildering. One could only guess wildly at his weight. To add to the peculiarity of his appearance, he wore a huge black beard, which not only hung over his chest, but grew so high up his cheeks as almost to conceal his eyes.

Mr Howitt took the chair which was in front of the stranger. His eyes were never for a moment still, resting, as they passed, upon the bearded giant in front of him, then flashing quickly hither and thither about the room.

'Do you stay in Jersey long?'

'No.'

The reply was monosyllabic, but, though it was heard so briefly, at the sound of the stranger's voice Mr Howitt half rose, grasped the arm of his chair, and gasped. The stranger seemed surprised.

'What's the matter?'

Mr Howitt dropped back on to his seat. He took out his handkerchief to wipe his forehead. His smile, which had changed into a stare of terror on its reappearance, assumed a sickly hue.

'Nothing. Only a curious similarity.'

'Similarity? What do you mean?'

Whatever Mr Howitt might mean, every time the stranger opened his mouth it seemed to give him another shock. It was a moment or two before he regained sufficient control over himself to enable him to answer.

'Your voice reminds me of one which I used to hear. It's a mere fugitive resemblance.'

'Whose voice does mine remind you of?'

'A friend's.'

'What was his name?'

'His name was – Cookson.'

Mr Howitt spoke with a perceptible stammer.

'Cookson? I see.'

There was silence. For some cause, Mr Howitt seemed on a sudden to have gone all limp. He sat in a sort of heap on his chair. He smoothed his hands together, as if with unconscious volition. His sickly smile had degenerated into a fatuous grin. His shifty eyes kept recurring to the stranger's face in front of him. It was the stranger who was the next to speak.

'Did you hear what those men were talking about?'

'Yes.'

'They were talking of murders.'

'Yes.'

'I heard rather a curious story of a murder as I came down to Weymouth in the train.'

'It's a sort of talk I do not care for.'

'No. Perhaps not; but this was rather a singular tale. It was about a murder which took place the other day at Exeter.'

Mr Howitt started.

'At Exeter?'

'Yes; at Exeter.'

The stranger stood up. As he did so, one realised how grotesquely unwieldy was his bulk. It seemed to be as much as he could do to move. The three pockets in the front of his overcoat were protected by buttoned flaps. He undid the buttons. As he did so the flaps began to move. Something peeped out. Then hideous things began to creep from his pockets – efts, newts, lizards, various crawling creatures. Mr Howitt's eyes ceased to stray. They were fastened on the crawling creatures. The hideous things wriggled and writhed in all directions over the stranger. The huge man gave himself a shake. They all fell from him to the floor. They lay for a second as if stupefied by the fall. Then they began to move to all four quarters of the room. Mr Howitt drew his legs under his chair.

'Pretty creatures, aren't they?' said the stranger. 'I like to carry them about with me wherever I go. Don't let them touch you. Some of them are nasty if they bite.'

Mr Howitt tucked his long legs still further under his chair. He regarded the creatures which were wriggling on the floor with a degree of aversion which was painful to witness. The stranger went on.

'About this murder at Exeter, which I was speaking of. It was a case of two solicitors who occupied offices together on Fore Street Hill.'

Mr Howitt glanced up at the stranger, then back again at the writhing newts. He rather gasped than spoke.

'Fore Street Hill?'

'Yes – they were partners. The name of one of them was Rolt – Andrew Rolt. By the way, I like to know with whom I am talking. May I inquire what your name is?'

This time Mr Howitt was staring at the stranger with wide-open eyes, momentarily forgetful even of the creatures which were actually crawling beneath his chair. He stammered and he stuttered.

'My name's – Howitt. You'll see it in the hotel register.'

'Howitt? – I see – I'm glad I have met you, Mr Howitt. It

seems that this man, Andrew Rolt, murdered his partner, a man named Douglas Colston.'

Mr Howitt was altogether oblivious of the things upon the floor. He clutched at the arms of his chair. His voice was shrill.

'Murdered! How do they know he murdered him?'

'It seems they have some shrewd ideas upon the point, from this.'

The stranger took from an inner pocket of his overcoat what proved, when he had unfolded it, to be a double-crown poster. He held it up in front of Mr Howitt. It was headed in large letters, 'MURDER! £100 REWARD.'

'You see, they are offering £100 reward for the apprehension of this man, Andrew Rolt. That looks as if someone had suspicions. Here is his description: Tall, thin, stoops; has sandy hair, thin on top, parted in the middle; restless grey eyes; wide mouth, bad teeth, thin lips; white face; speaks in a low, soft voice; has a nervous trick of rubbing his hands together.' The stranger ceased reading from the placard to look at Mr Howitt. 'Are you aware, sir, that this description is very much like you?'

Mr Howitt's eyes were riveted on the placard. They had followed the stranger as he read. His manner was feverishly strained.

'It's not. Nothing of the sort. It's your imagination. It's not in the least like me.'

'Pardon me, but the more I look at you the more clearly I perceive how strong is the resemblance. It is you to the life. As a detective' – he paused, Mr Howitt held his breath – 'I mean supposing I were a detective, which I am not' – he paused again, Mr Howitt gave a gasp of relief – 'I should feel almost justified in arresting you and claiming the reward. You are so made in the likeness of Andrew Rolt.'

'I'm not. I deny it! It's a lie!'

Mr Howitt stood up. His voice rose to a shriek. A fit of trembling came over him. It constrained him to sit down again. The stranger seemed amused.

'My dear sir! I entreat you to be calm. I was not suggesting for one moment that you had any actual connection with the miscreant Rolt. The resemblance must be accidental. Did you not tell me your name was Howitt?'

'Yes; that's my name, Howitt – William Howitt.'

'Any relation to the poet?'

'Poet?' Mr Howitt seemed mystified; then, to make a dash at it, 'Yes; my great-uncle.'

'I congratulate you, Mr Howitt, on your relationship. I have always been a great admirer of your great-uncle's works. Perhaps I had better put this poster away. It may be useful for future reference.'

The stranger, folding up the placard, replaced it in his pocket. With a quick movement of his fingers he did something which detached what had seemed to be the inner lining of his over-coat from the coat itself – splitting the garment, as it were, and making it into two. As he did so, there fell from all sides of him another horde of crawling creatures. They dropped like lumps of jelly on to the floor, and remained for some seconds, a wrig-gling mass. Then, like their forerunners, they began to make incursions towards all the points of the compass. Mr Howitt, already in a condition of considerable agitation, stared at these ungainly forms in a state of mind which seemed to approach to stupefaction.

'More of my pretty things, you perceive. I'm very fond of reptiles. I always have been. Don't allow any of them to touch you. They might do you an injury. Reptiles sometimes do.' He turned a little away from Mr Howitt. 'I heard some particu-lars of this affair at Exeter. It seems that these two men, Rolt and Colston, were not only partners in the profession of the law, they were also partners in the profession of swindling. Thorough-paced rogues, both of them. Unfortunately, there is not a doubt of it. But it appears that the man Rolt was not only false to the world at large, he was false even to his partner. Don't you think, Mr Howitt, that it is odd that a man should be false to his partner?'

The inquiry was unheeded. Mr Howitt was gazing at the crawling creatures which seemed to be clustering about his chair.

'Ring the bell!' he gasped. 'Ring the bell! Have them taken away!'

'Have what taken away? My pretty playthings? My dear sir, to touch them would be dangerous. If you are very careful not to move from your seat, I think I may guarantee that you will be safe. You did not notice my question. Don't you think it odd that a man should be false to his partner?'

'Eh? – Oh! – Yes; very.'

The stranger eyed the other intently. There was something in Mr Howitt's demeanour which, to say the least of it, was singular.

'I thought you would think it was odd. It appears that one night the two men agreed that they would divide spoils. They proceeded to do so then and there. Colston, wholly unsuspicious of evil, was seated at a table, making up a partnership account. Rolt, stealing up behind him, stupefied him with chloroform.'

'It wasn't chloroform.'

'Not chloroform? May I ask how you know?'

'I – I guessed it.'

'For a stranger, rather a curious subject on which to hazard a guess, don't you think so? However, allowing your guess, we will say it was not chloroform. Whatever it was it stupefied Colston. Rolt, when he perceived Colston was senseless, produced a knife – like this.'

The stranger flourished in the air a big steel blade, which was shaped like a hunting-knife. As he did so, throwing his overcoat from him on to the floor, he turned right round towards Mr Howitt. Mr Howitt stared at him voiceless. It was not so much at the sufficiently ugly weapon he was holding in his hand at which he stared, as at the man himself. The stranger, indeed, presented an extraordinary spectacle. The upper portion of his body was enveloped in some sort of oilskin – such as sailors wear in dirty weather. The oilskin was inflated to such an extent that the upper half of him resembled nothing so much as a huge ill-shaped bladder. That it was inflated was evident, with something, too, that was conspicuously alive. The oilskin writhed and twisted, surged and heaved, in a fashion that was anything but pleasant to behold.

'You look at me! See here!'

The stranger dashed the knife he held into his own breast, or he seemed to. He cut the oilskin open from top to bottom. And there gushed forth, not his heart's blood, but an amazing mass of hissing, struggling, twisting serpents. They fell, all sorts and sizes, in a confused, furious, frenzied heap, upon the floor. In a moment the room seemed to be alive with snakes. They dashed hither and thither, in and out, round and round, in search either of refuge or revenge. And, as the snakes came on, the efts, the newts, the lizards, and the other creeping things, in their desire to escape them, crawled up the curtains, and the doors, and the walls.

Mr Howitt gave utterance to a sort of strangled exclamation. He retained sufficient presence of mind to spring upon the seat of his chair, and to sit upon the back of it. The stranger remained standing, apparently wholly unmoved, in the midst of the seeming pandemonium of creepy things.

'Do you not like snakes, Mr Howitt? I do! They appeal to me strongly. This is part of my collection. I rather pride myself on the ingenuity of the contrivance which enables me to carry my pets about with me wherever I may go. At the same time you are wise in removing your feet from the floor. Not all of them are poisonous. Possibly the more poisonous ones may not be able to reach you where you are. You see this knife?' The stranger extended it towards Mr Howitt. 'This is the knife with which, when he had stupefied him, Andrew Rolt slashed Douglas Colston about the head and face and throat like this!'

The removal of his overcoat, and, still more, the vomiting forth of the nest of serpents, had decreased the stranger's bulk by more than one-half. Disembarrassing himself of the remnants of his oilskins, he removed his soft felt hat, and, tearing off his huge black beard, stood revealed as a tall, upstanding, muscularly-built man, whose head and face and neck were almost entirely concealed by strips of plaster, which crossed and recrossed each other in all possible and impossible directions.

There was silence. The two men stared at each other. With a gasp Mr Howitt found his voice.

'Douglas!'

'Andrew!'

'I thought you were dead.'

'I am risen from the grave.'

'I am glad you are not dead.'

'Why?'

Mr Howitt paused as if to moisten his parched lips.

'I never meant to kill you.'

'In that case, Andrew, your meaning was unfortunate. I do mean to kill you – now.'

'Don't kill me, Douglas.'

'A reason, Andrew?'

'If you knew what I have suffered since I thought I had killed you, you would not wish to take upon yourself the burden which I have had to bear.'

'My nerves, Andrew, are stronger than yours. What would crush you to the ground would not weigh on me at all. Surely you knew that before.' Mr Howitt fidgeted on the back of his chair. 'It was not that you did not mean to kill me. You lacked the courage. You gashed me like some frenzied cur. Then, afraid of your own handiwork, you ran to save your skin. You dared not wait to see if what you had meant to do was done. Why, Andrew, as soon as the effects of your drug had gone, I sat up. I heard you running down the stairs, I saw your knife lying at my side, all stained with my own blood – see, Andrew, the stains are on it still! I even picked up this scrap of paper which had fallen from your pocket on to the floor.'

He held out a piece of paper towards Mr Howitt.

'It is the advertisement of an hotel – Hôtel de la Couronne d'Or, St. Hélier's, Jersey. I said to myself, I wonder if that is where Andrew is gone. I will go and see. And if I find him I will kill him. I have found you, and behold, your heart has so melted within you that already you feel something of the pangs of death.' Mr Howitt did seem to be more dead than alive. His face was bloodless. He was shivering as if with cold.

'These melodramatic and, indeed, slightly absurd details' – the stranger waved his hand towards the efts, and newts, and snakes, and lizards – 'were planned for your especial benefit. I was aware what a horror you had of creeping things. I take it, it is constitutional. I knew I had but to spring on you half a bushel or so of reptiles, and all the little courage you ever had would vanish. As it has done.'

The stranger stopped. He looked, with evident enjoyment of his misery, at the miserable creature squatted on the back of the chair in front of him. Mr Howitt tried to speak. Two or three times he opened his mouth, but there came forth no sound. At last he said, in curiously husky tones –

'Douglas?'

'Andrew?'

'If you do it they are sure to have you. It is not easy to get away from Jersey.'

'How kind of you, Andrew, and how thoughtful! But you might have spared yourself your thought. I have arranged all that. There is a cattle-boat leaves for St Malo in half an hour on the tide. You will be dead in less than half an hour – so I go in that.'

Again there were movements of Mr Howitt's lips. But no words were audible. The stranger continued.

'The question which I have had to ask myself has been, how shall I kill you? I might kill you with the knife with which you endeavoured to kill me.' As he spoke, he tested the keenness of the blade with his fingers. 'With it I might slit your throat from ear to ear, or I might use it in half a hundred different ways. Or I might shoot you like a dog.' Producing a revolver, he pointed it at Mr Howitt's head. 'Sit quite still, Andrew, or I may be tempted to flatten your nose with a bullet. You know I can shoot straight. Or I might avail myself of this.'

Still keeping the revolver pointed at Mr Howitt's head, he took from his waistcoat pocket a small syringe.

'This, Andrew, is a hypodermic syringe. I have but to take firm hold of you, thrust the point into one of the blood-vessels of your neck, and inject the contents; you will at once endure exquisite tortures which, after two or three minutes, which will seem to you like centuries, will result in death. But I have resolved to do myself, and you, this service, with neither of the three.'

Again the stranger stopped. This time Mr Howitt made no attempt to speak. He was not a pleasant object to contemplate. As the other had said, to judge from his appearance he already seemed to be suffering some of the pangs of death. All the manhood had gone from him. Only the shell of what was meant to be a man remained. The exhibition of his pitiful cowardice afforded his whilom partner unqualified pleasure.

'Have you ever heard of an author named De Quincey? He wrote on murder, considered as a fine art. It is as a fine art I have had to consider it. In that connection I have had to consider three things: 1. That you must be killed. 2. That you must be killed in such a manner that you shall suffer the greatest possible amount of pain. 3. – and not the least essential – That you must be killed in such a manner that under no circumstances can I be found guilty of having caused your death. I have given these three points my careful consideration, and I think that I have been able to find something which will satisfy all the requirements. That something is in this box.'

The stranger went to the box which was on the table – the square box which had, as ornamentation, the hideously alternating stripes of blue and green and yellow. He rapped on it with his knuckles. As he did so, from within it there came a peculiar sound like a sullen murmur.

'You hear? It is death calling to you from the box. It awaits its prey. It bids you come.'

He struck the box a little bit harder. There proceeded from it, as if responsive to his touch, what seemed to be a series of sharp and angry screeches.

'Again! It loses patience. It grows angry. It bids you hasten. Ah!'

He brought his hand down heavily upon the top of the box. Immediately the room was filled with a discord of sounds, cries, yelpings, screams, snarls, the tumult dying away in what seemed to be an intermittent, sullen roaring. The noise served to rouse the snakes, and efts, and lizards to renewed activity. The room seemed again to be alive with them. As he listened, Mr Howitt became livid. He was, apparently, becoming imbecile with terror.

His aforetime partner, turning to him, pointed to the box with outstretched hand.

'What a row it makes! What a rage it's in! Your death screams out to you, with a ravening longing – the most awful death that a man can die. Andrew – to die! And such a death as this!'

Again he struck the box. Again there came from it that dreadful discord. 'Stand up!'

Mr Howitt looked at him, as a drivelling idiot might look at a keeper whom he fears. It seemed as if he made an effort to frame his lips for the utterance of speech. But he had lost the control of his muscles. With every fibre of his being he seemed to make a dumb appeal for mercy to the man in front of him. The appeal was made in vain. The command was repeated.

'Get off your chair, and stand upon the floor.'

Like some trembling automaton Mr Howitt did as he was told. He stood there like some lunatic deaf mute. It seemed as if he could not move, save at the bidding of his master. That master was careful not to loosen, by so much as a hair's-breadth, the hold he had of him.

'I now proceed to put into execution the most exquisite part of my whole scheme. Were I to unfasten the box and let death loose upon you, some time or other it might come out – these things do come out at times – and it might then appear that the deed had, after all, been mine. I would avoid such risks. So you shall be your own slayer, Andrew. You shall yourself unloose the box, and you shall yourself give death its freedom, so that it may work on you its will. The most awful death that a man can die! Come to me, here!'

And the man went to him, moving with a curious, stiff gait, such as one might expect from an automaton. The creatures writhing on the floor went unheeded, even though he trod on them.

'Stand still in front of the box.' The man stood still. 'Kneel down.'

The man did hesitate. There did seem to come to him some consciousness that he should himself be the originator of his own volition. There did come on to his distorted visage an agony of supplication which it was terrible to witness.

The only result was an emphasised renewal of the command.

'Kneel down upon the floor.'

And the man knelt down. His face was within a few inches of the painted box. As he knelt the stranger struck the box once more with the knuckles of his hand. And again there came from it that strange tumult of discordant sounds.

'Quick, Andrew, quick, quick! Press your finger on the spring! Unfasten the box!'

The man did as he was bid. And, in an instant, like a conjurer's trick, the box fell all to pieces, and there sprang from it, right into Mr Howitt's face, with a dreadful noise, some dreadful thing which enfolded his head in its hideous embraces.

There was a silence.

Then the stranger laughed. He called softly –

'Andrew!' All was still. 'Andrew!' Again there was none that answered. The laughter was renewed.

'I do believe he's dead. I had always supposed that the stories about being able to frighten a man to death were all apocryphal. But that a man could be frightened to death by a thing like this – a toy!'

He touched the creature which concealed Mr Howitt's head and face. As he said, it was a toy. A development of the old-fashioned jack-in-the-box. A dreadful development, and a dreadful toy. Made in the image of some creature of the squid class, painted in livid hues, provided with a dozen long, quivering tentacles, each actuated by a spring of its own. It was these tentacles which had enfolded Mr Howitt's head in their embraces.

As the stranger put them from him, Mr Howitt's head fell, face foremost, on to the table. His partner, lifting it up, gazed down at him.

Had the creature actually been what it was intended to represent it could not have worked more summary execution. The look which was on the dead man's face as his partner turned it upwards was terrible to see.

Stephen Gregory

THE PROGRESS OF
JOHN ARTHUR CRABBE

STEPHEN GREGORY *is the author of seven novels, the first three of which,* The Cormorant *(1986; winner of the Somerset Maugham Award),* The Woodwitch *(1988), and* The Blood of Angels *(1992) have recently been republished by Valancourt Books. Author Mark Morris has written that Gregory is 'one of the best and most underrated novelists in the world', and has noted the ways in which nature and the natural world play a prominent role in his fiction, particularly (as in this story) birds, which appear in Gregory's fiction as 'malign, destructive spirits or harbingers of doom'. This rare early tale first appeared in the* Illustrated London News *on December 6, 1982, and is reprinted here for the first time.*

Mrs Crabbe gave birth to a son one month after the death of her husband. She named the boy John Arthur, in memory of him. Mr Crabbe had been overjoyed at the news of his wife's unexpected pregnancy. A middle-aged man, disappointed for many years by his wife's failure to produce a child, he was delighted at the prospect of a son who would transform the marriage he saw as adequate and comfortable into something much more satisfactory. So it was tragic that he should die before the child was born.

John Arthur was a remarkable little boy. For one thing, it was realized within 18 months of his birth that he was severely mentally handicapped. As he grew into a strapping toddler it was obvious that his mind was defective. For such a young child he had a disconcerting, rasping, even sonorous voice, which he produced from his chest in a series of garbled speeches made up of sounds not unlike real words. In spite of his mother's sustained efforts to teach John Arthur the beginnings of a

vocabulary, the boy continued to clamour in his own clang-
ing language, as though half remembering words and phrases
from some distant past. He developed a shock of unruly black
hair which flopped over his brow, although it did not grow to
such an extent on the crown or the back of his head. Most striking of all was his bulging forehead which protruded over his
eyes, shadowing them. They retreated into his head like two
dangerous eels in an underwater crevice.

But Mrs Crabbe soon discovered that her growing son, so
inwardly disturbed and so incommunicative, had an unusual
gift. He had the power in his hands to heal. The first manifesta-
tion of this was when he came into the house from the bushes
of the garden holding the broken body of a fledgling bird. It
stared from his cupped hands and beat itself against his palms.
But soon it became calm, even torpid. As Mrs Crabbe watched,
John Arthur caressed the wound on the bird's breast until his
fingers were smeared with its blood. Then he raised the tiny
creature to his lips and kissed it on the crown of its head. Its
eyes flickered suddenly, like gems struck from a rock. The bird
hopped from the boy's hands on to the carpet. The only traces
of any wound were the blood which stained John Arthur's
hands and a tiny feather which clung to his lips. So Mrs Crabbe
realized that her son had an affinity with wild creatures. She
could hardly help noticing his tendency to bring into the house
all sorts of wounded animals, birds and insects. Each time,
however severely damaged the sparrow, the spider or the shrew,
it was soon whole again, and happy to stay with John Arthur in
his room.

The boy continued to grow sturdy. He carried himself well,
if occasionally with a stoop, cultivated from the almost con-
tinual nursing of injured creatures. The mass of hair still fell on
his forehead and still his eyes seemed buried under his powerful brow. John Arthur's hands were long and thin, even fragile.
They held the dusty wings of a moth or the limbs of a daddy-
longlegs with a tenderness which Mrs Crabbe found touching.
As she watched her son's strong body and his ponderous head
hunched over his latest find she marvelled at the gentleness of

his fine fingers. Then she felt her love for John Arthur and her regret for her dead husband mingling and aching inside her.

The boy did not go to school. Instead, he stayed at home and tended his ever-growing collection of specimens. His bedroom was full of small creatures which came and went from his window. They were not imprisoned. They were free to go, once heated by the warmth of John Arthur's fingers, but sometimes the grateful creatures would return to the boy. John Arthur could not wash or dress himself. He could not feed himself without making a fearful mess. He could not communicate with other human beings although he still held forth at length, and with a seemingly increasing vocabulary, in his own discordant language. But John Arthur had the heat in his hands and the breath from his lips to salve and restore the broken limbs of his many patients.

Naturally, word of John Arthur's power spread among Mrs Crabbe's friends, the circle that had grown up as her husband had become more successful. They had consoled her on the death of Mr Crabbe and had followed the development of John Arthur. But much as Mrs Crabbe enjoyed the company of her friends, she often felt that their interest in her and her curious son was ghoulish. She imagined them discussing John Arthur with a sort of unhealthy relish whenever she was not there. She could hear them describing the inhabitants of his bedroom, the voles, the mice and the moths, the leathery bat and the ducking, sidling jackdaw which never blinked. Mrs Crabbe particularly resented the dashing Mrs Sylvester, who pried into John Arthur's every small sign of progress, who chuckled at his rasping cries. She was gaudy, metallic. Mrs Crabbe resented her almost predatory interest in the boy.

Mrs Sylvester had a son who was as pert as herself. He was a success at school, regarding his fellows with a lift of his eyebrows and a mocking smile. Sometimes he accompanied his mother on her visits to Mrs Crabbe's house, but he was plainly uncomfortable in the presence of John Arthur. He flushed under the distant gaze of John Arthur's eyes and seemed overwhelmed, dominated by the weight of John Arthur's brow. But his mother remained jaunty, and her son gained in confidence until he, too, had developed a kind of growing curiosity about the power of John Arthur's fragile hands.

Then tragedy struck the Sylvester family. Within a few hours of being bright and swift, Mrs Sylvester's son fell gravely ill. He lay inert on his bed, his eyes open but unseeing. The doctors diagnosed that the boy had had the seed of a tumour growing within his skull, unsuspected until now. With the sudden pressure of the tumour against his brain, he was immediately paralysed in every limb. Furthermore, the tumour, at present the size of a small fist, would continue to grow, unclenching like a fist threatening to burst within the boy's head. He would die. Meanwhile, he lay with his eyebrows raised and with his mouth fixed in the faint smile which he had so often carried in the swift brightness of his health. More doctors were consulted. All of them were pessimistic, even advising against the boy's removal from the house to a hospital. It would be in vain; better to leave him lying on his own bed, breathing faintly and with the hard smile caught on his lips.

One evening Mrs Crabbe was astonished, on answering the door, to see the figure of Mrs Sylvester standing in the porch. The powerful, still glinting woman held the motionless body of her son in her arms. She stepped silently into the house. John Arthur stood at his mother's elbow and watched the progress of the woman who came into the hall. His chin was up, his eyes caught the light and threw it back at the limp boy in Mrs Sylvester's arms. There was an electric, crackling interchange between the sunken eyes of John Arthur and those of the unseeing, dying boy. And instantly John Arthur began to chatter in his harsh voice, releasing a torrent of half recognizable, half remembered sounds. Mrs Crabbe followed her son towards his bedroom and Mrs Sylvester carried her son behind them.

John Arthur opened his door. As he went into the room there started from all corners of the darkness the whispers of his other patients. Mrs Sylvester swallowed her apprehension and advanced towards the bed. She placed her motionless son on it. Still John Arthur poured out his dry, shouting sounds, echoed around the room by the rustling of the bat and the crow, the movement of the mole and the moth. Then Mrs Crabbe took Mrs Sylvester firmly by the arm and led her back to the door, out of the room. They left John Arthur and the stricken boy alone, in the muttering darkness.

John Arthur's cries stopped as the door closed. The two women waited outside the room, looking away from each other, along the corridor. Then, as though no time had passed at all, they were woken from their confusion, their doubts, by a barely perceptible click as the door opened and slowly swung wide. The light from the hallway spilled into the bedroom. John Arthur stood near his bed. His hair swept back from his brow, his eyes challenged the light, boldly staring towards the door.

There was no one, no figure, no boy lying on the bed. Only the rumpled blankets showed the imprint of a body. Two things seemed to happen as one, two outbursts of sound and colour simultaneously. Up from the bed there rose the metallic brightness of a bird, a jay. It beat across the room, blue, black, white and blue again. The jay struck the mirror with a loud crack, a dazzling duplicate of itself, dropping to the carpet and releasing a torrent of guttural shrieks. At the same time, with a mocking smile on his lips, John Arthur Crabbe began to speak in a clear, measured voice, welcoming his mother.

John Trevena

THE FROZEN MAN

The career of JOHN TREVENA (1870-1948), *whom a critic for the* Times Literary Supplement *in 2013 called 'one of England's lost novelists, a writer of startling ability', was a strange one. From 1897 to 1907 he built a minor reputation for himself under his birth name, Ernest G. Henham, publishing a number of moderately successful novels, including the weird decadent tale* Tenebrae (1898) *and the haunted house novel* The Feast of Bacchus (1907), *both republished by Valancourt. But for reasons of health, Henham was obliged to move to Dartmoor, where he apparently disowned his earlier works, adopting the pseudonym John Trevena and publishing a series of highly accomplished mystical novels which were ranked by a contemporary* Los Angeles Times *critic as being on par with the classics of Turgenev and Dostoevsky. The virtuosity of Trevena's prose is on full display in 'The Frozen Man', which originally appeared in the collection* Written in the Rain (1912) *and which is reprinted for the first time here.*

THE COUNTRY WAS THE HOME of the cold genius of the north: a ridiculous ball of sun, no warmer than the moon, surrounded by coronae, the air glittering with crystals, every bush and bough coated with glazed frost; I had but to kick up the snow to see a shower of diamonds; and above the steel-blue of the horizon hung a mirage, a deserted city of ice, a place of dreams and folklore. While I was staring at the spires and pinnacles shooting upward from silent streets of cloud, looking in vain for the snow-clad ghosts which should have been walking there, Chief Factor Armstrong came across, drew the corn-cob from his mouth, and spoke:

'It's real good of you to go with Mac. I couldn't send him out by himself, as you might say, for Sinapis as a companion is no better than a dog. The boy isn't right either – swears he is, but I know better. I believe he's sick. He must go, for I've no one else.'

'Old Mac is a good sort,' I said.

'The best in the world, when you can keep him off religion and whisky. He's fond of preaching, and the other thing. Here come the dogs,' Armstrong went on heartily. 'Good-luck to you, good weather, and lots of thanks.'

The assistant-factor, MacDonald, and myself were about to start upon an expedition to the north. Game of every kind had been scarce that season, not a fox came near the fort, even wolves appeared to have deserted us: so we were going to explore the country for signs of the fur-bearers, as we couldn't place much reliance upon the reports of wandering natives, although these same individuals had lately supplied Armstrong with information which made a journey of investigation necessary. According to them a party of Germans were passing through the country further north, trapping and shooting all the furs they could find, thereby infringing upon the rights of the Governor and Company of Adventurers of England trading into Hudson's Bay.

'There's no truth in the yarn,' Armstrong had said. 'Anyway, it's like this: if I make a search for these fellows, it will be found that the story is false. If I don't look for them, it will be true, and I shall hear something about neglect of duty.'

The long sleigh lay upon the glistening snow before the fort, packed with provisions and furs, while Sinapis with a heavy whip attempted to control the team of twenty-four dogs, the finest lot in the country, and the pride of the chief factor's heart. Well they might be, for the famous breed of sleigh dog, or husky, as the animal is generally named, is well-nigh extinct today. These powerful brutes are more like bears than dogs. Their strength and staying powers are enormous, and their ferocity is on a par with their hardiness, which is indeed almost abnormal, as I have driven a team for a week on nothing but a little hard biscuit, with a few scraps of deer pemmican and frozen fish strips once in the twenty-four hours. Yet they have snapped as fiercely and been to all appearance as lusty on the last few miles as at the start.

Sinapis crawled into the back of the sleigh, the long lash curled out, the leaders yelped impatiently and bit each other. The next moment we were gliding along swiftly, enveloped in the smoke-like breath of the dogs, while old Armstrong waved a farewell from the fort. There is nothing half so exhilarating as a good scamper over the northern plains, wrapped up to the nose tip, lying full length along the sleigh, with a score of thoroughbred dogs in front. Away on all sides extended the snow-covered wastes, broken here and there by dark-green fir bluffs, their tresses blue with ice. Not a man, not an animal, nor bird, nor insect could be seen for miles. But what of that? It was glorious to see the pale-blue sky spotted with fragile cirri, to watch the frost dancing around, and to feel the sharp prick of the crystals against the exposed cheeks and nose, and to hear the comfortable swish of the sleigh as it slid along, and the quick panting of the dogs.

That first day we travelled at a great rate, for the snow was solid and fairly even, although at times we would glance with a sudden shock off a hidden point of rock, or grate over a fallen tree trunk which the last sprinkle of snow had managed to cover. At evening we camped well inside a bluff, keeping up a huge fire, which was indeed needed, for our little spirit ther-mometer marked forty-six below zero when I read it at ten o'clock, and it would sink lower than that before morning.

It was not until we had finished supper, and were bending to light our pipes at the fire, that MacDonald put a suspicion I had been harbouring for the last hour into words.

'Say,' he remarked; 'been watching the boy lately?'

Sinapis appeared restless and miserable. He never spoke, moved listlessly, and accomplished his tasks without any show of alacrity, working slowly and heavily, although that was no new thing with him.

I answered MacDonald's question with another, 'What's wrong with him?'

He snorted impatiently. 'Sick, and dead sick, too. He was bad when we started, but wouldn't own to it, darn him.'

'He'll be all right to-morrow.'

'That's a silly thing to say. You know what a flimsy affair an Indian's constitution is. He's sick one day, dead the next. Doing his usual chores in the morning, taking his long rest at night. It's no use kicking back because you don't want to go on. What we want to do is to face the question.'

'Let's put him in the sleigh, cover him up, and if he is all right in the morning the better for us. If he isn't, we'll have done all we can. You might have been worse off, Mac. If I hadn't come –'

'If you weren't here I shouldn't think twice about it,' he interrupted. 'I should hitch up the huskies first thing in the morning, and start to work crossing those tracks we made to-day.'

Unluckily next morning there could be no question about the seriousness of the man's illness. What the disease was I couldn't tell; but his strength had gone, his head and body were racked with pains, and altogether he seemed in a bad way. However, we started off north as soon as we had partaken of some food, and made good progress all forenoon. Then evil fortune overtook us. We reached bad country, covered with rocks, and protected upon either side by a deep bank of pines. Here the snow-bed was uneven. The sleigh, instead of gliding over the surface, broke through the crust, while the dogs sank up to their bellies, tugging ineffectually, and filling the air with their short angry barks.

MacDonald and I looked at each other. Anger was visible all over his face, as he shouted sulkily to the dogs, who ceased from their labours willingly enough.

'Just what I told you,' he grumbled. 'Directly Sinapis is struck down, this sort of job crops up. We're going to have a happy day, I tell ye.'

There was no help for it. We lashed on the snowshoes and walked ahead of the dogs, breaking a trail for them. It was hard work, and took all the breath we could spare, so there was little talk until we reached a good camping-place and began to fix up for the night. Luckily the last few miles had been fairly easy, so we looked forward to good going on the morrow. It was worthy of note that during the whole of the day's journey we had never sighted a living thing.

Sinapis was better, I thought. He was quieter and had stopped groaning. He lay still, and did not appear to notice either of us. We did what we could – little enough – then left him and tried to get to sleep ourselves. The night was milder, if twenty-five below may be called warm, but we were well sheltered by bluffs on every side.

I was beginning to doze when MacDonald hit me in the ribs with the stem of his pipe, and I saw his quaint hairy face near mine.

'Man,' he whispered, 'have ye seen the boy?'

'Not for the last hour or two. What's wrong?' I said.

'Have ye seen his eyes?'

'Get away, Mac,' I muttered.

'I saw his eyes,' he went on, 'I waved my hand up and down and they never winked. Man, he's crazy.'

'Look here, Mac,' I said, 'keep your horrors to yourself, and let me get to sleep.'

'Crazy,' he repeated unpityingly. 'Knows he's going to die, and the fear o' death has crazed his brain because he's a papist, and knows – '

I put out an arm, pushed him off – I dare say I cursed. Mac-Donald returned to his own side of the fire, quoted Scripture at me, expressed a wish for a Bible that he might quote some more, and the last thing I heard as he settled down for sleep was a fervent whisper, 'Man, I'd give a year of my life for a wee bottle o' Glenlivet.'

Our luck improved when we made a start in the morning. The bad country was soon left behind, and we scudded over a level bed at high speed, covering a large area of country that day; but we saw no game, only a few snow-birds with a wolf slinking away here and there. It was indeed a barren season. Nor did we discover any tracks of the band of trappers we had come out to look for, so we attributed the story to the imagination of the native brain, although it transpired later that the report was true. The men were never caught; but they quarrelled when nearing the flats of Hudson's Bay, and the result was that two men, both Russians and not Germans, were picked up by the Indians fearfully hacked with knives about face and body.

About four o'clock that afternoon we were gliding along briskly in the mysterious semi-darkness, when I found that my eyes troubled me. They smarted, and the lids twitched continually. Hanging my arm over the side of the sleigh, I caught up some snow to rub on my face. While raising my hand I happened to glance towards stolid old MacDonald, and to my amazement discovered a pink halo round his grizzled head. Turning my throbbing eyes towards the dogs, I noticed a soft pink radiance glowing round their bodies, while the steam-like breath pouring from their mouths floated away in roseate clouds, which to a poetical mind might have suggested an effect of sunrise.

While I was wondering at the meaning of this phenomenon, MacDonald turned his head, and gazed at me solemnly with eyes that blinked and twitched like mine.

'Hello, Angel!' he exclaimed, without a vestige of humour in his voice.

I stared at him, and he continued, 'I don't want to flatter ye, but you'd make a good Catholic idol just now. There's a red ring round your head any saint might envy.'

'You've got one too,' I said.

'Darn the lights, anyway,' he muttered. '''Tis bad enough to see 'em when you're snug at home. When they strike ye out here 'tis death for somebody. He's going.'

'Keep off that,' I muttered.

'If Sinapis isn't going off, one of us is. I guess it's better him than you or me.'

The long lash curled savagely over the brightly coloured backs of the dogs, and we bounded along in silence, while I fixed my eyes upon a thick clump of firs which looked as though they were on fire. Presently a gruff exclamation at my shoulder made me start.

'Here they come – the devil's lights!'

I put my head back and glanced at the sky. Lurid tongues were creeping up from the magnetic north, and advancing with slow movements across the sky. They resembled flames of fire seen indistinctly through a cloud of smoke. On the opposite side flaming spindles shot upward in a clear sky, as though striking at invisible foes with their spear-like tips; and at the same time I heard a low moaning, like wind round a street corner on a wintry night. Otherwise there was silence, awful silence. Gradually the red hue became more pronounced, the air grew ghastly, figures seemed to creep by, the snow around might have marked the scene of a great carnage. MacDonald's face looked livid and awesome. I glanced once at the still countenance of Sinapis, but recoiled at the sight.

Few words passed, and presently we reached the pine bluff we had long been heading for. A cloud of fire crested the summit. We began to prepare our camp, between the slender columns stretching in lengthy corridors on each side, faintly illumined, as if to receive us, with the lambent lights.

We examined Sinapis, and one look passed between us. Amateur doctor that I was, a glance was enough to convince me the man was worse. His limbs were hot and covered with red spots. With his feeble arms he endeavoured to toss off the furs; and if he could suffer from an excess of heat in that atmosphere, I knew he must be sick indeed. I looked at the thermometer, feeling that the temperature must be nearing an exceptional point. The spirits were skulking away at the bottom, and the index marked sixty-one. I returned with the intelligence to my companion.

'Ninety-three degrees of frost, Mac.'

He raised his shaggy head. 'Well, Angel, that's about the limit. A few more degrees and we shall be smothered. I knew it was something low. The air strikes like fire.'

'A steady blow of wind now –'

'And we should be shrivelled up like dead leaves.'

We made four large fires at a slight distance from each other. For a couple of hours we toiled with axe and saw, felling wood to keep us in fuel for the night; but every other minute we had to pause and gasp for breath. Meantime the heavens were growing scarlet; the snow might have been soaked in blood;

my companion's face grew more corpse-like. Load after load
of resinous wood we carried to the camp, then settled down
to nibble at what food we could manage to thaw. After an altogether insufficient meal, we sat down opposite each other to
enjoy our only pleasure, a good pipeful of tobacco. The dogs
gathered round, snapping at one another, lying so close to the
fires that the air soon became filled with the odour of singeing
fur, and we had to drive them back, lest they should place us in a
quandary by committing suicide. Hard by lay Sinapis, wrapped
up in the sleigh, never moving nor speaking.

Nature has especially ordained that when the temperature
reaches an extremely low point two things may not happen: a
fire cannot burn dully, nor may the wind blow. Were it otherwise
human existence in the far north would often be impossible.

We smoked silently for an hour or more, only rising at inter-
vals for fresh supplies of wood. The mysterious atmosphere
bathed us in its red waves; the fiery cones and spindles above
kept on darting and flashing; the shuddering shadows crept
upon the trees. It was a remarkable night indeed.

Presently MacDonald drew the last mouthful of smoke
from his pipe. As he drew the little canvas bag out of his pocket
– in winter he always carried his tobacco cut – he eyed me in a
solemn fashion, and said, 'Do ye see, Angel?'

'I'm not blind,' I answered a bit testily, for I looked upon him
as a superstitious old fool.

'Do ye hear, Angel?' he continued in the same monotonous
voice.

'Quit calling me Angel!' I shouted. 'And talk of something
else. It's nothing but the aurora.'

'That's what they say. What makes the sounds? What makes
the red lights jump around in the sky? What makes the shadows
we see crawling around? Men whose heads are too big for their
bodies talk about electricity and terrestrial magnetism, and
clever enough they think themselves I have no doubt. But get
'em together, drive 'em in a bunch, and ask 'em straight what is
electricity an' what is terrestrial magnetism? You'll see them sit
down and suck their thumbs.'

'There are wiser men than us, Mac.'

'There's a clever and common-sense way of looking at things,' he said stubbornly. 'One man wants to find the height of a wall. He takes a sheet of paper and a lot of fiddling tools, draws pictures, and decorates them with half the letters in the alphabet. At last he works out a sort of answer, mostly wrong. Another man slips to the top of the wall, drops a plumb-line down, makes a knot in the line, and measures it. One's the clever way of finding the height of that wall and the other is the natural way. Give me the last.'

'What's your idea, then, about the red lights?'

'The devil fixes 'em up to scare us lonely fellows, and to warn us there's trouble coming.'

'Why do we only see them out here? Why only in the extreme cold?'

'Don't you try and corner the devil. He uses different methods to scare folk in other places. The red lights do show further south, and harm always comes with them. Sinapis will die.'

'Because the aurora happens to be red once in a way, it's no reason why a man should die.'

'Two years ago there was just such another night, the sky on fire and the snow bloody,' went on MacDonald, in his unhappiest voice. 'Factor Robinson went out on the ice of the bay to look for his little dog, which had strayed from the fort. We picked him up next morning, smashed by a bear, so that his own mother wouldn't ha' known him. I helped to carry him back, took the shoulders, I did, and his head was like a rotten apple some one had set their foot on. Kept touching my legs, too. Man, I had to shut my eyes.'

I tried to laugh his words away, but only a dry sound came from my throat. No man could have been light-hearted amid such weird surroundings.

'This night, further south, no electric instruments will obey the hand of any man,' my cheerful comrade rambled on. 'Telephones, telegraphs, all the rest of 'em, won't work, or will perform on their own account. Aye, on nights of this sort messages come along the wires, and the operators are called up by hands which have no flesh on 'em.'

'Free electricity has powers of which we know little,' I said.

'There ye are again. You're welcome to your notion and all you can make of it. Here's a little story, and if it isn't true, may my tongue be frost-bitten. In a small town, a year or two agone, the red lights came along, and all the telegraph stations were closed. Late at night one of the operators went into the office for something, and while there the signal sounded. He stepped up and prepared to take down the message. The needle ticked away, only one word was transmitted, only one word, Angel. They say he fainted right off.'

'What was it?'

'Death. Just that one word. Three months later it came for him.'

'You've got queer notions, Mac.'

'Maybe, Angel. There are queerer round us. I remember a fellow telling me once how, when the lights were bad, he switched on his telephone and listened. He wasn't a chap of powerful imagination, but he fairly made me shiver when he described how he heard the things twisting and turning round the wire outside, whispering and chattering, and groaning – '

'Quit it, Mac,' I interrupted. 'If you haven't got anything better to talk about, let's sit quiet.'

He bent to tuck the buffalo robe beneath his knees. That moment I heard a sound, a movement. We looked up together, and saw Sinapis leap out of the sleigh and dash across the snow with the wild motions of a maniac: this man whom we supposed was unconscious and too weak to lift his head – here he was running like an athlete, a man hunted by death, and looking for a place to hide himself. He had been a trapper of beasts, a hunter, all his life, and now he was running with the strength lent him by madness, running from the grisly trapper who sought his life.

'Man!' groaned MacDonald. 'I wish it warn't so lonesome.'

'You're scared, Mac?' I said hoarsely.

'Aye,' he said. 'I've got it down my back. Same with you,' he shouted. 'If it warn't for the red lights, your face would be as white as pudding. You ha' your eyes shut.'

'If I could shut them, I would,' was my answer. 'He'll never get out o' sight. He'll run and run all night, and we'll sit and watch. Man, I'd like a good black British night.'

Sinapis ran on, and as I gazed, unable to remove my eyes, his direction changed, and his motion became parallel with us; he seemed to be coming back, but it was not so; he passed, giving us a wide berth, and sped on, old MacDonald's head following his course, sheep-like. We perceived he was running in a circle of which we formed the centre.

'Run out and catch hold of him. I'll see him running to the end of my days,' MacDonald whispered.

I shuddered, but did not move.

'We were angels a while ago, church-window paintings wi' holy colours round our heads. Now we're devils. Who was that fellow who went to hell and saw the papists burn?'

'Don't know,' I muttered, never having heard of Dante in those days; and I was also angry, being myself a Catholic – as was Sinapis – and I did not like MacDonald's sneers at my religion.

'Bunyan or Gulliver; some such name,' he rambled on. 'If ever I go back to Tobermorey, I'll tell 'em I've been there, too.'

Again the Indian approached us, on another and smaller circle, and again he passed, but his speed was decreasing. We thought his strength was failing, but it was not that altogether. He went on describing circles, each drawing him nearer to us, and presently he fell on the snow and began to crawl.

'Played out,' muttered MacDonald.

'Come on, Mac,' I said, when I saw the poor wretch beginning to describe another circle on his hands and knees.

'Bide a wee. My breath ain't easy.'

A few more minutes passed, then I shook off the cold and the terror of the ghastly lights, crossed to MacDonald's side, and heaved him up. He came to his feet with as many groans as a dying man; together we crossed the snow and secured the Indian; but we let him go again and gasped.

Before leaving the sleigh, some mood of madness had provoked him to tear off his socks and moccasins; and he had been running over that red snow – I do not know how long – with bare feet.

He made no resistance. We carried him to the sleigh and wrapped him up, averting our eyes from those wax-like feet, then returned to our sleeping-bags by the fire, glancing across at each other, afraid to speak for some time; but I heard a lot of gulping going on, and at last a queer hoarse voice, 'Man, you're a Christian, and I used to be. Shall we put a bullet through his head? What's the sin, when 'tis a kindness?'

'Quit it, Mac,' I said; and he put his head down and took to his pipe again.

We could do nothing for Sinapis; only sit there and doze and wait for him to die. My eyes closed after a time, and I felt myself nodding, almost overbalancing. Suddenly I became wide awake, with a wild shudder, for I imagined something was leaning over, reaching out great hands to strangle me. I saw the red lights, and my excited imagination made me believe I saw also luminous faces revolving in one of those hideous circles, gradually advancing towards me with hollow eyes and bleeding jaws. I thought of Indian legends which I had laughed at when the sun was shining and Nature had been normal; and then I heard a low, dull, scraping sound which woke me up.

MacDonald had heard it too, but was not frightened. He wagged his head and grinned across the fire. He was nearer the sleigh than I was, and I supposed he could see what was going on.

'When a man's dying he gets a child again,' he muttered. 'The boy's having a game. He's sawing a bit of wood.'

Neither of us wondered what was taking place in that wild, unhappy mind, struggling against its destiny of death, what agony was there, what love of life and home. He was only an Indian; we looked upon him rather as a dog, and were sorry he was about to die, chiefly because it would inconvenience us.

'I was fond of sawing a bit of wood when I was a youngster,' MacDonald murmured lazily. 'Specially if 'twas the Sabbath. I'd get father's hand-saw and scrape for an hour at some log, and call myself a mighty fine carpenter when I saw what a pile of sawdust I was making. Eh, man, it was good to be a kiddie.'

He went on murmuring a little, and as I watched his lips something appeared to cross my eyesight and strike MacDonald on the head. It was not my fancy, for he shouted, 'The boy's thrown a chunk of wood at me.' Then he yelled, 'It's a moccasin'; and the next instant started up and lurched towards me blubbering.

'Man!' he panted. 'Take it away. It moves! Eh, man, it's a dead lump. He threw it away like an old boot. Take it away – my stomach's gone. Eh, man, man!'

I saw the thing lying in the light of the fire with the toes pointing towards it. Sinapis could have felt nothing while he sawed, because all feeling had been frozen out, and yet it was horrible – there. I could not move with MacDonald hanging to me; I dreaded the idea of touching the thing; but two of the dogs made for it, sniffing, one quicker than the other carried it away, and – we saw it no more.

MacDonald was like an hysterical girl. I made him lie down, covered him over, then went to the side of the sleigh, looking down upon the sick man, but not at his feet. He had fallen back, the mad strength had given out at last, he was breathing with difficulty, and still struggling, not only against madness and disease, but, as I could not help thinking, for I was more than a little upset, he was still striving to avoid the clutches of some invisible power, other than death, which hovered above his resting-place.

I sat down again, while MacDonald's groans died gradually away. I never slept. I nodded dreamily, all the time conscious of my companion's terrified eyes peering at me over the bowl of his pipe, through a continually rising cloud of smoke. Nothing could have frightened MacDonald from his pipe. He was a hard smoker, and used to say the only thing he had against sleep was that it deprived a man of his tobacco. I remained conscious of what was taking place around, and I perceived that whiteness was gradually returning to the snow and the fire was dying out of the sky. Luminous clouds, with swords of light flashing round the edges, moved slowly up; streamers quivered in the north, lengthening or shortening as the whim seized them. Falling back and resting my head against a pile of wood, I watched the strange forms, which were never for a moment at rest, hurrying always from one side to another, until it occurred to me that the prevailing movement was that of descent. These cloud spirits in their diaphanous robes of light, were inclined to leave the sky vault, to drop down towards us, to wrap us in their fleecy raiment, and carry us away to that land beyond the ice mountains, towards which men are always struggling, which they never have reached.

I had laughed, before that night, at the foolishness of the Indians. When these lights are bright, they will creep from their tents, uplift their arms towards the descending masses, cry aloud, then hurriedly re-seek the partial shelter of their homes. Why? Because at the sound of the human voice the descending motion ceases. The lights break up, scatter and flee away to all parts of the heavens, removing themselves until the atmosphere ceases to vibrate with the echo of the voice. Then they steal down once more, flock together in a ghostly band, and begin again to drop towards the brown tents.

'Should we not do this,' says the native, 'should we refrain from shouting with our voices, the spirits would descend, draw us away, and bear us to the land of the unmelting snow; for spirits drink the blood of mortals.'

Wild thoughts such as these coursed through my brain as I lay in a half somnolent state. The luminous clouds were descending with steady movements. They appeared larger, and a fire might now be perceived burning within the heart of each. Down, still down, nearer and closer, until my blinking eyes discovered long attenuated limbs, loosely robed, with hooked, blood-stained extremities working towards their prey. Still down, and the cloak fell aside. Hideous faces peered forth, malignant eyes revolving like red-hot wheels, huge mouths with gruesome fangs gnashing for a victim. But no other features, except ears, long and pointed, held erect for sounds of human life. I struggled to free myself, but an unseen power held me chained. It was the devil's hunt, and these were his hounds. They were in full cry and we were the quarry. But which was it to be? It must be the one who failed to send the cry ringing forth into the night.

Again I struggled, still the hand crushed me to the icy ground. MacDonald was bending over me, a pitying smile upon his face, on his lips the words:

'So, you are the chosen. Well, I am sorry; but I warned you against the death lights. You see, they have proved too strong, after all.'

There my dream was broken by a cry. I started up with dry throat, my body shivering with cold and the horror of the vision. As I dragged myself up, those grim lights darted swiftly away, and the next second were hurrying across the heavens, whispering in triumph, as though they had succeeded in their quest and were not returning empty-handed.

I heard MacDonald's voice, but when I turned, my fear came back.

'What is it, Mac? Did I scare you?'

'You!' he cried, in a high-pitched voice. 'How could ye scare any one, lying dead asleep?'

'Didn't I cry out?'

'You never made a sound. He did. He shouted one word.'

'What?'

'*Mascha* – go away! A nice thing to say with his last breath.'

'His last breath?'

'Man, look at him!' he cried fiercely. 'Don't lie there. Go and look at the boy.'

I rose, though my knees shook. I made my way to the side of the sleigh, through a ring of snoring dogs. I bent over the side, and looked upon the brown face which stared up surrounded by a frost-covered pile of furs.

Sinapis was dead.

Morning came at last, the sun glittered upon the snow plains, dispelling the unnatural colours of the night. As the day was only of a few hours' duration we had to make the most of it. When it was time for departure, we came to a disagree-ment concerning the disposal of the body. We had stripped away the furs, applying them to our own use, and the figure lay beneath the pines, stretched out straight and stiff, frozen by the inexorable cold into a mass as solid as a block of marble. I had touched the dark face with the tip of an unprotected finger, scraping away a line of ice-crystals, and in doing so froze the skin with that contact against the inanimate stone – I could not call it flesh.

MacDonald, superstitious to the end of his nails, though brave enough now that it was day, averred that he would not travel in such ghastly company. On the other side, I declared it would be an act of wickedness to leave the body behind, seeing that Sinapis had been a Christian, and therefore deserved a proper burial. There happened to be a priest near the fort, and as the body would keep for ever in that temperature, I argued that it was our duty to take it back. But MacDonald waxed wrathful.

'Plant him in the snow right here, and have done with it.'

'What's left of Sinapis is going back with us, if only for the sake of satisfying Armstrong. So it's no good you talking,' I said firmly.

At length, being Britishers, we compromised. The body was to follow us, lashed upon a little sleigh, which we improvised out of pine branches and attached to the back of our own. Even so MacDonald was uncomfortable, and continually glanced over his shoulder to satisfy himself that the body was, as he expressed it, 'keeping dead.'

During that short day we travelled swiftly over the dusty snow, approaching our journey's limit. Still we saw scarcely any game, although wolves and foxes grew more plentiful; nor could we discover any mark of moccasin, no trellis-work pattern where the snowshoe had pressed, no parallel grooves where runners had passed. Onward we swept towards the end-less ice-fields, swifter as afternoon grew, for the bed was solid; and along our trail bounded the stone-like image of the frozen man.

That night we encamped in the open. At least, there were banks of firs on all sides as wind breaks, but we made our fire in a space at the bottom of a slight dip, which we found to be natural and not a freak of the snow. The first thing was to isolate ourselves from our companion, so we unlashed the figure, dragged it over the ridge, and left it stiffly stretched upon its bier of pine branches in the valley beyond, out of sight, yet not more than seventy-five yards away. We had supper, commenced our tobacco and conversation, the latter of which did not continue long, since we had little of a pleasant nature to talk about, and were both tired.

A more beautiful sight I have rarely witnessed than the calm splendour of that night. White light poured over the dark summits of the pines, making their silvery tresses flash like a woman's hair with diamonds in it. When the great moon appeared, with a stately movement, the snow plains looked as soft and warm as a bed of feathers, and, opposite, the shivering arch of the aurora was a thing of beauty, not, as on the former night, a thing of horror. Silver streamers darted from the arch, illumining the sky with narrow bands; and countless spindles, dwindling away to nothingness, moved slowly, lengthening and shortening, one springing from the side of another.

I lay in a fine drowsy comfort, wrapped up to the eyes, in the sleigh. I heard the dogs snarling. I could see MacDonald endeavouring to clear the stem of his pipe, which was blocked, and smiled lazily when I perceived his lips moving, as he silently cursed his best friend. I watched the frost crystals dancing joyously everywhere. I followed the course of sparks carried from the keenly burning fire, and regretfully considered that I might have to bestir myself in an hour or so to haul in more fuel. There was not a breath of wind. I watched the tops of the pines for ten minutes together, in the hope of seeing some motion, but I could not declare I ever saw one stir an inch. I might have been gazing upon a panorama.

My brain was active, and passed rapidly from one subject to another. I wondered how many men in the course of the world's history had crossed the spot where we then rested. I tried to imagine the surroundings when this inhospitable land was a tropical country, infested by monsters now nothing more than skeletons, and tried to guess what the next change would be, when men had dug up all the vegetation of the coal period. My next idea was to guess at the nearest human beings. There would be Esquimaux along the bay, perhaps two hundred miles east by north, but closer might probably be found a wandering band of Swampy Crees. Finally I spared a thought for the silent figure in the valley. I had trusted Sinapis, for he was somewhat of an exception to the rule that a Christian Indian is sure to be an unprincipled rogue. He was an excellent hunter, and more than once had led me along the fresh trail of the moose; he was a good servant, rarely shirking his duties unless liquor came in his way. Now he had finished his life in the remote north, very far from cities and learning: he had been dragged into the vortex of the unknown: perhaps at that moment he knew of more mysteries than the wisest of us have ever dared to guess at.

It was not wonderful, in such a place, at such a time, that my last thoughts should turn towards sentiment, as I sank imperceptibly into slumber, but I am certain this insensibility was of short duration, and of the nature of a dog sleep, for my senses were active, and alive to every sound or motion.

So I became presently convinced that I had for some little time been listening to a scuffling noise, probably at no great distance, although in that abnormally clear atmosphere a sound would travel for miles. The moon was well up in the heavens, and looked down upon us coldly. An unearthly cry certainly rang in my ears; then a shadow fell upon the snow. I looked up and saw a tawny owl, with big horns and round eyes. He wheeled down, flapped his great wings, and glided away.

I was half awake only, yet there surely were sounds in the valley adjoining. Bodies in motion, pattering of feet upon crisp snow, stealthy glidings and whisperings. I pulled myself upright to listen more intently. And, as I did so, an awful cry burst forth, rending the still night air like a trumpet blast, every syllable of the message beating with accompanying echo in my ears:

'*Siphaytay! mascha!*'

The silence that followed was worse than the voice. I shook like a man with ague, my teeth went chattering together, my heart thumped furiously. I heard a gasp, as though some one was choking. Then I managed to look round at MacDonald.

His face was all manner of colours, and his hands were beating together in a fashion that might have been ludicrous at any other time. I could no longer doubt that those words had been spoken, or rather shouted, in appeal to us; and who could have given them utterance except the grim figure of the frozen man?

It was no use trembling there, waiting for the cry to be repeated; but it is a curious fact that when a man is really frightened he imagines himself safer while he remains quiescent. The act of motion suggests a challenging of unseen powers. However, I spoke, though there was a tremor in my voice which had a savour of cowardice.

'You heard, Mac?'

It was a foolish remark, but it opened a way between us.

He came shambling towards me, on hands and knees, grabbing hold of my arm when he reached the side of the sleigh.

'I told ye 'twould be bad travelling wi' that. I knew the boy wouldn't rest. He'll be running now, running round and round.'

'What's the matter with it?'

'How can a body frozen through and through scream out? 'Twas his voice, but scared and crazy. Mascha was his last word. He said it because he was afraid to die.'

'His body is in danger.' I tumbled out of the sleigh. 'Come, Mac, we must see what he wants. He was calling to us. He was telling them to leave his body alone.'

'Telling who?'

'I don't know.'

'Perhaps he's not dead. Perhaps the frost is keeping his – what do you papists call it?'

'His soul from departing.'

'Aye, something that way.'

'We must go and look.'

'Let's keep hold of your arm. The fear isn't so bad when you halve it up wi' another. The Lord only knows what devilry the boy may be up to.'

We ascended the incline with slow steps, both of us dreading to look down from the top of the ridge.

' 'Twas his own voice. Just the voice he used when he was scared,' muttered MacDonald, nearly pulling me down with his weight.

We neared the summit, a few more steps and the ridge would have been surmounted; when, without a note of warning, the cry darted out into the night, and we both sank upon our knees to the ground, shivering, awe-struck:

'Siphaytay! mascha!'

'Come away!' wailed MacDonald, catching at my legs as I tottered up, and bringing me down again. 'There are things we can't look at. Come back and hitch up the dogs, and let's get away. He's running – I know he's running.'

I fought with my breath, which was like a flame of fire. 'We can stand it now, Mac. We're ready for it. Another two steps and we shall see.'

I pulled him up, but he didn't hang to my arm. He clapped both hands to his ears. In this fashion we crossed the ridge, but when I looked down on the valley my courage returned, while the same word fell from the lips of us both:

'Wolves!'

A score or so round the motionless figure of the frozen man, hungrily struggling to tear that marble flesh. One part of the mystery was explained.

'Come away down, Mac,' I cried. 'There's nothing to fear.'

My companion recovered wonderfully when he perceived that the dead man was not running. He raised his great voice, bellowed lustily, and we floundered into the valley, while the animals sullenly dispersed.

Sinapis lay just as we had left him, upon his back, the face, covered with glittering frost, gazing up at the white moon, the scanty garments torn into shreds by the fangs of the wolves. There was nothing to tell us how that cry had been uttered. We could only wonder, as so many had done before us, trying in vain to tear away the veil which hangs between us and the mystery of death.

Each of us took an end of rope, and we retraced our steps to the camp fire dragging the bier and left it not far behind us in a position of safety away from the heat. This task accomplished, we settled in the sleigh, tucked ourselves up, and presently MacDonald said, 'We'll make for home first thing, and we won't take him with us.'

I had weakened in my resolution. 'Perhaps we'd best leave him. We'll bury him as decently as we can.'

'Aye,' he said. Then there was silence again.

'I'm not religious, though I quote Scripture,' MacDonald confessed. ''Tis a habit merely. I'd like to understand it. 'Twould help a man.'

'It's beyond us, Mac. Folks used to say the soul of a dead man couldn't rest unless the body was properly buried. If the wolves had torn Sinapis to pieces, the funeral would never have taken place. They would say that the spirit, which must have been looking after the body, used the power of human speech for the purpose of appealing to us.'

'He never did – not us. He was calling out to any one.'

'Well, it came to the same thing. It told us the body required help, and we were the only ones who could give it.'

'I guess you're right,' he said. 'Anyway, 'tis no use my disagreeing, for I've not your education.'

This from MacDonald was a great concession.

'There's nothing to keep us out longer,' I observed.

'We'll start back in the morning, first thing. Armstrong can do all the talking he likes. The furs have left this district, and as for those trappers, they never did have any existence outside of a lie –'

'*Siphaytay! mascha!*'

We sprang up with a yell, for this shock was worse than the first. The voice was so close, the tones were so distinct and agonised. During that first moment I felt sure the body must have moved, and, when I turned, gave a gasp of relief at not seeing the awful face of the frozen man at my shoulder. As for Mac-

Donald, I was afraid he had gone off his head, for he danced in front of me, gesticulating wildly.

'O Lord! O Lord! It cut all round me like a whip.'

The scuffling noise came again, but this time accompanied by angry barks and snarls.

Again we found a partial explanation. Now it was the dogs who had made an attack upon the frozen body. As I reached out my hand for the whip, I saw one of the leaders, a tremendous brute, standing upon the dead man's chest, licking the icy face with his great tongue. The next moment he sprang back with a howl as the thong struck him across the head. A few more strokes, and the rest of the ravenous pack were driven off.

I pulled the frozen man to the side of the sleigh and tumbled him in, unassisted by MacDonald, who refused to approach the mysterious remains. Then I sat down beside it and watched until morning. Better a loss of sleep than any repetition of that horrible cry.

And in the raw red light of the dawn we buried him. Hitching up the dogs, we drove to a thick bluff, south of our encampment. Here we found a snow hill, crested by a lofty dome like a miniature cathedral, with dark rounded columns of pines stretching away in a kind of religious darkness. With our axes we cut a deep hole, laid the frozen man in his resting-place, a strange dark figure in the midst of perfect whiteness, then piled the snow, like inodorous flowers, upon the unquiet body.

Before leaving, I felt it my duty to commend the dead Indian to the safe keeping of Providence as best I could, although I was well aware MacDonald was eyeing me askant and often grunting. When I concluded he muttered, 'Man, I can beat that,' flopped down upon the snow, and began to pour forth a long recitation, which, as far as I could make out, was nothing but a rebuke to me and others of my creed, until I became very cold and weary. At length he rose, and said to me proudly, 'Never repeated myself. I could have gone on for half an hour.'

We turned from that quiet pine bluff and the dome of snow which protected the remains of Sinapis. Again we glided over the plains to the music of the sleigh bells, but now we were on the homeward trail, travelling at full speed over the dazzling plain, with a cold sun above and loneliness on every side. Home! The word had a pleasant sound after what we had undergone. Even though it was nothing better than a solitary log-built fort in the centre of a frozen land.

Michael Blumlein

CALIFORNIA BURNING

The output of short fiction by MICHAEL BLUMLEIN, *a physician by profession, has not been vast, but it has been of unvarying and exceptional quality. He first gained widespread notice with the collection* The Brains of Rats (1989), *which was nominated for a World Fantasy Award and earned lavish praise both from main-stream critics and from leading writers in the horror community. More recently a new collection from Blumlein,* What the Doctor Ordered, *appeared from Centipede Press, and he is at work on a new novel. 'California Burning' first appeared in* Asimov's Science Fiction *in August 2009. Like most of Blumlein's fiction – and like some of the other tales in this book – it is not a traditional 'horror story', but this story of a corpse that refuses to be cremated is certainly macabre and features a dose of dark humor that makes a nice contrast with some of the more grimly serious tales.*

T HE GUY AT THE CREMATORIUM said it would take about three hours. A little less if he was lean, a little more if he was fat, as fat burns slower. 'Which is why it's so hard to get rid of,' he added, patting his ample belly. He was a congenial man, of a different congeniality than the people at the mortuary, who were hushed, respectful, reserved, sedate, watchful, and preternaturally composed. The sort of people whose every mannerism and facial expression assured you it was perfectly all right to get emotional, to rend your clothes, pound your fists, sob till your throat was raw. They were all for showing your grief. And if you didn't, you felt a little embarrassed, as if you hadn't performed up to par. And if you did, you also felt embar-rassed, for making such a fuss. The difference being that in the latter case you felt you'd done the right thing.

Greg, the crematorium guy, was not reserved at all. He was the opposite, chatty and matter-of-fact. Fat burned slower, he explained, because it had more calories than muscle. You could get it to burn faster by raising the temperature in the oven, but then you ran the risk of blackening the air with smoke and pollution, which were no-no's these days. They had a camera trained on the rooftop chimney that was hooked to a monitor to check what was coming out, which at the moment was nothing. Or rather, nothing worse than the air itself, which was hazy from a nearby fire. It was summer, and where I live, summer meant fires. 'Good day to be inside,' he said.

There was a box in the room. *The* box, I should say. Six feet long, one foot high, it sat on a gurney, and without so much as a word of explanation or warning, Greg lifted the lid.

I was determined to be cool. But it didn't turn out that way. My stomach lurched, and I choked back emotion.

The box was plain and anonymous, but the bag inside was body shaped. My father's name was printed in large letters, once at the foot of the bag and once at the head. There was a tag with a number that Greg removed for me to check against the number on a form I had. I was shaken by the sight of the bag and so relieved that he hadn't opened it and asked me to identify the body that I barely gave the number a glance. Dad's name was on the bag, not once but twice, and that was good enough for me. And even if by some fluke it was someone else, who would ever know? Ashes were ashes. A little more, weight-wise, if you were big, a little less if you were small. But quality-wise the same: a kind of gritty mixture of the soft ash of fully-combusted flesh and organs combined with the coarse ash of bone. This, according to Greg, who was free with the info. Gold and silver fillings that might identify a person vaporized, and personal prosthetic devices like knees and hips and artificial heart valves were confiscated as potentially biohazardous and not included in the remains. There was a stainless steel tray where the bones that hadn't crumbled completely in the heat were pulverized by hand, then fed, along with the rest, through a funnel-shaped sieve, rather like sifting flour to get a more homogeneous blend. Attached to the tray was a container half-filled with blackened metal prosthetic parts. Like jewelry, but scorched. Of everything I had seen so far, this was the most disturbing. Strange how the mind works.

I didn't flinch, for example, when he raised the door of the brick-lined oven and, again without a word, pushed my father in. I didn't flinch when the door snapped closed. And as the gas ignited with a soft hiss, I watched the temperature needle slowly rise without emotion. Perhaps it was this composure of mine that made Greg veer from normal procedure. Perhaps he admired me for it. Or maybe he thought that something was subtly wrong. At any rate, after the body was in the oven for a while, he opened the door. The cardboard coffin was on fire, somber red flames punctuated by bright curlicues of yellow. Centered almost exactly in the middle was the dark globe of my father's skull. He'd been bald in life, and I recognized the shape. It was him, and not only that, he seemed at peace. By which I mean it comforted me to think that. The flames appeared to be cradling him. They licked at his head but had not yet set it on fire, as though to honor him – his life, his achievements, his spirit – by not consuming him too fast.

I left the crematorium at 8 A.M., called at one (allowing time for the ashes to cool) to pick up the remains. I was told to call back later. I called again at two, and then at three, and then four. Greg said it was taking longer than expected. I asked if there was a problem.

'Sometimes the ovens act up. Don't heat like they're supposed to.'

'Which means what? That he can't be cremated?'

'Oh, he'll be cremated all right. It just takes longer.'

'How much longer?'

'Why don't you call back in a few hours.'

'Like when? Tonight?'

'No problem. We operate around the clock. Twenty-four, seven.'

'You don't sleep?'

'Can't afford to. They don't.'

In my mind's eye I saw a line of gray and expressionless men and women, waiting impassively to be slid in the oven and baked. It was a dreadful image. I wanted this to be done.

'Are you busy?' I asked.

'Most of the time we are. It's steady.'

'I mean now.'

'Now? Not too busy.'

'Can you fix it?'

'Fix it?'

'The oven.'

There was a pause, as if this was not exactly the right question. 'Sure. We fix them all the time.'

'So tonight then? I can pick them up tonight?'

'Right. Tonight. Call back. Everything'll be fine.'

As it turned out, everything wasn't fine, not by nine that night, when the swing shift guy suggested I call back in the morning. And not by the morning.

I got Greg again, a guy whom, in the short time I'd known him, I'd come to more or less trust. He was straight with me, and not unfeeling.

'It's not the oven. Sorry, man.'

'What do you mean?'

'My boss wants to talk to you.'

'*You* talk to me. What do you mean, it's not the oven?'

'He'll explain.'

'Just tell me.'

There was silence.

'Please.'

He was a decent guy. He cared about his job, and in this case his job meant caring for me.

My father, it seemed, did not want to burn. His skin and nails and organs, yes. They were gone. But his bones, no. Somehow they had resisted twenty-four hours of thirteen hundred degree heat and flame. Greg had never seen anything like it.

His boss, however, had. He'd been in the business almost thirty years and had seen, in his words, 'a little bit of everything.' We met in his office, which adjoined the crematorium. There was an old-fashioned oak desk piled with papers, a chair behind it and one in front of it, a dirty window, a concrete floor. By the look of things he wasn't used to visitors.

At another time I might have been interested in what he meant by 'a little bit of everything'. He was certainly interested in telling me, as though the existence of other unusual happenings and odd occurrences would be a comfort. Rather like expecting someone with a broken bone to be comforted by the news that other people were in pain.

I didn't want to hear about it. 'What's the problem with my father's bones?'

He was leaning against the front edge of his desk, his shirt collar open, his thick, calloused hands on his thighs. He looked like he could have been a fighter at one time. His face was carefully composed.

'They don't want to burn,' he said.

'And why is that?'

'I wish I had an answer. We gave it all we got.'

'Greg mentioned something about the oven. Thought maybe it was acting up.'

'Nothing wrong with the oven. We just had it serviced. It's working fine.'

'But this is what you do, right? You cremate bodies.'

'Twenty-nine years,' he said.

'But not mine.' I meant my father's, of course.

He rubbed his thighs, as if to clean his hands, or expel something. It reminded me of my father in his hospital bed, just a few days before he died. Picking at his gown over and over, at a thread or piece of lint or something that no one else could see, something that simply wasn't there, then tossing it over the side of the bed. I would take his hand and hold it, but he would pull it away, again and again, so in the end I stopped trying and instead just sat beside him and watched, transfixed and disturbed by what he was doing. There was no purpose to it. He wasn't himself. Or else he was (who else could he be?), and the purpose of this repetitive and disconcerting activity was hidden to me.

'I'm fully prepared to give you your money back,' the man said.

'And then what?'

'You can use it to bury him.'

'We don't want to bury him.'

He didn't reply.

'No offense, but maybe we should try someone else.'

'Sure. By all means. Do that.'

'Wouldn't you?'

'I told you what I'd do,' he said.

My father actually had suggested that when the time came, he be buried, but my mother was opposed. Her mind was set on cremation. She wanted to scatter his ashes and be done. She didn't want a grave to have to visit. Her mother and father, whom she adored, were buried in graves, and she didn't enjoy the feelings that visiting them stirred up in her. She didn't like being tied to her loved ones in that particular way. Ever the gentleman, my father had agreed.

'You said you'd seen this before.'

He nodded. 'One time. Six, seven years ago. We were using higher temperatures then. Didn't matter. Same thing.'

'Man or woman?'

'Man.'

'What did he die of?'

He didn't even have to think. 'Heart attack. What did your dad die of?'

The strange thing was, no one knew. He went into the hospital complaining of shortness of breath and twelve days later he was dead. Having lost his mind completely – also for unknown reasons – in the process.

'Not his heart. His heart was fine. What did you do? The other time?'

'I called around. Talked to some guys in the business. Everyone had had a case or two. Or if they didn't, they knew of one.'

'So this is not unheard of.'

'No. It's not.'

'It happens a lot?'

He shrugged. 'It happens.'

Knowing this, that we weren't alone, did, in fact, help. But only a little.

'So with the other one. The other body. What did you end up doing?'

'Same thing I'm doing now. I talked to the involved parties. I let them know this was not the outcome we planned. Not the one we wanted. I tried to help, just like I'm trying to help you.'

'Did they have a burial? The other time?'

'Don't know. They didn't say what they were going to do. Like you, they were upset.'

If my dad were alive, he would have been embarrassed at having caused a problem, embarrassed at being the center of attention, embarrassed at the fuss. If you told him he wasn't crematable, he wouldn't have asked why. He'd have said fine, do what you have to. Or rather, he would have said, don't upset your mother. Make it easy on her. Do whatever she wants.

'I'll have to talk to my mother.'

'Of course.'

I stood.

He said, 'Can I get you to sign some papers before you go?'

He produced them, I signed them, he punched a number into his phone. He lifted the receiver and spoke into it briefly, and a minute later, Greg came through the door. He was carrying a plain cardboard box about the size of a crate of oranges. It had a fitted top and cut-outs for handles at either end. He placed it on the desk.

It took me a moment to understand what it contained.

'I packed them real good. Nice and snug. There shouldn't be any problem with shifting or rubbing or slippage.' He stared at his feet, hesitating. 'The top I wrapped separate. And I put it in a bag. Just in case, you know, you don't want to look at it.'

'The top?'

His hand drifted up to his head.

Suddenly, I didn't feel so well. Weak in the knees, unsteady upstairs. Strangely, or maybe not so strangely, I wanted to throw up. Or cry. Or both (can a person do that?).

'I made an inventory, just so you know. It's on a piece of paper. In an envelope.'

I was afraid to ask what he meant by 'inventory'.

His boss, however, felt obliged to explain. There were a lot of bones in the body. He didn't know how many, but a lot. And they weren't held together anymore, because whatever it was that held them was all burned up. The ashes – what there were of them, which wasn't much – were in a small plastic bag. The bones, none of them touching, were packed separately, according to shape and size, not to how they fit together naturally. So I might not recognize which was which, and unless I happened to know anatomy, which I didn't, I certainly wouldn't be able to say that all the bones were there, that the body was complete.

'Which is why we made the list.'

I nodded, but I barely heard a word he said. I was thinking of my poor mother. I was thinking of my father's skull. I was also trembling. I felt like a little boy, being asked to be brave. My father, I sensed, was watching, not unsympathetically. He more than anyone would have understood. Inventory? You've got to be kidding. There was no way I was opening that box.

But I did have to take it. At first I put it beside me in the passenger seat, but after a block or two I moved it to the back. That was still too close, and a few blocks later, I put it in the trunk.

When it comes to disposing of a person's ashes, it seems that it's hard to go wrong. You can toss them to the wind, spread them around and dig them into the ground, charter a boat and scatter them at sea. You can do it as soon as you get them from the crematorium. You can wait a month, or a year, keeping them in an urn or a box, in private or in plain view on a shelf. You can keep them forever and never dispose of them at all. By some common decree, ashes are immune to misuse. Just about anything you do is acceptable.

But, aside from burying them or bequeathing them to science, what are you supposed to do with bones?

I put them in the living room, on a side table. My cat Chester made an exhaustive study of the box, seeing and smelling things, no doubt, far beyond my pale human senses. To me it looked gray and smelled like cardboard. The more I studied it, the more I should have stopped. For where Chester excelled in senses that were grounded in reality, I excelled in ones that were not. I fantasized, for example, that my father was alive and trapped inside. I fantasized he was a ghost. I fantasized he was troubled, restless, and was going to haunt me . . . not necessarily because he wanted to but because that's what people with unfinished business did.

This was not good. Not good at all. What was I going to tell my mother?

That was a Monday. The nearby fire, which was mostly brush, had been contained, but now there were other fires, and on Tuesday, the forest to the north of us went up in flame, filling the sky with billows of black smoke. It was the driest summer on record, and by Wednesday there were a hundred fires, and more igniting every hour. For mile after mile in every direction the air was thick and gray and nasty. People with respiratory conditions were advised to stay indoors, then that was amended to include everybody. I watched TV, transfixed by news of the fires, witness to something that seemed both terrifying and monumental, historic, apocalyptic, a turning point of some sort. Four hundred fires, eight hundred, a thousand, all up and down the state. 'California Burning', the headlines read. My father's resistance to flame – his unburnability – seemed somehow part and parcel of this. Sphinx-like, inscrutable, the box sat on the side table as if daring me to understand. What was I to do?

The doorbell rang, and I nearly jumped. Two men were at the door. For an instant I feared that I was being evacuated. Like most people, I didn't want to go.

One was tall, the other stocky and broad. The tall one looked to be in his sixties; the stocky one, in his late thirties or so, a good ten years older than me. They were dressed conservatively in suits and ties.

They introduced themselves and said how sorry they were

to hear of my father's death. I thanked them and asked how they knew him.

'We didn't know him personally,' the older one, Michaels, said.

'Felt like we did,' said the other one, whose name was Neal. 'It was nice what they said in the paper. Good man.'

'Exceptional,' said Michaels. 'Outstanding. I wish I had known him. A fine man all around.'

The younger one, Neal, handed me a card. 'We were wondering if we could have a minute of your time.'

I looked at it, then him. 'Bereavement counselor?'

He frowned. His buddy Michaels snatched the card out of my hand, read it, then narrowed his eyes.

'Wrong card,' he told Neal, who stammered something and blushed. 'He's only been doing this a little while,' he explained to me, returning the card to Neal, who pocketed it, fished out his wallet and withdrew another one. After a moment's hesitation he offered it to me, but Michaels took it first. He examined it, gave a little nod, looked me in the eye in a friendly sort of way, and passed it on. This one read 'Department of Public Health.'

'Which one are you?' I asked.

'We're health officers,' said Michaels. 'We received a notice of an irregularity. We're following up.'

'Strictly routine,' said Neal. 'Nothing to worry about.'

Michaels seemed to tense slightly. 'Larry. Why would he worry?'

'He wouldn't. Like I said . . .'

'We know it's a difficult time,' said Michaels, cutting him off, 'but we'd like to ask you a few questions. Do you have a minute? It won't take long.'

'Is there a problem?'

'No problem.'

'None at all,' added Neal. 'Routine visit. We'll be gone before you know it.'

The two of them stood there for a while, not looming exactly, but not going away. At length Michaels said, 'May we come in?'

There is something gravitational about authority, compelling in an almost physical way. Without thinking, you find yourself drawn to it. And you want to be, that's the thing. You like the feeling. You want a piece of the action, whether or not you believe in it or plan to obey.

I opened the door wider. Then I remembered the box.

'Hold on a minute.' I hurried to the living room, picked it up and carried it to my bedroom. But the bedroom seemed too obvious, which was a strange thought to have, unless, like me, the only thing stronger than your trust in authority is your distrust of it. My apartment is small, and room-wise, all that was left was the kitchen. The box didn't fit in the oven, and hastily, I stowed it under the sink.

'Something cooking?' Michaels asked when I returned.

'Cooking?'

He motioned toward the kitchen. I was caught off-guard.

'You guys want coffee?' I asked.

They didn't, and I ushered them into the living room. We all sat down, and under Michaels' watchful eye, Neal began.

'Again, our condolences.'

'Thank you.'

'We understand your father passed away unexpectedly. And rather fast.'

For some reason that irked me. 'He was twelve days in the hospital and eighty-three years old. Is that fast?'

'And of unknown causes.'

'Like I said, he was eighty-three.'

'But not especially sick before he went into the hospital. Say a day or two before.'

'No. Not especially.'

He nodded in a knowing sort of way, then cleared his throat. 'Forgive me for asking, but did you consider doing an autopsy?'

'No. I didn't.'

'Any particular reason why not?'

In fact, the thought had crossed my mind, but only briefly. He was eighty-three, after all.

'I didn't see how it would have helped.'

'How about your mother? Was she interested?'

I thought of her expression the day she came in and he didn't recognize her, or anyone, the day he became delirious. How her face had crumpled, and her eyes had teared up, and she couldn't speak, except in little sobs. And how after a minute she gathered herself and sat beside him, taking his hand in hers and speaking to him in a calm, reassuring, almost chatty, voice, reminding him who and where he was, affectionately chiding him for not knowing. The eleven days between his entering the hospital and his dying were for me a blur, but for my mother, I think, it was the opposite: time slowed to a crawl. She was not shocked or surprised when he died; she was relieved more than anything, both for his sake and hers. She had known him for more than forty years, and no autopsy would have enabled her to know him any better, or changed how she felt.

'No. She wasn't. Not at all.'

'Interesting.'

'Why is that interesting?'

Michaels was quick to reply. 'What Mr Neal means is, you can understand our interest. From a public health standpoint. Rapid death. Unknown cause.'

'There is a cause. The cause was old age.'

He regarded me for a few seconds, then inclined his head. 'It gets the best of us. Why don't we leave it at that.'

'I do have another question,' said Neal.

I was beginning to grow impatient. Neal especially was getting on my nerves.

'What is it?'

'It has to do with his bones.'

'What about them?'

'We understand there was an irregularity.'

'Is that right?'

He nodded.

'Word gets around.'

Michaels, sensing the tension, intervened. 'Again, it's a regulatory matter. The crematorium is required to inform us of any unusual occurrence.'

I replied that it wasn't that unusual. It had happened before.

'Has it?'

'That's what the man said. Not often. But then my father didn't always do things the conventional way.'

It was a light-hearted comment. I meant nothing by it, and Michaels let it slide. But Neal was the sort who saw meaning and motive everywhere.

'How so?'

'I was joking.'

He frowned, then gave a bogus laugh. 'Oh. I see. Hah. You mean your father *was* conventional?'

'Sometimes. Sometimes not.'

'He was unpredictable?'

'I wouldn't say that.'

'In the end. How would you describe him then?'

'He was delirious.'

'Yes. That's what the hospital notes say.'

'He wasn't himself.'

'Did he talk to you?'

'He was babbling.'

'About?'

'Nothing. It was nonsense.'

'Could you understand it?'

'Sometimes. Most of the time not.'

He wasn't satisfied with this. 'Could you be more specific? You couldn't understand the words? Or the words were put together in a way you didn't understand?'

'I don't know. Both, I suppose.'

He exchanged a look with Michaels. 'Can you remember any of them? The words.'

'Not really.'

'Did you recognize any? Had he said them before?'

'Some of them. Sure.'

'The ones you didn't know.'

'What's this have to do with his bones?'

'Bear with us for just a moment,' said Michaels. 'We're almost done. Did any of the words sound foreign?'

'I don't remember. He mumbled a lot.'

'Had he ever acted that way before?'

'No. Never.'

'He never behaved unusually? Like, say, someone you didn't know?'

'A stranger,' said Neal. 'Did you ever think of your father like that?'

I'd had enough, especially of him. 'Do you have a father?'

'Is that a yes or a no?'

'It's a question. If you don't know the answer, maybe I can help.'

'Let's get back to his bones,' said Michaels. 'We'd like to have a look at them.'

'Would you? And why is that?'

'Because we're public health officials.'

'And it's the law,' said Neal, although the look he got from Michaels made me wonder if he'd made that up.

'Why are you so interested? Is there some danger to the public? Some sort of health risk?'

'We won't know until we examine them.'

'But what's the likelihood? Really.'

'I couldn't say.'

I suspected he could. Moreover, I began to feel the need to defend my father, as though his honor and integrity were at stake. Which was ironic, because of all his qualities these were the ones that he, and I, and nearly everyone who knew him, valued most.

'They've cooked for a whole day at more than a thousand degrees. Is there anything you know of that survives that kind of heat for that long? Anything that could possibly harm anybody?'

There was a pause. Somehow the word 'harm' changed the whole tenor of the conversation. Neal glanced at Michaels, who wore a grave expression, then at me.

'If you don't mind, we'd like a look.'

'They're not here.'

'Where are they?'

I had to think fast. 'Somewhere else.'

Lame? What can I say? Neal started to reply, but Michaels stopped him.

'Can you arrange for us to see them?' he asked.

'When?'

'Tomorrow, say.'

I wanted to get rid of these guys, and the quickest way, it seemed was to agree. Besides, I was out of snappy rejoinders. 'Tomorrow it is.'

'Excellent. We'll see you in the morning.'

What is it about health officials that leaves you feeling anxious, worried, vulnerable, agoraphobic, headachy, sick to your stomach, tight in the chest, sweaty, itchy and insecure? Bacteria in the food supply, pesticides in the water supply, smoke in the air supply, obesity, cigarettes, heart disease, ADD, depression ... it's a dangerous world out there, hazards everywhere, and these functionaries seem to delight in reminding us of this, bludgeoning us with statistics and sharing, if not manufacturing, the most alarming trends. But how bad really is it? The people I see look like people I've seen all my life, only more of them, and, I have to say, on the whole they look better. Take my father, for example. He used to smoke, like nearly everyone his age, then he stopped. Then he got fat, like ex-smokers do, then he got rid of the fat. He looked good when he was seventy, he looked good when he was eighty, and he looked pretty darn good for an eighty-three year old, all the way up to the last two weeks of his life. A stranger? Yes, he was, in those final few days. And before? Who isn't a stranger to some degree, even to his closest companions? I knew my father as a son, but what did I know of him as a husband, or a friend, or a son himself? What secrets did he have? And what thoughts and experiences that weren't secrets at all, merely too pedestrian and numerous to mention, or too far in the past, too dim, to recall? Of course he was a stranger. On some level, we're all strangers to each other. But I feared those men meant something more.

After they left and I calmed down, I called my mother. Some

friends were making a condolence call, so she couldn't talk long. She asked how I was doing, which is how she starts every conversation, and I told her everything was fine.

'How about you? How are you?'

'Everyone's being very nice,' she said.

'Are you sleeping?'

'Not too bad. I'm not eating much. I don't have much of an appetite.' There was a pause. 'Why is that?'

She sounded puzzled, as if she'd never known anyone who'd lost a loved one and heard them describe what it was like: the loss of appetite, the sleepless nights, the sudden and recurrent shock of being alone. In fact, she had paid countless condolence calls of her own and had many widowed friends.

'Because your husband just died. People lose their appetite. It's pretty normal.'

'So I shouldn't worry?'

'Are you eating anything at all?'

'Some soup. I had a piece of toast.'

'Then no. You shouldn't. You'll be fine.'

'But everybody's bringing things. Chicken salad. Meatloaf. Lasagna. The food's just piling up.'

'But you like those things.'

'I'm not hungry. But they keep bringing them anyway.'

'You'll be hungry later. You can freeze them.'

'I'm not helpless. I can cook for myself.'

'You might not feel like cooking.'

I could see the look on her face. 'It's annoying. Just so you know. *I* didn't die. Your father did.'

Grieving, for my mother, was a relatively new condition, but being aggrieved was not. The latter for her was sometimes an expression of discontent but more often of worry, which itself was an expression of fear. What she feared most was losing something: her independence, her self-control, someone she loved. In this case, she had lost all those things to one degree or another, and I did my best to reassure her. We made a date to see each other the next day, and I hung up, relieved, temporarily, to have avoided the subject of my dad.

The fire situation worsened that afternoon. At one point there were a reported fourteen hundred blazes throughout the state. One would get contained, and a score of others would take its place. Forests were being consumed, homes destroyed, thousands upon thousands of firefighters mobilized, countless lives imperiled. The closest blaze to us was a scant twenty miles away, and the air outside my window had to be the epicenter of the smoke. I could barely see across the street. The sun was a blur, and the light was brown and eerie.

This is how the world will end, I thought. Maybe it's ending now. Not with a bang but in a slow, deepening, sunless shadow.

I stayed inside and watched the news. I made some calls. I searched the Internet on the subject of bones: bone conditions, bone diseases, skeletons, burials, decomposition, cremation. I learned that in acromegaly the bones are unusually thick. And in something called osteogenesis imperfecta, unusually thin and fragile. I learned that the monks of a certain Catholic sect in Rome collected the bones of their brethren and made sculptures out of them. I learned many fascinating facts, but nothing that helped me in the matter of my father.

His bones were still under the kitchen sink, an ignoble hiding place, but the living room was too exposed, and, call me squeamish, but I did not want them in the bedroom. So I left them where they were and said goodnight, paused, then said 'I'm sorry about this, Dad', paused again, then said 'I miss you, Dad', turned, turned back and said 'I love you, Dad', then went to bed.

In the morning there were ashes everywhere: on the trees, on the cars, in the street. There was barely a county in the state that wasn't on fire. The governor had declared a state of emergency. The President, bless his heart, sent condolences.

I had decided, for the time being, to leave my father's remains where they were. My mother, of course, had to be told, and I was thinking about that when the doorbell rang.

It was Neal and Michaels again. I was nonplussed. I had called and left a message to cancel our date the night before.

'Didn't you get it?' I asked.

They frowned and looked at each other.

'Did you get a message?' Michaels asked Neal.

Neal shook his head. 'Did you?'

Michaels shook his. 'This is a bad time? It's inconvenient?'

'Yes. It is.'

'I'm sorry.' And he looked it.

A moment passed.

'When did you leave it?' he asked.

'Leave it?'

'The message.'

'Last night.'

'What number?'

The air was burning my eyes. By the looks of things, theirs too. Common courtesy obliged me to invite them inside, which I did.

'I don't know. The number you gave me. The one on the card.'

'That's funny,' said Neal.

Michaels agreed. 'Maybe you punched it in wrong.'

'I've done that,' said Neal. 'Plenty of times.'

'It's not as easy as it looks. Those little pads. Those tiny little phones.'

'It's not easy at all. Anyone can make a mistake. Don't worry about it.'

'Not for a second. Please. Do me that favor.'

'It's not worth the trouble.'

'That's what I'm saying. Stuff happens.' He glanced at Neal. 'Am I right?'

Neal rolled his eyes. 'You got to be kidding. All the time.'

'Like yesterday.'

Neal gave a nod. 'Yesterday's a case in point.'

'You probably thought we were stringing you along.'

'Lying to you.'

'Lying's strong, Larry.'

'Misinforming you then. Not laying our cards on the table. Maybe you thought that.'

'You didn't trust us.'

'You weren't sure who we were or what to do. You suffered a tragedy. You're trying to sort things out. You've got a lot on your mind. A lot of feelings. Some this way, some that.'

'You didn't trust yourself,' said Michaels.

'You had the bones, but you didn't want to tell us. You thought it was disrespectful to your dad.'

'You weren't sure what to think. You wanted to help, but you didn't want to do the wrong thing.'

'That's exactly right.' Neal pointed a finger at Michaels, as if to single out his razor-sharp intellect. 'You hit the nail on the head, Mike. He wanted to help, just like he wants to help now.' He turned the finger on me. 'He wants to help, but he doesn't want to make a mistake. Doesn't want to blow it. Like before.'

'With the phone. The wrong number.'

'The phone, the information, the car, whatever.'

'What about the car?' I asked.

He gave me a look.

'The car,' I repeated. 'What's wrong with it?'

He transferred his look to Michaels.

'He's asking about the car,' said Michaels.

'What about it?'

Michaels shrugged and turned to me. 'What's the deal? Is something wrong?'

'*You* said car.'

He frowned. 'No, sir. I did not.'

'*He* did.' I pointed at Neal.

Michaels turned to him. 'He said it was you.'

Neal looked thoughtful. 'Interesting.'

'Maybe he didn't hear you right.'

'It's possible. Mistakes happen.' He addressed me. 'Can you hear me now?'

'I heard you before.'

'Say it. What you thought you heard. The word.'

I was annoyed. This was ridiculous. 'Car.'

'Not this?' He made a sort of gurgling in his throat, very brief and, I have to say, weird. Like water running over rocks, where sometimes you think you can almost make out words.

'Larry, behave.'

'Familiar?' he asked.

I felt like it should have been, but I shook my head.

He looked disappointed.

Michaels intervened. 'Maybe you said cart. Or Carl.'

'Who's Carl?' asked Neal.

'Or card. Maybe card.'

He scratched his head. 'Coulda been that. Come to think of it, I was thinking about a card.'

He reached in his pocket, pulled out his wallet and slid a card out. He handed it to Michaels, who glanced at it before giving it to me. 'Now please, don't take this the wrong way.'

Advice, naturally, that ensures you will.

I looked at it, and my heart froze.

Embossed on it, in large, no-nonsense, steel blue letters were the three initials no one ever wants to see. Who among us is not guilty of something?

The two of them watched me, waiting, it seemed, for some reaction.

'You look worried,' said Neal.

Michaels nodded. 'He does. I think he's taking it the wrong way.'

'You said not to.'

'I did. But obviously we're not communicating well. Do *you* understand me?'

'Sure.'

'I don't talk with an accent?'

Neal grinned. 'Not to me.'

'And the words, they're clear?'

'Like crystal.'

'But still there's a fundamental problem. Like a dog talking to a cat. Like different languages.'

'But related.'

'Definitely related.'

Neal nodded. 'It happens. Between people. Communication difficulties.'

'All the time,' said Michaels, taking the card from me and

tearing it in half. 'It's just a card, for chrissake. Anyone can make a card. What you should be looking at is the deliverer. Look at me.'

I did, and what I saw was not what I expected. His eyes held a depth I hadn't seen before. They were warm, and, dare I say it, friendly.

I was almost taken in. 'You want me to trust you? Is that it?'

'Sure I do. Who doesn't want that?'

'Good cop, bad cop.'

He looked chagrined. 'Larry's not bad.'

I gave Larry a glance. 'He's not exactly reassuring.'

'Vive la différence. And we're not cops.'

'Excuse me. Federal agents.'

'You have a suspicious mind, my friend.'

'You make me suspicious. With all your questions and innu-endoes. And your stupid cards.'

He considered this for a moment. 'The cards, perhaps, were a mistake. I apologize.'

I nodded at the one he held in his hand, torn in half like a losing lottery ticket. 'How do you expect a person to react to that?'

'It's a problem, I admit.'

'Those letters . . .'

'We should change them,' said Neal.

Michaels agreed. 'We should. They're not what you think.'

Neal said something in a rapid, fluty voice, like birdsong.

'That's how it sounds in the native tongue,' said Michaels. 'Or how we think it did. It translates roughly into "Friends of our Deceased."'

The 'F' was right, but the 'O's and the 'D' were nowhere on the card. 'You're pulling my leg.'

He shook his head. 'We're not.'

'Friends of our Deceased.'

'F – O – O – D,' said Neal. 'Maybe we should put that.'

And I thought, are you dumb or something?

Neal smiled at me. 'Pretty dumb idea, huh?'

I stared at him. 'What native tongue?'

Michaels said a word I hadn't heard. 'It's more or less extinct.'

'What the hell is it? Friends of our Deceased?'

He rattled off some names, two or three I recognized as friends or acquaintances of my father.

'It's a group?'

He thought for a second. 'Sure. A group. You could call it that.'

'What do you do?'

'Why this.' He gestured, as though it were obvious.

'What?'

'Visit people.'

'You visit people.'

'Sure. And talk to them. Help out.'

'That's it?'

'We do other stuff too.'

'Like what?'

He looked apologetic. 'We don't usually talk about that with outsiders.'

'So it's a secret group.'

'Not secret. Private.'

'And my dad was a member.'

He seemed to understand how this might be troubling to me. 'I'm sure he was a member of other groups too,' he said gently.

This was true. He was a member of a number of groups. And maybe some, like this one, I didn't know about.

'So you're here on behalf of this group. To help me.'

'That's right.'

'Fair enough. So tell me this: how is it going to help me for you to see my father's bones?'

'We can help you decide what to do with them,' he said.

'Do you have a way to cremate him?'

'No. We don't.'

'Then I don't think you can.'

He protested, as did Neal, and repeated their request to see the bones.

I had this to say: 'The message I left. The one you didn't get? To cancel our meeting today? Maybe it was a bad connection. You didn't hear it right. The words were garbled. Maybe you didn't understand.' I paused, expressing my regret. 'I'm so sorry.'

'You're not.'

'If you give me a number – maybe one that's more reliable – I'll call you if anything new comes up.'

More protests, but I was done. Neal didn't take it well. He issued various veiled and not so veiled threats, but he had no power, as it turned out, legal or otherwise, to back them up. Michaels was more resigned, as though he half expected this. He handed me a new card, this one with his name on it. He lingered a moment, then suddenly and without warning reached out and gave me a hug. He said my father would be proud of me. He said to call if I changed my mind. Then he and Neal left.

I saw my mother later that day. She lived on the other side of town. Ash was in the air and on the ground, floating like snowflakes and stirring around my feet like dust. The heat and smoke were insane. Traffic was light, proving that people can, if they put their hearts, minds and souls to it, use common sense. I would have liked to use common sense too, but mom and I had some things to discuss, and the phone just wouldn't cut it. This had to be face-to-face.

She had made iced tea, a drink best taken outside, but we stayed in the kitchen. She wore shorts and a blouse and no makeup. Her cheeks were naturally pink, her eyes naturally large and dark, her face unnaturally drawn. The first order of business, to show that the world had not come to a halt with her husband's death and that she was okay, was to complain about her hair. This she did more by gesture than by word, grabbing it, scowling, looking annoyed and exasperated, shaking her head. She hadn't been to the hairdresser since the week before he died. Initially, she hadn't wanted to, and then it didn't seem proper.

'It looks fine,' I told her, for which I received a look that said 'Are you an imbecile? Who raised you because I know it couldn't have been me.'

'I made an appointment for Saturday. Do you think that's all right?'

'Sure.'

'Really?'

'Mom. You're the widow. You get to do what you want.'

'I don't want to offend anyone.'

She did have the power to offend, typically with her tongue, and usually without meaning to, or even knowing. But maybe now that dad was gone and she was alone, things would be different. The fact that she was concerned enough to mention it was a positive sign.

'Look how much you'll offend people if you don't get it done,' I pointed out.

'Really? It looks that bad?'

'It looks fine. You have beautiful hair.' And she did, salt and pepper and spry, at the grand old age of seventy. I felt a wave of affection for her and planted a kiss on her head.

'How are you?' she asked, relaxing a little.

I mentioned the fires, which she hadn't been following. News and current events were not at the forefront of her mind.

'How awful,' she said. 'Are you okay?'

'So far.' It was a thoughtless reply, and I regretted it instantly. 'I'm fine.'

'Your father would have left.'

'They're not advising us to. Not yet.'

'There was a big fire here . . . god, it must have been nearly thirty years ago. You were a baby. They weren't telling us to leave then either, but he packed us all up and took us to a motel.'

Playing it safe . . . this sounded like dad.

'Once we were settled in and he was sure we were okay, he drove back and helped fight it.'

'You're kidding?'

'I'm not.'

'Dad did that?'

She nodded, and her eyes shone. 'Your father was full of surprises.'

'What else?'

'I don't know. Whatever they do. Hosed things down. Dug things out. He came back and got us in a couple of days.'

'I mean other surprises. What other ones?'

'Oh, that.' She thought for a moment. 'A surprise birthday party for me. A surprise vacation. He loved planning surprises. And keeping them to himself. He prided himself on that, and with good reason. I can't remember a time he gave a secret away.'

She paused, smiling at something.

'What?' I asked.

'Oh, I was thinking about you. You were another surprise your father gave me. Completely unexpected. I was forty-two. Who would have thought? But what a gift. Really. What a miracle. The best ever.'

The memory of it lingered on her face. Tenderly, she asked if she could fix me something to eat. I wasn't hungry, but she opened the refrigerator anyway. Within seconds, she was scowling.

'Why do they keep bringing me things? It's such a waste. All this food. I wish they'd stop.'

'Mom. Come sit. I have something to tell you.'

Her face became utterly still. 'What's the matter? What's wrong?

I coaxed her beside me, then told her about the remains. She was puzzled at first, as if she didn't understand what I was saying. I had to tell her again, then test her further with the small detail that no one had an explanation. She wasn't happy with the news – who could be happy – but, leave it to her, she wasn't derailed.

'Call someone else,' she said.

'I did. They won't take him. Not the way he is.'

'What does that mean?'

It meant that word had gotten around. That no one thought they could do any better. No one had offered to try.

'It means I want to talk to you about alternatives.'

She folded her arms and pressed her lips together, girding herself.

'I want you to consider burying him.'

In the past two weeks she had lost weight. There were hollows at her temples and in her cheeks, making her eyes, which were large to begin with, more striking than ever. And those eyes regarded me, and it was a wonder I didn't turn to stone.

'Just consider it. Not necessarily do it. But think about it.'

'No, thank you.'

'Why not?'

'We discussed it already. I don't want your father somewhere in the ground. I don't like it. I've never liked it. Okay?'

'Things have changed. We have to change too.'

'Not in this.'

'Mom. Please. Be reasonable.'

She looked at me, and slowly her face softened, and I felt the change that every child feels, or longs to feel, and maybe sometimes fears to feel, as her attention shifted from herself to me and her motherliness took center stage.

'You're upset. I'm so sorry, sweetheart. I wish there were something I could do.'

'You're not upset?'

'It's your father,' she said, as if this explained everything.

'Is it?'

'He can be difficult. You know that. And stubborn. Lord, I never met a man so stubborn.'

And I thought, was that what this was? A character trait?

'I learned long ago not to argue with him. It only makes things worse.'

'So what do you suggest we do?'

'Explain to me again why they can't . . . why he won't . . .' She couldn't quite finish the sentence.

'No one could tell me. No one knew.'

'Well maybe we should find someone who does. A bone specialist.'

'A doctor?'

'Why not?'

Coming from her, this was a remarkable – really, an extraordinary – suggestion. The woman had a lifelong distrust of the medical profession, rivaled only by her deification of it. And sure enough, a moment later she reconsidered.

'Well, some kind of expert.' She paused to think. 'Maybe Adolph.'

'Adolph?'

'You know Adolph.'

'Adolph Krantz?'

'Why not? He went to college. He studied chemistry. He's a smart man. And he was very fond of your father.'

I hadn't seen Adolph since I was a boy. He was one of my father's oldest friends. I didn't see how he could help, but if my mother thought he might, it was worth a try.

'If I talk to him, will you listen to what he has to say? Will you take his advice, even if it's different from what you think? From what your mind is set on?'

'He wrote a very sweet note.'

'Will you?'

'He'll get a kick out of seeing you.'

'Mom.'

'You're pestering me.'

'Will you listen to him?'

She didn't say no, I'll give her that. 'Talk to him. Let's see what he says.'

There was one more item, which was apt to upset her, though with mom you never knew. The smallest thing could cause the biggest reaction, and the biggest, she could take in stride. As it turned out, she didn't know either of the men, nor the group which they claimed to be members of. But she wasn't particularly alarmed or surprised that they knew my dad. He and she shared many of the same beliefs and memberships, but not all. And in the interest of marital peace and harmony, some things they kept to themselves.

I asked if Dad ever seemed strange to her.

She laughed. 'Your father? Very odd. But you get used to it. Look, we were married forty-three years.'

'How?'

'How what?'

'Was he odd.'

'You knew your father. He had his way of doing things. It wasn't my way. Which, as you know, is perfect.'

'Did he ever seem different from other people?'

She gave me a look. 'You ask the weirdest questions. Of course he was different. Everybody's different.'

'I mean different from normal. Different in some other way.'

The look narrowed. 'What are you driving at?'

'I'm not sure.'

'Then let me tell you something. Your father was an exceptional man. He had his quirks ... who doesn't? But when it counted, he was always there. For both of us. If you have any doubts about that, my advice to you is, don't.'

I didn't have doubts, not about that, and for her the conversation was over. I had some food, which always made her happy, agreed to take some home, which made her even happier, kissed her goodbye and left.

The men visited me once more, this time in a dream. They were dressed the same, but they looked different. Their faces were rubbery and their arms and legs were long and loose. They moved like seaweed underwater, like eels, like smoke. I couldn't take my eyes off them ... I think maybe they were hypnotizing me. I wanted to be with them, but they were underwater and I couldn't breathe. I tried to go after them, but I could hardly move. And my chest was starting to hurt. I opened my mouth, but I couldn't get any air. I tried and tried, but something was blocking my windpipe. The men were watching without emotion, while I was suffocating. My chest was ready to burst. Which is how it must have felt to my father the night he was hospitalized. He couldn't breathe either. It's a terrifying feeling. Thank god, I awoke.

The person who invents the twistless, tangleless, knotless

sheet will be enshrined in the Sleepless Hall of Fame. Along with the one who invents the sweatless, soakless, self-cleaning pajamas. What did this dream mean? Aside from the fact that I was afraid to go back to sleep. That these men were not what they seemed? No surprise there. That I felt threatened by them? I did feel threatened. My heart was racing. But why?

Eventually, I did get back to sleep, a very light and fitful one, as I tried to strike that hopeless balance between vigilance and repose. I woke tired and grumpy, with the sense that something had to be done and the desire that someone would do it for me. After a strong cup of coffee, I was ready to take action myself.

I hadn't seen Adolph Krantz since I was a child, and I'd never been to his home. He lived outside a small town a couple of hours north of me in an old ranch house in a quiet neighborhood of parched fields and beautiful, stately oaks. The air was dry and caustic with smoke when I arrived. A cinder, or even the thought of a cinder, and the house, and everything near it, would be toast.

I parked at the curb, passed through a chain link gate and up a cracked concrete path to the front door. I rang the bell. After a minute I rang it again, and at length the door opened.

An old man peered out. Day old whiskers, hawk-shaped nose, boxy black-rimmed glasses that magnified his eyes two or three-fold, a flurry of white hair.

I gave him my name.

A moment passed, and then he offered his hand. 'I'm Krantz. Call me Adolph. I was sorry to hear about your dad. Come in.'

He led me inside, moving slowly but steadily, down a hall and into a small, paneled room full of books and odds and ends. There were two leather armchairs facing each other across a chess board. Only a few pieces remained in play.

He took one of the chairs. 'Do you play?'

'I know how the pieces move. That's about it.'

He studied the board for a moment, then leaned forward and advanced one of the pawns. 'Your father never liked the game.

Though he'd play if I asked him to, back in the day. He hated this part. Endgame. Too slow for him. Not enough action.'

He pointed to a pawn on my side of the table and asked me to move it. He studied the board a minute or two more, and satisfied, sat back and studied me.

'You look like your father. You have his eyes. People used to say I looked like him too. To me that was a great compliment. I admired him enormously. There're not a lot of us left.'

'Us?'

'That's right. Hardly any.'

'What do you mean "us"?'

'The gang. The tribe.' He paused. 'What did we call ourselves?' He couldn't remember.

'FOOD?' I ventured.

'What about it?'

'Was that the name?'

He gave me a look. 'Food?'

I nodded.

'What kind of name is that?'

I told him what it stood for, at which point, I believe, he ceased to take me seriously.

'You're needling me.'

'I'm not.'

'Your dad used to needle.'

'I'm only telling you what they said.'

'Such a needler. The King of Needling. The Needlemeister. What an education, watching him work. A thing of beauty, your father. He had the softest touch.' He fell silent, and I could see him remembering. The years seemed to melt away. A smile lit his old, craggy face.

'We did pretty well for ourselves, didn't we, Mickey? Considering what we had to work with. Where we came from. What we had to do. Pretty damned well.'

Mickey was my father's nickname, from the old days. Only a handful of people used it. Evidently, Adolph was talking to him.

'We've got nothing to be ashamed of. You a high school dropout. Me a college bum.'

'Adolph?'

He glanced at me.

'Mickey's not here.'

He looked lost, but only for a moment. 'Why would he be? But you. Listen. Be proud of your father. He was a good man. A wonderful person. You know how we met? The story. You know the story?'

Some of it I did, but only bits and pieces, mostly from my mom. Dad didn't talk much about the past.

'I came over when I was just a kid. Your father was a year or two older and already here. My family took a room in a house in the neighborhood. Five of us in a single room. I didn't know anybody. I didn't speak the language. I didn't know my way from a hole in the ground. Scared? You bet I was scared. Excited too. Scared and excited at the same time. Everything was so different, so strange and unusual, and one day I walked out the door, and there was your father. He was sitting on a fire hydrant, playing with a piece of string. He smiled when he saw me. "I've been waiting for you," he said.'

'He spoke your language? He spoke German?'

'Your father? German? Never. Not a word.'

'So how'd you understand him?'

'How do you think I understood him? He made himself understood. He took me under his wing. Became a big brother to me. That's how they worked it. The buddy system. Everything in pairs.'

'Who worked it?'

'The ones who sent us. The program. For me, mandatory. Your dad, if I'm not mistaken, was a volunteer.'

'For what? A volunteer for what?'

He thought for a moment, and a smile spread across his face. 'The rest of his life. And then some. That's for what. Don't ask me how long, because I can't tell you. As you see, I'm still here.'

Apparently, he found this amusing. To me it was annoyingly obtuse.

'You said you were sent. By whom?'

'The senders.'

'Who are the senders?'

'I was five. What does a kid know when he's five?' He gave me a look. 'Your father never talked to you about this?'

'No.'

'Never?'

I shook my head.

'Then I assume he didn't want you to know.'

'Know what?'

'Some do, some don't. Tell people. It's an individual deci-sion. It's not up to me to decide otherwise. Out of respect for your father, may he rest in peace. Out of respect for your mother. And for you.'

This wasn't good enough, not by a long shot. I asked him again what it was I didn't know, but he refused to say another word. I wasn't about to get down on my knees. Not literally. I did, however, let a certain plaintive, importuning tone enter my voice. But he wouldn't budge.

So I tried a different tactic. 'The men who visited me. Are they part of this thing? Do they know?'

He didn't recognize either of their names, but my descrip-tion of Michaels seemed to ring a bell.

'They came to pay their respects?'

'They wanted a look at him. At his bones. Who are they, Adolph?'

'I'd imagine another unit. Another pair. Did you let them see?'

'No. I didn't trust them.'

'They were secretive?'

'Extremely.'

'And you found that annoying. Distasteful. Unpleasant.'

'Yes.'

He nodded, then fell silent. Nearly a minute passed before he spoke. 'I understand. I do. But imagine for a moment if they weren't.'

'What do you mean?'

'Imagine if they were completely open and honest. Imagine if everyone was. Now take that one step further and imagine if everyone shared everything. If there were no secrets, no hidden thoughts, no privacy. If everyone knew everything about everybody. No separation between people. No boundaries. No mystery. Imagine a world like that. Every channel open all the time. Everything revealed. How does that sound to you?'

He didn't wait for an answer. 'We've tried it. It fried our little brains. Almost fried our future too. Better a little privacy. A little ignorance. Trust me, it's no crime to know a little less.'

Then I'm in good shape, I thought. I had no idea what he was talking about.

'Why won't his bones burn, Adolph?'

'Ah, yes. That question. Do you have them?'

As a matter of fact, I did. 'They're in the car.'

He nodded, as if he'd expected no less. 'The answer to your question is I don't know why. I only know what you know, that they won't.'

He removed his glasses and rubbed his eyes. He did resemble my father, and the look he gave me – searching and warm – resembled him too.

'Have you thought of burying him?' he asked.

'My mother won't allow it.'

'It's a common custom, you know.'

'I do know. But it's not up to me.'

'Throughout the world. Among a great many groups, as different and diverse as they can be. To hazard a guess, I'd say the custom is quite universal. And I use that term in the broadest possible way.'

He replaced his glasses and leveled his eyes at me. 'Did it ever occur to you that the men were there for that?'

'What? To bury my father?'

'Yes. To bury him. Simply that.'

'They didn't mention it. And it didn't occur to me. Not once.'

'A failure of communication perhaps. But it doesn't matter, does it? Your mother won't permit it.'

'She has that right.'

'Certainly she does. The right of the survivor. We should

do our best to honor her wishes. Perhaps it's time you brought him in.'

Him was not exactly how I thought of what I had, but I did agree that it was time, and I left the house and went to the car. By now it was late afternoon, and the sun through all the smoke and haze was a blurry ball of red. A woman pushing a stroller passed me on the sidewalk. She smiled, and I smiled back. A brief but warm and very human connection. But then I asked myself, what did her smile signify, what did it mean? And what did mine mean, and were our meanings the same? What did it mean to share something? To understand someone? To be inside another's skin or their head? And then I thought, us. The word Adolph had used. *They sent us.* Who was us? And the senders, who were they?

The box was in the trunk. I hadn't opened it, and I didn't intend to, but I had a feeling that Adolph did. I was willing to let him, as long as I didn't have to watch. It was my dad after all, not some random bag of bones. And frankly, in my mind he was still living. Though not, I admit, living very well: the image I had of him was an elderly man who in his last days was not at all the man he was. That's the trouble, if you can call it that, of someone living to a ripe old age: you tend to remember them as old. If they happened to be sick, especially if the sickness was prolonged, you remember them that way. I'm sure it gets better with time, easier, that is, to recall earlier days and younger selves, but at the moment what was freshest in my mind was dad in the hospital, restless and agitated, not recognizing me or my mother, awake but clearly somewhere, if not someone, else. The word 'possession' comes to mind, but it was more the absence of possession, as if something structured and maybe even made up, like a façade, were gone. Stripped away, to reveal a deeper – and frankly, deeply disturbing – inner self. Had I seen this person before? The one with barely a thread of connection to the real world, the world, that is, that most of us lived in and knew? Maybe I had. Once when he got so mad while driving he had a near fatal accident. Once when he got so drunk he started singing in someone else's voice. Another time, or several times, when he and my mother fought. Mostly he was not this way, and I loved him, but he did have a temper, which, when it came, made me think of him as monstrous: those bulging eyes, usually so mild, that strained and frightening voice, that blood red face.

So yes, I do have memories. But pretty thin evidence for his being other than what he was. Because that's what we're talking about. The A word. No one's using it … too scared, too diplomatic, too worried about what the family might say or do or think, too protective of us and our feelings. Whatever. But that's what they mean.

So maybe last night's dream was a message. Maybe it was the voice of truth. Those weird, inhuman bodies. Those shifting, watery faces.

Not that I believe in such things.

Not that I necessarily don't.

It does raise some questions though. Like, where did you come from, Dad? How many of you are there? Any special powers? Weaknesses? Does Mom know?

At a certain age – I'm not sure what, but I think pre-teen – if you'd told me my dad was an alien, I'd have said cool. Go Dad. Part of it bravado, part of it pride, part a confirmation of how I was feeling anyway about him and the world. Face it, when you're a kid, everything's alien to some degree. But at an older age, like now, it's different. I want to know what it means, and what it meant then, and why he didn't tell me. I want to know who the hell I was living with, and listening to, and trying to impress. Who was I modeling myself after (and doing a pretty good job, judging by the result), and what does that make me?

The fact is, my dad did have powers. He was good at business. He was super good at cards. He was super modest. When it came to sports, he was super slow.

And vulnerabilities? His kryptonite? He didn't always believe in himself. He had a weakness for food and drink. He got angry over and over at the same things. He was stubborn to a fault.

The bones were a perfect example of his stubbornness: their

resistance to being burned really shouldn't have surprised me at all. When dad didn't want to do something, he wouldn't do it. The more you tried to get him to, the harder he'd dig in. If he does have a spirit, it's a good bet that it resides in this: the hard-headed, infuriating, refusal-to-budge persistence of his damn bones.

They weren't much heavier than the box they were packed in, but when I removed them from the trunk, I felt a weight much like what I felt when he and I would square off. The weight of expectation, but more than anything, the weight, the sheer mass, of that stubbornness of his, and not knowing how to respond to it: give in, and let him have his way? Be stubborn back and show my mettle? Should I open the box and force myself to look at him? Would that prove something? If he were watching, what would he think? If he were in my place, what would he do?

Adolph was waiting when I returned. He'd cleared the table of the chess board, and I placed the box there. He looked at it for a long time before speaking.

'You've not opened it?'

'No.'

'But you want to.'

I shook my head.

He looked at me and at the same time laid his palm on the box, pressing it there as though to steady himself, or else to steady and maybe comfort who or what was inside. He didn't reply, and at length I said, 'I do and I don't.'

He nodded. 'You have an urge.'

'A small one.'

'A sense of obligation.'

I shrugged.

'Have you ever seen a man's bones?' he asked.

'In books. And museums.'

'Up close?'

'Not so very close.'

'Ever held a skull?'

'No.'

'It's an interesting business, skulls and bones. But not so interesting that a man should have to look at his own father. I advise against it. Unless you're used to such things, the sight can be more than a little unsettling. There's no reason to inflict it on yourself. It can leave an indelible scar.'

I thanked him. I did feel an obligation, and his words helped relieve it.

'So what do we do? What's the plan?'

'You're asking my advice?'

'Yes. Please.'

He folded his hands. 'Very well. Leave the box with me.'

'Leave it?'

'Come back tomorrow and I'll give you his ashes.'

'How are you going to do that?'

'Not by fire,' he said.

'How?'

He didn't reply, and I recalled that he had been a chemist. Possibly he was going to use some chemical method. Possibly that method was illegal, and he didn't want to implicate me.

'I'd like you to trust me,' he said.

'I'd like to.'

'Good.' A moment passed. He gave a knowing smile. 'The question is, will you?'

'If you tell me how you're going to do it.'

'And if I can't?'

'Can't or won't?'

'Can't,' he said.

'Then I'd want to know why.'

The smile deepened. 'Of course. And I'd say that why is unimportant. Or rather, secondary. Inessential at this time. Our job is to honor your father and take care of your mother. And of you. That's the business at hand. We can continue our conversation later, though I'm not sure you'll end up knowing more than you do now. The older you get, the more you learn to be satisfied with less. At any rate, now we should do what we have to.'

'Who is he, Adolph?'

'You know who he is.'

'I don't.'

'Forgive me, but you do.'

This was my father's oldest friend. My mother trusted him, and I wanted to trust him, too. I longed to trust him. But I couldn't, not in this.

I thanked him for everything and left the house, the box in my arms. He watched from the doorway as I slid it in the trunk, doing nothing to interfere. I pulled away and drove a few blocks, then stopped and moved the box to the back seat. A few blocks later, and I moved it to the front.

The sun had set, and the moon was low in the sky, shrouded gray. It looked like a hole through which all the smoke and soot might pour and disappear, leaving the world, my world, clean and whole again. In the distance along the edge of a hill was a smudge of red where another fire raged. My heart was heavy. I stopped the car.

Adolph was right. I did know who he was. And that person wasn't in the box, or behind some secret door, or in what people thought or hinted about him. Who he was was inside me. And knowing this was knowing a lot, and it made the decision of what to do next easy.

The fires continued to ravage the state, until it seemed we had entered an era of flame. If you didn't see one, then you saw smoke, and breathed it in and tasted it. But then one day, miraculously, the sun rose in a sky that was nearly blue. And the air was nearly fresh. And that was the day we scattered his ashes.

Some, at mom's insistence, we sprinkled on a pathetic little planting strip beside Oak Mall, which was all that remained of a park where she and dad had courted. The rest we scattered on a hilltop overlooking town. Adolph had sealed them in a heavy-duty plastic bag, which he had thoughtfully placed in a stainless steel urn. My mother, who normally notices such things, made no comment, but to me the urn looked suspiciously like a large martini shaker.

Were they my father's remains? My mom certainly thought they were. And I was inclined to think so too. If they weren't, they were doing what they had to. They were fulfilling their purpose.

It's a terrible thing to live in a constant state of doubt. It's hard, sometimes excruciatingly hard, to always be unsure. Whoever my father was and wherever he came from, the earth had him now. But we had him before, and without question he had us.

Mary Cholmondeley

LET LOOSE

MARY CHOLMONDELEY (1859-1925) (*pronounced 'Chumley'*) *was a popular novelist of the late Victorian period, best known as an author of 'Sensation' fiction, including* Red Pottage (1899), *a bestseller on both sides of the Atlantic. Another sensational tale,* Diana Tempest (1893), *was well received by critics and has been reprinted by Valancourt in a scholarly edition. 'Let Loose' first appeared in* Temple Bar *magazine in April 1890. Preceding Bram Stoker's famous novel by seven years, Cholmondeley's tale has been recognized by critics as an early vampire story of sorts.*

> The dead abide with us! Though stark and cold
> Earth seems to grip them, they are with us still.

SOME YEARS AGO I TOOK UP ARCHITECTURE, and made a tour through Holland, studying the buildings of that interesting country.

I was not then aware that it is not enough to take up art. Art must take you up, too. I never doubted but that my passing enthusiasm for her would be returned. When I discovered that she was a stern mistress, who did not immediately respond to my attentions, I naturally transferred them to another shrine. There are other things in the world besides art. I am now a landscape gardener.

But at the time of which I write I was engaged in a violent flirtation with architecture. I had one companion on this expedition, who has since become one of the leading architects of the day. He was a thin, determined-looking man with a screwed-up face and heavy jaw, slow of speech, and absorbed in his work to a degree which I quickly found tiresome. He was possessed of a certain quiet power of overcoming obstacles which I have rarely seen equalled. He has since become my brother-in-law, so I ought to know; for my parents did not like him much and opposed the marriage, and my sister did not like him at all, and refused him over and over again; but, nevertheless, he eventually married her.

I have thought since that one of his reasons for choosing me as his travelling companion on this occasion was because he was getting up steam for what he subsequently termed 'an alliance with my family,' but the idea never entered my head at the time. A more careless man as to dress I have rarely met, and yet, in all the heat of July in Holland, I noticed that he never appeared without a high, starched collar, which had not even fashion to commend it at that time.

I often chaffed him about his splendid collars, and asked him why he wore them, but without eliciting any response. One evening, as we were walking back to our lodgings in Middleberg, I attacked him for about the thirtieth time on the subject.

'Why on earth do you wear them?' I said.

'You have, I believe, asked me that question many times,' he replied, in his slow, precise utterance; 'but always on occasions when I was occupied. I am now at leisure, and I will tell you.'

And he did.

I have put down what he said, as nearly in his own words as I can remember them.

Ten years ago, I was asked to read a paper on English Frescoes at the Institute of British Architects. I was determined to make the paper as good as I could, down to the slightest details, and I consulted many books on the subject, and studied every fresco I could find. My father, who had been an architect, had left me, at his death, all his papers and note-books on the subject of architecture. I searched them diligently, and found in one of them a slight unfinished sketch of nearly fifty years ago that specially interested me. Underneath was noted, in his clear, small hand – *Frescoed east wall of crypt. Parish Church. Wet Waste-on-the-Wolds, Yorkshire (viâ Pickering.)*

The sketch had such a fascination for me that I decided to go there and see the fresco for myself. I had only a very vague idea as to where Wet Waste-on-the-Wolds was, but I was ambitious for the success of my paper; it was hot in London, and I set off on my long journey not without a certain degree of pleasure, with my dog Brian, a large nondescript brindled creature, as my only companion.

I reached Pickering, in Yorkshire, in the course of the afternoon, and then began a series of experiments on local lines which ended, after several hours, in my finding myself deposited at a little out-of-the-world station within nine or ten miles of Wet Waste. As no conveyance of any kind was to be had, I shouldered my portmanteau, and set out on a long white road that stretched away into the distance over the bare, tree-less wold. I must have walked for several hours, over a waste of moorland patched with heather, when a doctor passed me, and gave me a lift to within a mile of my destination. The mile was a long one, and it was quite dark by the time I saw the feeble glim-mer of lights in front of me, and found that I had reached Wet Waste. I had considerable difficulty in getting any one to take me in; but at last I persuaded the owner of the public-house to give me a bed, and, quite tired out, I got into it as soon as pos-sible, for fear he should change his mind, and fell asleep to the sound of a little stream below my window.

I was up early next morning, and inquired directly after break-fast the way to the clergyman's house, which I found was close at hand. At Wet Waste everything was close at hand. The whole village seemed composed of a straggling row of one-storied grey stone houses, the same colour as the stone walls that sep-arated the few fields enclosed from the surrounding waste, and as the little bridges over the beck that ran down one side of the grey wide street. Everything was grey. The church, the low tower of which I could see at a little distance, seemed to have been built of the same stone; so was the parsonage when I came up to it, accompanied on my way by a mob of rough, uncouth children, who eyed me and Brian with half-defiant curiosity.

The clergyman was at home, and after a short delay I was admitted. Leaving Brian in charge of my drawing materials, I followed the servant into a low panelled room, in which, at a latticed window, a very old man was sitting. The morning light fell on his white head bent low over a litter of papers and books.

'Mr er – ?' he said, looking up slowly, with one finger keeping his place in a book.

'Blake.'

'Blake,' he repeated after me, and was silent.

I told him that I was an architect; that I had come to study a fresco in the crypt of his church, and asked for the keys.

'The crypt,' he said, pushing up his spectacles and peering hard at me. 'The crypt has been closed for thirty years. Ever since –' and he stopped short.

'I should be much obliged for the keys,' I said again.

He shook his head.

'No,' he said. 'No one goes in there now.'

'It is a pity,' I remarked, 'for I have come a long way with that one object;' and I told him about the paper I had been asked to read, and the trouble I was taking with it.

He became interested. 'Ah!' he said, laying down his pen, and removing his finger from the page before him, 'I can understand that. I also was young once, and fired with ambition. The lines have fallen to me in somewhat lonely places, and for forty years I have held the cure of souls in this place, where, truly, I have seen but little of the world, though I myself may be not unknown in the paths of literature. Possibly you may have read a pamphlet, written by myself, on the Syrian version of the Three Authentic Epistles of Ignatius?'

'Sir,' I said, 'I am ashamed to confess that I have not time to read even the most celebrated books. My one object in life is my art, you know.'

'You are right, my son,' said the old man, evidently disappointed, but looking at me kindly. 'There are diversities of gifts, and if the Lord has entrusted you with a talent, look to it. Lay it not up in a napkin.'

I said I would not do so if he would lend me the keys of the crypt. He seemed startled by my recurrence to the subject and looked undecided.

'Why not?' he murmured to himself. 'The youth appears a good youth. And superstition! What is it but distrust in God!'

He got up slowly, and taking a large bunch of keys out of his pocket, opened with one of them an oak cupboard in the corner of the room.

'They should be here,' he muttered, peering in; 'but the dust of many years deceives the eye. See, my son, if among these parchments there be two keys; one of iron and very large, and the other steel, and of a long and thin appearance.'

I went eagerly to help him, and presently found in a back drawer two keys tied together, which he recognized at once.

'Those are they,' he said. 'The long one opens the first door at the bottom of the steps which go down against the outside wall of the church hard by the sword graven in the wall. The second opens (but it is hard of opening and of shutting) the iron door within the passage leading to the crypt itself. My son, is it necessary to your treatise that you should enter this crypt?'

I replied that it was absolutely necessary.

'Then take them,' he said, 'and in the evening you will bring them to me again.'

I said I might want to go several days running, and asked if he would not allow me to keep them till I had finished my work; but on that point he was firm.

'Likewise,' he added, 'be careful that you lock the first door at the foot of the steps before you unlock the second, and lock the second also while you are within. Furthermore, when you come out lock the iron inner door as well as the wooden one.'

I promised I would do so, and, after thanking him, hurried away, delighted at my success in obtaining the keys. Finding Brian and my sketching materials waiting for me in the porch, I eluded the vigilance of my escort of children by taking the narrow private path between the parsonage and the church which was close at hand, standing in a quadrangle of ancient yews.

The church itself was interesting, and I noticed that it must have arisen out of the ruins of a previous building, judging from the number of fragments of stone caps and arches, bearing traces of very early carving, now built into the walls. There were incised crosses, too, in some places, and one especially caught my attention, being flanked by a large sword. It was in trying to get a nearer look at this that I stumbled, and, looking down, saw at my feet a flight of narrow stone steps green with moss and mildew. Evidently this was the entrance to the crypt. I at once descended the steps, taking care of my footing, for they were damp and slippery in the extreme. Brian accompanied me, as nothing would induce him to remain behind. By the time I had reached the bottom of the stairs, I found myself almost in darkness, and I had to strike a light before I could find the keyhole and the proper key to fit into it. The door, which was of wood, opened inwards fairly easily, although an accumulation of mould and rubbish on the ground outside showed it had not been used for many years. Having got through it, which was not altogether an easy matter, as nothing would induce it to open more than about eighteen inches, I carefully locked it behind me, although I should have preferred to leave it open, as there is to some minds an unpleasant feeling in being locked in anywhere, in case of a sudden exit seeming advisable.

I kept my candle alight with some difficulty, and after groping my way down a low and of course exceedingly dank passage, came to another door. A toad was squatting against it, who looked as if he had been sitting there about a hundred years. As I lowered the candle to the floor, he gazed at the light with unblinking eyes, and then retreated slowly into a crevice in the wall, leaving against the door a small cavity in the dry mud which had gradually silted up round his person. I noticed that this door was of iron, and had a long bolt, which, however, was broken. Without delay, I fitted the second key into the lock, and pushing the door open after considerable difficulty, I felt the cold breath of the crypt upon my face. I must own I experienced a momentary regret at locking the second door again as soon as I was well inside, but I felt it my duty to do so. Then, leaving the key in the lock, I seized my candle and looked round. I was standing in a low vaulted chamber with groined roof, cut out of the solid rock. It was difficult to see where the crypt ended, as further light thrown on any point only showed other rough archways or openings, cut in the rock, which had probably served at one time for family vaults. A peculiarity of the Wet Waste crypt, which I had not noticed in other places of that description, was the tasteful arrangement of skulls and bones which were packed about four feet high on either side. The skulls were symmetrically built up to within a few inches of the top of the low archway on my left, and the shin bones were arranged in the same manner on my right. *But the fresco!* I looked round for it in vain. Perceiving at the further end of the crypt a very low and very massive archway, the entrance to which was not filled up with bones, I passed under it, and found myself in a second smaller chamber. Holding my candle above my head, the first object its light fell upon was – the fresco, and at a glance I saw that it was unique. Setting down some of my things with a trembling hand on a rough stone shelf hard by, which had evidently been a credence table, I examined the work more closely. It was a reredos over what had probably been the altar at the time the priests were proscribed. The fresco belonged to the earliest part of the fifteenth century, and was so perfectly preserved that I could almost trace the limits of each day's work in the plaster, as the artist had dashed it on and smoothed it out with his trowel. The subject was the Ascension, gloriously treated. I can hardly describe my elation as I stood and looked at it, and reflected that this magnificent specimen of English fresco painting would be made known to the world by myself. Recollecting myself at last, I opened my sketching bag, and, lighting all the candles I had brought with me, set to work.

Brian walked about near me, and though I was not other-wise than glad of his company in my rather lonely position, I wished several times I had left him behind. He seemed restless, and even the sight of so many bones appeared to exercise no soothing effect upon him. At last, however, after repeated commands, he lay down, watchful but motionless, on the stone floor.

I must have worked for several hours, and I was pausing to

rest my eyes and hands, when I noticed for the first time the intense stillness that surrounded me. No sound from *me* reached the outer world. The church clock which had clanged out so loud and ponderously as I went down the steps, had not since sent the faintest whisper of its iron tongue down to me below. All was silent as the grave. This *was* the grave. Those who had come here had indeed gone down into silence. I repeated the words to myself, or rather they repeated themselves to me.

Gone down into silence.

I was awakened from my reverie by a faint sound. I sat still and listened. Bats occasionally frequent vaults and underground places.

The sound continued, a faint, stealthy, rather unpleasant sound. I do not know what kinds of sounds bats make, whether pleasant or otherwise. Suddenly there was a noise as of something falling, a momentary pause – and then – an almost imperceptible but distinct jangle as of a key.

I had left the key in the lock after I had turned it, and I now regretted having done so. I got up, took one of the candles, and went back into the larger crypt – for though I trust I am not so effeminate as to be rendered nervous by hearing a noise for which I cannot instantly account; still, on occasions of this kind, I must honestly say I should prefer that they did not occur. As I came towards the iron door, there was another distinct (I had almost said hurried) sound. The impression on my mind was one of great haste. When I reached the door, and held the candle near the lock to take out the key, I perceived that the other one, which hung by a short string to its fellow, was vibrating slightly. I should have preferred not to find it vibrating, as there seemed no occasion for such a course; but I put them both into my pocket, and turned to go back to my work. As I turned, I saw on the ground what had occasioned the louder noise I had heard, namely, a skull which had evidently just slipped from its place on the top of one of the walls of bones, and had rolled almost to my feet. There, disclosing a few more inches of the top of an archway behind was the place from which it had been dislodged. I stooped to pick it up, but fearing to displace any more skulls by meddling with the pile, and not liking to gather up its scattered teeth, I let it lie, and went back to my work, in which I was soon so completely absorbed that I was only roused at last by my candles beginning to burn low and go out one after another.

Then, with a sigh of regret, for I had not nearly finished, I turned to go. Poor Brian, who had never quite reconciled himself to the place, was beside himself with delight. As I opened the iron door he pushed past me, and a moment later I heard him whining and scratching, and I had almost added, beating, against the wooden one. I locked the iron door, and hurried down the passage as quickly as I could, and almost before I had got the other one ajar there seemed to be a rush past me into the open air, and Brian was bounding up the steps and out of sight. As I stopped to take out the key, I felt quite deserted and left behind. When I came out once more into the sunlight, there was a vague sensation all about me in the air of exultant freedom.

It was already late in the afternoon, and after I had sauntered back to the parsonage to give up the keys, I persuaded the people of the public-house to let me join in the family meal, which was spread out in the kitchen. The inhabitants of Wet Waste were primitive people, with the frank, unabashed manner that flourishes still in lonely places, especially in the wilds of Yorkshire; but I had no idea that in these days of penny posts and cheap newspapers such entire ignorance of the outer world could have existed in any corner, however remote, of Great Britain.

When I took one of the neighbour's children on my knee – a pretty little girl with the palest aureole of flaxen hair I had ever seen – and began to draw pictures for her of the birds and beasts of other countries, I was instantly surrounded by a crowd of children, and even grown-up people, while others came to their doorways and looked on from a distance, calling to each other in the strident unknown tongue which I have since discovered goes by the name of 'Broad Yorkshire.' The following morning, as I came out of my room, I perceived that something was amiss in the village. A buzz of voices reached me as I passed the bar, and in the next house I could hear through the open window a high-pitched wail of lamentation.

The woman who brought me my breakfast was in tears, and in answer to my questions, told me that the neighbour's child, the little girl whom I had taken on my knee the evening before, had died in the night.

I felt sorry for the general grief that the little creature's death seemed to arouse, and the uncontrolled wailing of the poor mother took my appetite away.

I hurried off early to my work, calling on my way for the keys, and with Brian for my companion descended once more into the crypt, and drew and measured with an absorption that gave me no time that day to listen for sounds real or fancied. Brian, too, on this occasion seemed quite content, and slept peacefully beside me on the stone floor. When I had worked as long as I could, I put away my books with regret that even then I had not quite finished, as I had hoped to do. It would be necessary to come again for a short time on the morrow. When I returned the keys late that afternoon, the old clergyman met me at the door, and asked me to come in and have tea with him.

'And has the work prospered?' he asked, as we sat down in the long, low room, into which I had just been ushered, and where he seemed to live entirely.

I told him it had, and showed it to him.

'You have seen the original, of course?' I said.

'Once,' he replied, gazing fixedly at it. He evidently did not care to be communicative, so I turned the conversation to the age of the church.

'All here is old,' he said. 'When I was young, forty years ago, and came here because I had no means of mine own, and was much moved to marry at that time, I felt oppressed that all was so old; and that this place was so far removed from the world, for which I had at times longings grievous to be borne; but I had chosen my lot, and with it I was forced to be content. My son, marry not in youth, for love, which truly in that season is a mighty power, turns away the heart from study, and young children break the back of ambition. Neither marry in middle life, when a woman is seen to be but a woman and her talk a weariness, so you will not be burdened with a wife in your old age.'

I had my own views on the subject of marriage, for I am of opinion that a well-chosen, companion of domestic tastes and docile and devoted temperament may be of material assistance to a professional man. But, my opinions once formulated, it is not of moment to me to discuss them with others, so I changed the subject, and asked if the neighbouring villages were as anti-quated as Wet Waste.

'Yes, all about here is old,' he repeated. 'The paved road lead-ing to Dyke Fens is an ancient pack road, made even in the time of the Romans. Dyke Fens, which is very near here, a matter of but four or five miles, is likewise old, and forgotten by the world. The Reformation never reached it. It stopped here. And at Dyke Fens they still have a priest and a bell, and bow down before the saints. It is a damnable heresy, and weekly I expound it as such to my people, showing them true doctrines; and I have heard that this same priest has so far yielded himself to the Evil One that he has preached against me as withholding gospel truths from my flock; but I take no heed of it, neither of his pamphlet touching the Clementine Homilies, in which he vainly contradicts that which I have plainly set forth and proven beyond doubt, concerning the word *Asaph*.'

The old man was fairly off on his favourite subject, and it was some time before I could get away. As it was, he followed me to the door, and I only escaped because the old clerk hob-bled up at that moment, and claimed his attention.

The following morning I went for the keys for the third and last time. I had decided to leave early the next day. I was tired of Wet Waste, and a certain gloom seemed to my fancy to be gathering over the place. There was a sensation of trouble in the air, as if, although the day was bright and clear, a storm were coming.

This morning, to my astonishment, the keys were refused to me when I asked for them. I did not, however, take the refusal as final – I make it a rule never to take a refusal as final – and after a short delay I was shown into the room where, as usual, the clergyman was sitting, or rather, on this occasion, was walking up and down.

'My son,' he said with vehemence, 'I know wherefore you have come, but it is of no avail. I cannot lend the keys again.'

I replied that, on the contrary, I hoped he would give them to me at once.

'It is impossible,' he repeated. 'I did wrong, exceeding wrong. I will never part with them again.'

'Why not?'

He hesitated, and then said slowly:

'The old clerk, Abraham Kelly, died last night.' He paused, and then went on: 'The doctor has just been here to tell me of that which is a mystery to him. I do not wish the people of the place to know it, and only to me he has mentioned it, but he has discovered plainly on the throat of the old man, and also, but more faintly on the child's, marks as of strangulation. None but he has observed it, and he is at a loss how to account for it. I, alas! can account for it but in one way, but in one way!'

I did not see what all this had to do with the crypt, but to humour the old man, I asked what that way was.

'It is a long story, and, haply, to a stranger it may appear but foolishness, but I will even tell it; for I perceive that unless I furnish a reason for withholding the keys, you will not cease to entreat me for them.

'I told you at first when you inquired of me concerning the crypt, that it had been closed these thirty years, and so it was. Thirty years ago a certain Sir Roger Despard departed this life, even the Lord of the manor of Wet Waste and Dyke Fens, the last of his family, which is now, thank the Lord, extinct. He was a man of a vile life, neither fearing God nor regarding man, nor having compassion on innocence, and the Lord appeared to have given him over to the tormentors even in this world, for he suffered many things of his vices, more especially from drunkenness, in which seasons, and they were many, he was as one possessed by seven devils, being an abomination to his household and a root of bitterness to all, both high and low.

'And, at last, the cup of his iniquity being full to the brim, he came to die, and I went to exhort him on his death-bed; for I heard that terror had come upon him, and that evil imaginations encompassed him so thick on every side, that few of them that were with him could abide in his presence. But when I saw him I perceived that there was no place of repentance left for him, and he scoffed at me and my superstition, even as he lay dying, and swore there was no God and no angel, and all were damned even as he was. And the next day, towards evening, the pains of death came upon him, and he raved the more exceedingly, inasmuch as he said he was being strangled by the Evil One. Now on his table was his hunting knife, and with his last strength he crept and laid hold upon it, no man withstanding him, and swore a great oath that if he went down to burn in hell, he would leave one of his hands behind on earth, and that it would never rest until it had drawn blood from the throat of another and strangled him, even as he himself was being strangled. And he cut off his own right hand at the wrist, and no man dared go near him to stop him, and the blood went through the floor, even down to the ceiling of the room below, and thereupon he died.

'And they called me in the night, and told me of his oath, and I counselled that no man should speak of it, and I took the dead hand, which none had ventured to touch, and I laid it beside him in his coffin; for I thought it better he should take it with him, so that he might have it, if haply some day after much tribulation he should perchance be moved to stretch forth his hands towards God. But the story got spread about, and the people were affrighted, so, when he came to be buried in the place of his fathers, he being the last of his family, and the crypt likewise full, I had it closed, and kept the keys myself, and suffered no man to enter therein any more; for truly he was a man of an evil life, and the devil is not yet wholly overcome, nor cast chained into the lake of fire. So in time the story died out, for in thirty years much is forgotten. And when you came and asked me for the keys, I was at the first minded to withhold them; but I thought it was a vain superstition, and I perceived that you do but ask a second time for what is first refused; so I let you have them, seeing it was not an idle curiosity, but a desire to improve the talent committed to you, that led you to require them.'

The old man stopped, and I remained silent, wondering what would be the best way to get them just once more.

'Surely, sir,' I said at last, 'one so cultivated and deeply read as yourself cannot be biased by an idle superstition.'

'I trust not,' he replied, 'and yet – it is a strange thing that since the crypt was opened two people have died, and the mark is plain upon the throat of the old man and visible on the young child. No blood was drawn, but the second time the grip was stronger than the first. The third time, perchance –'

'Superstition such as that,' I said with authority, 'is an entire want of faith in God. You once said so yourself.'

I took a high moral tone which is often efficacious with conscientious, humble-minded people.

He agreed, and accused himself of not having faith as a grain of mustard seed; but even when I had got him so far as that, I had a severe struggle for the keys. It was only when I finally explained to him that if any malign influence *had* been let loose the first day, at any rate, it was out now for good or evil, and no further going or coming of mine could make any difference, that I finally gained my point. I was young, and he was old; and, being much shaken by what had occurred, he gave way at last, and I wrested the keys from him.

I will not deny that I went down the steps that day with a vague, indefinable repugnance, which was only accentuated by the closing of the two doors behind me. I remembered then, for the first time, the faint jangling of the key and other sounds which I had noticed the first day, and how one of the skulls had fallen. I went to the place where it still lay. I have already said these walls of skulls were built up so high as to be within a few inches of the top of the low archways that led into more distant portions of the vault. The displacement of the skull in question had left a small hole just large enough for me to put my hand through. I noticed for the first time, over the archway above it, a carved coat-of-arms, and the name, now almost obliterated, of Despard. This, no doubt, was the Despard vault. I could not resist moving a few more skulls and looking in, holding my candle as near the aperture as I could. The vault was full. Piled high, one upon another, were old coffins, and remnants of coffins, and strewn bones. I attribute my present determination to be cremated to the painful impression produced on me by this spectacle. The coffin nearest the archway alone was intact, save for a large crack across the lid. I could not get a ray from my candle to fall on the brass plates, but I felt no doubt this was the coffin of the wicked Sir Roger. I put back the skulls, including the one which had rolled down, and carefully finished my work. I was not there much more than an hour, but I was glad to get away.

If I could have left Wet Waste at once I should have done so, for I had a totally unreasonable longing to leave the place; but I found that only one train stopped during the day at the station from which I had come, and that it would not be possible to be in time for it that day.

Accordingly I submitted to the inevitable, and wandered about with Brian for the remainder of the afternoon and until late in the evening, sketching and smoking. The day was oppressively hot, and even after the sun had set across the burnt stretches of the wolds, it seemed to grow very little cooler. Not a breath stirred. In the evening, when I was tired of loitering in the lanes, I went up to my own room, and after contemplating afresh my finished study of the fresco, I suddenly set to work to write the part of my paper bearing upon it. As a rule, I write with difficulty, but that evening words came to me with winged speed, and with them a hovering impression that I must make haste, that I was much pressed for time. I wrote and wrote, until my candles guttered out and left me trying to finish by the moonlight, which, until I endeavoured to write by it, seemed as clear as day.

I had to put away my MS., and, feeling it was too early to go to bed, for the church clock was just counting out ten, I sat

down by the open window and leaned out to try and catch
a breath of air. It was a night of exceptional beauty; and as I
looked out my nervous haste and hurry of mind were allayed.
The moon, a perfect circle, was – if so poetic an expression be
permissible – as it were, sailing across a calm sky. Every detail
of the little village was as clearly illuminated by its beams as
if it were broad day; so, also, was the adjacent church with its
primeval yews, while even the wolds beyond were dimly indi-
cated, as if through tracing paper.

I sat a long time leaning against the windowsill. The heat
was still intense. I am not, as a rule, easily elated or readily cast
down; but as I sat that night in the lonely village on the moors,
with Brian's head against my knee, how, or why, I know not, a
great depression gradually came upon me.

My mind went back to the crypt and the countless dead who
had been laid there. The sight of the goal to which all human
life, and strength, and beauty, travel in the end, had not affected
me at the time, but now the very air about me seemed heavy
with death.

What was the good, I asked myself, of working and toiling,
and grinding down my heart and youth in the mill of long and
strenuous effort, seeing that in the grave folly and talent, idle-
ness and labour lie together, and are alike forgotten? Labour
seemed to stretch before me till my heart ached to think of it,
to stretch before me even to the end of life, and then came, as
the recompense of my labour – the grave. Even if I succeeded,
if, after wearing my life threadbare with toil, I succeeded, what
remained to me in the end? The grave. A little sooner, while the
hands and eyes were still strong to labour, or a little later, when
all power and vision had been taken from them; sooner or later
only – *the grave*.

I do not apologise for the excessively morbid tenor of these
reflections, as I hold that they were caused by the lunar effects
which I have endeavoured to transcribe. The moon in its various quarterings has always exerted a marked influence on what
I may call the sub-dominant, namely, the poetic side of my
nature.

I roused myself at last, when the moon came to look in upon me where I sat, and, leaving the windows open, I pulled myself together and went to bed.

I fell asleep almost immediately, but I do not fancy I could have been asleep very long when I was wakened by Brian. He was growling in a low, muffled tone, as he sometimes did in his sleep, when his nose was buried in his rug. I called out to him to shut up; and as he did not do so, turned in bed to find my match box or something to throw at him. The moonlight was still in the room, and as I looked at him I saw him raise his head and evidently wake up. I admonished him, and was just on the point of falling asleep when he began to growl again in a low, savage manner that waked me most effectually. Presently he shook himself and got up, and began prowling about the room. I sat up in bed and called to him, but he paid no attention. Suddenly I saw him stop short in the moonlight; he showed his teeth, and crouched down, his eyes following something in the air. I looked at him in horror. Was he going mad? His eyes were glaring, and his head moved slightly as if he were following the rapid movements of an enemy. Then, with a furious snarl, he suddenly sprang from the ground, and rushed in great leaps across the room towards me, dashing himself against the furniture, his eyes rolling, snatching and tearing wildly in the air with his teeth. I saw he had gone mad. I leaped out of bed, and rushing at him, caught him by the throat. The moon had gone behind a cloud; but in the darkness I felt him turn upon me, felt him rise up, and his teeth close in my throat. I was being strangled. With all the strength of despair, I kept my grip of his neck, and, dragging him across the room, tried to crush in his head against the iron rail of my bedstead. It was my only chance. I felt the blood running down my neck. I was suffocating. After one moment of frightful struggle, I beat his head against the bar and heard his skull give way. I felt him give one strong shudder, a groan, and then I fainted away.

When I came to myself I was lying on the floor, surrounded by the people of the house, my reddened hands still clutching

Brian's throat. Some one was holding a candle towards me, and the draught from the window made it flare and waver. I looked at Brian. He was stone dead. The blood from his battered head was trickling slowly over my hands. His great jaw was fixed in something that – in the uncertain light – I could not see.

They turned the light a little.

'Oh, God!' I shrieked. 'There! Look! look!'

'He's off his head,' said some one, and I fainted again.

I was ill for about a fortnight without regaining consciousness, a waste of time of which even now I cannot think without poignant regret. When I did recover consciousness, I found I was being carefully nursed by the old clergyman and the people of the house. I have often heard the unkindness of the world in general inveighed against, but for my part I can honestly say that I have received many more kindnesses than I have time to repay. Country people especially are remarkably attentive to strangers in illness.

I could not rest until I had seen the doctor who attended me, and had received his assurance that I should be equal to reading my paper on the appointed day. This pressing anxiety removed, I told him of what I had seen before I fainted the second time. He listened attentively, and then assured me, in a manner that was intended to be soothing, that I was suffering from an hallucination, due, no doubt, to the shock of my dog's sudden madness.

'Did you see the dog after it was dead?' I asked.

He said he did. The whole jaw was covered with blood and foam; the teeth certainly seemed convulsively fixed, but the case being evidently one of extraordinarily virulent hydrophobia, owing to the intense heat, he had had the body buried immediately.

My companion stopped speaking as we reached our lodgings, and went upstairs. Then, lighting a candle, he slowly turned down his collar.

'You see I have the marks still,' he said, 'but I have no fear of dying of hydrophobia. I am told such peculiar scars could not have been made by the teeth of a dog. If you look closely you see the pressure of the five fingers. That is the reason why I wear high collars.'

Bernard Taylor

OUT OF SORTS

One of the finest authors to emerge from the horror publishing boom of the late 1970s and early '80s, BERNARD TAYLOR *is the author of ten novels and several nonfiction true crime books. His first novel,* The Godsend (1976), *the story of the horrible things that happen to an ordinary family who adopt a sweet-looking little girl, was a bestseller and adapted for a film.* Sweetheart, Sweetheart (1977) *was chosen for inclusion in* Horror: 100 Best Books (1990) *and was named by Charles L. Grant as the best ghost story he had ever read. Both of these novels, along with* The Moorstone Sickness (1982), *are available from Valancourt Books. 'Out of Sorts' first appeared in Grant's anthology* Gallery of Horror (1983).

'OH, *not the twenty-first!*' Paul Gunn said. 'Whatever made you choose *that* date?'

'I didn't *choose* it. That's the day the meeting falls – third Friday in the month.' Sylvia shook her head. 'I told you – there was nothing I could do about it.'

'You could have arranged to hold the bloody thing somewhere else, couldn't you? Does it have to be here?'

'It's *my turn*,' Sylvia said with a sigh. 'Besides, I'm president. And apart from that I just wasn't thinking, I suppose. I can't be expected to remember everything.'

'No, but I do expect you to remember the *important* things.' He made a sound of exasperation. 'Can't you change it? It's bad enough at the best of times, but when the bloody house is filled with people – '

'It's only three days away,' Sylvia said reasonably. 'Look, Paul, we planned it weeks ago and it's too late to alter it now.' She looked at him entreatingly. 'Oh, please don't be angry. You'll be all right. No one will bother you.'

He refused to be entreated or pacified, though, and she

watched as he angrily snatched up his newspaper, opened it
unnecessarily roughly and submerged himself in its contents.
End of conversation, as always.

His large, tanned hands looked very dark against the white
of the paper. It was the hair on them. Thick and black, it made
his hands look larger than they were. It was probably a turn-on
for some women, she thought. Not to herself, though; not now
– if it had ever been . . . It was to Norma Russell, though, she
was quite certain. Norma, with her model's 35 x 25 x 36 figure,
her high cheek bones and sleek blonde hair. Paul's hirsute body
would be just the thing to appeal to *her.*

If it came to looks, she reflected, it was quite obvious that
she herself couldn't compete with anyone like Norma. Oh,
once she'd been pretty in a vague, mousey kind of way, but not
for years now. Well, she hadn't made any effort, had she? And
why should she try, now, when there was no point?

And there was no point anymore. More than that, in her eyes
it would have seemed the height of stupidity to go to the bother
of dressing up, when practically the only man who ever looked
at you was your husband – and even when he *did* he didn't even
see you. Yes, pointless, to say the least.

Paul, on the other hand, seemed to have grown sleeker and
better-looking in an overfed kind of way over the years. Success showed clearly on him; in his clothes and his body – and
his women. Yes, he did look better. That, she supposed, was
what contentment and complacency did. She shot him a look
of hatred as he lounged, protected by the shield of his paper.
Then she turned and went upstairs.

This place, too, was a sign of his success. Set apart in this
tiny Yorkshire village of Tallowford, the house was huge and
rambling, exquisitely furnished; further testimony to the years
of effort he'd put into his engineering company, now one of the
most profitable small businesses in nearby Bradford.

In her study Sylvia sat down at her elegant desk, Louis XIV,
genuine. Opening her diary she looked again at the date of
the meeting. The 21st. No mistake. Then she checked over the
Women's Circle committee list. There would be six of them.

On the past three occasions there'd been only five of them – Pamela Horley, Jill Marks, Janet True, and Mary Hanley. This time, though, there'd be six again. A replacement had been found for Lilly Sloane who had moved away – a replacement proposed by her and voted in unanimously by the others: Norma Russell.

Norma, of course, had so eagerly accepted the offered place on the committee. 'Well, if you really want me and you think I can be of help,' she'd said. But she hadn't fooled Sylvia for one minute. Sylvia knew quite well that Norma's eagerness stemmed from the fact that as every third meeting was held at the Gunns' house it could only lead to more encounters between herself and Paul...

Methodically Sylvia went through the list, telephoning the members to check that each was okay for the 21st. All except Norma. *Her* number was engaged. Not that Sylvia needed to worry; if there was one member she knew she could count on, that one was Norma.

Pushing her papers away from her she turned in her chair and looked around her. No expense had been spared in this room. The rest of the furniture was as elegant as the desk on which her elbow rested, as elegant as that in the bedroom next door – the bedroom in which she slept alone – except on those nights when Paul would come to her and use her for the release of frustrations ...

That's how it had gone on. That's how it *would* go on – unless something was done to stop it. Oh, she was safe enough, she knew; secure enough in the continuing of her material comforts. As much as Paul would like to see the back of her he'd never divorce her – or even leave her. He knew which side his bread was buttered, all right. Hence the comfort in which he kept her. And that, surely, was partly the reason for his resentment of her – the fact that he knew that they were irrevocably tied – in sickness and in health, for as long as they both should live – by his dependence upon her.

And why, she sometimes asked herself, didn't *she* leave *him*? But what would she do if she did? Paul wouldn't support her,

and she'd been trained for no particular occupation. For the
past twenty-five years she'd known only this life – marriage to
a man whose gratitude for her understanding had in no time
worn threadbare.

But for all of that, she thought, she could have put up with
it – had it not been for his affairs. One after the other they had
punctuated the years of their married life. And for that she was
resentful – not just because of his infidelity and his rejection of
her, but because he gave to those *other* women what he never
gave, never *had* given, to her – not after the first few months
of their courtship, anyway. Those other women – they were
allowed to see only the *best* side of him – the cheerfulness, the
gentlemanliness, the solicitousness. She, through her near-total
acceptance of the real person, the person they never saw, was
doomed to live with it, warts and all.

She got up from the desk and stood there in the silent room.
It couldn't go on, though. And it *wouldn't*. *No*, after the 21st it
wouldn't be the same. Come the 21st there'd be some changes
made. Norma Russell would be the last, she'd make sure of
that. After Norma there wouldn't be any more affairs.

When she got downstairs she found Paul on the phone. He
started slightly when she suddenly appeared before him, and
said shakily into the receiver, voice thick with guile and not a
little guilt:

'Well, Frank, I think we ought to leave it until our meeting next week ... we can discuss it fully then ...' And Sylvia
smiled to herself as she went by him, realizing why Norma's
telephone had been engaged, and at the realization that *they*
thought she was so easily fooled. Not she. *Frank*, indeed. She
was a lot smarter than they dreamed. Certainly a damn sight
smarter than that vacuous, simpering Norma with her Gucci
shoes, Charlie perfume, and Dior sunglasses. Norma Russell,
with her sophisticated approach and smug, know-it-all manner
didn't know it all by any means.

Not yet. She would in time.

Paul left his office early that Friday, came into the house and flopped down onto the sofa saying he had a headache. From past experience Sylvia guessed well enough how he was feeling, but any sympathy she once might have felt for him had long ago vanished.

They ate an early dinner and as soon as it was over he went upstairs to the attic. Sylvia followed after a while, and quietly opened the door and looked in. He was sound asleep. Backing out again, she turned the key and softly pushed home the heavy bolts. For a second she listened, her ear to door, but no sound came to her through the thick, heavy oak. After a moment she turned and went back downstairs to get ready for the meeting.

The women all arrived within a few minutes of each other around eight o'clock, and with the coffee already made they got down fairly quickly to the business of the evening. That business was the forthcoming summer fête and the Women's Circle's part in it. The discussion went smoothly, and so it should have, for each of them – with the exception of Norma – had helped organize a dozen similar events in the past.

Finally, after much discussion and note-taking it was seemed to be all sorted out. Sylvia summed up the results of their discussion.

'All right, then,' she said, 'I think that's it. So you, Pam, and you, Janet, will get together and organize the refreshments and the baking competition. And you, Jill and Mary, will work on the jumble. And you all know your individual tasks.' Smiling at Norma, who returned the smile, she went on: 'And that leaves Norma and me to take care of the Fancy Goods and the white elephant stall. Is that okay?'

The next forty minutes were spent in drinking more coffee and generally talking over the finer points of their various tasks. There was much talk of 'willing hands' and 'helpers' and 'generous donors'; various names were bandied about, and there were the endlessly expressed hopes that on the day the weather would be kind to them. Sylvia began to get the feeling that the meeting would never end; never before had the conversation of her friends seemed quite so meaningless. But there, never before had she herself had quite such serious matters on her mind.

At last, though, it was nine-forty-five, and the meeting was over. As they all got up to go, chattering their goodnights, Sylvia caught at Norma's sleeve, saying, 'Oh, Norma – are you in a particular hurry to get away?'

Norma's eager-to-please expression didn't fool Sylvia for one moment. 'Not at all,' she said. 'Why? Is there something else I can do?' Now she was like the cat that had found the cream; not only had she been voted onto the committee but she had furthermore been chosen to work closely with Sylvia. From now on she'd have a cast-iron excuse for phoning or calling at the house at practically any time.

Sylvia smiled as sweetly and as naturally as she could under the circumstances. 'I was just wondering whether you'd care to stay behind for a little while so that we can go over – in more detail – a few of the things that you and I will be looking after . . .'

'Of course, I'd be glad to. Anytime at all, Sylvia. You just let me know.' She'd picked up her bag but now she set it down again at the side of the sofa.

'Fine,' said Sylvia. 'I'll just see the other girls out, then we can talk.'

When the other members had all gone out into the night Sylvia came back into the sitting room. As she sat down, Norma said to her: 'I suppose Paul hates being around when these – these hen parties are in session, doesn't he?'

Sylvia nodded. 'Oh, loathes it, my dear. Absolutely.'

'Does he – er – get back late . . . ?'

Oh, thought Sylvia, so obviously Norma had told Paul that she'd be coming to the meeting – and it was equally obvious that he'd told her he'd be out somewhere. Well, that was understandable. 'I'm sorry?' Sylvia said, ' – what did you ask me?'

'Paul – does he usually stay out late when you have your meetings here?'

'Oh, yes, usually he does. Not tonight, though.' That, Sylvia thought, should get her going. It did.

'Oh,' said Norma, ' – is there something different about tonight?' She sounded very casual.

Sylvia thought, Yes, you could say that. Then she said aloud, 'The poor love didn't go out this evening. He can't.'

'Oh – you mean he's still in the house?'

'Yes. He couldn't go out. He's just not up to it, poor man.' Sylvia eyed Norma's expression, seeing the look of concern that briefly clouded Norma's green eyes.

'Is he ill?' Norma asked.

'Well, not exactly ill,' Sylvia replied. 'He's just – well, just a little out of sorts.'

'Oh, dear, what a shame.' Norma sighed. 'Perhaps you should have phoned and cancelled the meeting. Won't he have been disturbed by all our chatter?'

Sylvia shook her head. 'Oh, no, don't worry about that. He won't have heard a thing. He's up in the attic.'

'In the attic?'

'Yes,' Sylvia's smile was indulgent. 'It's his little den, as he calls it. His little retreat. He's got a bed up there – well away from it all. It's much the best place for him at a time like this, when he's not himself. Anyway ...' She pulled her notepad towards her as if to signify that it was time for them to get on with their work, then, suddenly, with a look of dismay, she dropped her pencil and clapped her hand to her mouth. 'Oh, my God!' she said.

'What's the matter?' Norma stared at her in surprise. Her concern looked genuine.

'I think I'm losing my mind,' Sylvia said. 'It's going, I swear it's going. My memory. Oh, dear.'

'What is it? What's up?'

'I promised faithfully that I'd drop a few little things over to Mrs Harrison this afternoon. Poor old lady – she can't get out, what with her bad leg, and she's got her daughter coming for lunch tomorrow. I did all her shopping for her this afternoon – and it's still out there in the kitchen.' She glanced at the clock. 'Just ten o'clock. I'll bet she's been expecting me all day. How dreadful.' She sat as if pondering for a moment, then said: 'I know she doesn't go to bed till quite late. I think I'll just give her a ring and then take the stuff round to her. I shan't get a chance in the morning, I know . . .'

Even as she finished speaking she was opening her address book and looking up Mrs Harrison's number. She dialled it and Mrs Harrison answered almost immediately. She sounded so pleased to hear Sylvia's voice. No, she said, she wasn't been in bed; she was watching the telly darts championship – adding with a little giggle that she quite liked big men. Sylvia, refusing to take no for an answer, then said that she was going to get straight on her bike and bring the groceries round. After all, it was only a couple of miles and no one ever came to harm in Tallowford.

The call at an end, Sylvia had put on her coat and was picking up the shopping basket before she seemed to remember that Norma was still there.

'Oh, Norma, my dear,' she said. 'After asking you to stay behind I now go rushing off like this. I do apologise. Whatever must you think of me?'

'I think you're a very kind person,' Norma simpered. 'That's what I think.'

And Sylvia, in spite of her loathing for the creature, found herself thinking, How very true.

She hitched the handle of the basket more securely over her arm. 'My bike's just round the side,' she said. 'I'm sorry to go dashing off like this, but I've got to go.' She paused. 'You don't mind letting yourself out, do you?'

'Of course not. Not at all.'

'Oh, bless you. And I wonder, would you be an angel and make sure that I've turned off the gas under the kettle and see that there are no cigarettes burning anywhere . . . Oh, and if Paul *should* by any chance call out, just tell him I'll be back in an hour or so – or maybe a little longer. Would you mind?' She moved to the door. 'You can let yourself out, can't you?'

'Yes, of course.'

'Oh, thank you so much. Goodnight, then.'

'Goodnight.'

Hardly hearing Norma's reply, Sylvia opened the front door and went to her bicycle in the garage. After carefully securing the basket, she got on and pedalled away. The night was so bright as she sped down the lonely country road that she really had hardly any need of her bicycle lamp at all.

From the window Norma watched the red glow of Sylvia's tail light till it disappeared. Then she made a lightning check of the gas taps and the ashtrays. Everything was fine.

Yes, everything was fine. Everything was perfect.

In the hall she stood quite still and looked up the stairs. Then, after a second or two, she began to climb. She didn't put on the lights; she didn't want to take the chance of being seen through a window by some passing villager.

So Paul was in the attic, Sylvia had said. Norma continued up the stairs, past the first floor and on up the next flight – narrower now and turning. At the top she came to a stop, hesitated a moment and then softly called out:

'Paul – ?'

Silence. And then she heard a sound. It came from the door a few yards to her right. Moving towards it she saw to her horror that there were two heavy bolts pulled across. Sylvia had locked him in! How could she?!

There was a key in the lock too. She turned it, releasing the lock. How could Sylvia have done such a thing? Some people! She turned her attention then to the bolts, and with an effort slid them back. It was done. Then, turning the handle, she opened the door a fraction.

From the faint glow filtering in from the landing she could see that there was no light in the room, and none coming in from the small, uncurtained window. 'Paul – ?' She whispered his name. She could hear him breathing, heavily, as if he was in a very deep sleep, or . . .

Opening the door wider, she stepped into the room and closed the heavy door behind her.

Now in deep darkness she whispered his name again. 'Paul?' There came no answer. 'Paul,' she said, a little louder now,

' – are you there? It's me – Norma. I've come to pay you a little surprise visit.'

The room was swallowed up in shadow. She could see nothing. She could hear nothing but the breathing.

'Paul – darling, is that you?' she said. She listened. The breathing – somehow it didn't sound like him. It didn't sound quite – right. 'Paul,' she said, 'Sylvia told me you weren't quite yourself tonight – so I've come to cheer you up a bit – if I can!' She laughed lightly, nervously into the dark. The sound of his breathing was growing louder, coming a little nearer. 'Paul,' she said, ' – oh, come on, darling. Don't fool about . . .'

Suddenly the moon, the full moon, was no longer obscured by the clouds. Suddenly the room was bathed in light. And she saw the bars at the window – thick, metal bars. She noticed, too, the complete absence of furniture. There was only straw on the floor. She became aware, too, of the strong, rank animal smell that permeated the air around her.

And then she saw Paul coming towards her.

In the brilliant silver light of the full moon he lunged towards her and she felt him reach out with one huge clawed paw, felt herself wrenched forward, towards the great snout, the great fangs that opened wide, dripping in anticipation. She heard the guttural sound from deep in his throat.

The sound that came from her own throat, a small, pleading cry of terror, was cut off before she'd hardly had a chance to utter it.

At Mrs Harrison's, Sylvia looked at her watch. It was almost eleven. She put down her cup, got to her feet and took up her empty basket. It had been so nice, she said, but she really must get back. There'd be a lot of cleaning up to do. Besides, Paul might start to wonder where she was. He didn't usually worry, but he could get very funny when he was out of sorts. There was just no telling.

'It's probably the full moon,' Mrs Harrison said with a little chuckle. 'Did you notice there's a full moon tonight? I swear it makes a difference to some people. You might not believe this, but I'm sure it used to affect my Ralph. He used to go right off his food. Wouldn't eat a thing. No appetite at all.'

Sylvia looked out of the window at the moon's big, white, smiling face. 'Oh,' she said with a little smile, 'I can't say it takes Paul like that. Just the opposite in fact. When he's not his usual self, like today – a bit out of sorts – he gets absolutely ravenous. Such an appetite you wouldn't believe! Like he hasn't eaten in a month.'

Christopher Priest

THE HEAD AND THE HAND

One of the most acclaimed science fiction authors of our time, CHRISTOPHER PRIEST *was born in Cheshire, England in 1943 and first gained notice with his stories in magazines such as* Impulse *and* New Worlds *in the late 1960s. He has gone on to receive widespread praise for his novels, including the modern classics* Inverted World (1974), The Affirmation (1981) *and* The Glamour (1984). *Priest is probably best known for* The Prestige (1995), *the only novel to win the mainstream James Tait Black Memorial Prize for best novel of the year and the World Fantasy Award; it was later adapted for a major Hollywood film.* The Separation (2002), *which tells the intertwining stories of two brothers in World War II across alternate timelines, won both the Arthur C. Clarke and BSFA Awards for best novel. 'The Head and the Hand', which the* Times Literary Supplement *praised as 'a fabulously disgusting story' worthy of Roald Dahl, was first published in* New Worlds Quarterly *in 1972 and first collected in* Real-Time World (1974). *Four of Priest's best novels are available from Valancourt in paperback, and* The Prestige *is available as an electronic book.*

O N THAT MORNING AT RACINE HOUSE we were taking exer-cise in the grounds. There had been a frost overnight, and the grass lay white and brittle. The sky was unclouded, and the sun threw long blue shadows. Our breath cast clouds of vapour behind us. There was no sound, no wind, no movement. The park was ours, and we were alone.

Our walks in the mornings had a clearly defined route, and as we came to the eastern end of the path at the bottom of the long sloping lawn I prepared for the turn, pressing down hard on the controlling handles at the back of the carriage. I am a large man, and well-muscled, but the combined weight of the invalid carriage and the master was almost beyond the limit of my strength.

That day the master was in a difficult mood. Though before we set out he had clearly stated that I was to wheel him as far as the disused summer lodge, as I tried to lift him round he waved his head from side to side.

'No, Lasken!' he said irritably. 'To the lake today. I want to see the swans.'

I said to him: 'Of course, sir.'

I swung the carriage back into the direction in which we had been travelling, and continued with our walk. I waited for him to say something to me, for it was unusual that he would give me untempered instructions without qualifying them a few moments later with some more intimate remark. Our relationship was a formal one, but memories of what had once existed between us still affected our behaviour and attitudes. Though we were of a similar age and social background, Todd's career had affected us considerably. Never again could there be any kind of equality between us.

I waited, and in the end he turned his head and said: 'The park is beautiful today, Edward. This afternoon we must ride through it with Elizabeth, before the weather gets warmer. The trees are so stark, so black.'

'Yes sir,' I said, glancing at the woods to our right. When he bought the house, the first action he had taken was to have all the evergreen trees felled, and the remainder sprayed so that their greenery would be inhibited. With the passage of years they had regained their growth, and now the master would spend the summer months inside the house, the windows shuttered and the curtains drawn. Only with the coming of autumn would he return to the open air, obsessively watching the orange and brown leaves dropping to the ground and swirling across the lawns.

The lake appeared before us as we rounded the edge of the wood. The grounds dropped down to it in a shallow and undulating incline from the house, which was above us and to our left.

A hundred yards from the water's edge I turned my head and looked towards the house, and saw the tall figure of Elizabeth moving down towards us, her long maroon dress sweeping across the grass.

Knowing he would not see her, I said nothing to Todd.

We stopped at the edge of the lake. In the night a crust of ice had formed on its surface.

'The swans, Edward. Where are they?'

He moved his head to the right, and placed his lips on one of the switches there. At once, the batteries built into the base of the carriage turned the motors of the servos, and the backrest slid upwards, bringing him into a position that was almost upright.

He moved his head from side to side, a frown creasing his eyebrow-less face.

'Go and find their nests, Lasken. I must see them today.'

'It's the ice, sir,' I said. 'It has probably driven them from the water.'

I heard the rustle of silk on frosted grass, and turned. Elizabeth stood a few yards behind us, holding an envelope in her hands.

She held it up, and looked at me with her eyebrows raised. I nodded silently: that is the one. She smiled at me quickly. The master would not yet know that she was there. The outer membrane of his ears had been removed, rendering his hearing unfocused and undirectional.

She swept past me in the peremptory manner she knew he approved of, and stood before him. He appeared unsurprised to see her.

'There's a letter, Todd,' she said.

'Later,' he said without looking at it. 'Lasken can deal with it. I have no time now.'

'It's from Gaston I think. It looks like his stationery.'

'Read it to me.'

He swung his head backwards sharply. It was his instruction to me: move out of earshot. Obediently I stepped away to a place where I knew he could not see me or hear me.

Elizabeth bent down and kissed him on his lips.

'Todd, whatever it is, please don't do it.'

'Read it to me,' he said again.

She slitted the envelope with her thumb and pulled out a sheet of thin white paper, folded in three. I knew what the letter contained; Gaston had read it to me over the telephone the day before. He and I had arranged the details, and we knew that no higher price could be obtained, even for Todd. There had been difficulties with the television concessions, and for a while it had looked as if the French government was going to intervene.

Gaston's letter was a short one. It said that Todd's popularity had never been higher, and that the Théâtre Alhambra and its consortium had offered eight million francs for another appearance. I listened to Elizabeth's voice as she read, marvelling at the emotionless monotone of her articulation. She had warned me earlier that she did not think she was going to be able to read the letter to him.

When she'd finished, Todd asked her to read it again. She did this, then placed the open letter in front of him, brushed her lips against his face and walked away from him. As she passed me she laid a hand on my arm for a moment, then continued on up towards the house. I watched her for a few seconds, seeing her slim beauty accentuated by the sunlight that fell sideways across her face, and strands of her hair blown behind by the wind.

The master waved his head from side to side.

'Lasken! Lasken!'

I went back to him.

'Do you see this?'

I picked it up and glanced at it.

'I shall write to him of course,' I said. 'It is out of the question.'

'No, no, I must consider. We must always consider. I have so much at stake.'

I kept my expression steady.

'But it is impossible. You can give no more performances!'

'There is a way, Edward,' he said, in as gentle a voice as I had ever heard him use. 'I must find that way.'

I caught sight of a water-fowl a few yards from us, in the reeds at the edge of the lake. It waddled out on to the ice, confused by the frozen surface. I took one of the long poles from the side of the carriage and broke a section of the ice. The bird slithered across the ice and flew away, terrified by the noise.

I walked back to Todd.

'There. If there is some open water, the swans will return.'

The expression on his face was agitated.

'The Théâtre Alhambra,' he said. 'What shall we do?'

'I will speak to your solicitor. It is an outrage that the theatre should approach you. They know that you cannot go back.'

'But eight million francs.'

'The money does not matter. You said that yourself once.'

'No, it is not the money. Nor the public. It is everything.'

We waited by the lake for the swans, as the sun rose higher in the sky. I was exhilarated by the pale colours of the park, by the quiet and the calm. It was an aesthetic, sterile reaction, for the house and its grounds had oppressed me from the start. Only the transient beauty of the morning – a frozen, fragile countenance – stirred something in me.

The master had lapsed into silence, and had returned the backrest to the horizontal position he found most relaxing. Though his eyes were closed I knew he would not be asleep.

I walked away from him, out of his earshot, and strolled around the perimeter of the lake, always keeping a watch for movement on the carriage. I wondered if he would be able to resist the offer from the Théâtre Alhambra, fearing that if he did there would he no greater attraction.

The time was right ... he had not been seen in public for nearly four and a half years. The mood of the public was right ... for the media had recently returned their interest to him, criticising his many imitators and demanding his return. None of this was lost on the master. There was only one Todd Alborne, and only he could have gone so far. No one could compete with him. Everything was right, and only the participation of the master was needed to complete it.

The electric klaxon I had fitted to the carriage sounded.

Looking back at him across the ice I saw that he had moved his face to the switch. I turned back, and went to him.

'I want to see Elizabeth,' he said.

'You know what she will say.'

'Yes. But I must speak to her.'

I turned the carriage round, and began the long and difficult return up the slope to the house.

As we left the side of the lake I saw white birds flying low in the distance, headed away from the house. I hoped that Todd had not seen them.

He looked from side to side as we moved past the wood. I saw on the branches the new buds that would burst in the next few weeks; I think he saw only the bare black twigs, the stark geometry of the naked trees.

In the house I took him to his study, and lifted his body from the carriage he used for outside expeditions to the motorised one in which he moved about the house. He spent the rest of the day with Elizabeth, and I saw her only when she came down to collect for him the meals I prepared. In those moments we had time only to exchange glances, to intertwine fingers, to kiss lightly. She would say nothing of what he was thinking.

He retired early and Elizabeth with him, going to the room next to his, sleeping alone as she had done for five years.

When she was sure he was asleep, she left her bed and came to mine. We made love at once. Afterwards we lay together in the dark, our hands clasped possessively; only then would she tell me what she thought his decision would be.

'He's going to do it,' she said. 'I haven't seen him as excited as this for years.'

I have known Todd Alborne since we were both eighteen. Our families had known one another, and chance brought us together one year during a European holiday. Though we did not become close friends immediately, I found his company fascinating and on our return to England we stayed in touch with each other.

The fascination he held over me was not one I admired, but neither could I resist it: he possessed a fanatical and passionate dedication to what he was doing, and once started he would be deterred by nothing. He conducted several disastrous love-affairs, and twice lost most of his money in unsuccessful business ventures. But he had a general aimlessness that disturbed me; I felt that once pressed into a direction he could control, he would be able to exploit his unusual talents.

It was his sudden and unexpected fame that separated us. No one had anticipated it, least of all Todd. Yet when he recognised its potential, he embraced it readily.

I was not with him when it began, though I saw him soon after. He told me what happened, and though it differs from the popular anecdote I believe it.

He was drinking with some friends when an accident with a knife occurred. One of his companions had been cut badly, and had fainted. During the commotion that followed, a stranger made a wager with Todd that he would not voluntarily inflict a wound on his own body.

Todd slashed the skin of his forearm, and collected his money. The stranger offered to double the stake if Todd would amputate a finger.

Placing his left hand on the table in front of him, Todd removed his index finger. A few minutes later, with no further encouragement from the stranger – who by this time had left – Todd cut off another finger. The following day a television company had picked up the story, and Todd was invited to the studio to relate what had happened. During the live transmission, and against the wishes of the interviewer, Todd repeated the operation.

It was the reaction to this first broadcast – a wave of prurient shock from the public, and an hysterical condemnation in the media – that revealed to Todd the potential in such a display of self-mutilation.

Finding a promoter, he commenced a tour of Europe, performing his act to paying audiences only.

It was at this point – seeing his arrangements for publicity, and learning of the sums of money he was confident of earning – that I made the effort of dissociating myself from him. Purposely, I isolated myself from news of his exploits and would take no interest in the various public stunts he performed. It was the element of ritual in what he did that sickened me, and his native flair for showmanship only made him the more offensive to me.

It was a year after this alienation that we met again. It was he who sought me out, and though I resisted him at first I was unable to maintain the distance I desired.

I learned that in the intervening period he had married.

At first I was repelled by Elizabeth, for I thought that she loved Todd for his obsession, in the way the blood-hungry public loved him. But as I grew to know her better I realised that she saw herself in some messianic role. It was then that I understood her to be as vulnerable as Todd – though in an entirely different way – and I found myself agreeing to work for Todd and to do for him whatever he requested. At first I refused to assist him with the mutilations, but later did as he asked. My change of mind in this instance was initiated by Elizabeth.

The condition of his body when I started to work for him was so bad that he was almost entirely crippled. Though at first he had had several organs grafted back on to his body after mutilation, such operations could be carried out only a limited number of times, and while healing, prevented further performances.

His left arm below the elbow had been removed; his left leg was almost intact beyond the two removed toes. His right leg was intact. One of his ears had been removed, and he had been scalped. All fingers but the thumb and index on his right hand had been removed.

As a result of these injuries he was incapable of administering the amputations himself, and in addition to the various assistants he employed for his act he required me to operate the mutilating apparatus during the actual performances.

He attested a disclaimer form for the injuries to which I was to be an accessory, and his career continued.

And it went on, between spells for recovery, for another

two years. In spite of the apparent contempt he had for his body, Todd bought the most expensive medical supervision he could find, and the recovery from each amputation was strictly observed before another performance.

But the human body is finite, and his eventual retirement was inevitable.

At his final performance, his genital organs were removed amid the greatest storm of publicity and outrage he had known. Afterwards, he made no further public appearance, and spent a long spell of convalescence in a private nursing-home. Elizabeth and I stayed with him, and when he bought Racine House fifty miles from Paris, we went there with him.

And from that day we had played out the masque; each pretending to the others that his career had reached its climax, each knowing that inside the limbless, earless, hairless, castrated man there was a flame burning still for its final extinguishment.

And outside the gates of Racine House, Todd's private world waited for him. And he knew they waited, and Elizabeth and I knew they waited.

Meanwhile our life went on, and he was the master.

There was an interval of three weeks between my confirming to Gaston that Todd was to make another appearance and the actual night itself. There was much to be done.

While we left the publicity arrangements to Gaston, Todd and I began the job of designing and building the equipment for the show. This was a process that in the past had been one of extreme distaste to me. It wrought an unpleasant tension between Elizabeth and myself, for she would not allow me to tell her about the equipment.

This time, though, there was no such strain between us. Halfway through the work she asked me about the apparatus I was building, and that night, after Todd had fallen asleep, I took her down to the workshop. For ten minutes she walked from one instrument to another, testing the smoothness of the mechanism and the sharpness of the blades.

Finally, she looked at me without expression, then nodded.

I contacted Todd's former assistants, and confirmed with them that they would be present at the performance. Once or twice I telephoned Gaston, and learned of the wave of speculation that was anticipating Todd's return.

As for the master himself, he was taken with a burst of energy and excitement that stretched to its limits the prosthetic machinery which surrounded him. He seemed unable to sleep, and several nights would call for Elizabeth. For this period she did not come to my room, though I often visited her for an hour or two. One night Todd called her while I was there, and I lay in bed listening to him talk to her, his voice unnaturally high-pitched, though never uncontrolled or over-excited.

When the day of the performance arrived I asked him if he wanted to drive to the Alhambra in our specially built car, or to use the carriage and horses that I knew he preferred for public appearances. He chose the latter.

We departed early, knowing that in addition to the distance we had to cover there would be several delays caused by admirers.

We placed Todd at the front of the carriage, next to the driver, sitting him up in the seat I had built for him. Elizabeth and I sat behind, her hand resting lightly on my leg. Every so often, Todd would half turn his head and speak to us. On these occasions, either she or I would lean forward to acknowledge him and reply.

Once we were on the main road into Paris we encountered many large groups of admirers. Some cheered or called; some stood in silence. Todd acknowledged them all, but when one woman tried to scramble up into the carriage he became agitated and nervous and screamed at me to get her away from him.

The only place where he came into close contact with any of his admirers was during our stop to change horses. Then he spoke volubly and amiably, though afterwards he was noticeably tired.

Our arrival at the Théâtre Alhambra had been planned in

great detail, and the police had cordoned off the crowd. There was a broad channel left free through which Todd could be wheeled. As the carriage halted the crown began to cheer, and the horses became nervous.

I wheeled Todd in through the stage door, responding in spite of myself to the hysteria of the crowds. Elizabeth was close behind us. Todd took the reception well and professionally, smiling round from side to side, unable to acknowledge the acclaim in any other way. He appeared not to notice the small but determined and vociferous section of the crowd chanting the slogans that they bore on placards.

Once inside his dressing-room we were able to relax for a while. The show was not scheduled to start for another two and a half hours. After a short nap, Todd was bathed by Elizabeth, and then dressed in his stage costume.

Twenty minutes before he was due to give his performance, one of the female staff of the theatre came into the dressing-room and presented him with a bouquet of flowers. Elizabeth took them from the woman and laid them uncertainly before him, knowing well his dislike of flowers.

'Thank you,' he said to the woman. 'Flowers. What beautiful colours.'

Gaston came in fifteen minutes later, accompanied by the manager of the Alhambra. Both men shook hands with me, Gaston kissed Elizabeth on her cheek, and the manager tried to strike up a conversation with Todd. Todd did not reply, and a little later I noticed that the manager was weeping silently. Todd stared at us all.

It had been decided by Todd that there was to be no special ceremony surrounding this performance. There were to be no speeches, no public remarks from Todd. No interviews to be granted. The act on the stage would follow carefully the instructions he had dictated to me, and the rehearsals that the other assistants had been following for the last week.

He turned to Elizabeth, and put his face up towards her. She kissed him tenderly, and I turned away.

After nearly a minute he said: 'All right, Lasken. I'm ready.'

I took the handle of his carriage and wheeled him out of the dressing-room and down the corridor towards the wings of the stage.

We heard a man's voice talking in French of Todd, and a great roar of applause from the audience. The muscles of my stomach contracted. The expression on Todd's face did not change.

Two assistants came forward, and lifted Todd into his harness. This was connected by two thin wires to a pulley in the flies, and when operated by one of the assistants in the wings would move Todd around the stage. When he was secure, his four false limbs were strapped in place.

He nodded to me, and I prepared myself. For a second, I saw the expression in Elizabeth's eyes. Todd was not looking in our direction, but I made no response to her.

I stepped on to the stage. A woman screamed, then the whole audience rose to its feet. My heart raced.

The equipment was already on the stage, covered with heavy velvet curtains. I walked to the centre of the stage, and bowed to the audience. Then I walked from one piece of apparatus to another, removing the curtains.

As each piece was revealed the audience roared its approval. The voice of the manager crackled over the P.A. system, imploring them to return to their seats. As I had done at previous performances, I stood still until the audience was seated once more. Each movement was provocative.

I finished revealing the equipment. To my eye it was ugly and utilitarian, but the audience relished the appearance of the razor-sharp blades.

I walked to the footlights.

'Mesdames. Messieurs.' Silence fell abruptly. 'Le maître.'

I moved downstage, holding out my hand in the direction of Todd. I tried purposely to disregard the audience. I could see Todd in the wings, hanging in his harness beside Elizabeth. He was not talking to her or looking at her. His head was bent forward, and he was concentrating on the sound from the audience.

They were still in silence . . . the anticipatory motionlessness of the voyeur.

Seconds passed, and still Todd waited. Somewhere in the audience a voice spoke quietly. Abruptly, the audience roared.

It was Todd's moment. He nodded to the assistant, who wound the pulley ropes and propelled Todd out on to the stage.

The movement was eerie and unnatural. He floated on the wire so that his false legs just scraped the canvas of the stage. His false arms hung limply at his side. Only his head was alert, greeting and acknowledging the audience.

I had expected them to applaud . . . but at his appearance they subsided again into silence. I had forgotten about that in the intervening years. It was the silences that had always appalled me.

The pulley-assistant propelled Todd to a couch standing to the right of the stage. I helped him lie down on it. Another assistant – who was a qualified medical doctor – came on to the stage, and carried out a brief examination.

He wrote something on a piece of paper, and handed it to me. Then he went to the front of the stage and made his statement to the audience.

I have examined the master. He is fit. He is sane. He is in full possession of his senses, and knows what he is about to undertake. I have signed a statement to this effect.

The pulley-assistant raised Todd once more, and propelled him around the stage, from one piece of equipment to another. When he had inspected them all, he nodded his agreement.

At the front of the stage, in the centre, I unstrapped his false legs. As they fell away from his body, one or two men in the audience gasped.

Todd's arms were removed.

I then pulled forward one of the pieces of equipment: a long, white-covered table with a large mirror above it.

I swung Todd's torso on to the table, then removed the harness and signalled for it to be lifted away. I positioned Todd so that he was lying with his head towards the audience, and with his whole body visible to them in the mirror. I was working amidst silence. I did not look towards the audience. I did not look towards the wings. I was perspiring. Todd said nothing to me.

When Todd was in the position he required, he nodded to me and I turned towards the audience, bowing and indicating that the performance was about to commence. There was a ripple of applause, soon finished.

I stood back, and watched Todd without reaction. He was feeling the audience again. In a performance consisting of one solitary action, and a mute one at that, for best effect his timing had to be accurate. There was only one piece of apparatus on the stage which was to be used this evening; the others were there for the effect of their presence.

Todd and I both knew which one it was to be: I would wheel it over at the appropriate time.

The audience was silent again, but restless. I felt that it was poised critically; one movement would explode it into reaction. Todd nodded to me.

I walked again from one piece of apparatus to the next. On each one I put my hand to the blade, as if feeling its sharpness. By the time I had been to each one, the audience was ready. I could feel it, and I knew Todd could.

I went back to the apparatus Todd had selected: a guillotine made from tubular aluminium and with a blade of finest stainless steel. I trundled it over to his table, and connected it with the brackets for that purpose. I tested its solidity, and made a visual check that the release mechanism would work properly.

Todd was positioned now so that his head overhung the edge of the table, and was directly underneath the blade. The guillotine was so constructed that it did not obscure the view of his body in the mirror.

I removed his costume.

He was naked. The audience gasped when they saw his scars, but returned to silence.

I took the wire loop of the release mechanism and, as Todd had instructed me, tied it tightly around the thick meat of his tongue. To take up the slack of the wire, I adjusted it at the side of the apparatus.

I leaned over him, and asked if he was ready. He nodded.

'Edward,' he said indistinctly. 'Come closer.'

I leaned forward so that my face was near his. To do this I had to pass my own neck under the guillotine blade. The audience approved of this action.

'What is it?' I said.

'I know, Edward. About you and Elizabeth.'

I looked into the wings, where she was still standing.

I said: 'And you still want to . . . ?'

He nodded again, this time more violently. The wire release on his tongue tightened and the mechanism clicked open. He nearly caught me in the apparatus. I jumped away as the blade plummeted down. I turned from him, looking desperately into the wings at Elizabeth as the first screams from the audience filled the theatre.

Elizabeth stepped out on to the stage. She was looking at Todd. I went to her.

Todd's torso lay on the table. His heart was still beating, for blood spurted rhythmically in thick gouts from his severed neck. His hairless head swung from the apparatus. Where the wire gripped his tongue, it had wrenched it nearly from his throat. His eyes were still open.

We turned and faced the audience. The change that had come over them was total; in under five seconds they had panicked. A few people had fainted; the rest were standing. The noise of their shouting was unbelievable. They moved towards the doors. None looked at the stage. One man swung his fist at another; was knocked down from behind. A woman was having hysterics, tearing at her clothes. No one paid her any attention. I heard a shot, and ducked instinctively, pulling Elizabeth down with me. Women screamed; men shouted. I heard the P.A. click on, but no voice came through. Abruptly, the doors of the auditorium swung open simultaneously on all sides, and armed riot-police burst in. It had been planned carefully. As the police attacked them, the crowd fought back. I heard another shot, then several more in rapid succession.

I took Elizabeth by the hand, and led her from the stage.

In the dressing-room we watched through a window as the police attacked the crowds in the street. Many people were shot. Tear-gas was released, a helicopter hovered overhead.

We stood together in silence, Elizabeth crying. We were obliged to stay within the safety of the theatre building for another twelve hours. The next day we returned to Racine House, and the first leaves were spreading.

Florence Marryat

THE GHOST OF CHARLOTTE CRAY

FLORENCE MARRYAT (1833-1899) *was the daughter of Captain Frederick Marryat, author of* The Phantom Ship (1839), *and went on to become a popular and prolific author in her own right. She published sixty-eight novels during her career, many of them falling into the genre of the 'Sensation' novel popular in late-Victorian England and often dealing with then-shocking themes such as marital cruelty, adultery, and alcoholism. Later in life, she became known for her involvement in the Spiritualist movement, and her highly successful nonfiction volume* There Is No Death (1891) *compiled her experiences with séances and mediums, including numerous anecdotes tending to prove the existence of a life after death. Over the past decade or so, critical and scholarly interest in Marryat has been high, particularly in her strange novel* The Blood of the Vampire (1897), *which Valancourt reissued in 2009. Originally published the same year as* Dracula, *Marryat's novel was a very different sort of vampire tale, focusing on a beautiful young woman – the daughter of a mad scientist and a voodoo priestess – who seems to possess the power to psychically drain victims of their life essence. 'The Ghost of Charlotte Cray', taken from* A Moment of Madness, and Other Stories (1883), *is a classic, creepy Victorian ghost story written by a woman who believed wholeheartedly in the paranormal.*

M R SIGISMUND BRAGGETT was sitting in the little room he called his study, wrapped in a profound – not to say a mournful – reverie. Now, there was nothing in the present life nor surroundings of Mr Braggett to account for such a demon-stration. He was a publisher and bookseller; a man well to do, with a thriving business in the city, and the prettiest of all pretty villas at Streatham. And he was only just turned forty; had not a grey hair in his head nor a false tooth in his mouth; and had been married but three short months to one of the fairest and most affectionate specimens of English womanhood that ever transformed a bachelor's quarters into Paradise.

What more could Mr Sigismund Braggett possibly want? Nothing! His trouble lay in the fact that he had got rather more than he wanted. Most of us have our little peccadilloes in this world – awkward reminiscences that we would like to bury five fathoms deep, and never hear mentioned again, but that have an uncomfortable habit of cropping up at the most inconvenient moments; and no mortal is more likely to be troubled with them than a middle-aged bachelor who has taken to matrimony.

Mr Sigismund Braggett had no idea what he was going in for when he led the blushing Emily Primrose up to the altar, and swore to be hers, and hers only, until death should them part. He had no conception a woman's curiosity could be so keen, her tongue so long, and her inventive faculties so correct. He had spent whole days before the fatal moment of marriage in burning letters, erasing initials, destroying locks of hair, and making offerings of affection look as if he had purchased them with his own money. But it had been of little avail. Mrs Braggett had swooped down upon him like a beautiful bird of prey, and wheedled, coaxed, or kissed him out of half his secrets before he knew what he was about. But he had never told her about Charlotte Cray. And now he almost wished that he had done so, for Charlotte Cray was the cause of his present dejected mood.

Now, there are ladies *and* ladies in this world. Some are very shy, and will only permit themselves to be wooed by stealth. Others, again, are the pursuers rather than the pursued, and chase the wounded or the flying even to the very doors of their stronghold, or lie in wait for them like an octopus, stretching out their tentacles on every side in search of victims.

And to the latter class Miss Charlotte Cray decidedly belonged. Not a person worth mourning over, you will naturally say. But, then, Mr Sigismund Braggett had not behaved well to her. She was one of the 'peccadilloes.' She was an authoress – not an author, mind you, which term smacks more of the profession than the sex – but an 'authoress,' with lots of the 'ladylike' about the plots of her stories and metre of her rhymes. They had come together in the sweet connection of publisher and writer – had met first in a dingy, dusty little office at the back of his house of business, and laid the foundation of their friendship with the average amount of chaffering and prevarication that usually attend such proceedings.

Mr Braggett ran a risk in publishing Miss Cray's tales or verses, but he found her useful in so many other ways that he used occasionally to hold forth a sop to Cerberus in the shape of publicity for the sake of keeping her in his employ. For Miss Charlotte Cray – who was as old as himself, and had arrived at the period of life when women are said to pray 'Any, good Lord, any!' – was really a clever woman, and could turn her hand to most things required of her, or upon which she had set her mind; and she had most decidedly set her mind upon marrying Mr Braggett, and he – to serve his own purposes – had permitted her to cherish the idea, and this was the Nemesis that was weighing him down in the study at the present moment. He had complimented Miss Cray, and given her presents, and taken her out a-pleasuring, all because she was useful to him, and did odd jobs that no one else would undertake, and for less than anyone else would have accepted; and he had known the while that she was in love with him, and that she believed he was in love with her.

He had not thought much of it at the time. He had not then made up his mind to marry Emily Primrose, and considered that what pleased Miss Cray, and harmed no one else, was fair play for all sides. But he had come to see things differently now. He had been married three months, and the first two weeks had been very bitter ones to him. Miss Cray had written him torrents of reproaches during that unhappy period, besides calling day after day at his office to deliver them in person. This and her threats had frightened him out of his life. He had lived in hourly terror lest the clerks should overhear what passed at their interviews, or that his wife should be made acquainted with them.

He had implored Miss Cray, both by word of mouth and

letter, to cease her persecution of him; but all the reply he received was that he was a base and perjured man, and that she should continue to call at his office, and write to him through the penny post, until he had introduced her to his wife. For therein lay the height and depth of his offending. He had been afraid to bring Emily and Miss Cray together, and the latter resented the omission as an insult. It was bad enough to find that Sigismund Braggett, whose hair she wore next her heart, and whose photograph stood as in a shrine upon her bedroom mantelpiece, had married another woman, without giving her even the chance of a refusal, but it was worse still to come to the conclusion that he did not intend her to have a glimpse into the garden of Eden he had created for himself.

Miss Cray was a lady of vivid imagination and strong aspirations. All was not lost in her ideas, although Mr Braggett *had* proved false to the hopes he had raised. Wives did not live for ever; and the chances and changes of this life were so numerous, that stranger things had happened than that Mr Braggett might think fit to make better use of the second opportunity afforded him than he had done of the first. But if she were not to continue even his friend, it was too hard. But the perjured publisher had continued resolute, notwithstanding all Miss Cray's persecution, and now he had neither seen nor heard from her for a month; and, manlike, he was beginning to wonder what had become of her, and whether she had found anybody to console her for his untruth. Mr Braggett did not wish to comfort Miss Cray himself; but he did not quite like the notion of her being comforted.

After all – so he soliloquised – he had been very cruel to her; for the poor thing was devoted to him. How her eyes used to sparkle and her cheek to flush when she entered his office, and how eagerly she would undertake any work for him, however disagreeable to perform! He knew well that she had expected to be Mrs Braggett, and it must have been a terrible disappointment to her when he married Emily Primrose.

Why had he not asked her out to Violet Villa since? What harm could she do as a visitor there? particularly if he cautioned

her first as to the peculiarity of Mrs Braggett's disposition, and
the quickness with which her jealousy was excited. It was close
upon Christmas-time, the period when all old friends meet
together and patch up, if they cannot entirely forget, everything that has annoyed them in the past. Mr Braggett pictured
to himself the poor old maid sitting solitary in her small rooms
at Hammersmith, no longer able to live in the expectation of
seeing his manly form at the wicket-gate, about to enter and
cheer her solitude. The thought smote him as a two-edged
sword, and he sat down at once and penned Miss Charlotte a
note, in which he inquired after her health, and hoped that they
should soon see her at Violet Villa.

He felt much better after this note was written and des-
patched. He came out of the little study and entered the cheerful drawing-room, and sat with his pretty wife by the light of
the fire, telling her of the lonely lady to whom he had just proposed to introduce her.

'An old friend of mine, Emily. A clever, agreeable woman,
though rather eccentric. You will be polite to her, I know, for
my sake.'

'An *old* woman, is she?' said Mrs Braggett, elevating her
eyebrows. 'And what do you call "old," Siggy, I should like to
know?'

'Twice as old as yourself, my dear – five-and-forty at the very
least, and not personable-looking, even for that age. Yet I think
you will find her a pleasant companion, and I am sure she will
be enchanted with you.'

'I don't know that: clever women don't like me, as a rule,
though I don't know why.'

'They are jealous of your beauty, my darling; but Miss Cray
is above such meanness, and will value you for your own sake.'

'She'd better not let me catch her valuing me for *yours*,' re-
sponded Mrs Braggett, with a flash of the eye that made her husband ready to regret the dangerous experiment he was about to
make of bringing together two women who had each, in her
own way, a claim upon him, and each the will to maintain it.

So he dropped the subject of Miss Charlotte Cray, and took

to admiring his wife's complexion instead, so that the evening passed harmoniously, and both parties were satisfied.

For two days Mr Braggett received no answer from Miss Cray, which rather surprised him. He had quite expected that on the reception of his invitation she would rush down to his office and into his arms, behind the shelter of the ground-glass door that enclosed his chair of authority. For Miss Charlotte had been used on occasions to indulge in rapturous demonstrations of the sort, and the remembrance of Mrs Braggett located in Violet Villa would have been no obstacle whatever to her. She believed she had a prior claim to Mr Braggett. However, nothing of the kind happened, and the perjured publisher was becoming strongly imbued with the idea that he must go out to Hammersmith and see if he could not make his peace with her in person, particularly as he had several odd jobs for Christmastide, which no one could undertake so well as herself, when a letter with a black-edged border was put into his hand. He opened it mechanically, not knowing the writing; but its contents shocked him beyond measure.

'HONOURED SIR, – I am sorry to tell you that Miss Cray died at my house a week ago, and was buried yesterday. She spoke of you several times during her last illness, and if you would like to hear any further particulars, and will call on me at the old address, I shall be most happy to furnish you with them. – Yours respectfully,

'MARY THOMPSON.'

When Mr Braggett read this news, you might have knocked him over with a feather. It is not always true that a living dog is better than a dead lion. Some people gain considerably in the estimation of their friends by leaving this world, and Miss Charlotte Cray was one of them. Her persecution had ceased for ever, and her amiable weaknesses were alone held in remembrance. Mr Braggett felt a positive relief in the knowledge that his dead friend and his wife would never now be brought in contact with each other; but at the same time he blamed himself more than was needful, perhaps, for not having seen nor communicated with Miss Cray for so long before her death. He came down to breakfast with a portentously grave face that morning, and imparted the sad intelligence to Mrs Braggett with the air of an undertaker. Emily wondered, pitied, and sympathised, but the dead lady was no more to her than any other stranger; and she was surprised her husband looked so solemn over it all. Mr Braggett, however, could not dismiss the subject easily from his mind. It haunted him during the business hours of the morning, and as soon as he could conveniently leave his office, he posted away to Hammersmith. The little house in which Miss Cray used to live looked just the same, both inside and outside: how strange it seemed that *she* should have flown away from it for ever! And here was her landlady, Mrs Thompson, bobbing and curtseying to him in the same old black net cap with artificial flowers in it, and the same stuff gown she had worn since he first saw her, with her apron in her hand, it is true, ready to go to her eyes as soon as a reasonable opportunity occurred, but otherwise the same Mrs Thompson as before. And yet she would never wait upon *her* again:

'It was all so sudden, sir,' she said, in answer to Mr Braggett's inquiries, 'that there was no time to send for nobody.'

'But Miss Cray had my address.'

'Ah! perhaps so; but she was off her head, poor dear, and couldn't think of nothing. But she remembered you, sir, to the last; for the very morning she died, she sprung up in bed and called out, "Sigismund! Sigismund!" as loud as ever she could, and she never spoke to anybody afterwards, not one word.'

'She left no message for me?'

'None, sir. I asked her the day before she went if I was to say nothing to you for her (knowing you was such friends), and all her answer was, "I wrote to him. He's got my letter." So I thought, perhaps, you had heard, sir.'

'Not for some time past. It seems terribly sudden to me, not having heard even of her illness. Where is she buried?'

'Close by in the churchyard, sir. My little girl will go with you and show you the place, if you'd like to see it.'

Mr Braggett accepted her offer and left.

When he was standing by a heap of clods they called a grave, and had dismissed the child, he drew out Miss Cray's last letter, which he carried in his pocket, and read it over.

'You tell me that I am not to call at your office again, except on business' (so it ran), 'nor to send letters to your private address, lest it should come to the knowledge of your wife, and create unpleasantness between you; but I *shall* call, and I *shall* write, until I have seen Mrs Braggett, and, if you don't take care, I will introduce myself to her and tell her the reason you have been afraid to do so.'

This letter had made Mr Braggett terribly angry at the time of reception. He had puffed and fumed, and cursed Miss Charlotte by all his gods for daring to threaten him. But he read it with different feelings now Miss Charlotte was down there, six feet beneath the ground he stood on, and he could feel only compassion for her frenzy, and resentment against himself for having excited it. As he travelled home from Hammersmith to Streatham, he was a very dejected publisher indeed.

He did not tell Mrs Braggett the reason of his melancholy, but it affected him to that degree that he could not go to office on the following day, but stayed at home instead, to be petted and waited upon by his pretty wife, which treatment resulted in a complete cure. The next morning, therefore, he started for London as briskly as ever, and arrived at office before his usual time. A clerk, deputed to receive all messages for his master, followed him behind the ground-glass doors, with a packet of letters.

'Mr Van Ower was here yesterday, sir. He will let you have the copy before the end of the week, and Messrs. Hanley's foreman called on particular business, and will look in to-day at eleven. And Mr Ellis came to ask if there was any answer to his letter yet; and Miss Cray called, sir; and that's all.'

'*Who* did you say?' cried Braggett.

'Miss Cray, sir. She waited for you above an hour, but I told her I thought you couldn't mean to come into town at all, so she went.'

'Do you know what you're talking about, Hewetson? You said *Miss Cray!*'

'And I meant it, sir – Miss Charlotte Cray. Burns spoke to her as well as I.'

'Good heavens!' exclaimed Mr Braggett, turning as white as a sheet. 'Go at once and send Burns to me.' Burns came.

'Burns, who was the lady that called to see me yesterday?'

'Miss Cray, sir. She had a very thick veil on, and she looked so pale that I asked her if she had been ill, and she said "Yes." She sat in the office for over an hour, hoping you'd come in, but as you didn't, she went away again.'

'Did she lift her veil?'

'Not whilst I spoke to her, sir.'

'How do you know it was Miss Cray, then?'

The clerk stared. 'Well, sir, we all know her pretty well by this time.'

'Did you ask her name?'

'No, sir; there was no need to do it.'

'You're mistaken, that's all, both you and Hewetson. It couldn't have been Miss Cray! I know for certain that she is – is – is – not in London at present. It must have been a stranger.'

'It was not, indeed, sir, begging your pardon. I could tell Miss Cray anywhere, by her figure and her voice, without seeing her face. But I *did* see her face, and remarked how awfully pale she was – just like death, sir!'

'There! there! that will do! It's of no consequence, and you can go back to your work.'

But any one who had seen Mr Braggett, when left alone in his office, would not have said he thought the matter of no consequence. The perspiration broke out upon his forehead, although it was December, and he rocked himself backward and forward in his chair with agitation.

At last he rose hurriedly, upset his throne, and dashed through the outer premises in the face of twenty people waiting to speak to him. As soon as he could find his voice, he hailed a hansom, and drove to Hammersmith. Good Mrs Thompson opening the door to him, thought he looked as if he had just come out of a fever.

'Lor' bless me, sir! whatever's the matter?'

'Mrs Thompson, have you told me the truth about Miss Cray? Is she really dead?'

'*Really dead*, sir! Why, I closed her eyes, and put her in the coffin with my own hands! If she ain't dead, I don't know who is! But if you doubt my word, you'd better ask the doctor that gave the certificate for her.'

'What is the doctor's name?'

'Dodson; he lives opposite.'

'You must forgive my strange questions, Mrs Thompson, but I have had a terrible dream about my poor friend, and I think I should like to talk to the doctor about her.'

'Oh, very good, sir,' cried the landlady, much offended. 'I'm not afraid of what the doctor will tell you. She had excellent nursing and everything as she could desire, and there's nothing on my conscience on that score, so I'll wish you good morning.' And with that Mrs Thompson slammed the door in Mr Braggett's face.

He found Dr Dodson at home.

'If I understand you rightly,' said the practitioner, looking rather steadfastly in the scared face of his visitor, 'you wish, as a friend of the late Miss Cray's, to see a copy of the certificate of her death? Very good, sir; here it is. She died, as you will perceive, on the twenty-fifth of November, of peritonitis. She had, I can assure you, every attention and care, but nothing could have saved her.'

'You are quite sure, then, she is dead?' demanded Mr Braggett, in a vague manner.

The doctor looked at him as if he were not quite sure if he were sane.

'If seeing a patient die, and her corpse coffined and buried, is being sure she is dead, *I* am in no doubt whatever about Miss Cray.'

'It is very strange – most strange and unaccountable,' murmured poor Mr Braggett, in reply, as he shuffled out of the doctor's passage, and took his way back to the office.

Here, however, after an interval of rest and a strong brandy and soda, he managed to pull himself together, and to come to the conclusion that the doctor and Mrs Thompson *could* not be mistaken, and that, consequently, the clerks *must*. He did not mention the subject again to them, however; and as the days went on, and nothing more was heard of the mysterious stranger's visit, Mr Braggett put it altogether out of his mind.

At the end of a fortnight, however, when he was thinking of something totally different, young Hewetson remarked to him, carelessly, –

'Miss Cray was here again yesterday, sir. She walked in just as your cab had left the door.'

All the horror of his first suspicions returned with double force upon the unhappy man's mind.

'Don't talk nonsense!' he gasped, angrily, as soon as he could speak. 'Don't attempt to play any of your tricks on me, young man, or it will be the worse for you, I can tell you.'

'Tricks, sir!' stammered the clerk. 'I don't know what you are alluding to. I am only telling you the truth. You have always desired me to be most particular in letting you know the names of the people who call in your absence, and I thought I was only doing my duty in making a point of ascertaining them – '

'Yes, yes! Hewetson, of course,' replied Mr Braggett, passing his handkerchief over his brow, 'and you are quite right in following my directions as closely as possible; only – in this case you are completely mistaken, and it is the second time you have committed the error.'

'Mistaken!'

'Yes! – as mistaken as it is possible for a man to be! Miss Cray *could* not have called at this office yesterday.'

'But she did, sir.'

'Am I labouring under some horrible nightmare?' exclaimed the publisher, 'or are we playing at cross purposes? Can you mean the Miss Cray I mean?'

'I am speaking of Miss Charlotte Cray, sir, the author of "Sweet Gwendoline," – the lady who has undertaken so much of our compilation the last two years, and who has a long nose, and wears her hair in curls. I never knew there was another Miss Cray; but if there are two, that is the one I mean.'

'Still I *cannot* believe it, Hewetson, for the Miss Cray who has been associated with our firm died on the twenty-fifth of last month.'

'*Died*, sir! Is Miss Cray dead? Oh, it can't be! It's some humbugging trick that's been played upon you, for I'd swear she was in this room yesterday afternoon, as full of life as she's ever been since I knew her. She didn't talk much, it's true, for she seemed in a hurry to be off again, but she had got on the same dress and bonnet she was in here last, and she made herself as much at home in the office as she ever did. Besides,' continued Hewetson, as though suddenly remembering something, 'she left a note for you, sir.'

'A note! Why did you not say so before?'

'It slipped my memory when you began to doubt my word in that way, sir. But you'll find it in the bronze vase. She told me to tell you she had placed it there.'

Mr Braggett made a dash at the vase, and found the three-cornered note as he had been told. Yes! it was Charlotte's handwriting, or the facsimile of it, there was no doubt of that; and his hands shook so he could hardly open the paper. It contained these words:

'You tell me that I am not to call at your office again, except on business, nor to send letters to your private address, lest it should come to the knowledge of your wife, and create unpleasantness between you; but I *shall* call, and I *shall* write until I have seen Mrs Braggett, and if you don't take care I will introduce myself to her, and tell her the reason you have been afraid to do so.'

Precisely the same words, in the same writing of the letter he still carried in his breast pocket, and which no mortal eyes but his and hers had ever seen. As the unhappy man sat gazing at the opened note, his whole body shook as if he were attacked by ague.

'It is Miss Cray's handwriting, isn't it, sir?'

'It looks like it, Hewetson, but it cannot be. I tell you it is an impossibility! Miss Cray died last month, and I have seen not only her grave, but the doctor and nurse who attended her in her last illness. It is folly, then, to suppose either that she called here or wrote that letter.'

'Then *who could it have been*, sir?' said Hewetson, attacked with a sudden terror in his turn.

'That is impossible for me to say; but should the lady call again, you had better ask her boldly for her name and address.'

'I'd rather you'd depute the office to anybody but me, sir,' replied the clerk, as he hastily backed out of the room.

Mr Braggett, dying with suspense and conjecture, went through his business as best he could, and hurried home to Violet Villa.

There he found that his wife had been spending the day with a friend, and only entered the house a few minutes before himself.

'Siggy, dear!' she commenced, as soon as he joined her in the drawing-room after dinner; 'I really think we should have the fastenings and bolts of this house looked to. Such a funny thing happened whilst I was out this afternoon. Ellen has just been telling me about it.'

'What sort of a thing, dear?'

'Well, I left home as early as twelve, you know, and told the servants I shouldn't be back until dinner-time; so they were all enjoying themselves in the kitchen, I suppose, when cook told Ellen she heard a footstep in the drawing-room. Ellen thought at first it must be cook's fancy, because she was sure the front door was fastened; but when they listened, they all heard the noise together, so she ran upstairs, and what on earth do you think she saw?'

'How can I guess, my dear?'

'Why, a lady, seated in this very room, as if she was waiting for somebody. She was oldish, Ellen says, and had a very white face, with long curls hanging down each side of it; and she wore a blue bonnet with white feathers, and a long black cloak, and –'

'Emily, Emily! Stop! You don't know what you're talking about. That girl is a fool: you must send her away. That is, how could the lady have got in if the door was closed? Good heavens! you'll all drive me mad between you with your folly!' exclaimed Mr Braggett, as he threw himself back in his chair, with an exclamation that sounded very like a groan.

Pretty Mrs Braggett was offended. What had she said or done that her husband should doubt her word? She tossed her head in indignation, and remained silent. If Mr Braggett wanted any further information, he would have to apologise.

'Forgive me, darling,' he said, after a long pause. 'I don't think I'm very well this evening, but your story seemed to upset me.'

'I don't see why it should upset you,' returned Mrs Braggett. 'If strangers are allowed to come prowling about the house in this way, we shall be robbed some day, and then you'll say I should have told you of it.'

'Wouldn't she – this person – give her name?'

'Oh! I'd rather say no more about it. You had better ask Ellen.'

'No, Emily! I'd rather hear it from you.'

'Well, don't interrupt me again, then. When Ellen saw the woman seated here, she asked her her name and business at once, but she gave no answer, and only sat and stared at her. And so Ellen, feeling very uncomfortable, had just turned round to call up cook, when the woman got up, and dashed past her like a flash of lightning, and they saw nothing more of her!'

'Which way did she leave the house?'

'Nobody knows any more than how she came in. The servants declare the hall door was neither opened nor shut – but, of course, it must have been. She was a tall gaunt woman, Ellen says, about fifty, and she's sure her hair was dyed. She must have come to steal something, and that's why I say we ought to have the house made more secure. Why, Siggy! Siggy! what's the matter? Here, Ellen! Jane! come, quick, some of you! Your master's fainted!'

And, sure enough, the repeated shocks and horrors of the day had had such an effect upon poor Mr Braggett, that for a moment he did lose all consciousness of what surrounded him. He was thankful to take advantage of the Christmas holidays, to run over to Paris with his wife, and try to forget, in the many marvels of that city, the awful fear that fastened upon him at the mention of anything connected with home. He might be enjoying himself to the top of his bent; but directly the remembrance of Charlotte Cray crossed his mind, all sense of enjoyment vanished, and he trembled at the mere thought of returning to his business, as a child does when sent to bed in the dark.

He tried to hide the state of his feelings from Mrs Braggett, but she was too sharp for him. The simple, blushing Emily Primrose had developed, under the influence of the matrimonial forcing-frame, into a good watch-dog, and nothing escaped her notice.

Left to her own conjecture, she attributed his frequent moods of dejection to the existence of some other woman, and became jealous accordingly. If Siggy did not love her, why had he married her? She felt certain there was some other horrid creature who had engaged his affections and would not leave him alone, even now that he was her own lawful property. And to find out who the 'horrid creature' was became Mrs Emily's constant idea. When she had found out, she meant to give her a piece of her mind, never fear! Meanwhile Mr Braggett's evident distaste to returning to business only served to increase his wife's suspicions. A clear conscience, she argued, would know no fear. So they were not a happy couple, as they set their faces once more towards England. Mr Braggett's dread of re-entering his office amounted almost to terror, and Mrs Braggett, putting this and that together, resolved that she would fathom the mystery, if it lay in feminine *finesse* to do so. She did not whisper a word of her intentions to dear Siggy, you may be sure of that! She worked after the manner of her amiable sex, like a cat in the dark, or a worm boring through the earth, and appearing on the surface when least expected.

So poor Mr Braggett brought her home again, heavy at heart indeed, but quite ignorant that any designs were being made against him. I think he would have given a thousand pounds to be spared the duty of attending office the day after his arrival.

But it was necessary, and he went, like a publisher and a Briton. But Mrs Emily had noted his trepidation and his fears, and laid her plans accordingly. She had never been asked to enter those mysterious precincts, the house of business. Mr Braggett had not thought it necessary that her blooming loveliness should be made acquainted with its dingy, dusty accessories, but she meant to see them for herself to-day. So she waited till he had left Violet Villa ten minutes, and then she dressed and followed him by the next train to London.

Mr Sigismund Braggett meanwhile had gone on his way, as people go to a dentist, determined to do what was right, but with an indefinite sort of idea that he might never come out of it alive. He dreaded to hear what might have happened in his absence, and he delayed his arrival at the office for half-an-hour, by walking there instead of taking a cab as usual, in order to put off the evil moment. As he entered the place, however, he saw at a glance that his efforts were vain, and that something had occurred. The customary formality and precision of the office were upset, and the clerks, instead of bending over their ledgers, or attending to the demands of business, were all huddled together at one end whispering and gesticulating to each other. But as soon as the publisher appeared, a dead silence fell upon the group, and they only stared at him with an air of horrid mystery.

'What is the matter now?' he demanded, angrily, for like most men when in a fright which they are ashamed to exhibit, Mr Sigismund Braggett tried to cover his want of courage by bounce.

The young man called Hewetson advanced towards him, with a face the colour of ashes, and pointed towards the ground-glass doors dumbly.

'What do you mean? Can't you speak? What's come to the lot of you, that you are neglecting my business in this fashion to make fools of yourselves?'

'If you please, sir, she's in there.'

Mr Braggett started back as if he'd been shot. But still he tried to have it out.

'*She!* Who's *she?*'

'Miss Cray, sir.'

'Haven't I told you already that's a lie.'

'Will you judge for yourself, Mr Braggett?' said a grey-haired man, stepping forward. 'I was on the stairs myself just now when Miss Cray passed me, and I have no doubt whatever but that you will find her in your private room, however much the reports that have lately reached you may seem against the probability of such a thing.'

Mr Braggett's teeth chattered in his head as he advanced to the ground-glass doors, through the panes of one of which there was a little peephole to ascertain if the room were occupied or not. He stooped and looked in. At the table, with her back towards him, was seated the well-known figure of Charlotte Cray. He recognised at once the long black mantle in which she was wont to drape her gaunt figure – the blue bonnet, with its dejected-looking, uncurled feather – the lank curls which rested on her shoulders – and the black-leather bag, with a steel clasp, which she always carried in her hand. It was the embodiment of Charlotte Cray, he had no doubt of that; but how could he reconcile the fact of her being there with the damp clods he had seen piled upon her grave, with the certificate of death, and the doctor's and landlady's assertion that they had watched her last moments?

At last he prepared, with desperate energy, to turn the handle of the door. At that moment the attention of the more frivolous of the clerks was directed from his actions by the entrance of an uncommonly pretty woman at the other end of the outer office. Such a lovely creature as this seldom brightened the gloom of their dusty abiding-place. Lilies, roses, and carnations vied with each other in her complexion, whilst the sunniest of locks, and the brightest of blue eyes, lent her face a girlish charm not easily described. What could this fashionably-attired Venus want in their house of business?

'Is Mr Braggett here? I am Mrs Braggett. Please show me in to him immediately.'

They glanced at the ground-glass doors of the inner office.

They had already closed behind the manly form of their employer.

'This way, madam,' one said, deferentially, as he escorted her to the presence of Mr Braggett.

Meanwhile, Sigismund had opened the portals of the Temple of Mystery, and with trembling knees entered it. The figure in the chair did not stir at his approach. He stood at the door irresolute. What should he do or say?

'Charlotte,' he whispered.

Still she did not move.

At that moment his wife entered.

'Oh, Sigismund!' cried Mrs Emily, reproachfully, 'I knew you were keeping something from me, and now I've caught you in the very act. Who is this lady, and what is her name? I shall refuse to leave the room until I know it.'

At the sound of her rival's voice, the woman in the chair rose quickly to her feet and confronted them. Yes! there was Charlotte Cray, precisely similar to what she had appeared in life, only with an uncertainty and vagueness about the lines of the familiar features that made them ghastly.

She stood there, looking Mrs Emily full in the face, but only for a moment, for, even as she gazed, the lineaments grew less and less distinct, with the shape of the figure that supported them, until, with a crash, the apparition seemed to fall in and disappear, and the place that had known her was filled with empty air.

'Where is she gone?' exclaimed Mrs Braggett, in a tone of utter amazement.

'Where is *who* gone?' repeated Mr Braggett, hardly able to articulate from fear.

'The lady in the chair!'

'There was no one there except in your own imagination. It was my great-coat that you mistook for a figure,' returned her husband hastily, as he threw the article in question over the back of the arm-chair.

'But how could that have been?' said his pretty wife, rubbing her eyes. 'How could I think a coat had eyes, and hair, and features? I am *sure* I saw a woman seated there, and that she rose and stared at me. Siggy! tell me it was true. It seems so incomprehensible that I should have been mistaken.'

'You must question your own sense. You see that the room is empty now, except for ourselves, and you know that no one has left it. If you like to search under the table, you can.'

'Ah! now, Siggy, you are laughing at me, because you know that would be folly. But there was certainly some one here – only, where can she have disappeared to?'

'Suppose we discuss the matter at a more convenient season,' replied Mr Braggett, as he drew his wife's arm through his arm. 'Hewetson! you will be able to tell Mr Hume that he was mistaken. Say, also, that I shall not be back in the office today. I am not so strong as I thought I was, and feel quite unequal to business. Tell him to come out to Streatham this evening with my letters, and I will talk with him there.'

What passed at that interview was never disclosed; but pretty Mrs Braggett was much rejoiced, a short time afterwards, by her husband telling her that he had resolved to resign his active share of the business, and devote the rest of his life to her and Violet Villa. He would have no more occasion, therefore, to visit the office, and be exposed to the temptation of spending four or five hours out of every twelve away from her side. For, though Mrs Emily had arrived at the conclusion that the momentary glimpse she caught of a lady in Siggy's office must have been a delusion, she was not quite satisfied by his assertions that she would never have found a more tangible cause for her jealousy.

But Sigismund Braggett knew more than he chose to tell Mrs Emily. He knew that what she had witnessed was no delusion, but a reality; and that Charlotte Cray had carried out her dying determination to call at his office and his private residence, *until she had seen his wife!*

M. G. Lewis

THE GRIM WHITE WOMAN

MATTHEW GREGORY LEWIS (1775-1818) *was the author of one of the earliest – and still one of the best – horror novels in English,* The Monk (1796). *An enormous bestseller in its day, Lewis's novel also created a scandal. That a Member of Parliament should publish a novel featuring Satanic pacts, murder, infanticide, rotting corpses, rape, and blasphemy shocked the arbiters of morality. But as outrage grew, so did sales of the book. Lewis's other successes included* Tales of Wonder (1801), *a compilation of tales in verse, some written or translated by Lewis,* The Bravo of Venice (1805), *a translation of a German Gothic novel, and* Romantic Tales (1808), *a four-volume collection of Gothic stories in prose and verse, from which 'The Grim White Woman' is taken. Lewis's* The Monk *is available from Valancourt in a hardcover edition introduced by Stephen King.*

Lord Ronald was handsome, Lord Ronald was young;
The green wood he traversed, and gaily he sung;
His bosom was light, and he spurr'd on amain,
When lo! a fair lass caught his steed by the rein.

She caught by the rein, and she sank on her knee;
—'Now stay thee, Lord Ronald, and listen to me!'—
She sank on her knee, and her tears 'gan to flow,
—'Now stay thee, Lord Ronald, and pity my woe!'—

—'Nay, Janet, fair Janet, I needs must away;
I speed to my mother, who chides my delay.'—
—'Oh! heed not her chiding; though bitter it be,
Thy falsehood and scorn are more bitter to me.'—

—'Nay, Janet, fair Janet, I needs must depart;
My brother stays for me to hunt the wild hart.'—
—'Oh! let the hart live, and thy purpose forego,
To soothe with compassion and kindness my woe.'—

—'Nay, Janet, fair Janet delay me no more;
You please me no longer, my passion is o'er:
A leman more lovely waits down in yon dell,
So, Janet, fair Janet, for ever farewell!'—

No longer the damsel's entreaties he heard;
His dapple-grey horse through the forest he spurr'd;
And ever, as onwards the foaming steed flew,
Did Janet with curses the false one pursue.

—'Oh! cursed be the day,' in distraction she cries,
'When first did thy features look fair in my eyes!
And cursed the false lips, which beguiled me of fame;
And cursed the hard heart, which resigns me to shame!

'The wanton, whom now you forsake me to please—
May her kisses be poison, her touch be disease!
When you wed, may your couch be a stranger to joy,
And the Fiend of the Forest your offspring destroy!

'May the Grim White Woman, who haunts this wood,
The Grim White Woman, who feasts on blood,
As soon as they number twelve months and a day,
Tear the hearts of your babes from their bosoms away.'—

Then frantic with love and remorse home she sped,
Lock'd the door of her chamber, and sank on her bed;
Nor yet with complaints and with tears had she done,
When the clock in St Christopher's church struck—'one!'—

Her blood, why she knew not, ran cold at the sound;
She lifted her head; she gazed fearfully round!

When lo! near the hearth, by a cauldron's blue light,
She saw the tall form of a female in white.

Her eye, fix'd and glassy, no passions express'd;
No blood fill'd her veins, and no heart warm'd her breast!
She seem'd like a corse newly torn from the tomb,
And her breath spread the chillness of death through the room.

Her arms, and her feet, and her bosom were bare;
A shroud wrapp'd her limbs, and a snake bound her hair.
This spectre, the Grim White Woman was she,
And the Grim White Woman was fearful to see!

And ever, the cauldron as over she bent,
She mutter'd strange words of mysterious intent:
A toad, still alive, in the liquor she threw,
And loud shriek'd the toad, as in pieces it flew!

To heighten the charm, in the flames next she flung
A viper, a rat, and a mad tiger's tongue;
The heart of a wretch, on the rack newly dead,
And an eye, she had torn from a parricide's head.

The flames now divided; the charm was complete;
Her spells the White Spectre forbore to repeat;
To Janet their produce she hasten'd to bring,
And placed on her finger a little jet ring!

—'From the Grim White Woman,' she murmur'd, 'receive
A gift, which your treasure, now lost, will retrieve.
Remember, 'twas she who relieved your despair,
And when you next see her, remember your prayer!'—

This said, the Fiend vanish'd! no longer around
Pour'd the cauldron its beams; all was darkness profound;
Till the gay beams of morning illumined the skies,
And gay as the morning did Ronald arise.

With hawks and with hounds, to the forest, rode he:
—'Trallira! trallara! from Janet I'm free!
Trallira! trallara! my old love, adieu!
Trallira! trallara! I'll get me anew!'—

But while he thus caroll'd in bachelor's pride,
A damsel appear'd by the rivulet's side:
He rein'd in his courser, and soon was aware,
That never was damsel more comely and fair.

He felt at her sight, what no words can impart;
She gave him a look, and he proffer'd his heart:
Her air, while she listen'd, was modest and bland:
She gave him a smile, and he proffer'd his hand.

Lord Ronald was handsome, Lord Ronald was young,
And soon on his bosom sweet Ellinor hung;
And soon to St Christopher's chapel they ride,
And soon does Lord Ronald call Ellen his bride.

Days, weeks, and months fly.—'Ding-a-ding! ding-a-ding!'—
Hark! hark! in the air how the castle-bells ring!
—'And why do the castle-bells ring in the air?'—
Sweet Ellen hath born to Lord Ronald an heir.

Days, weeks, and months fly.—'Ding-a-ding; ding-a-ding!'—
Again, hark! how gaily the castle-bells ring!
—'Why again do the castle-bells carol so gay?'—
A daughter is born to Lord Ronald to-day.

But see'st thou yon herald so swift hither bend?
Lord Ronald is summon'd his king to defend:
And see'st thou the tears of sweet Ellinor flow?
Lord Ronald has left her to combat the foe.

Where slumber her babies, her steps are address'd;
She presses in anguish her son to her breast;

Nor ceases she Annabel's cradle to rock,
Till—'one!'—is proclaim'd by the loud castle-clock.

Her blood, why she knows not, runs cold at the sound!
She raises her head; she looks fearfully round!
And lo! near the hearth, by a cauldron's blue light,
She sees the tall form of a female in white!

The female with horror sweet Ellen beholds:
Still closer her son to her bosom she folds;
And cold tears of terror bedew her pale cheeks,
While, nearer approaching, the Spectre thus speaks.—

—'The Grim White Woman, who haunts yon wood,
The Grim White Woman, who feasts on blood,
Since now he has number'd twelve months and a day,
Claims the heart of your son, and is come for her prey.'—

—'Oh! Grim White Woman, my baby now spare!
I'll give you these diamonds so precious and fair!'—
—'Though fair be those diamonds, though precious they be,
The blood of thy babe is more precious to me!'—

—'Oh! Grim White Woman, now let my child live!
This cross of red rubies in guerdon I'll give!'—
—'Though red be the flames from those rubies which dart,
More red is the blood of thy little child's heart.'—

To soften the dæmon no pleading prevails;
The baby she wounds with her long crooked nails:
She tears from his bosom the heart as her prey!
' 'Tis mine!'—shriek'd the Spectre, and vanish'd away.

The foe is defeated, and ended the strife,
And Ronald speeds home to his children and wife.
Alas! on his castle a black banner flies,
And tears trickle fast from his fair lady's eyes.

—'Say, why on my castle a black banner flies,
And why trickle tears from my fair lady's eyes?'—
—'In your absence the Grim White Woman was here,
And dead is your son, whom you valued so dear.'—

Deep sorrow'd Lord Ronald; but soon for his grief,
He found in the arms of sweet Ellen relief:
Her kisses could peace to his bosom restore,
And the more he beheld her, he loved her the more;

Till it chanced, that one night, when the tempest was loud,
And strong gusts of wind rock'd the turrets so proud,
As Ronald lay sleeping he heard a voice cry,
—'Dear father, arise, or your daughter must die!'—

He woke, gazed around, look'd below, look'd above;
—'Why trembles my Ronald? what ails thee, my love?'—
—'I dreamt, through the skies that I saw a hawk dart,
Pounce a little white pigeon, and tear out its heart.'—

—'Oh hush thee, my husband; thy vision was vain.'—
Lord Ronald resign'd him to slumber again:
But soon the same voice, which had roused him before,
Cried—'Father, arise, or your daughter's no more!'—

He woke, gazed around, look'd below, look'd above;
—'What fears now, my Ronald? what ails thee, my love?'—
—'I dreamt that a tigress, with jaws open'd wide,
Had fasten'd her fangs in a little lamb's side!'—

—'Oh! hush thee, my husband; no tigress is here.'—
Again Ronald slept, and again in his ear
Soft murmur'd the voice,—'Oh! be warn'd by your son;
Dear father, arise, for it soon will strike—"one!"'—

'Your wife, for a spell your affections to hold,
To the Grim White Woman her children hath sold;

E'en now is the Fiend at your babe's chamber door;
Then father, arise, or your daughter's no more!'—

From his couch starts Lord Ronald, in doubt and dismay,
He seeks for his wife—but his wife is away!
He gazes around, looks below, looks above;
Lo! there sits on his pillow a little white dove!

A mild lambent flame in its eyes seem'd to glow;
More pure was its plumage than still-falling snow,
Except where a scar could be seen on its side,
And three small drops of blood the white feathers had dyed.

—'Explain, pretty pigeon, what art thou, explain?'—
—'The soul of thy son, by the White Dæmon slain;
E'en now is the Fiend at your babe's chamber door,
And thrice having warn'd you, I warn you no more!'—

The pigeon then vanish'd; and seizing his sword,
The way to his daughter Lord Ronald explored;
Distracted he sped to her chamber full fast,
And the clock it struck—'one!' as the threshold he past.

And straight near the hearth, by a cauldron's blue light,
He saw the tall form of a female in white;
Ellen wept, to her heart while her baby she press'd,
Whom the Spectre approaching, thus fiercely address'd.

'The Grim White Woman, who haunts yon wood,
The Grim White Woman, who feasts on blood,
Since now she has numbered twelve months and a day,
Claims the heart of your daughter, and comes for her prey!'

This said, she her nails in the child would have fix'd;
Sore struggled the mother; when, rushing betwixt,
Ronald struck at the Fiend with his ready drawn brand,
And, glancing aside, his blow lopp'd his wife's hand!

Wild laughing, the Fiend caught the hand from the floor,
Releasing the babe, kiss'd the wound, drank the gore;
A little jet ring from the finger then drew,
Thrice shriek'd a loud shriek, and was borne from their view!

Lord Ronald, while horror still bristled his hair,
To Ellen now turn'd;—but no Ellen was there!
And lo! in her place, his surprise to complete,
Lay Janet, all cover'd with blood, at his feet!

—'Yes, traitor, 'tis Janet!'—she cried;—'at my sight
No more will your heart swell with love and delight;
That little jet ring was the cause of your flame,
And that little jet ring from the Forest-Fiend came.

'It endow'd me with beauty, your heart to regain;
It fix'd your affections, so wavering and vain;
But the spell is dissolved, and your eyes speak my fate,
My falsehood is clear, and as clear is your hate.

'But what caused my falsehood?—your falsehood alone;
What voice said—"be guilty?"—seducer, your own!
You vow'd truth for ever, the oath I believed,
And had you not deceived me, *I* had not deceived.

'Remember my joy, when affection you swore!
Remember my pangs, when your passion was o'er!
A curse, in my rage, on your children was thrown,
And alas! wretched mother, that curse struck my own!'—

And here her strength fail'd her!—the sad one to save
In vain the Leech labour'd; three days did she rave;
Death came on the fourth, and restored her to peace,
Nor long did Lord Ronald survive her decease.

Despair fills his heart! he no longer can bear
His castle, for Ellen no longer is there:

From Scotland he hastens, all comfort disdains,
And soon his bones whiten on Palestine's plains.

If you bid me, fair damsels, my moral rehearse,
It is that young ladies ought never to curse;
For no one will think her well-bred, or polite,
Who devotes little babes to Grim Women in White.

Charles Birkin

THE TERROR ON TOBIT

CHARLES LLOYD BIRKIN (1907-1985) *was an important figure in early 20th-century British horror fiction, editing over a dozen volumes in the* Creeps *series, published by Philip Allan in the 1930s. These books, with colorful, eye-catching dust jacket artwork and titles like* Creeps *(1932),* Shudders *(1933), and* Monsters *(1934), were the precursors of later horror series like the* Pan Books of Horror Stories *and featured tales by well-known horror writers of the day, including H. R. Wakefield, Tod Robbins, and Elliott O'Donnell, as well as contributions by Birkin himself. In 1936, Birkin collected his contributions to the* Creeps *volumes in* Devils' Spawn. *He did not publish again until 1964, when he released – perhaps with the encouragement of the popular novelist Dennis Wheatley, who championed Birkin's work – two volumes,* The Kiss of Death *and* The Smell of Evil. *Six more volumes would follow over the course of the decade, mostly consisting of* contes cruels *rather than supernatural tales. For Birkin, the cruelty of which human beings are capable was far more horrific than imaginary ghosts or goblins. As prolific horror editor Hugh Lamb wrote, Birkin's stories 'are not for the squeamish. Be warned, if you are at all sensitive, leave him well alone. He deals unflinchingly with such subjects as murder, rape, concentration camps, patricide, mutilation and torture.' 'The Terror on Tobit', first published in* Terrors *(1933), is an exception: a wholesome, old-fashioned monster story. Two of Birkin's collections are available from Valancourt.*

'I SUPPOSE YOU REALISE,' said Daphne, 'that in three more days we shall be back in London – for another year?'

'You needn't remind me of that ... the last fortnight has simply flown,' Anne replied, shutting her book with a snap. 'And I for one have never enjoyed a holiday so much.'

The oil-lamp stood, squat and homely, on the plain table

in the girls' sitting-room. Outside, the warm August night crept close to the windows, only a slight breeze disturbing the checked curtains. The cottage was one of the dozen modest dwellings that comprised the village of St Mark's on one of the smaller of the Scilly Islands – relics of that lost land of Lyonesse.

'I hope that you're glad I persuaded you to come?' Daphne, vivid in her dark beauty, smiled at her friend.

'Oh, Daphne, you know I am. It's been absolutely heavenly!'

'Better than Torquay?'

'I've never liked anything better. I can't say more than that, can I?'

There was a knock on the door, and Mrs Arraway, the mother of the fisherman who owned the cottage, came in for the supper tray. Anne turned to her. 'That lobster was delicious. If you only knew how I hated the thought of going back to London.'

Mrs Arraway laughed. She was a pleasant, full-bosomed woman of the islands, where, with the exception of rare visits to Penzance, she had spent her whole life. 'I shall be very sorry to lose you, missie. I hope as how you've been comfortable here?'

'It's been perfect,' Daphne broke in. 'But we've got a favour to ask you.'

Mrs Arraway raised her eyebrows, waiting for her to continue.

'We wondered if Jean would row us over to Tobit to-morrow evening. We want to camp there for the night. It would be such a marvellous ending to our holiday. He could come back for us the next morning. Do you think he would?'

'Well, miss, what do two young ladies like you want to do a thing like that for?' Mrs Arraway was doubtful.

'Because we want to sleep under the stars – on an uninhabited island. Could anything be more romantic? Oh it would be such fun! Please persuade Jean to take us.'

Mrs Arraway frowned. It was clear that the idea was distasteful to her. But what could one do? Girls were so self-willed nowadays.

'Tobit isn't healthy,' she replied after a pause, 'that is, not exactly. There's no water on it anyway,' she concluded triumphantly.

'That's all right. We can take what we want in a thermos. Please say yes, Mrs Arraway,' Daphne implored.

'Well, I don't know, I'm sure,' the landlady answered. 'I'll tell you what I will do, miss. I'll send Jean to you and you can see what he says – although I'm certain as how he'll never consider such a mad-cap notion.' She picked up the supper tray, and went out of the door, still muttering to herself.

Anne stood by the window looking into the night, with her hands parting the curtains. Against a sky of almost midnight blue, loomed the wild chaos of scarred and riven rocks. The fantastic rocks of the Scilly Isles, that had by day a different and more friendly appearance; calm and less harsh – bearded shaggily with moss and lichen.

'I wonder why these islands have such an atmosphere of enchantment. I've never had the same impression anywhere else. They seem so sad – like gentle faded beauties, dreamily remembering past glories . . . and waiting for the end.'

Before Daphne could reply there was a quiet knock at the door.

'I expect that is Jean. Daphne, we *must* persuade him to take us. It would be the most heavenly experience. Come in!'

Jean Arraway strode into the small parlour. He was in the middle twenties, and remarkably handsome, in a strange gipsy way that was unusual among the islanders – but his dark eyes had the faraway dreamy expression that is so often found among those whose mother is the sea.

'Yes, missie?'

'Jean! We want you to help us. Will you?'

'What is it you want me to do, missie?'

'Take us to Tobit to-morrow. We want to stay there for the night. And you can fetch us early on Friday morning. You will, won't you?' Anne smiled at him, exercising her not inconsiderable charm.

'You can't spend the night on Tobit, missie!'

'Why not?' Daphne asked.

'It isn't healthy.'

'What do you mean – it isn't healthy? Your mother used the same expression,' Anne broke in impatiently.

Jean glanced at her strangely. It was obvious that he was ill at ease; and unwilling to elaborate his statement. There was a short silence in the little room. The girls waited for him to continue.

'It's kind of difficult to explain,' he said at last. 'But things have happened there. . . .'

'What sort of things?' Daphne was interested.

'Queer things.'

'But I thought no one lived there?'

'No one does. But people have gone there once or twice. There was an artist chap the year before last.'

'And what happened to him?'

'I don't rightly know.'

'Then, why all this mystery?' Anne demanded.

'You see, missie, he never came back. Kind of disappeared.'

'But that's impossible. Where could he have disappeared to?'

Jean shrugged his shoulders.

'*No one* rightly knows. There's mighty queer stories about Tobit. It's not meant for us humans.'

'What stories?' This was thrilling.

'Well, that artist chap wasn't the only one what went. The year before, there was a lady. A writer I think she was. Insisted on staying there the night – same as you want to do.'

'I don't believe it. You're just saying that to put us off. Anyway we're going, if you take us or not – aren't we, Anne?'

'Certainly. A lot of ridiculous superstition.'

'I shouldn't if I was you, missie. You wouldn't get none of the islanders to take you. It's real bad. Tobit belongs to the sea, and the sea's creatures.'

'Don't be absurd, Jean. Am I to understand that you refuse to take us?'

'I'm sorry, missie.'

Fingering his belt, he avoided Anne's eyes.

'Then we'll row ourselves over. And if we aren't back by lunch-time on Friday you'll know the Bogey's got us – and can come over and look for us!' Daphne laughed.

Jean made no reply. He stood there in an awkward silence as if wishing to add some further remonstrance; but realising the uselessness of any such action, contented himself by saying:

'Good night, missies. Maybe in the morning you'll have changed your minds.'

Left alone, Anne turned to her friend. 'Did you ever hear anything so absurd? It's just because Jean's too lazy to take us – that's all. We'll still go – won't we?'

'Of course we will,' Daphne replied. 'I wouldn't be put off by a string of lies like that. Although if there was any truth in them, it would be rather . . . curious, wouldn't it?'

The next day, when Daphne and Anne were unlatching the little gate that divided the flower-filled garden of their cottage from the road – little more than a track – that formed the main street of village, they encountered Mrs Arraway, who, her arms full of vegetables, wished them good morning.

'We didn't have much encouragement from your son last night,' said Anne laughingly.

Mrs Arraway's mouth tightened into a thin line, and an anxious frown wrinkled the placid expanse of her forehead.

'Oh, miss, do give up this mad idea of yours. Jean told me he'd tried to dissuade you. You don't know these islands like we do. Indeed, how could you?'

'But, Mrs Arraway, what *is* it exactly we have to fear – smugglers or such shady doings?'

'No, miss – smugglers are flesh and blood – but the Thing on Tobit . . . well, no one knows rightly quite what it is, tho' they do say that Tobit belongs to the sea; and that each year the sea demands a sacrifice – in return for all it gives to us.'

In spite of the brilliant sunshine and the cheerfulness of the bright island scenery, Daphne felt a chill of foreboding. After all, these islanders might be much nearer to the truth of things than she and Anne.

'The sea missed its sacrifice last year – didn't it? How about that?' Anne teased.

'Don't joke about such a subject, miss – and don't, I beg of you, go to Tobit to-night.'

'Nonsense, Mrs Arraway, we simply must go. We'll be alright ... don't worry. Would you be very kind, and make us up a picnic basket? We're starting about seven to give ourselves plenty of time to settle down before it's dark' – and the girls swung down the road, two gay figures in their coloured cotton dresses, their towels and bathing suits over their arms.

A group of fishermen was clustered round the few wooden sheds that formed the tiny harbour, overhauling their nets; or sitting silent in companionable groups.

Nothing could have been less sinister or more secure than the tranquil sun-soaked scene. The sea, its calm scarcely broken by a ripple, lay smiling in the sun, flaunting its motley of blues and greens and rich purples – a sea more of the tropics than of our dour northern climate – yet a sea that could on occasion be lashed into a pitiless titan devoid of mercy, a monster of tossing crests and crashing spume-flecked waves that flayed the rocks and crushed the pebbles in grinding torment.

It was after six o'clock when Daphne and Anne, after a long and lazy day on the beach, returned to the cottage. They were full of content, and a pleasurable fatigue, the outcome of hours of amphibian existence; of bathing, and basking, and bathing once more. Their skins were bronzed to a deep tan that made their young prettiness the more effective. Health and well-being wrapped them in their cheerful embrace.

They were met by Jean, his dark hair ruffled, his face sullen. He wore a bleached blue shirt, his sleeves rolled up to his elbows, exposing the tense muscles of his arms; light canvas shoes, and well-worn flannel trousers completed his dress.

'Good evening, Jean.'

'Good evening, missie.'

The two girls started to walk up the stone flags of the path, Jean following. At the door he spoke.

'You're going to Tobit?'

'Yes.'

'Then I'll take you, missie.'

'But I thought nothing would persuade an islander to go there?'

Jean flushed. He was intensely uncomfortable. 'You see, missie. It isn't right for you to go alone. I'd feel happier myself, like, if you'd let me take you.'

'Thank you, we're very grateful.' Daphne spoke with sincerity, for she knew the effort that had prompted Jean's offer.

'But you mustn't sleep on the island. That would spoil everything, wouldn't it, Daphne?' then, seeing the man's embarrassment, Anne hurried on, 'I mean, you must drop us there, and either come back for us in the morning, or sleep in the boat.'

'As you say, missie. And what time will you want to be starting?'

'In about half an hour. We'll meet you at the harbour.'

Up in their bedroom, while they were collecting the blankets and rugs necessary for their night's adventure, Daphne said, 'You know, Anne, I'm rather pleased Jean will be near us.'

'Why, I believe you're scared.'

'I'm not at all – but it will mean we can get away if we want to.'

'We shan't. Hurry up – we've got to get the food yet – and don't forget the matches.'

They found Jean waiting for them in the boat; and in a very few minutes their various packages were stowed away and their journey had begun. Tobit lay about a mile to the west of St Mark's – a last defiant rock against the barrage of the Atlantic. To their left Daphne saw the island of Samson, uninhabited save for the sea-gulls, although a ruined hut showed where once a shepherd had grazed a few sheep. Tobit itself lay low in the sea – a queer, dark shape, a gigantic beast of a long-forgotten age, stricken and petrified, wallowing in the mill of the waters. Its rocky and forbidding shores riddled with caves gave scant welcome to visitors from the neighbouring islands. On the higher land a coarse sea-grass faintly coloured its spine, dotted with giant and fantastic boulders, monuments of a race lost in the dim ages of the past, perhaps a mountain outpost of Atlantis itself.

Daphne was surprised to find that the boat was nearly there, so lost had she been in her musings. Jean sprang into the sea and waded ashore with the blankets and picnic basket.

From the boat the girls noticed that the rocks had caught a liberal supply of driftwood, so that there would be no likelihood of their fire dying down through lack of fuel.

In a few minutes Jean returned; he had not spoken during the journey, and was evidently liking the expedition no more than in the morning.

'Shall I carry you, missie?'

'No – we'll wade, too,' Anne answered.

'Then I'll be helping you to get settled. There's a sandy hollow at the far end of the island that should be sheltered.'

They splashed after him to the shore; stumbling over the treacherous rocks slippery with seaweed of a peculiar red colour, and studded with deep pools. Five minutes' walking brought them to a narrow peninsula on the main end of which was a circular patch of sand almost entirely surrounded by great wind-eaten rocks.

'I say, Daphne,' her friend said, 'looks like a druid's circle, doesn't it?'

'It's one of the fairies' rings,' Jean broke in. 'There are several such on the islands. The pixies made them.'

Daphne laughed. 'Yes? I must thank them in that case for our bedroom. By the way, are *you* going to sleep in the boat to-night?'

'It's not right for you to be here by yourselves. It's dangerous, I tell you. Tobit's cursed. It belongs to the sea.'

'If you're afraid, why don't you go back to St Mark's? You can come back for us in the morning.' There was a taunt in Anne's question.

'I won't be denying that I *be* afraid. But I won't be leaving you.'

'Then you'll sleep – in the boat?'

'No. I'll be on the main part of the island. Near like, in case you're needing me. I'd best stay within hearing.'

'Very well.' Daphne turned to Anne. 'I think we should collect the wood for the fire. Jean and I will get it while you "unpack."'

They walked away; and Anne started to make their camp. In her heart of hearts she was none too confident now that night was actually falling . . . and there was no going back. She shivered. Why should her thoughts say that?

There is no going back! She mustn't be hysterical. It might have serious consequences. Still, the feeling remained – a feeling of uneasiness, of dread, almost as if something was menacing them – something unseen watching – and waiting.

Ten o'clock. The firelight flickered eerily, throwing into brief illumination the faces of the two girls, and causing dark shadows to dart momentarily to the very edge of the crackling, salt-saturated fire.

'Don't you think we should try to sleep?' Daphne suggested. 'It's after ten.'

'Yes. Daphne – I hate to admit it – but I'm frightened. Where's Jean?'

'Over there to the left – about a hundred yards.'

'Is he asleep?'

'No, he said he'd . . . watch.'

'What for?'

'Goodness only knows. The Bogey, perhaps!' Anne snuggled down more comfortably into her blankets. It was so easy to imagine things, she told herself.

'Good night.'

'Good night.'

And the waves splashed softly on the shore.

Two hours passed. Daphne stirred restlessly. Then she sat up.

What was that?

The air seemed to vibrate with a high singing sound – oddly

penetrating, like the noise of a swarm of giant mosquitoes. It rose and fell in a monotonous cadence. Paralysed with foreboding she lay motionless. She knew she could not bear to listen to it alone for another moment.

'Anne!' her voice was urgent.

Anne did not stir.

'Anne!' she called more loudly.

'Yes. What is it? What's the matter?' She raised herself drowsily on her elbow.

'Don't . . . don't you hear it?'

'Hear what?'

They listened intently. The sea murmured, caressing the rocks with soft, secretive whisperings, glutting the myriad little caves, reluctant to withdraw. But above the whispering of the sea rose that other sound – a high, uncanny whistling, growing more insistent every moment.

'It's the wind in the rocks. Try and go to sleep again.'

The fire had burnt down to a heap of glowing embers, and Daphne stretched out her hand to the pile of driftwood. The sticks spluttered and popped as they lay on the hot ashes; but gradually little blue flames crept up into a cone of warmth.

Soon Anne was asleep once more; and Daphne lay on her back gazing wide-eyed at the sky, peppered with a million stars. She was frightened . . . that whistling – what could it be?

'Tobit belongs to the sea – humans have no right there.'

Where had she heard those words? Who had spoken them?

She was beginning to feel sleepy. If only that whistling would stop, she might go to sleep. If only it would stop. It seemed that she tossed the victim of insomnia for hours.

Daphne awoke with a start. She was shivering as with an ague. . . . Even now she could not put that terrible dream out of her head.

She had been alone – quite alone by the seashore; and suddenly she had heard a voice cry:

'Two . . . this time it shall be two,' and the words had filled her with an indescribable fear, and she had turned to run; but her way had been blocked by a figure, gigantic in stature – and its monstrous shape had moved towards her, and she knew it was the incarnation of evil itself. If it had touched her Daphne was certain that she would have gone mad. . . .

She looked at her watch. Two o'clock. A few more hours and it would be dawn. The fire had died down once more. She stretched out her hand for more wood; but there were only a few sticks left. Anne must have used their supply while she was sleeping.

Without the security of the fire slumber would be impossible. She looked at Anne. Her head lay on her left shoulder, her fair hair falling back from her forehead. Daphne thought she looked very young and very, very sweet. No, she wouldn't disturb her.

The whistling had grown in volume, it seemed to fill the air in a pæan of triumph. She must collect more sticks. . . . The darkness would be unbearable. She got up and walked out of the circle away from the sandy patch and the friendly embers into the sombre mystery of the island.

The night closed round her. . . . She was alone, quite alone. But that was ridiculous. After all, Jean was there, and Anne.

She felt afraid: she would walk towards the huge monolith where Jean was watching. She remembered his face, reddened by the light of his fire. His determined expression . . . the set look, akin to martyrdom, in his eyes; he knew the danger they were threatened by . . . he could only wait.

It was difficult walking. There was no moon; and the tough sea-grass tore at her legs. Where was Jean? There! She caught the glow of the ashes of his fire. She stumbled towards it. But where *was* Jean? She stood on a small hillock peering into the darkness.

'Jean! Jean!' Her voice sounded strangled and strange.

She moved towards the fire; and as she drew nearer she noticed something glistening in the dim light, glistening with a pale phosphorescence. She bent down, the better to discover what it could be. She started back with an exclamation of disgust. The side of the fire where Jean had been sitting was a pool of slime – reeking and foul; the thought came to her that a giant slug might have made that mark – a giant sea-slug. And then real fear gripped her. She was rooted to the spot; stricken with the paralysis of fear. She gazed at the filthy trail at her feet.

'Daphne!' It was Anne's voice – and terror was in it – incredible terror.

'Daphne! . . . Jean! . . . Daphne! Help! Help! Oh, my God!'

The cries suddenly ceased, and a silence, more significant than any clamour, froze her heart.

With an effort she staggered towards their camp, her lips gasping, 'I'm coming . . . I'm coming.'

She tottered to the top of the rise below which was their sleeping place.

'Anne!' Her scream rose shrilly in the air. 'What is it? I'm coming, Anne.'

She ran to their camp. Where Anne had lain was a second pool of slime – the same odour of putrefaction . . . and the same trail that led – towards the sea.

Now, if ever courage was needed, she must have it. Such horrors could not be allowed to happen – and she was alone. Anne was gone; and so was Jean. *Something* had taken them. She gazed in horror at the slimy track; remembered the story of the artist who had disappeared. Jean had said, 'No one rightly knows what happened to him.'

She stumbled on trying to follow the trail of the Thing that had taken Anne. It was difficult to see by the starlight. Occasionally a smear of slime shone on some exposed rock. And always the way led to the sea. Several times she fell, her hands were torn and bleeding, her legs cut by the rocks and the sharp blade-like grass.

'Anne! Anne!'

But the only answer was the faint beating of the waves on the shore. Everything seemed uncannily quiet. Daphne sobbed aloud in her fear.

She realised that the whistling had stopped.

Mrs Arraway sat in the stern of the boat, her eyes fixed on

the island they were approaching. Tobit, in the mellow sun of the late afternoon, presented an appearance of impressive beauty. The jagged outline of her coasts bravely challenged the surrounding waters; the blood-red seaweed gently rose and fell on the waves.

Mrs Arraway's face was grim, and her eyes were anxious. In the boat were four islanders – sturdy fishermen with muscles of steel, and they rowed in silence. The boat grounded. Mrs Arraway was the first to reach the shore. She ran to the higher ground.

'Jean! Jean! Miss Daphne! Jean!'

And the caves echoed, 'Jean! Jean!' And the sea chuckled as it churned in the channels between the rocks.

Behind her the fishermen padded, heavy-footed, scrambling up the rocks.

'There's one of 'em!' Jim Tregarth shouted.

Mrs Arraway turned quickly. On the shore below her Daphne sat by a deep pool, her hands full of the red seaweed. She appeared to be unaware of the presence of the fishermen.

Mrs Arraway ran towards her. She bent down and shook her by the shoulder. Daphne looked up, and there was a great wisdom and understanding in her eyes.

'Jean . . . where's Jean?'

'Jean?' Daphne shook her head. 'Jean?'

'And Miss Anne? Tell me, what's happened? Where are they?'

'You'd like to know, wouldn't you? I can see you would. But you won't. . . . You won't. Because nobody knows rightly what happened to them.' She laughed to herself. She possessed a great secret, and one that nobody must share. She gave the woman a cunning look; and stroked the seaweed that she held between her fingers. 'No,' she continued, 'nobody will rightly know what happened to them. This time it claimed two. This time. Tobit has taken two!'

For a long time she would not consent to leave the island.

And if you care to go and see her in the square yellow brick building where she was sent, she will beckon you over to her, and drawing your head down to hers will begin to confide her secret to you. But she will never finish it, for she is afraid that if she does the Thing on Tobit will know that she has told – and Tobit belongs to the sea.

Forrest Reid

FURNISHED APARTMENTS

FORREST REID (1875-1947) *is still regarded by most critics as the finest writer ever to emerge from the North of Ireland. Though popular success eluded him during his lifetime (and after), his novels were almost universally praised by contemporary critics, and* Young Tom (1944), *perhaps his greatest achievement, was awarded the James Tait Black Memorial Prize for best novel of the year, the equivalent of today's Booker Prize. Though Reid is widely recognized as a great writer, he is not often discussed as a practitioner of supernatural fiction, an odd omission, given that the supernatural runs through almost all his work, from* The Spring Song (1916), *in which a ghostly tune seems to be luring a boy to the world of the dead, to* Uncle Stephen (1931), *in which a young lad has a spectral playmate, to* Denis Bracknel (1947), *the story of an unworldly boy who practices strange occult rituals by moonlight. Reid's literary idol was Henry James, and like that master, he was concerned not only with telling a story, but telling it perfectly, in pellucid prose and always employing 'le mot juste'. This attention to detail is evident in the typescript of 'Furnished Apartments' – found among his papers at Queen's University Belfast and never before published – which is filled with Reid's handwritten emendations. This wonderfully atmospheric tale is an exciting discovery that provides a new opportunity to reevaluate the works of Reid, an exceptionally talented writer with a lifelong interest in the supernatural who still awaits the popular recognition he is due.*

'WELL – HAVE YOU MOVED IN YET?' Bingham asked, staring at me through floating clouds of tobacco smoke, in the midst of which his plump pale face, with its thick-lensed spectacles perched on an absurdly babyish nose, appeared like a full moon. Or the dial of a kitchen clock; it had more the expression of that – something plain, honest, homely, but certainly neither brilliant nor romantic. Yet Bingham, in a sense, *was* romantic: I also found him subtle and ironic; and the artlessness of his freckled countenance added a piquancy, an element of unexpectedness, to the more daring flights of his conversation. Spiritually he was alert, restless, adventurous: and corporeally he was sluggish, a consumer of patent medicines, a creature of habit. That is why I had known exactly where I should find him, and exactly how he would be occupied, on this damp muggy evening, which, but for its temperature, might have been an evening in November. It was not November; it was July; but times and seasons meant little to Bingham, their passing did not affect him – except that towards the end of May he ceased to wear socks, and resumed these again in October. A hygienic measure, I imagine, extremely uncomfortable and of doubtful efficacy, like so many of his other prophylactic experiments. There had been a period when he had lived entirely upon half-raw chops; there had been a period when he had taken iron till his hair had turned a weird rusty colour; there had been a period when he had swallowed sulphur in such frequent doses that it had begun to ooze out through the pores of his skin, and had actually tarnished the keys in his pocket. Before I had time to sit down he had pushed an electric bell behind him, and before the barman had time to answer it he had pushed it again.

That also was habit, an eccentricity, Bingham invariably was in a hurry for his drinks; though once the stuff was there he would sit for long enough with the tumbler untasted before him, lost in what appeared to be an aesthetic appreciation of its rich and cream-topped darkness. I had seen him so often in this particular attitude that in his absence I found it difficult to picture him in any other, or in any other surroundings than those of a public-house. Elsewhere, he presented a timid, vaguely lost appearance; but in a 'pub' he was at home, like a snail in his shell – from which he could peep out at a variegated, complex world, and weave his impressions into boldly speculative designs. He had a theory on the subject; he once told me he could think better in a public-house than anywhere else; and he certainly talked better, though not just any kind of 'pub' would do. There were 'pubs' and 'bars', and for those latter gilded and brightly illuminated establishments, where the sexes are mixed, Bingham had no use at all. *His* public-house was not of the kind to which opulent customers brought vivacious lady friends; it was of a strictly democratic order, a blend of the homely and the decently, comfortably gross. He liked the murky atmosphere, the smoke-darkened ceiling and woodwork, the rough uneducated voices, the complete absence of everything genteel. He called such places 'taverns', and maintained that they gave him much the same pleasure as a picture by Rembrandt – the later Rembrandt – the interesting Rembrandt – for of course the only beauty that was really interesting was the beauty created out of ugliness. That was another theory – they were numerous as mites in cheese – theories of art, of religion, of philosophy, of life; and the only place where one could do them justice, expound them at one's ease, was a 'pub'. . . .

When the barman had served us, and swabbed the small square table with a damp cloth; when he had been paid and had retired, leaving us in our comparatively secluded corner, Bingham repeated his question.

This time I answered it. 'I haven't moved,' I said. 'And I don't know that I ever shall. At least, not to the place you mean.'

'But why? Last week you were full of it. You even described it as ideal. Ideal and cheap. I happen to remember the combination because it struck me at the time as ominous.'

'It *is* cheap,' I answered, ignoring his ironical tone. 'On the other hand, it has several disadvantages.'

'What's the matter with it?' Bingham persisted. 'I mean, what is your real reason – apart from the several disadvantages?'

'I see. . . . Well, if you want to know, I went there last night – late – just to take a few measurements for bookshelves, and – I didn't like it.'

Bingham looked at me searchingly, but he only said, 'Nothing more than that? Nothing definite?'

'No,' I answered. 'The place struck me as depressing – that is all.'

He sighed faintly – perhaps at my inability, or reluctance, to pursue a subject which lent it itself so invitingly to the kind of imaginative speculation he loved.

'You don't think there's much in such impressions?' I suggested. 'You think they're entirely fanciful?'

Bingham, I was sure, thought nothing of the sort; but he did not reply at once, and during the ensuing pause we both sat listening to the melancholy notes of a flute, which drifted in from the street. I guessed that he was on the brink of a theory, or perhaps a story bearing on the matter, and I was quite content to wait in silence. Nor was I surprised when presently, leaning across the table, he made this oracular statement: 'Houses are like sponges. They absorb.'

'Absorb what?' I asked, and saw him cast a quick glance over his shoulder at a group of revellers perched on three-legged stools close by the counter. At the same time, and I suppose suggested by his words, there floated into my mind the memory of a room in a house I had known in childhood – a room which had been kept locked up for years simply because somebody had died of cancer in it – a room I myself one afternoon had peeped into, half expecting I know not what secret and ghastly spectacle.

Bingham's judiciously lowered voice brought me back to the present. 'That depends,' he was saying, 'depends on who lives in them. But they absorb: they're absorbing all the time; night and day. And when they're saturated they begin to give out.'

'Still,' I objected – for now that he appeared to have condoned it, I began to regard my behaviour as weak – 'to sacrifice what was in many ways a suitable flat – and you know how hard it is to find one –'

He did not give me time to finish. 'It can't have been suitable if it affected you in that way. And if you had moved in it would have got worse. That sort of thing spreads and deepens – like a damp spot on a wall. I mean, when it once gets at you it doesn't stop there. The barrier, or whatever it is, breaks down: your mind comes into tune: in the end you begin both to see and to hear.' He paused, and gazing down at the table, began to draw circles and triangles of stout on its damp surface with his forefinger. Then, abruptly, and in a voice surprisingly morose, he said: 'Did you ever hear of the Wace affair?'

I shook my head: the name was unfamiliar.

'It got into the papers,' Bingham muttered, 'for all that. . . . And it would have been a good deal more in them if it had happened nowadays. Fortunately there were then no Sunday papers specializing in such things.'

'You mean it was unpleasant,' I said, and he replied, 'Yes, very unpleasant. . . . damned unpleasant to be mixed up with.'

I gazed at him: there was no mistaking this particular note: Bingham had been mixed up with it. What was more, unless I was greatly mistaken he was going to tell me how and why – a most unusual proceeding on his part, for he rarely indulged in autobiography. And it suddenly occurred to me that beyond his ideas and fads I really knew remarkably little about him, except that he wrote musical criticisms for a newspaper I seldom read, and that his journalism appeared to provide him with sufficient means to satisfy his wants, which were few, since he was a bachelor, middle-aged, and prudent.

'I never told you, did I,' he went on, 'of how I first came to London – many years ago – when I was a boy – and a boy, I may add, who had lived all his life in a small country town.'

'You've never told me anything,' I replied. 'Anything about yourself, I mean. You're the least communicative person I know.'

He looked surprised, but did not dispute the statement. 'That's odd,' he said. 'It hadn't occurred to me I didn't talk.'

I laughed. 'Oh, you talk,' I assured him. 'You talk more than most people; only not in that way.'

Again he pondered my words. 'It isn't because I wish to be secretive,' he explained. 'It's because I didn't think you'd be interested. My childhood and boyhood *weren't* interesting, you know. For one thing, I never properly woke up till I was seventeen. I had no definite tastes, except a love of music. When I was asked what I wanted to be, what I wanted to do, I couldn't tell. I didn't want to do anything – or so it must have seemed. I was torpid. At the same time I was extremely docile, and there wasn't really very much choice. Anyhow, when my father decided to put me into a bank I accepted his decision.'

Bingham paused, and seemed to be staring at what might have been the wooden partition behind my head, but what was, I felt sure, something much less palpable. Then, as if dismissing an irrelevant vision or reflection, he resumed his story.

'The bank was in London. My father himself was a country parson; and I had several brothers and sisters, all of whom had to be educated and given some sort of start in life. My start happened to be a bad one. . . . Perhaps I ought not to blame my father, for if he was unimaginative and fatally slack, I, on my side, was stupidly submissive. Chance, of course, entered into it too; because originally both my parents had intended to come up to London with me to look for lodgings, and had they done so all would have been well. Unluckily, when train-time came my mother was prostrate with an attack of neuralgia, so my father and I set out alone.

'We had selected Westminster for our hunting ground – I suppose that I might be near the office where I was going to work – and it was in a quiet, dingy street, within a few minutes walk of the Abbey, that eventually we found what we wanted. Or rather what *he* wanted; or rather what he thought would do. Number 10 Anselm Terrace – that was the address; and the locality, I dare say, had once been highly respectable. Indeed, it was its obviously reduced respectability which in the first place discouraged me. The house was half way down a side street leading to the entrance of a mews. A narrow, commonplace, brick house, with a tall flight of steps mounting up to the hall-door, and rusty iron railings facing an underground basement. The basement suggested cockroaches; the steps were dirty; the paint and plaster blistered and begrimed; the very card in the window, which had attracted my father's attention, looked to me as if it had been there for years. Certainly, it was a quiet neighbourhood (the only living thing I saw was a cat crossing the entrance to the mews), but the quiet did not appeal to me; I should have preferred cheerfulness.

'We knocked twice (the bell was broken), and I had begun to hope the house was empty, when we heard footsteps in the hall. The door was opened by a small and unexpectedly pretty servant in a neat cap and apron. She was quite young, almost childish, and she looked timidly at my father when he asked to see the rooms, keeping her hand on the door, as if ready to shut it at any moment in our faces. It was perfectly clear to me that we were not wanted, and equally clear that she did not know how to tell us this. 'I don't think there are any rooms, sir,' she said at last.

' "But you've a card in the window!" my father exclaimed. "Why is it there if the rooms are taken?"

' "A card?"

' "Yes, yes; a card." My father, though incorrigibly dilatory himself, was never very patient with others. "A card with 'Apartments' printed on it – 'Furnished Apartments'."

' "I expect she forgot," faltered the small maid – and the door began to close.

' "You mean the rooms *have* been taken," my father persisted.

'But to this there was no reply, and as she faced us, in the now narrowed slit of doorway, she reminded me of a kitten I had once seen holding the road against two bullying dogs. My father's persistence annoyed me, and I made a sign to him to come away, while she still gazed at him – never once at me – and only his clerical dress, I fancy, kept her from straying into the path of fibs. Her lips, indeed, moved soundlessly as if rehearsing a few, and then: "No, sir; there's nobody taken rooms," she whispered – "not since I was here. . . . But I don't think the card should be there. . . . He must have – "

' "Come away," I muttered, and my father might have done so had we not heard from invisible back regions the sound of an opening door, followed by the call of an abnormally high-pitched masculine voice.

' "What is it, Maggie? Who is there?" At the same moment a shuffle of loosely-slippered feet approached, and the hall-door was suddenly pulled wide, revealing a man.

'He was distinctly not a gentleman; neither did he seem

to me to belong to the working class – something half way between. Moreover, he looked ill; he had the unhealthy complexion of a chronic invalid; though the illness, I now imagine, was more mental than physical. He was dressed in a loose, badly-fitting, rather flashy suit; he had a thin, greyish beard, and dark bright eyes. Altogether, there was something gimcrack about him, meretricious, shoddy, cheap.

'"I called to see about lodgings for my son," my father began, "but I'm told you have none to let."

'"Who told you that? What are you thinking of, Maggie? Of course there are rooms. Come in – come in. Why, nobody lives in the house but my wife and myself and Maggie here, and it's a big house, though it doesn't look so from the street. . . . I don't know how many rooms your son may require," he went on, with a quick glance at me, "but I dare say we can give him half a dozen." This last remark I supposed was a joke, since it was followed by a shrill soprano cackle. "My name is Wace," he continued jauntily. "Mrs Wace has gone out, but I can show you the rooms." He waved towards the staircase, and that thin yellowish hand strengthened the feeling of aversion he had already inspired in me. At the same time I was puzzled by the manner of the small servant. She evidently wished to tell her master something, and equally evidently he was determined not to listen. At last she faltered, "Please, sir, there was a gentleman called the other day and the mistress told him she didn't take lodgers."

'Mr Wace tapped her good-naturedly on the cheek with one finger. "Nonsense, Maggie, nonsense. You must have misunderstood her. I expect she didn't like the look of that particular gentleman," he added significantly to us. "Naturally, she doesn't want people who may turn out to be undesirable."

'"Naturally – naturally," my father agreed, and I could see that Mrs Wace's exclusiveness was greatly in her favour. She was just the landlady for me; obviously particular; one who would look after me, take care that I formed no dangerous acquaintances.

'The small servant, having done her duty, said no more;

she retired, while the rest of us, the three of us, in single file, mounted the stairs to inspect the rooms.

'At the head of the first flight was a landing roofed by a semi-opaque glass dome, and from this landing there stretched back a long passage, off which several rooms opened, one behind the other, their doors, which had triangular fan-lights above them, facing a blank wall. "Queer, the way they built these old houses," Mr Wace rattled on. "You'd have no idea, from the street, that they ran back so far. I don't call them well-planned myself; because, as you can see, the only light in this passage comes from the dome in the landing. . . . Not at all our modern idea of comfort. Too much work for servants – basements and all that. . . . That's why most of them are empty and have been allowed to get out of repair. *We* don't use the basement; we keep it locked up; and speaking personally I'd sell the house for what it would fetch and move into a smaller one, or into rooms, only Mrs Wace is so attached to it. It's hers; it belongs to Mrs Wace; she's lived in it all her life, and her father lived in it all *his* life." He had reached the door of the end room as he produced this information, but he still kept us standing outside it in the dim grey light while he proceeded volubly: "Mrs Wace's father was a well-known scientist. Might have made pots of money, but instead devoted himself to unremunerative research – experiments – experiments with animals – down in the base-ment. Edwards was his name – Dr Edwards – you may possibly have heard of him. If you have, you can take it from me that all those ridiculous stories circulated at the time were the inven-tions of cranks and busybodies. They were lies, my dear sir, lies – malicious distortions of the truth – when they had any truth in them at all, which was seldom. Dr Edwards was a charming man. A trifle unconventional, I don't dispute, but incapable of hurting a fly. That is, of course, except in the interests of sci-ence. I'm not denying that he went in for vivisection; but I'd like to ask some of those people who talked so freely – and wrote – actually in the end they wrote – to the papers: – I'd like to ask them just where they think surgical science would be to-day if it weren't for such experiments!"

' "Quite quite," my father murmured, to show that the church at least recognized the legitimacy of Dr Edwards' efforts in the cause of an afflicted humanity.

'Mr Wace, by a bow, accepted the acknowledgement. At the same time he flung the door open with a flourish. "How will this do?" he asked, stepping politely to one side that we might enter first.

'My father turned to me, smiling. "You'll certainly not be cramped for space, Henry."

'And it was, I don't mind admitting, a finely proportioned room – far larger and far loftier than any bedroom in the rectory at home: yet, though I tried to smile in response, I didn't like it. From the first moment of entering that house I had felt a spiritual distress. Not all the geniality of Mr Wace (whom I suspected to be cracked), supported by that of my father, could blind me. I knew there was something wrong. Cheap – cheap and ideal – like that flat of yours – a combination to be avoided like the devil.'

'I *have* avoided it, Bingham,' I reminded him.

'Yes, but my father didn't: he took the apartments – furnished – and furnished most strikingly – for the furniture had character! The bed was a huge wooden four-poster hung with a fringed and crimson canopy – a feather bed, with two wooden steps to help you to climb into it. The bell-pulls – those old-fashioned rope things – were crimson also, and so were the curtains. The whole room, in my first rapid view of it, seemed to me to be flooded with the same sinister colour. Then this impression faded, leaving everything threadbare and drab, like the spiders' webs in the corners under the ceiling. There were no blinds, the carpet was in holes, and there was a large chip out of the water jug; but the permanent stuff, the big mahogany wardrobe, the oval-mirrored dressing-table, the chest of drawers – those were solid as the house itself. And it was the same in my sitting-room – really the dining-room – when we went down to it; all the larger furniture was sombre, massive and old, built to defy the attacks of time; but there were rents in the chairs, through which the stuffing was visible; the screen in front of the grate was broken; the gas globes were dusty; the windows uncleaned; and the paper in one corner had begun to peel from the wall. My father thought I should be "very snug here".'

Bingham laughed rather sourly, 'You don't see the joke, perhaps; but then you didn't see the rooms. Even if they had been spick and span it would have been difficult to find them snug. But my father was like that, not so much optimistic as incurably easy-going and indolent. He gave me another surprise on the way to the station, when he remarked that Mrs Wace appeared to be a motherly kind of person. It may sound incredible; nonetheless, he really used those words; and I, in my turn, could not help asking upon what he based this opinion. "We haven't seen her," I pointed out, "and what we heard was chiefly about her father. It was in the basement, wasn't it, that he tortured the animals?"

'I mention this little outburst just to show, that though tiresomely submissive, I wasn't absolutely a fool. I could picture, you see, all the cheerful colours in which Number 10 Anselm Terrace would be painted for my mother, and this exasperated me – none the less, because my deepest misgivings were incommunicable. In the meantime we walked up and down the platform, having arrived at the station much too soon.

'When the train was gone I collected my traps and drove in a hansom back to Anselm Terrace. It was already dusk. I knocked – without result. I knocked twice more, and still nobody came. There was the noise of an upper window being opened in one of the houses opposite, but Number 10 remained silent as the tomb. The situation was becoming ridiculous, and if my cab still had been there I believe I should have put my portmanteau back into it and gone in search of a lodging on my own account. As it was, for several minutes I must have waited before I heard a soft yet heavy tread on the other side of the door. There was even a further delay, as if I were being inspected through the keyhole; then the door was slowly drawn back, and in the aperture a rather portentous figure loomed.

'At least, she looked to me portentous, though it was only

the "motherly" Mrs Wace, and I confess I gazed at her with a sinking of the heart. For she was not prepossessing, though, as with the house itself, I couldn't have told you what I felt to be wrong. She uttered not a word of apology for having kept me; she remained absolutely still – a dark, massive figure, black against the thickening dusk behind her – black from head to foot, except for the white face, with its many chins and expressionless boot-button eyes.

'I don't suppose I can describe Mrs Wace dispassionately, but I can describe the impression she produced on me. She had not the distressingly common appearance of her husband; she probably was by birth a lady; but she was grotesque, extravagant, abnormal. For one thing, she seemed to me enormous; even her hands, her feet, might have been a man's, and a big man's. On her feet she wore felt slippers; on her wrists were black lace mittens; round her neck was a chain of jet beads, from which depended an oval locket of the kind that opens to reveal a portrait, or somebody's hair twisted into a neat little plait. A memorial locket – a locket enshrining some memento of the dead. I am sure I stared at her, and I know she stared at me, or rather examined me, deliberately, appraisingly, from the crown of my head down to my feet, and then slowly up again. "You are Mr Bingham, I suppose," she said at last, speaking in a husky voice that appeared to have travelled a long distance before it actually issued from her lips. And I answered with a meekness from which no one could have guessed the indignation I had felt while waiting on the doorstep. For that matter, Mrs Wace still appeared to be in no hurry to admit me. "There seems to have been some mistake," she remarked, renewing her embarrassing inspection of my person. "There were no rooms to let." She paused for quite a long time, during which I stood there tongue-tied, like an awkward schoolboy – and indeed I was no more. "Mr Wace must have put that card back into the window. It isn't the first time he has done so, though when I speak to him about it he promises not to do it again. But he forgets. However, now you *are* here, I suppose you must stay. Can you carry your bag upstairs? Maggie is out; she has gone a message."

'I followed her into the hall, mumbling an apology. I didn't want to stay, and if only she had not kept on looking at me I might have bolted even then. On the other hand, beneath the light of the hall lamp Mrs Wace's attitude underwent an abrupt change. "Why, you're only a boy!" she exclaimed. "I doubt if you're as old as Maggie. Young people always interest me, and I'm afraid I spoil them." She smiled, and I had a sudden feeling that it would be better not to be spoiled by Mrs Wace. "Mr Wace," she continued, "let you the rooms, Maggie says. I think I'd better tell you at once that Mr Wace has never quite recovered from a bad nervous breakdown. He has little lapses now and then, in which he gets strange notions and does odd things. I only mention it to clear up the misunderstanding."

'I made no comment on this pleasant addition to my knowledge of the household, nor am I sure that it *was* an addition. Slowly, and despite her weight noiselessly, Mrs Wace preceded me upstairs to the bedroom I had already visited. "You'll want some tea," she murmured, as if it had just struck her. "Maggie will get it for you when she comes in. I can't give you dinner: if you want dinner you will have to go out for it."

'I assured her that tea would do me very well, and that I was accustomed to dine in the middle of the day. I hoped she would now go, and leave me to unpack alone, but she stood at the foot of the bed, watching me with an interest that I suppose my father would have described as "motherly". "We must give you a latchkey," she said, while a smile spread across her white face. "Then you can come and go just as you wish." Her tongue flickered for a moment between her parted teeth with a startling suggestion of active and separate life. "How old are you, Mr Bingham?"

' "Seventeen."

' "Seventeen!" She glanced at the label on my portmanteau. "Then I suppose I may call you by your christian name, which I see is Henry. . . . And you are going to be a banker, Mr Wace says!"

' "Yes," I answered shortly, for I did not relish the note of a rather heavy playfulness underlying her last words.

She fumbled with a matchbox, struck a match, and lit a second gas-burner, which cast its crude glare on her upturned and, as I now saw, distinctly ravaged countenance. "Shall I help you to unpack?" she suggested, and though I told her I could manage by myself, I might as well have held my peace. Not that she really did more than watch me, and occasionally lift up some garment and smooth it with a lingering caressing touch, as one might stroke an animal.

'There was nothing very alarming, you may think, in all this, yet my discomfort remained. I knew little about life, and not much about human nature, but subconsciously I received a warning; Mrs Wace made me uneasy. Even when my back was turned I could feel her gaze fixed upon me, and no matter how soundlessly she might move in those large felt slippers, I was sure I should always know when she was near. "You are very shy!" she murmured.

'I blushed still more. I was beginning to feel acutely unhappy; for beneath her half-bantering manner – which was in itself far too intimate – I became aware of something that, without fully understanding it, alarmed me – something I should now describe as a kind of veiled amorousness.

' "I hope you'll be happy with us, Henry," she pursued unctuously, "though I'm afraid you'll find us very commonplace, ordinary people, not at all interesting."

' "I don't think you're so very ordinary," I plucked up courage to retort, but I kept my head bent while I said it.

'A strange, low, not unmusical sound broke upon my ears, and looking up I perceived that Mrs Wace was laughing, and possibly for the first time quite unaffectedly. "He says that as if he meant it," she chuckled richly, and I felt a firm warm hand drawn slowly over my hair. "Now don't start away like that, as if I had done something dreadful! I believe you're half afraid of me. And there's Maggie – Maggie who would do anything for me! But it is always so: we're mere bundles of prejudices – sympathies and antipathies, equally irrational. And what a little can alter them – and alter *us*! A stumble on the stairs – a fall – no bones broken – nothing apparently beyond a slight concussion: yet the difference ever afterwards!" Her eyes were fixed on mine. "That happened to Mr Wace, Henry – the least imaginative, the least fanciful of men. . . . And now he believes in ghosts!"

'I did not answer, and as if at my embarrassed silence, once more she laughed. "Ghosts," she went on, in half-humorous deprecation – "poor harmless creatures! Why should we be afraid of them? Aren't we all of us, in a sense, trying to leave ghosts behind us? In other words, memories – memories to cheer and comfort those we love: and I'm sure at your age, Henry, whatever you may think of ghosts, you believe in love." She had lifted my Sunday jacket from the bed, and now held the dark cloth against her mouth, while she looked at me over the top of it, much as a sentimental vulture might regard some particularly appetizing lamb. "I, too, believe in love," she sighed, "so it turns out that in this at least we are very much alike."

'Here, though more from nervousness than amusement, I suddenly laughed myself, which perhaps pleased her, for she went on: "You must humour Mr Wace; make allowances for him: he suffers from fits of depression which come on quite suddenly, for no reason at all, and are, the doctors have warned us, the great, the real danger."

' "Does he think the house is haunted?" I asked.

'Mrs Wace put a finger to her lips and leaned her head sidelong, so that she seemed both to be enjoining silence and to be listening, though I heard nothing. "Haunted!" she at last breathed. "Well, I sometimes ask myself, could one be so deeply attached to it if it weren't? But haunted only by thoughts, memories, and things that happened long ago. All my life, Henry, has been lived in this house."

' "What were you listening to just now?" I questioned, plucking up a bolder spirit in sheer defiance.

'Mrs Wace, I think, noticed this, for she laid a big white hand confidently on my shoulder. "Was I listening?" she rallied me. "Thoughts and memories are soundless." And on that she turned slowly round, like an unwieldy sailing-ship, and left me.

'I continued to put away my things, and by the time I had

finished the unblinded windows were filled with night. On opening my door I was both surprised and annoyed to find the passage outside as black as pitch. I struck a match, and by its feeble glimmer made my way to the landing, and from there on down to the lighted hall. In my sitting-room, too, the gas had been lit and the table laid, so, after ringing the bell, I sat down in a rather more reconciled state of mind. Very soon the small servant came in with a rack of toast, which she placed on the table, and then retired. A further ten minutes elapsed without her reappearance. What could she be doing? I wondered, and how long did it take them to make a pot of tea? My impatience rapidly became indignation. If I was neglected in this barefaced fashion on the very evening of my arrival, what would it be like later? and I made up my mind that I would leave next day even if it meant going to an hotel. In the meantime I was determined to assert myself, and gave the bell a second and more violent tug.

'All I heard was the rattle of a loose wire and the falling of some plaster; but in remote regions I must have succeeded in arousing a din, for after a minute or two Maggie returned, bearing a tray on which were a tea-pot and other essentials to a not very elaborate meal. As she set the things on the table I watched her with a dawning suspicion. There was something very strange about her. Her movements were somnambulistic, her eyes vacant, and the little smile on her lips was as fixed and meaningless as if it had been painted there. Placidly, deliberately, she arranged the tea-things, after which she laid a key upon the tablecloth. "This is the latchkey," she said, in a soft indifferent voice, and without looking at me. "She told me to ask you, if you do go out, would you please lock and bolt the door and turn out the gas when you come back."

' "Very well; and I want to be called in the morning at eight o'clock, please."

' "Yes, sir."

' "I'll have breakfast at half-past eight sharp, remember."

' "Yes, sir."

' "That's all." I added the last words because she had made

no movement to go, but seemed prepared to stand there in the same trance-like attitude for the rest of the evening. With a faint sigh, she turned and walked slowly from the room.

'While I munched my cold toast I puzzled over the alteration that had taken place in her since our first meeting. I could not understand it; nevertheless I should have been prepared to swear that her condition now was not normal. Nor was Mrs Wace's, if it came to that. But I could hit on no explanation that would fit the case, though a vague thought of drugs did occur to me. . . .

'When I had finished tea, I put on my hat and went out. I had no destination in view, but I didn't intend to sit all evening in that dreary room. For November the weather must have been unusually mild; I distinctly remember that I didn't wear an overcoat. I sauntered up one street and down another, till presently I reached Westminster Bridge and began to stroll along the Embankment. When I grew tired of this, I turned up a street on my left, leading to the Strand. It was all so new to me that doubtless I should have enjoyed myself had I not been haunted by the thought of my return to those dismal lodgings. This cast its lugubrious shadow over everything, and the shadow deepened – deepened perceptibly – when at last I decided that I must go back.

'It was a reluctant decision. Still, I could not walk the streets all night. In the morning I would send a telegram to my mother and word it so that it would bring her to town immediately. For I couldn't do much without her: to-morrow would be my first day at the bank, and I should have very little time. To reassure myself I argued that it was because the place was so uncomfortable that I was in such a hurry to leave it, and so loath to go back to it now. After all, though I disliked my landlady, what had I against her? She had, in her own fashion, been very friendly. True, her manner and conversation were eccentric – but what *else* was there? Then I thought I had better have this out with myself once for all, and actually came to a halt under a lamp to do so.

'No, there was nothing else – absolutely nothing. The

house was cheerless, shabby, and, I suspected, not too clean; its inmates were peculiar; the service was deplorable; and that was all. . . . "A motherly sort of person!" . . . The abysmal ineptitude of my father's remark still exasperated me. Nevertheless, I was determined to behave like a rational being, and walked on determinedly and quickly, disregarding an alarming simulacrum of Mrs Wace which suddenly took shape before me – the white, smiling face being followed by the complete form – voluminous, obese, draped from throat to heel in black, adorned with lace mittens and a mortuary locket. Yet all I knew about her was that she believed in love. . . . And Mr Wace believed in ghosts and suffered from fits of depression. If I had been near the station and the last train for home had not gone— But no: there was the bank in the morning.' Bingham leaned his elbows on the little table and stared with gloomy absorption at an advertisement of Somebody's Soda Water.

'You must think I was a very highly-strung youngster. I wasn't. I was never the kind of boy who is afraid of the dark, and at this period I was practically grown-up, distinctly stolid: there's a good deal of Scotch blood in me.'

'I should have guessed Irish,' I ventured.

'Irish? Why? Well, there may be; it doesn't matter; the point is that I returned to Anselm Terrace. I had to: I had to go to my work in the morning. Besides, there was something else which I haven't mentioned. I am naturally curious, and to tell the truth, at the back of everything, I had now a consuming curiosity to find out just what *was* the matter with Mrs Wace – with Mr Wace – with Maggie. . . .

'Late as it was, there were lights glimmering in several of the windows of Anselm Terrace when I reached it, and there was a street lamp immediately opposite Number 10. I climbed the five steps and opened the door with my latchkey. The gas in the hall had been turned down to a mere spark, but a candle and box of matches had been left on the side table, for which unexpected thoughtfulness I was grateful. On entering my room I lit the gas and sat down on the bed. It may have been that physical fatigue had blunted my sensibilities: at all events,

I felt more at ease. This didn't prevent me from making a careful tour of inspection. I examined the wardrobe and I peered under the bed: I would have locked the door, only there was no key. Finally, I undressed and turned out the gas. The softness of the feather mattress into which I sank was more strange to me than agreeable, but I had been on my feet more or less all day, and very soon I fell asleep. Nor were my last waking thoughts concerned with Mrs Wace. She had gone – I can't say how: I only know that a weight, an oppression, had been lifted from my mind, and that my last thoughts before dropping asleep were of the morning and of the bank.

'I had been sleeping for some hours, I suppose, before I began to dream. It was an uncomfortable dream, but not in the least terrifying, not a nightmare, and it began with an apparent waking. This was followed immediately by the discovery that I had lost the power to move my limbs or even utter a sound. Then, as one will in dreams, I remembered the thick festoons of cobwebs I had noticed under the corners of the ceiling, and guessed that two or three adventurous spiders must have spun their way down to me. I had no prejudice against spiders – even these – which I imagined to be much larger than usual. Their busyness and persistence, on the contrary, amused me, for it was as if they were trying to bind me down with a silken web. But all at once these childish fancies gave place to a sharp recoil from something else – indefinite, unknown, yet very near. Actually it reached me, I think, through my sense of smell – a sickly sweetness – and, still half dreaming, I opened my eyes. It was dark; it was night; yet darker than the darkness a motionless black form leaned over me. I struggled against the impotence that had glued me down to my bed: I struggled, and some kind of stifled sound must have issued from my throat, for I saw the stooping black shadow – like an incubus – lifting, receding, vanishing. . . .

'This time I awakened completely, yet a further moment or two elapsed before I realized that I was lying on my back, and that the bedclothes, which I had, as usual, carefully tucked in, must have come loose, for I was more or less uncovered. I must have done this in my dream, I told myself – unbelievingly, unhappily – for another feeling persisted. . . .

'I sat up, and it seemed to me that the sweet, slightly nauseating odour still lingered faintly on the air. Then I raised my eyes to the fanlight above my door and saw that it was not as it had been when I had gone to bed, but was now visible as a triangle of dim, wan light. The light must be coming from the passage; it could not be a reflection from outside, because the curtains were drawn across the windows, and the windows themselves did not overlook any street, but a walled yard with a narrow lane beyond it. The minutes passed, and I sat staring at this pallid light, till suddenly it was not there – there was nothing there but darkness.

'I did not lie down again, but neither did I strike a match. If I was afraid, at least it was not that kind of fear. What I felt was more spiritual dismay, following on the understanding, the half-understanding, of something not so much dangerous as shocking.

'The room was intensely quiet: no flapping curtain, no gnawing mouse, no rattling window-frame. I knew I was alone, yet I knew, also, that someone had been near, thinking, willing. . . . Blunderingly I groped for the matches and candlestick beside my bed. I touched them, I knocked them over, and at the same time the rickety little table itself overturned with a crash. That accident was fortunate. It dispersed something, diverted something; I was conscious of a relaxed tension so instantaneous and unqualified as to suggest the snapping of a spell. A drop of sweat fell on my hand, but I had escaped, and during the next few minutes the mere sense of relief excluded every other feeling. In this breathing-space, this perhaps only temporary truce, my mind and heart gathered courage. Sufficient at least to enable me to act, and I slipped noiselessly from the bed and, candle in hand, tip-toed across the room. With my ear at the keyhole I crouched, listening. Once I heard the creak of a board, but it was just such a sound as in an old house one can always hear at night, and it was not repeated. Cautiously I turned the handle and peeped out. The odour I had smelt in my dream lingered there, too, but the passage itself was empty.

'I returned to my room, closed the door, and lit the gas. I did not go back to bed, but dressed myself, and sat down with a book to wait for daylight. Of course I did not read; but gradually I grew more capable of cool and logical thought. I pulled my portmanteau from under the bed and packed it. I got my shoes, which I had left outside my door, and put them on. It was already daylight, or very nearly, when suddenly I heard sounds of commotion – a scream, a hurried flight of footsteps – succeeded by silence. I came out from my room; as far as the landing; and why I did not there and then leave the house I do not know; but that scream held me, though I made no attempt to discover the cause of it. Then I saw Maggie. She came running downstairs, she would have passed me had I not grabbed her by the arm. "What's the matter? What's wrong?" I found myself bawling these questions at the top of my voice, as if she were deaf, or half a mile away. A few moments ago I had been moving about with the utmost stealth; now, I don't know why, noise seemed essential. I held on to her; I even shook her when she tried to free herself from my grasp.

'Unexpectedly she burst into sobs, and throwing her arms round my neck, clung to me like a frightened child. She made the most extraordinary sounds, but it was several minutes before I could distinguish intelligible words. "Oh, sir! Something has happened! I must get a doctor. I must –"

' "What has happened?" I cried angrily, though still clasping her tightly, determined not to let her go. "Is anybody ill? Is it Mrs Wace?"

' "He's dead – lying in the bathroom. She found him. And she took me in there – she made me look. Let me go; let me go; before she comes."

'These words, wailed into my ears, brought me to my senses. I even stood for a few moments straining my ears, but there was not a sound from above. Nor did I now want to know what had happened or was happening. Nothing could have induced me to ascend that staircase. I asked no more questions, but we went down together, and out into the street in search of a doctor, though I myself felt it ought to have been a policeman. On our way, as it happened, we did meet a policeman, who looked at us rather strangely, pausing in his beat to do so. And this was my second day in London! An auspicious opening to my new career! It was now between seven and eight o'clock, and I was due at the bank at half-past nine. But luckily the doctor we eventually found was an elderly, kindly person, and when I had explained my position he offered to take charge of things, to give me breakfast at his house, and even to call round later in the day at the bank.'

Bingham paused, as if his story, or all he intended to tell me of it, were over; but presently he added, 'The police, too, were decent enough, though naturally they asked a great many questions. There was an inquest, of course, when a verdict of suicide was returned. But they didn't let it go at that, they weren't satisfied, there were things they wanted to know – things they seemed to think might possibly help to account for Mr Wace's determined escape to a happier world. I was cross-examined by a pertinacious, middle-aged inspector. Certain stories were being inquired into – suggestive if ambiguous stories – supplied by hitherto reserved but now loquacious neighbours. Boys of the lowest class – and girls also – had been seen at night entering or leaving the house. There was, I imagine, nothing more definite than that, but it gave the police a line they now followed up. Several of these visitors were traced, or came forward voluntarily in response to an advertisement (I don't know what methods are adopted in such cases), and their evidence left little room for doubt. What I could never explain – either then or later – was the attitude of Maggie. After that first momentary weakness when she had turned to me, she veered round completely to the side of her mistress. She did not deny that more than once certain persons had called at the house and been admitted by her (the instincts of Mrs Wace, it transpired, were philanthropic); but she denied tooth and nail that there was any truth in the tales they now told of what had taken place on these occasions. As for me, I held my tongue concerning my own experience. Naturally they had fastened at once on the circumstance of my having been up and dressed and apparently on the point of leaving the house at so early an hour; but my explanation that I had slept badly, and had thought a walk in the open air before breakfast might freshen me up, was accepted. After all, I had arrived only on the previous afternoon, so could not be expected to supply much information.'

'And what happened in the end?' I asked. 'It *was* suicide, I suppose?'

'Oh yes; no doubts, I believe, were ever thrown on that. After the inquest, indeed, it was regarded as a side-issue, bearing on the later investigation only because without it there would have been no investigation at all.'

'So it fizzled out?'

Bingham shook his head. 'Not exactly. Maggie got off – there was nothing against her except perhaps perjury, which was not pressed. Considering her age, she was regarded as a victim.' He hesitated. 'Mrs Wace really got off too – that is to say, after the police-court inquiry, and apart from the publicity, the unpleasant things that came out then, and the subsequent attitude of the neighbours.'

'What is your own opinion, Bingham?' I asked him bluntly. 'Do you think she was responsible?'

'If by that you mean normal, no. Otherwise, yes. But you haven't quite realized my point in telling you the story.'

'Which is?'

'That she was an active agent: Number 10 Anselm Terrace was filled with her. Mr Wace was right when he said the house was haunted; only it was she who haunted it – her mind, her spirit, those thoughts and memories she was so fond of. . . . I don't say there had been no other influences at work – that of her father, for instance, the eminent Dr Edwards, who conducted his experiments down in the basement. Doubtless she had been an intelligent and inquiring child – '

There was a crash. Bingham had upset his tumbler and it lay in fragments on the ground. A very large, obese woman, dressed in rusty black, had just entered through the swing-door.

At the noise, she turned a flushed, fuddled, good-natured face in our direction – a face nobody could have found alarming. One of the barmen had already come forward to tell her that they did not serve ladies.

Bingham apologized for his clumsiness, gave me a deprecating, rather shame-faced glance, and began to wipe the spilled stout from his clothes. Then he smiled sheepishly as we got up to go out.

Hugh Fleetwood

SOMETHING HAPPENED

Born in England in 1944, HUGH FLEETWOOD *is a writer and artist whom a critic for the London* Sunday Times *has dubbed 'the master of modern horror'. His second novel,* The Girl Who Passed for Normal, *won the John Llewellyn Rhys Prize, and his fifth,* The Order of Death, *was adapted for a film starring Harvey Keitel and John Lydon (Johnny Rotten of the Sex Pistols). More recently, in 2012 Fleetwood was cited by critic David Malcolm as a key figure in the development of the English short story. Fleetwood's third novel,* Foreign Affairs (1974), *a thriller about a famous concert pianist stalked by a deranged, crippled boy, is available from Valancourt, and we are very pleased to be able to present here the weird and haunting 'Something Happened', which is original to this collection.*

S OMETHING HAPPENED. Admittedly not very much: a visitor was announced. A friend of Boss's was to come and stay for a few days. But, Anya, Alexej and Gabriel agreed, one must be thankful for small mercies. It was four years now since anything had happened. Then, Marek had been polishing Boss's car, and had forgotten to put it back in the garage. There had been a freak hail-storm, with stones the size of ping-pong balls. The car had been badly dented, and Marek had been in disgrace. If Boss returned and saw the car, he would be furious; Marek might even lose his job. Of course Marek was slightly simple, and it was possible they could appeal to Boss's better nature. Even so – an expensive car like that! Stupid Marek! Careless Marek! We *all* might lose our jobs because of you. For ages Anya and Gabriel couldn't bring themselves to talk to Alexej's tall, gangling brother, to whom Alexej himself hadn't spoken for years.

Long before the incident of the car Alexej had considered

his brother a liability in his life – as before him their parents had considered Marek a liability in their lives – and had wanted as little as possible to do with him. Alas, after he had been working for Boss for two years, he was one day asked about his family, and had confessed that he had an elder brother. Being at times good-hearted, Boss had said, 'Wouldn't he like to come and work for me, too?'

'Oh no, thank you Boss,' Alexej had said. 'He's a bit – you know, soft in the head, my brother.'

'All the more reason,' Boss had said. 'Bring him over to England, Alexej. Tell him I want to meet him. I'll pay his fare. And if it doesn't work out – I'll pay his fare back again.'

Alexej had been furious. But one never argued with Boss. So over Marek had come, sure enough Boss had taken him on, and six years later, when Marek had left the car out of the garage, both brothers were still working for him – albeit in Switzerland now, in a house by a lake.

'He's a ball and chain round my ankle,' Alexej had complained to Anya and Gabriel. 'He's a curse. A stain.'

'Oh come now,' Anya had said. 'He means well.'

'Means is not enough,' Alexej had grunted, and vowed to himself that if he had not addressed a word to Marek since they had arrived in Switzerland, he would not address another to him until they left.

Six months after the freak hail-storm, Anya and Gabriel – who were husband and wife – had taken pity on Marek and started talking to him again. After all, Boss hadn't turned up in the meantime, and they supposed that when eventually he did come they could say that they had been taking the car out for its monthly run when they had been caught in the storm. And so long as Boss wasn't in one of his bad moods, he would probably shrug it off, and say, 'I'll get in touch with the insurance people.'

But Alexej had never relented. If he passed his brother in the corridor, he pretended he wasn't there. At table, he never included him in the conversation, or offered him a second helping. And when Marek returned from his three week annual holiday, he never asked him where he had been or if he

had enjoyed himself. He knew Marek hadn't enjoyed himself;
Marek never enjoyed himself, and only took an annual holiday
because Boss insisted that he take one. But he was damned if
he was going to get Marek to tell him that – as he would, had he
insisted – and simply raised his eyebrows when Anya or Gabriel
asked these questions, and Marek replied, 'Yes, thank you. I
enjoyed myself very much. I went home.'

Home, indeed! As if such a place existed for Marek. Or had
existed since he was seventeen, when his parents had thrown
him out of the house, telling him he was a lazy good-for-nothing.

Marek had looked at them as if he agreed, had packed a
small bag, and had disappeared. Not to be seen again by his
mother and father in their lifetime. And only to be seen by
his brother because when Alexej had been young he had been
kind. As Marek was loping away from the farm-labourer's cottage in which he had been born and raised, his twelve-year-old
brother had followed him and whispered, 'Please keep in touch
with me, Marek. Write to me. Look after yourself. I love you.'

Thereafter the brothers had met once or twice a year, much
to their parents' disapproval. Until, after Alexej had married and
his wife had said *she* didn't want a weirdo like that in their house
and didn't understand why Alexej bothered with him, Alexej
had started to make excuses when Marek phoned him or wrote
a note suggesting they meet; and would probably have never
seen his brother again had he not told the truth that day, when
Boss asked him if he had any siblings. Of course one never lied
to Boss; his wrath was terrible if he discovered someone had
deceived him. Nonetheless, he could have said, 'I used to have,
but I've lost touch with him. I don't know where he is.'

Oh, he had paid the price for his honesty – for his foolishness.
And he would no doubt go on paying it until either he or Marek
died. Unless Boss did unexpectedly return to the house by the
lake, kick up a fuss about the car and fire Marek. But none of
these eventualities seemed likely. It was almost ten years now
since he had come; suddenly turning up three months after he
had hired Marek, and two months after sending 'my four most
trusted employees' over to Switzerland 'to get the house ready

for my arrival. I'm planning to retire there.' He had flown in; he had expressed his satisfaction with the arrangements; he had said he had to do 'a few last things' before settling in definitively; and then, after just four days, he had flown out again, never to re-appear. He had sent messages, letters, emails, and even made the occasional phone call; giving instructions, asking questions, promising that any day now he *would* return. But so far, not a sign of him had there been. And while they waited, Anya, Alexej and Gabriel cleaned windows, patched up walls, tended the garden, occasionally checked that the humidity from the lake was not having any ill effect on the Old Master drawings and paintings that hung everywhere in the house, repaired anything that needed repairing, polished the car – that on Alexej's instructions had not been repaired after the hailstorm, ostensibly because Boss had to see it first before claiming for insurance, in fact in the hope that when he saw it he *would* fire Marek – and once a month took the great pock-marked vehicle out for a drive: Anya sitting up front, Gabriel behind, and Alexej at the wheel. All three feeling as if they were on a royal progress through the Swiss countryside, being gawped at by the natives, and all three relieved that, there again at Alexej's insistence, Marek was not with them.

Twice a year, those same three took it in turns to return to their native country: Anya and Gabriel to see their daughter, whom they had left with Anya's parents, and Alexej to see his wife and two children. They assured their families that just as soon as they had saved enough and made provision for the future, they would come home for good. 'It won't be long now,' they always said. 'Promise!'

After which, back to Switzerland they went, and back to their routine of cleaning, tending, repairing – and waiting. Waiting for Boss to keep his promise to return. Or waiting for something – anything – to happen.

And then a visitor was announced. So excited were they, that Alexej even forgot his vow, and coming into the kitchen after receiving a text message from Boss's secretary, blurted out to his brother, 'We're going to have a visitor, Marek!'

Marek stared at him as if he didn't recognise him, and was startled to be spoken to by a stranger. Then he nodded, and went back to stirring sugar into the coffee he had just made.

Even so, he must have been excited himself. Five minutes later Alexej noticed that he hadn't drunk his coffee; and when he looked out of the kitchen window he saw his brother raking up leaves and preparing a bonfire.

It was true that this was pretty much all that Marek ever did; forbidden by the others to touch anything in the house and almost anything out of it, he spent his days either wandering round the garden gazing at the trees as though hoping to learn some secret from them, or, if not raking up leaves, picking up pine needles, rooting out the tiniest weed he saw in the lawns and flower-beds, and fishing driftwood from the lake. All of which bounty he would stack into a pile until he deemed it large enough to set fire to. But since he had had a bonfire just yesterday, Alexej supposed he could hardly have enough material for another. That didn't stop him. They were to have a visitor. The place must be *spotless*. And as he was permitted to eradicate no other spots, those few fallen leaves he could gather must pay the price.

'I sometimes think,' Anya had once told Alexej, 'that Marek must have been a heretic-burner in another life.'

'Or,' Alexej had replied, 'a heretic.'

In another life, possibly. In this, Marek gave no sign of knowing what heresy was.

Like all those of his generation, from his part of the world, Marek had been brought up entirely without religion, and even gave the impression of not comprehending the meaning of the word. He would stare at the angels in Boss's fifteenth-century Italian paintings as if trying to work out what manner of bird they were; and when over lunch or dinner Alexej and Gabriel spoke sometimes of Jews or Muslims, he would shake his head, and seem to understand still less than normal.

Which made it all the odder that when the visitor arrived – Alexej having gone in the car to pick him up from the airport one Monday afternoon in early October – Marek treated the

man as if he were some heavenly apparition. Some messenger
of the gods, if not God, who had been sent to redeem him.

The man didn't look like an angel; certainly not like one of
those painted angels that Marek was wont to gawp at. Tall – as
tall as Marek – and thin – even thinner than Marek – with short
grey hair and a pale rather haggard face, he had more the air of
an unfrocked priest than one in the business of making Annun-
ciations, or whisking saints off to the clouds.

Nonetheless, from the moment Mr Smith – as Boss's secretary had said he was called – got out of the car, Marek gazed at
him as Alexej had never seen him gaze at anyone, and thereafter hung around the guest cottage that had been prepared
for the man ready, it seemed, to run any errand that might be
requested, or carry out any sort of order.

Mr Smith was quiet, reserved – so reserved that Gabriel said,
'He's even odder than Marek; that must be the attraction,' –
and appeared not to notice the gaunt East European dancing
attendance on him; albeit at a distance of some fifty metres.
For Marek never got close to the cottage; he just hovered in the
garden, picking up leaves and pine-needles, always in a position
that enabled him to keep an eye on the cottage door.

His first evening, the visitor came to the main house for
dinner, which he ate alone in the dining room. He murmured
that he would be quite happy to eat with 'you all' in the kitchen,
but Anya ignored that, and showed him the place at the table she
had set for him as if she didn't hold with fraternity or equality.
He then retired to his cottage and went, presumably, to sleep;
at any rate, Marek, who loitered in the garden until two-thirty,
saw his lights go out around ten-thirty and not come on again.
In the morning the man appeared for breakfast at eight, once
again returning to the cottage after he had eaten; at eleven, he
interrupted whatever he was doing to take a walk around the
garden. And it was during the course of this walk that he finally
spotted Marek tending his bonfire, and going over to him,
wished him a good morning.

'Good morning,' Marek replied, in a heavy accent and a
slightly surly fashion.

'Isn't it a beautiful day?' Mr Smith continued.

Marek looked around him, as though unaware till now of the blue sky, the still warm sun, the soft October breeze. 'Yes,' he conceded. 'It is very beautiful.'

But when Smith went on to comment, 'It's such a lovely spot, isn't it?' although Marek again looked around him, at the immaculately kept garden, the calm water of the lake, the distant mountains tipped with snow, he felt obliged to point out, 'I am here for work, not holiday.'

A comment that seemed to embarrass and sadden Smith. He flushed slightly, muttered, 'Oh yes, of course,' and having given Marek a searching look, quickly retreated; not to be seen now by anyone in the household until he once more appeared for dinner at eight.

That night, however – if Marek were to be believed – although as before his lights went out around ten-thirty, the man did not go to sleep after finishing his dinner.

Marek normally never spoke unless spoken to, and sometimes not then. So when, as he was drinking what was already his third coffee of the day, he suddenly announced over breakfast the following morning that he had seen Mr Smith down by the lake in the middle of the night, Anya, Alexej and Gabriel hardly knew whether they were more surprised by what he had said, than by the fact that he had said anything.

Alexej looked at his brother with a frown, in any case disapproving of the precedent that had been set; but Anya couldn't contain her curiosity.

'What were you doing down by the lake in the middle of the night?' she asked.

'He was spying,' Alexej muttered.

'And what was *he* doing down by the lake in the middle of the night?' Gabriel asked. 'Assuming you weren't dreaming.'

'I couldn't sleep,' Marek said. 'I went out to sit by the lake.' He didn't think it necessary to add that he often did. 'I was under the willow tree. He didn't see me. He came out, stood on the shore for a bit, then . . .' Marek hesitated. 'A lot of swans swam up, and he walked on the water and spoke to them.'

'Oh fuck,' Alexej murmured.

'What do you mean he walked on the water?' Anya snapped. She sounded alarmed.

'He walked *in* the water,' Marek muttered. 'He paddled.'

'In his bedroom slippers, I suppose?' Anya said.

Gabriel laughed.

When they had all arrived in Switzerland ten years ago, Alexej had had Gabriel inform his brother that one of his tasks was to keep the fore-shore free of driftwood.

'If I were you,' Gabriel had said, 'I would get some shorts and plastic shoes from the shop in the village. The stones are sharp on the shore, and you might hurt your feet.'

Marek had ignored him, and the following day, Anya had seen him wading knee-deep in the water at the lake's edge; still wearing his long trousers, and the crepe-soled felt bedroom slippers he wore everywhere, in the house and out.

'Marek!' Anya had yelled. 'You can't go in the water like that!'

But Marek was in the water like that, and in the water he remained until he was sure there was no more driftwood to be gathered; whereupon he resumed raking up leaves and pine-needles in his soaked pants and soggy slippers.

'Change,' Anya said. 'You'll catch your death.'

But Marek didn't change, nor catch his death; so the next time Anya saw him paddling fully clothed, she said nothing.

'He wasn't wearing slippers,' Marek said now to Gabriel, with lowered eyes.

'But he was talking to the swans?'

'Yes.'

'How many swans?'

'I don't know. A lot.' Marek hesitated again. 'More than I have ever seen.'

'And what was he saying?'

'I couldn't hear. He was too far away. And he was talking in English, I think.'

Alexej sighed, and stood up. 'What clever swans they have in Switzerland. They not only talk – they understand English.'

Marek's eyes suddenly filled with tears.

'I saw him,' he said. 'I did.'

Then he too stood and hurried from the room, even as Alexej was shaking his head and saying, 'Poor fellow, he's finally lost his marbles completely.'

At least Anya and Gabriel waited till Marek was out of earshot, before they nodded and agreed that they were seriously worried about Marek's mental health.

'I mean he's always been a *bit* strange. But – is he prone to Jesus fantasies?'

'Not that I know of,' Alexej replied. 'And if he is, I don't know where he gets 'em from.'

'Poor Marek,' Anya said. 'I've never really felt sorry for him before. He's always seemed reasonably content in his own little world. But now . . .'

'Do you think he's having a nervous breakdown?' Gabriel asked.

Alexej shrugged. For the first time in years he too felt a certain pity for his elder brother; so mocked and mistreated by his parents when small, who-knew how hurt by others since.

'Well let's hope Mr Smith doesn't walk too far onto or into the water, and drown,' Gabriel said. 'Then Boss would get really mad.'

'Possibly,' Alexej murmured. Then, 'I wonder how he knows Boss?' Then, 'I wonder if he's been sent here as a spy by Boss? To check up on us?'

'What's he checking up on?' Anya said. 'The paddling facilities? Or the welfare of the swans?'

The others laughed, uneasily.

Later that morning, having again emerged from his cottage to take a walk around the garden, and looking as if he wanted to make amends if he had given offence the previous day, Mr Smith once more approached Marek at his bonfire, and wished him good morning.

'Good morning,' Marek replied, in a more civil manner than he had twenty-four hours earlier. Then, though he hadn't heard his brother's speculation, he asked, 'Do you work for Boss?'

'Good heavens, no!' Mr Smith replied. 'I'm afraid I don't work for anyone. That is, I work for whoever will have me. I'm in show business,' he explained, sounding somewhat apologetic. 'I'm a professional magician. An . . . illusionist.' He paused before continuing slowly, not sure if Marek could understand him, 'I'm going to be hosting a new television series about magic next year. I came here to polish my script and work up a few new tricks.'

'Ah,' Marek said.

'I – I'm trying to incorporate certain . . . fairy stories, myths, into each episode. I mean . . . build each episode around a well-known tale that has elements of magic in it. Like – Little Red Riding Hood. Cinderella. Sleeping Beauty. Peter and the Wolf.' Again he paused, before adding, 'Swan Lake.'

'Ah,' repeated Marek, who had learned some English when first he had started working for Boss, and by dint of listening over and over to the CDs Boss had given him, now understood more than he generally let on. Even so, he had difficulty following Mr Smith, and anyway wasn't sure he wanted to follow him.

He had thought he recognised the man when first he had arrived, though he hadn't known how or where from. He had been puzzled. Now he realized he must have seen him on television at some stage. Made-up, no doubt, and wearing some fancy costume. Still, with that pale, haggard face, quite identifiable. So in a sense the man's explanation was a relief. On the other hand, he didn't like too many explanations. They solved mysteries, while at the same time they opened up other, often more complex mysteries. It was better to accept appearances as reality, Marek felt, and not question what went on off-stage, as it were, behind the scenes.

'Excuse me,' he told Mr Smith. 'I must get on with my work.'

'Yes, of course,' said the Englishman – at least Marek assumed he was English – giving Marek another of his searching looks, as if determined to make out what went on behind *his* scenes. 'And I must get on with mine. Good talking to you, Marek.'

To this Marek said nothing immediately, though he felt perplexed as he took the hand that Mr Smith offered, and shook it. He had never told the man his name; he couldn't imagine that the others had; and he was certain that Boss hadn't provided any personal details about his employees, before Smith had set out from London. So how –

Without really meaning to, Marek asked, 'How do you know my name?'

'We've met before,' Mr Smith said, with a slightly sad smile. 'When . . . er . . . Boss came down here soon after he bought the place, he invited me over to lunch one day. I was staying in Geneva at the time, and – I was introduced to everyone. I have a very good memory.'

Marek frowned, trying to remember. There had certainly been a lunch party, he recalled, at which a number of people had been present. But this gaunt, haunted man? There had been two Swiss sisters, one tiny and grey-haired, the other blonde and statuesque. There had been a middle-aged couple; she with a lot of make-up and a mini-skirt, he with a pony-tail. There had been a slightly younger couple: a good-looking man who had come into the kitchen and introduced himself, telling them that he was a writer, and his Chinese wife, who had been a doctor. Then there had been a tall dark-haired man of indeterminate age, who had also made it his business to meet and shake hands with everyone working in the house. Surely though, he couldn't be –

'I have rather aged in the past few years, I'm afraid,' Mr Smith said. 'I have had a few . . . contretemps, let's say, in both my personal and professional life. But – I was there, I assure you. I met you all. Your brother Alexej. Anya. And Gabriel. I remember you all most vividly.' A pause. 'But I remember you most vividly, Marek. You were in the garden – doing what you are doing now. And I thought . . . But forgive me,' he said. 'I am keeping you. Goodbye.'

With that, Mr Smith turned and went back to his cottage, and Marek resumed his tasks.

At lunch, however, with the others, he once again couldn't resist initiating a conversation.

'He has been here before, Mr Smith,' he announced. 'He remembers us all.'

'When?' Anya, Alexej and Gabriel said in unison. And on being told what Smith had told Marek, they all chorused, 'Rubbish!'

'I remember that lunch quite well,' Anya said. 'There were two Swiss sisters . . .'

'A Swiss writer and his Chinese wife,' chipped in Gabriel.

'A couple of middle-aged Bohemians . . .'

'And a dark-haired man who looked like a gangster,' Alexej said. 'But his name wasn't Smith and there's no *way* it was this man.'

'He has had some . . .' Marek announced, hesitating before he brought the word out, '*contretemps* in his life, he said.'

'I don't care whether he's had contretemps, car-crashes or cancer,' Gabriel snorted. 'He's not the same man who came to lunch with Boss that day. I'd bet my life on it. And no one else came the rest of the time Boss was here. I remember it like it was yesterday.'

'Yes, so do I,' Anya said.

'You're sure you're not making things up again?' Alexej asked his brother.

'I – no,' Marek said. Petulant, he went on, 'That's what he told me.' Then he got up and, as he had at breakfast, walked out of the room.

'Well *someone's* a liar,' Anya said, 'and for once I don't think it's Marek,' Alexej muttered. 'I can see that man quite clearly,' he went on.

'You're quite right,' Gabriel said. 'He did look like a gangster. There was something sleazy about him. Sinister. As if . . .'

'He was the only person I've ever seen who – I got the impression Boss was frightened of him in some way,' Anya said. 'As if he knew more about Boss than he should have. Or as if he had some sort of hold over Boss.'

'Maybe Marek misunderstood him,' Gabriel suggested. 'Or maybe . . .'

'We've all changed since we got here,' Alexej observed. 'In ten years everyone changes. But we're still *recognizable* as the people we once were.' He added, with what he hoped was a smile, 'Aren't we?'

The three of them considered. Yes, they all thought. Though perhaps . . .

They had been in their late twenties when Boss had first hired them; and just turned thirty when they had come to live in Switzerland. They had all felt young still, and looked it, they hoped. Buxom Anya, the qualified nurse who was to become Boss's housekeeper. Tough, wiry Gabriel, the mason, painter and decorator of the group. And handsome, charming – at times – Alexej, the electrician, plumber and if necessary carpenter. All fair-haired, blue-eyed and optimistic about the future.

Now, however, they felt middle-aged, they looked middle-aged. Anya had thickened, coarsened, and while she remained bright she was no longer cheerful; as if her light had shone too brightly on others' defects, and by exposing them, sickened her. As she had swelled, Gabriel had diminished, so that though he still looked tough, he looked mean with it; a thin, bitter runt. And as for Alexej: oh, his good looks had long since faded into flabbiness, and his charm was now so rare as to be virtually extinct. Anya had once suggested that Alexej's face and manner were the cause of Marek's initial disaffection; for surely, she had said to Gabriel, the older boy must have resented terribly the arrival of a brother so unlike him in every way. A child on whom their parents doted, and whose birth, they had made plain, went some way to cancelling the disappointment they had always felt with their first-born. But if those parents could see Alexej now, Anya thought – though this she did not say to Gabriel – they might feel still more disappointed in him than they had in Marek. At least Marek was the same . . .

Nevertheless, however much Alexej had changed, however much they had all changed, he and they *hadn't* changed out of all recognition. The three sitting round the table were convinced of that. Whereas Mr Smith, if Marek was right about his having been here before, had not merely changed; he had become an entirely other person. It was as if he were a magician, with the power to transform himself.

'Whoever he is, I hope he goes soon,' Anya said. 'Otherwise I'm afraid poor Marek might really be tipped over the edge.'

'Poor Marek,' Gabriel echoed.

'Poor Marek,' Alexej said.

Whether or not poor Marek was tipped over the edge by Mr Smith, the others could never agree. All they knew was what he told them over breakfast on the third morning of the visitor's stay, when they asked him if last night too Mr Smith had gone walking on – 'Sorry, I mean *in*, ha ha ha,' – the water, and talking to the swans.

Normally when he knew the others were laughing at him Marek ignored them; closed up like the proverbial clam determined to keep out the waters of derision. Today, however, detecting the real interest, real concern even, behind their mockery, he told them yes, and went on to describe what had happened.

He had once again gone down to sit under the willow. The moon had been even brighter than the night before; in fact it had been full. And at about two minutes to midnight, down Mr Smith had come from the cottage. 'I'm *sure* he didn't see me,' Marek murmured, for fear Alexej and the others would claim the man had put on a show for his benefit.

Smith was wearing a black shirt and black trousers. His feet were bare. He had waded into the water but – as on the previous night – it had looked as if he were walking *on* it. He had walked out a couple of metres. And then, again as on the previous night, as if from nowhere ten, fifteen, maybe twenty swans had appeared. They had glided up. They had circled round Mr Smith. He had murmured to them. And then – one of the swans had detached itself from the group. It was the largest, whitest and most beautiful of all the birds.

'I thought all swans looked alike,' Anya murmured, though in such a way as not to interrupt Marek's narrative. She didn't believe a word of what she was hearing; but she wanted to hear more.

This most beautiful of all the swans had left the circle. It had swum right up to Mr Smith. And then the man had raised his arms – 'only they didn't look like arms any longer,' Marek whispered. 'They looked like *wings*. Great black wings, as if he were becoming a swan himself. A black swan. Or – an angel.' He stopped, and waited for the others to jeer. They didn't. They were looking at him, rapt.

'And then the swan reared up out of the water and seemed to embrace Mr Smith, and – she became a woman,' Marek whispered. 'A white, beautiful woman *like* a swan. Like the moonlight. But still . . .' Marek hesitated. He didn't dare look at the others, but he was aware they were staring at him not even remotely with derision now but only, all three of them, with a pity they could scarcely bear. It was as if their hearts were breaking for him. Nevertheless, he had to go on. To tell them –

That the beautiful woman had glided out of the water. That she had glided – part walked, part floated, part flown – over to him, still under the willow. And that as he had stood to greet her, she had enfolded *him* in her wings, she had gazed at him with great tragic eyes, not merely as if she had come to redeem him but as if he had come to redeem *her*, and she had kissed him. She had kissed him as he had never been kissed before –

'You *have* never been kissed before,' Alexej whispered.

– and he had closed his eyes and – when he had opened them she had vanished. So had Mr Smith.

All Marek had seen were two or three swans gliding away from the shore, out into the darkness of the lake – and, by the water's edge, two feathers. One black, the other white.

'Oh yeah,' Gabriel said, clearing his throat, trying to sound unaffected by Marek's tale, but unable to look at the tears he was aware were running down Marek's cheeks. 'And what did you do with them?'

'I picked them up,' Marek said, reaching into the pocket of the denim jacket he was wearing. Without another word, he held out for the others to see two feathers: one black, the other white.

Gabriel, Anya and Alexej looked; and then they did at last raise their eyes to Marek himself. And though they gazed at him once more with scepticism, if not scorn, and still with pity, they saw that Marek, gaunt unlovely Marek, had been transfigured. He remained gaunt. He remained unlovely. But there was a radiance about him that made him appear – enchanted. It was as if *he* were glowing with moonlight, with happiness – and whatever he had or hadn't seen down by the lake last night, they couldn't begrudge him that happiness, and even felt he deserved it.

What was more, in the weeks, months and years that followed Mr Smith's visit, Marek never quite lost his radiance, his air of having been kissed, loved and redeemed. And when every now and then they caught a glimpse of the light that still seemed to shine from him, the others almost envied him his madness, and the two feathers he kept in a jar in his room, one black, the other white.

'*He's* all right,' Anya said, bitterly.

Partly because of their envy, Anya, Alexej and Gabriel prayed that they would never again see Mr Smith – who had left the same day that Marek had told them his story. They remained uncertain whether Marek had been tipped permanently over the edge by the man's visit, or whether he was still clinging on to remnants of his sanity – by his fingertips, so to speak. But they were sure that should Boss's friend reappear, Marek would be lost forever, with who knows what consequences for them all.

'He might run amok with an axe,' Anya murmured.

'Besides,' Gabriel said, 'with all that business about Smith saying he was who he wasn't, and that he'd been here before . . .'

Indeed, so unsettled had they been by their visitor that more and more, as the years passed, while Marek was neither asked for nor expressed an opinion, the others started to pray that Boss himself would never return to the house by the lake. To pray – and little by little, to believe . . . that Boss would never return; that their salaries would continue to be paid; and that nothing would ever again happen, to break the spell that had been cast on them.

Hugh Walpole

THE TARN

Like a number of the authors in this book, HUGH WALPOLE
*(1884-1941) was once an enormously successful and respected
novelist whose reputation waned significantly after his death and
who is only now being rediscovered. He published more than forty
volumes of fiction and during his lifetime was best known for the
quartet of 'Herries' novels set in 18th-century England and for his
stories of the beloved boy character Jeremy. Walpole was especially
popular in the United States, where he attracted crowds at his
lectures not seen since the tours of Charles Dickens. But Walpole
deserves to be remembered for what he called his 'macabre' fiction,
which includes several fine novels and a number of horror and
supernatural stories, some of which bear comparison with the best
such stories in the English language. Walpole's posthumous macabre novel,* The Killer and the Slain *(1942) and his story collection*
All Souls' Night *(1933) are available from Valancourt. 'The Tarn'
was originally published in the magazine* Success *in October 1923.*

A S FOSTER MOVED UNCONSCIOUSLY ACROSS THE ROOM, bent
towards the bookcase, and stood leaning forward a little,
choosing now one book, now another, with his eyes, his host,
seeing the muscles of the back of his thin, scraggy neck stand
out above his low flannel collar, thought of the ease with which
he could squeeze that throat, and the pleasure, the triumphant,
lustful pleasure, that such an action would give him.

The low, white-walled, white-ceilinged room was flooded
with the mellow, kindly Lakeland sun. October is a wonderful
month in the English Lakes, golden, rich, and perfumed, slow
suns moving through apricot-tinted skies to ruby evening glories; the shadows lie then thick about that beautiful country, in
dark purple patches, in long web-like patterns of silver gauze,
in thick splotches of amber and grey. The clouds pass in gal-

leons across the mountains, now veiling, now revealing, now
descending with ghost-like armies to the very breast of the
plains, suddenly rising to the softest of blue skies and lying thin
in lazy languorous colour.

Fenwick's cottage looked across to Low Fells; on his right,
seen through side windows, sprawled the hills above Ullswater.

Fenwick looked at Foster's back and felt suddenly sick, so
that he sat down, veiling his eyes for a moment with his hand.
Foster had come up there, come all the way from London, to
explain. It was so like Foster to want to explain, to want to put
things right. For how many years had he known Foster? Why,
for twenty at least, and during all those years Foster had been
for ever determined to put things right with everybody. He
could never bear to be disliked; he hated that anyone should
think ill of him; he wanted everyone to be his friends. That was
one reason, perhaps, why Foster had got on so well, had prospered so in his career; one reason, too, why Fenwick had not.

For Fenwick was the opposite of Foster in this. He did not
want friends, he certainly did not care that people should like
him – that is, people for whom, for one reason or another, he
had contempt – and he had contempt for quite a number of
people.

Fenwick looked at that long, thin, bending back and felt his
knees tremble. Soon Foster would turn round and that high,
reedy voice would pipe out something about the books. 'What
jolly books you have, Fenwick!' How many, many times in the
long watches of the night, when Fenwick could not sleep, had
he heard that pipe sounding close there – yes, in the very shadows of his bed! And how many times had Fenwick replied to it:
'I hate you! You are the cause of my failure in life! You have been
in my way always. Always, always, always! Patronizing and
pretending, and in truth showing others what a poor thing you
thought me, how great a failure, how conceited a fool! I know.
You can hide nothing from me! I can hear you!'

For twenty years now Foster had been persistently in Fenwick's way. There had been that affair, so long ago now, when
Robins had wanted a sub-editor for his wonderful review, the

Parthenon, and Fenwick had gone to see him and they had had a splendid talk. How magnificently Fenwick had talked that day; with what enthusiasm he had shown Robins (who was blinded by his own conceit, anyway) the kind of paper the *Parthenon* might be; how Robins had caught his own enthusiasm, how he had pushed his fat body about the room, crying: 'Yes, yes, Fenwick – that's fine! That's fine indeed!' – and then how, after all, Foster had got that job.

The paper had only lived for a year or so, it is true, but the connection with it had brought Foster into prominence just as it might have brought Fenwick!

Then, five years later, there was Fenwick's novel, *The Bitter Aloe* – the novel upon which he had spent three years of blood-and-tears endeavour – and then, in the very same week of publication, Foster brings out *The Circus*, the novel that made his name; although, Heaven knows, the thing was poor enough sentimental trash. You may say that one novel cannot kill another – but can it not? Had not *The Circus* appeared would not that group of London know-alls – that conceited, limited, ignorant, self-satisfied crowd, who nevertheless can do, by their talk, so much to affect a book's good or evil fortunes – have talked about *The Bitter Aloe* and so forced it into prominence? As it was, the book was stillborn and *The Circus* went on its prancing, triumphant way.

After that there had been many occasions – some small, some big – and always in one way or another that thin, scraggy body of Foster's was interfering with Fenwick's happiness.

The thing had become, of course, an obsession with Fenwick. Hiding up there in the heart of the Lakes, with no friends, almost no company, and very little money, he was given too much to brooding over his failure. He was a failure and it was not his own fault. How could it be his own fault with his talents and his brilliance? It was the fault of modern life and its lack of culture, the fault of the stupid material mess that made up the intelligence of human beings – and the fault of Foster.

Always Fenwick hoped that Foster would keep away from him. He did not know what he would not do did he see the man.

And then one day, to his amazement, he received a telegram:

Passing through this way. May I stop with you Monday and Tuesday? – Giles Foster.

Fenwick could scarcely believe his eyes, and then – from curiosity, from cynical contempt, from some deeper, more mysterious motive that he dared not analyse – he had telegraphed – *Come.*

And here the man was. And he had come – would you believe it? – to 'put things right'. He had heard from Hamlin Eddis that Fenwick was hurt with him, had some kind of grievance.

'I didn't like to feel that, old man, and so I thought I'd just stop by and have it out with you, see what the matter was, and put it right.'

Last night after supper Foster had tried to put it right. Eagerly, his eyes like a good dog's who is asking for a bone that he knows he thoroughly deserves, he had held out his hand and asked Fenwick to 'say what was up'.

Fenwick simply had said that nothing was up; Hamlin Eddis was a damned fool.

'Oh, I'm glad to hear that!' Foster had cried, springing up out of his chair and putting his hand on Fenwick's shoulder. 'I'm glad of that, old man. I couldn't bear for us not to be friends. We've been friends so long.'

Lord! How Fenwick hated him at that moment!

II

'What a jolly lot of books you have!' Foster turned round and looked at Fenwick with eager, gratified eyes. 'Every book here is interesting! I like your arrangement of them, too, and those open bookshelves – it always seems to me a shame to shut up books behind glass!'

Foster came forward and sat down quite close to his host. He even reached forward and laid his hand on his host's knee.

'Look here! I'm mentioning it for the last time – positively!
But I do want to make quite certain. There *is* nothing wrong
between us, is there, old man? I know you assured me last night,
but I just want . . .'

Fenwick looked at him and, surveying him, felt suddenly an
exquisite pleasure of hatred. He liked the touch of the man's
hand on his knee; he himself bent forward a little and, thinking
how agreeable it would be to push Foster's eyes in, deep, deep
into his head, crunching them, smashing them to purple, leaving the empty, staring, bloody sockets, said:

'Why, no. Of course not. I told you last night. What could
there be?'

The hand gripped the knee a little more tightly.

'I *am* so glad! That's splendid! Splendid! I hope you won't
think me ridiculous, but I've always had an affection for you
ever since I can remember. I've always wanted to know you
better. I've admired your talent so greatly. That novel of yours –
the – the – the one about the aloe –'

'*The Bitter Aloe?*'

'Ah, yes, that was it. That was a splendid book. Pessimistic,
of course, but still fine. It ought to have done better. I remember thinking so at the time.'

'Yes, it ought to have done better.'

'Your time will come, though. What I say is that good work
always tells in the end.'

'Yes, my time will come.'

The thin, piping voice went on:

'Now, I've had more success than I deserved. Oh yes, I have.
You can't deny it. I'm not falsely modest. I mean it. I've got
some talent, of course, but not so much as people say. And
you! Why, you've got so much more than they acknowledge.
You have, old man. You have indeed. Only – I do hope you'll
forgive my saying this – perhaps you haven't advanced quite as
you might have done. Living up here, shut away here, closed
in by all these mountains, in this wet climate – always raining –
why, you're out of things! You don't see people, don't talk and
discover what's really going on. Why, look at me!'

Fenwick turned round and looked at him.

'Now, I have half the year in London, where one gets the best of everything, best talk, best music, best plays; and then I'm three months abroad, Italy or Greece or somewhere, and then three months in the country. Now, that's an ideal arrangement. You have everything that way.'

Italy or Greece or somewhere!

Something turned in Fenwick's breast, grinding, grinding, grinding. How he had longed, oh, how passionately, for just one week in Greece, two days in Sicily! Sometimes he had thought that he might run to it, but when it had come to the actual counting of the pennies ... And how this fool, this fathead, this self-satisfied, conceited, patronizing...

He got up, looking out at the golden sun.

'What do you say to a walk?' he suggested. 'The sun will last for a good hour yet.'

III

As soon as the words were out of his lips he felt as though someone else had said them for him. He even turned half-round to see whether anyone else were there. Ever since Foster's arrival on the evening before he had been conscious of this sensation. A walk? Why should he take Foster for a walk, show him his beloved country, point out those curves and lines and hollows, the broad silver shield of Ullswater, the cloudy purple hills hunched like blankets about the knees of some recumbent giant? Why? It was as though he had turned round to someone behind him and had said: 'You have some further design in this.'

They started out. The road sank abruptly to the lake, then the path ran between trees at the water's edge. Across the lake tones of bright yellow light, crocus-hued, rode upon the blue. The hills were dark.

The very way that Foster walked bespoke the man. He was always a little ahead of you, pushing his long, thin body along with little eager jerks, as though, did he not hurry, he would miss something that would be immensely to his advantage. He talked, throwing words over his shoulder to Fenwick as you throw crumbs of bread to a robin.

'Of course I was pleased. Who would not be? After all, it's a new prize. They've only been awarding it for a year or two, but it's gratifying – really gratifying – to secure it. When I opened the envelope and found the cheque there – well, you could have knocked me down with a feather. You could, indeed. Of course, a hundred pounds isn't much. But it's the honour – '

Whither were they going? Their destiny was as certain as though they had no free-will. Free-will? There is no free-will. All is Fate. Fenwick suddenly laughed aloud.

Foster stopped.

'Why, what is it?'

'What's what?'

'You laughed.'

'Something amused me.'

Foster slipped his arm through Fenwick's.

'It *is* jolly to be walking along together like this, arm in arm, friends. I'm a sentimental man. I won't deny it. What I say is that life is short and one must love one's fellow-beings, or where is one? You live too much alone, old man.' He squeezed Fenwick's arm. 'That's the truth of it.'

It was torture, exquisite, heavenly torture. It was wonderful to feel that thin, bony arm pressing against his. Almost you could hear the beating of that other heart. Wonderful to feel that arm and the temptation to take it in your hands and to bend it and twist it and then to hear the bones crack . . . crack . . . crack. . . . Wonderful to feel that temptation rise through one's body like boiling water and yet not to yield to it. For a moment Fenwick's hand touched Foster's. Then he drew himself apart.

'We're at the village. This is the hotel where they all come in the summer. We turn off at the right here. I'll show you my tarn.'

IV

'Your tarn?' asked Foster. 'Forgive my ignorance, but what *is* a tarn exactly?'

'A tarn is a miniature lake, a pool of water lying in the lap of the hill. Very quiet, lovely, silent. Some of them are immensely deep.'

'I should like to see that.'

'It is some little distance – up a rough road. Do you mind?'

'Not a bit. I have long legs.'

'Some of them are immensely deep – unfathomable – nobody touched the bottom – but quiet, like glass, with shadows only – '

'Do you know, Fenwick, I have always been afraid of water – I've never learnt to swim. I'm afraid to go out of my depth. Isn't that ridiculous? But it is all because at my private school, years ago, when I was a small boy, some big fellows took me and held me with my head under the water and nearly drowned me. They did indeed. They went farther than they meant to. I can see their faces.'

Fenwick considered this. The picture leapt to his mind. He could see the boys – large, strong fellows, probably – and this skinny thing like a frog, their thick hands about his throat, his legs like grey sticks kicking out of the water, their laughter, their sudden sense that something was wrong, the skinny body all flaccid and still –

He drew a deep breath.

Foster was walking beside him now, not ahead of him, as though he were a little afraid and needed reassurance. Indeed, the scene had changed. Before and behind them stretched the uphill path, loose with shale and stones. On their right, on a ridge at the foot of the hill, were some quarries, almost deserted, but the more melancholy in the fading afternoon because a little work still continued there; faint sounds came from the gaunt listening chimneys, a stream of water ran and tumbled angrily into a pool below, once and again a black silhouette, like a question-mark, appeared against the darkening hill.

It was a little steep here, and Foster puffed and blew.

Fenwick hated him the more for that. So thin and spare and still he could not keep in condition! They stumbled, keeping below the quarry, on the edge of the running water, now green, now a dirty white-grey, pushing their way along the side of the hill.

Their faces were set now towards Helvellyn. It rounded the cup of hills, closing in the base and then sprawling to the right.

'There's the tarn!' Fenwick exclaimed; and then added, 'The sun's not lasting as long as I had expected. It's growing dark already.'

Foster stumbled and caught Fenwick's arm.

'This twilight makes the hills look strange – like living men. I can scarcely see my way.'

'We're alone here,' Fenwick answered. 'Don't you feel the stillness? The men will have left the quarry now and gone home. There is no one in all this place but ourselves. If you watch you will see a strange green light steal down over the hills. It lasts for but a moment and then it is dark.

'Ah, here is my tarn. Do you know how I love this place, Foster? It seems to belong especially to me, just as much as all your work and your glory and fame and success seem to belong to you. I have this and you have that. Perhaps in the end we are even, after all. Yes. . . .

'But I feel as though that piece of water belonged to me and I to it, and as though we should never be separated – yes. . . . Isn't it black?

'It is one of the deep ones. No one has ever sounded it. Only Helvellyn knows, and one day I fancy that it will take me, too, into its confidence, will whisper its secrets – '

Foster sneezed.

'Very nice. Very beautiful, Fenwick. I like your tarn. Charming. And now let's turn back. That is a difficult walk beneath the quarry. It's chilly, too.'

'Do you see that little jetty there?' Fenwick led Foster by the arm. 'Someone built that out into the water. He had a boat there, I suppose. Come and look down. From the end of the little jetty it looks so deep and the mountains seem to close round.'

Fenwick took Foster's arm and led him to the end of the jetty. Indeed, the water looked deep here. Deep and very black. Foster peered down, then he looked up at the hills that did indeed seem to have gathered close around him. He sneezed again.

'I've caught a cold, I am afraid. Let's turn homewards, Fenwick, or we shall never find our way.'

'Home, then,' said Fenwick, and his hands closed about the thin, scraggy neck. For the instant the head half turned, and two startled, strangely childish eyes stared; then, with a push that was ludicrously simple, the body was impelled forward, there was a sharp cry, a splash, a stir of something white against the swiftly gathering dusk, again and then again, then far-spreading ripples, then silence.

V

The silence extended. Having enwrapped the tarn, it spread as though with finger on lip to the already quiescent hills. Fenwick shared in the silence. He luxuriated in it. He did not move at all. He stood there looking upon the inky water of the tarn, his arms folded, a man lost in intensest thought. But he was not thinking. He was only conscious of a warm, luxurious relief, a sensuous feeling that was not thought at all.

Foster was gone – that tiresome, prating, conceited, self--satisfied fool! Gone, never to return. The tarn assured him of that. It stared back into Fenwick's face approvingly as though it said: 'You have done well – a clean and necessary job. We have done it together, you and I. I am proud of you.'

He was proud of himself. At last he had done something definite with his life. Thought, eager, active thought, was beginning now to flood his brain. For all these years he had

hung around in this place doing nothing but cherish griev-
ances, weak, backboneless – now at last there was action. He
drew himself up and looked at the hills. He was proud – and he
was cold. He was shivering. He turned up the collar of his coat.
Yes, there was that faint green light that always lingered in the
shadows of the hills for a brief moment before darkness came.
It was growing late. He had better return.

Shivering now so that his teeth chattered, he started off
down the path, and then was aware that he did not wish to leave
the tarn. The tarn was friendly – the only friend he had in all
the world. As he stumbled along in the dark this sense of loneliness grew. He was going home to an empty house. There had
been a guest in it last night. Who was it? Why, Foster, of course
– Foster with his silly laugh and amiable, mediocre eyes. Well,
Foster would not be there now. No, he never would be there
again.

And suddenly Fenwick started to run. He did not know why,
except that, now that he had left the tarn, he was lonely. He
wished that he could have stayed there all night, but because
it was cold he could not, and so now he was running so that he
might be at home with the lights and the familiar furniture –
and all the things that he knew to reassure him.

As he ran the shale and stones scattered beneath his feet.
They made a tit-tattering noise under him, and someone else
seemed to be running too. He stopped, and the other runner
also stopped. He breathed in the silence. He was hot now.
The perspiration was trickling down his cheeks. He could feel
a dribble of it down his back inside his shirt. His knees were
pounding. His heart was thumping. And all around him the
hills were so amazingly silent, now like india-rubber clouds
that you could push in or pull out as you do those india-rubber
faces, grey against the night sky of a crystal purple, upon whose
surface, like the twinkling eyes of boats at sea, stars were now
appearing.

His knees steadied, his heart beat less fiercely, and he began
to run again. Suddenly he had turned the corner and was out
at the hotel. Its lamps were kindly and reassuring. He walked

then quietly along the lake-side path, and had it not been for the certainty that someone was treading behind him he would have been comfortable and at his ease. He stopped once or twice and looked back, and once he stopped and called out, 'Who's there?' Only the rustling trees answered.

He had the strangest fancy, but his brain was throbbing so fiercely that he could not think, that it was the tarn that was following him, the tarn slipping, sliding along the road, being with him so that he should not be lonely. He could almost hear the tarn whisper in his ear: 'We did that together, and so I do not wish you to bear all the responsibility yourself. I will stay with you, so that you are not lonely.'

He climbed down the road towards home, and there were the lights of his house. He heard the gate click behind him as though it were shutting him in. He went into the sitting-room, lighted and ready. There were the books that Foster had admired.

The old woman who looked after him appeared.

'Will you be having some tea, sir?'

'No, thank you, Annie.'

'Will the other gentleman be wanting any?'

'No; the other gentleman is away for the night.'

'Then there will be only one for supper?'

'Yes, only one for supper.'

He sat in the corner of the sofa and fell instantly into a deep slumber.

VI

He woke when the old woman tapped him on the shoulder and told him that supper was served. The room was dark save for the jumping light of two uncertain candles. Those two red candlesticks – how he hated them up there on the mantelpiece! He had always hated them, and now they seemed to him to have something of the quality of Foster's voice – that thin, reedy, piping tone.

He was expecting at every moment that Foster would enter, and yet he knew that he would not. He continued to turn his head towards the door, but it was so dark there that you could not see. The whole room was dark except just there by the fireplace, where the two candlesticks went whining with their miserable twinkling plaint.

He went into the dining-room and sat down to his meal. But he could not eat anything. It was odd – that place by the table where Foster's chair should be. Odd, naked, and made a man feel lonely.

He got up once from the table and went to the window, opened it and looked out. He listened for something. A trickle as of running water, a stir, through the silence, as though some deep pool were filling to the brim. A rustle in the trees, perhaps. An owl hooted. Sharply, as though someone had spoken unexpectedly behind his shoulder, he closed the windows and looked back, peering under his dark eyebrows into the room.

Later on he went up to his bed.

VII

Had he been sleeping, or had he been lying lazily, as one does, half-dozing, half-luxuriously not thinking? He was wide awake now, utterly awake, and his heart was beating with apprehension. It was as though someone had called him by name. He slept always with his window a little open and the blind up. To-night the moonlight shadowed in sickly fashion the objects in his room. It was not a flood of light nor yet a sharp splash, silvering a square, a circle, throwing the rest into ebony darkness. The light was dim, a little green, perhaps, like the shadow that comes over the hills just before dark.

He stared at the window, and it seemed to him that something moved there. Within, or rather against, the green-grey light, something silver-tinted glistened. Fenwick stared. It had the look, exactly, of slipping water.

Slipping water! He listened, his head up, and it seemed to him that from beyond the window he caught the stir of water, not running, but rather welling up and up, gurgling with satisfaction as it filled and filled.

He sat up higher in bed, and then saw that down the wallpaper beneath the window water was undoubtedly trickling. He could see it lurch to the projecting wood of the sill, pause, and then slip, slither down the incline. The odd thing was that it fell so silently.

Beyond the window there was that odd gurgle, but in the room itself absolute silence. Whence could it come? He saw the line of silver rise and fall as the stream on the window-ledge ebbed and flowed.

He must get up and close the window. He drew his legs above the sheets and blankets and looked down.

He shrieked. The floor was covered with a shining film of water. It was rising. As he looked it had covered half the short stumpy legs of the bed. It rose without a wink, a bubble, a break! Over the sill it poured now in a steady flow, but soundless. Fenwick sat up in the bed, the clothes gathered up to his chin, his eyes blinking, the Adam's apple throbbing like a throttle in his throat.

But he must do something, he must stop this. The water was now level with the seats of the chairs, but still was soundless. Could he but reach the door!

He put down his naked foot, then cried again. The water was icy cold. Suddenly, leaning, staring at its dark, unbroken sheen, something seemed to push him forward. He fell. His head, his face was under the icy liquid; it seemed adhesive and, in the heart of its ice, hot like melting wax. He struggled to his feet. The water was breast-high. He screamed again and again. He could see the looking-glass, the row of books, the picture of Dürer's 'Horse', aloof, impervious. He beat at the water, and flakes of it seemed to cling to him like scales of fish, clammy to his touch. He struggled, ploughing his way towards the door.

The water now was at his neck. Then something had caught him by the ankle. Something held him. He struggled, crying:

'Let me go! Let me go! I tell you to let me go! I hate you! I hate you! I will not come down to you! I will not – '

The water covered his mouth. He felt that someone pushed in his eyeballs with bare knuckles. A cold hand reached up and caught his naked thigh.

VIII

In the morning the little maid knocked and, receiving no answer, came in, as was her wont, with his shaving-water. What she saw made her scream. She ran for the gardener.

They took the body with its staring, protruding eyes, its tongue sticking out between the clenched teeth, and laid it on the bed.

The only sign of disorder was an overturned water-jug. A small pool of water stained the carpet.

It was a lovely morning. A twig of ivy idly, in the little breeze, tapped the pane.

Gerald Kersh

THE GENTLEMAN ALL IN BLACK

The case of GERALD KERSH (1911-1968) *is another example of
the fickleness of authorial reputations. At one time, Kersh was
ubiquitous – not only in bookshops, where some thirty-five volumes
of his fiction were on sale over the years – but also in magazines:
hundreds of his stories appeared everywhere from* Playboy *to*
The Saturday Evening Post *to* Harper's *and dozens of others.
His most famous novel,* Night and the City *(1938), a noir classic, has been filmed twice, and his fiction has been championed by,
among others, Angela Carter, Harlan Ellison, Ian Fleming, and
Michael Moorcock. Yet today Kersh is too little known, which is
unfortunate, since his best short stories, tales like 'The Brighton
Monster' and 'Men Without Bones', are both brilliantly original
and undeniably horrific. 'The Gentleman All in Black', which features Kersh's trademark blend of humor and horror, is taken from
his collection* Neither Man Nor Dog *(1946), one of six Kersh
volumes available from Valancourt.*

T HERE IS A CRAZY OLD FELLOW who lives – or used to live, in
1937 – in a crazy old skylight room in Paris, and was known
as Le Borgne. He squinted horribly, and was well known for his
avarice. Although he was reputed to have a large sum of money
put by, he shuffled about in the ragged remains of a respectable black suit and tried to earn a few coppers doing odd jobs in
cafés. He was not above begging . . . a very unsightly, disreputa-
ble, ill-tempered old man. And this is the story he told me one
evening when he was trying to get two francs out of me.

'You needn't look down on me,' he said. (He adopted a
querulous, bullying tone even when asking a favor.) 'I have
been as well-dressed as you. I'm eighty years old, too. Ah yes, I
have seen life, I have. Why, I used to be clerk to one of the greatest financiers in the world, no less a man than Mahler. That

was before your time. That was fifty years ago. Mahler handled millions. I used to receive the highest of the high, the greatest of the great, in his office. There was no staff but me. Mahler worked alone, with me to write the letters. All his business was finished by three in the afternoon. He was a big man, and I was his right hand. I have met royalty in the office of Mahler. Why, once, yes, I even met the Devil.'

And when I laughed at him, Le Borgne went on, with great vehemence:

Mahler died rich. And yet it is I who can tell you that a week before his death things went wrong and Mahler was nearly twenty million francs in debt. In English money, a million pounds, let us say. I was in his confidence. He had lost everything and, gambling in a mining speculation, had lost twenty million francs which were not his to lose. He said to me – it was on the 19th, or the 20th of April, 1887 – 'Well, Charles, it looks as if we are finished. I have nothing left except my immortal soul; and I'd sell that if I could get the worth of it.' And then he went into his office.

I was copying a letter to the Bank, about five minutes later, when a tall, thin gentleman dressed all in black came into my room and asked to see Monsieur Mahler. He was a strange, foreign-looking gentleman, in a frock-coat of the latest cut and a big black cravat which hid his shirt. All his clothes were brand new, and there was a fine black pearl in his tie. Even his gloves were black. Yet he did not look as if he was in mourning. There was a power about him. I could not tell him that Mahler could not be disturbed. I asked him what name, and he replied, with a sweet smile: 'Say – a gentleman.' I had no time to announce him; I opened Mahler's door and this stranger walked straight in and shut the door behind him.

I used to listen to what went on. I put my ear to the door and listened hard, for this man in black intrigued me. And so I heard a very extraordinary conversation. The man in black spoke in a fine deep voice with an educated accent, and he said:

'Mahler, you are finished.'

'Nonsense,' said Mahler.

'Mahler, there is no use in your trying to deceive me. I can tell you positively that you are in debt to the tune of just over twenty million francs – to be exact, 20,002,907 francs. You have gambled, and have lost. Do you wish me to give you further details of your embezzlements?'

Calm as ice, Mahler said, 'No. Obviously, you are in the know. Well, what do you want?'

'To help you.'

At this Mahler laughed, and said, 'The only thing that can help me is a draft on, say, Rothschild's, for at least twenty millions.'

'I have more than that in cash,' said the gentleman in black and I heard something fall heavily on Mahler's desk, and Mahler's cry of surprise.

'There are twenty-five millions there,' said the stranger.

Mahler's voice shook a little as he replied, 'Well?'

'Now let us talk. Monsieur Mahler, you are a man of the world, an educated man. Do you believe in the immortality of the soul?'

'Why, no,' said Mahler.

'Good. Well, I have a proposition to make to you.'

'But who are you?' Mahler asked.

'You'll know that soon enough. I have a proposition. Let us say that I am a buyer of men's time, men's lives. In effect, I buy men's souls. But let us not speak of souls. Let us talk in terms of time, which we all understand. I will give you twenty million francs for one year of your life – one year in which you must devote yourself utterly to me.'

A pause: then Mahler said, 'No.' (Ah, he was a cunning man of business, poor Mahler!) 'No. That is too long. It's too cheap at that price. I've made fifty million in less than a year before now.'

I heard another little thud. The stranger said, 'All right my friend. Fifty million francs.'

'Not for a year,' said Mahler.

The stranger laughed. 'Then six months,' he said.

And now I could tell, by the tone of his voice, that Mahler

had taken control of the situation, for he could see that the strange man in black really wanted to buy his time. And Mahler had a hard, cold head, and was a genius at negotiation. Mahler said, 'Not even one month.'

Somehow, this affair brought sweat out on my forehead. It was too crazy. Mahler must have thought so too. The stranger said:

'Come. Do not let us quarrel about this. I buy time – any quantity of time, upon any terms. Time, my friend, is God's one gift to man. Now tell me, how much of your time, all the time that is yours, will you sell to me for fifty million?'

And the cold, even voice of Mahler replied, 'Monsieur. You buy a strange commodity. Time is money. But *my* time is worth more money than most. Consider. Once, when Salomon Gold Mines rose twenty points overnight, I made something like twenty million francs by saying one word, *Soit*, which took half a second. *My* time, at that rate, is worth forty million a second, and two thousand four hundred million francs a minute. Now think of it like that – '

'Very well,' said the visitor, quite unmoved. 'I'll be even more generous. Fifty million a second. Will you sell me one second of your time?'

'Done,' said Mahler.

The gentleman in black said, 'Put the money away. Have no fear; it is real. And now I have bought one second of your time.'

Silence for a little while. Then they both walked to the window, which was a first-floor one, and I heard the stranger say:

'I have bought one second of your time for fifty million francs. Ah well. Look down at all those hurrying people, my friend. That busy street. I am very old, and have seen much of men. Why, Monsieur Mahler . . . once, many years ago, I offered a man all the kingdoms of the earth. He would not take them. Yet in the end he got them. And I stood with him on a peak, and said to him what I say to you now – *Cast thyself down!*'

Silence. Then I seemed to come out of a sleep. The door of Mahler's office was open. Nobody was there. I looked out of the open window. There was a crowd. Mahler was lying in the street, sixteen feet below, with a broken neck. I have heard that a body falls exactly sixteen feet in precisely one second. That gentleman all in black was gone. I never saw him go. They said I had been asleep and dreamed him, and that Mahler had fallen by accident. Yet in Mahler's desk lay fifty million francs in bonds, which I had never seen there before. I am sure he never had them before. I believe, simply, that the gentleman in black was the Devil, and that he bought Mahler's soul. Think I am crazy if you like. On my mother's grave I swear that what I have told you is true. . . . And now can you give me fifty centimes? I want to buy a meal. . . .'

CPSIA information can be obtained
at www.ICGtesting.com
Printed in the USA
LVHW081113011021
699142LV00018B/542/J